FAMILY TRADE

JAMES CARROLL, author of the much admired *Mortal Friends*, has stepped into competition with authors like John Le Carré and Len Deighton in *Family Trade*, a compelling story of human emotion and international espionage. He is himself the son of an American intelligence officer. He and his wife, the author Alexandra Marshall, live in Boston.

JAMES CARROLL

Family Trade

FONTANA/Collins

First published in Great Britain
by William Collins Sons & Co. Ltd 1982
First issued in Fontana Paperbacks 1983

Copyright © 1982 by Morrissey Street Ltd

Made and printed in Great Britain by
William Collins Sons & Co. Ltd, Glasgow

CONDITIONS OF SALE:
This book is sold subject to the condition
that it shall not, by way of trade or otherwise,
be lent, re-sold, hired out or otherwise circulated
without the publisher's prior consent in any form of
binding or cover other than that in which it is
published and without a similar condition
including this condition being imposed
on the subsequent purchaser

For My Father

WASHINGTON, D.C.

1960

CHAPTER ONE

Jake McKay was drawn to the clown portraits by Rouault because he was eighteen years old. The whimsy of those faces, but also their gravity, appealed to him. Perhaps they, he thought, would make a fit subject for his paper.

It was his third day of college, he was a brand-new freshman at Georgetown, and he was already in a panic about all the course work. He and a classmate had come to the Phillips intending to get in, get an idea, and get out. But the gallery, with its intimate rooms and beautiful paintings, had snagged McKay. The museum had been the Phillips family home, and it was left with just enough furniture and domestic appointments to suggest how children and parents had lived there once. The Rouault paintings were arranged along an oak-panelled chamber that must have been the dining-room before. It was sombre. The leaded glass windows were small and high. Daylight had never been a feature of the room's charm. Jake could not imagine festive meals in there. But the room was warm and, despite its size, cosy. A large stone fireplace dominated the far wall. It was easy to conjure up a huge fire; that was the light that counted. The lively shadows would have flickered across the room and played upon Rouault's images. The three paintings were small, eighteen inches, perhaps, by twelve, and each was at the mercy of the same face.

Jake walked slowly along the line of paintings, and then slowly back again. How would his paper begin? 'The viewer is at first offended by the contradiction between the painting's subject – the clown, a figure of fun – and its mood, a bleak, crude despair. But then it becomes apparent that the artist's true subject is neither the clown's whimsy nor his unhappiness, but the way the one implies the other.'

The act of walking made Jake conscious of his stiff leg and his stick. He'd always been lame and he was used to it, and he'd long since learned to wear his walking stick as an item of apparel. He was tall and carried himself erectly, like a war hero, as if he expected other people to envy him his limp, not pity him for it.

Someone called Jake's name quietly behind him. It took a moment to remember that he'd come to the Phillips with Ned

Cooney his first friend at Georgetown.

'Hey, McKay,' Cooney whispered. 'I thought you were right behind me. I went all the way upstairs. They have a new part; it's better.'

'I like it here, Ned.'

'Too gloomy, if you ask me.'

'I'm thinking of writing about these guys.'

Cooney squinted at the Rouaults. 'What is it?'

'It's clowns.'

'Sad-looking clowns, if you ask me. You ought to come upstairs. There's some nudes.' Cooney fluttered his eyebrows. 'I think I found my topic. "The Crotch on Canvas".'

McKay smiled, but Cooney seemed a little crude to him, frankly, and McKay couldn't help but feel disappointed. He'd been drawn to Cooney for his ribald sense of humour, but one wanted more than that in a best friend. It was like Jake to be measuring already the limits on their relationship. It was a weakness of his, his mother told him, to want too much too soon. He had no right to feel disappointed in Cooney and he chided himself. But he also understood that there were some things he could never explain to this guy. Like about the sadness in those paintings. Like about his leg.

Jake had no memory of the air raid. He was in the house with his mother and neither of them, she said, heard the V-2 bomb before it hit. Jake's mother was a stately attractive woman, but when he imagined that scene in wartime London it wasn't her face he conjured, but young Deborah Kerr's, that brisk nobility, or Audrey Hepburn's, those sad eyes. The woman he knew as his mother was efficient, courtly and, if not reserved, dignified, not given in the slightest to impulse or spontaneity. But the wartime woman he imagined was a British beauty who had foolishly, on an impulse which horrified her parents, given herself to her Yank officer because she loved him, and because she was about to lose him to the noble struggle. It was all too heartbreaking. She wanted to give him a few moments of happiness. She wanted to give him a son.

Jake's parents were not self-dramatizing people, and they did not encourage him to consider his injury in romantic terms. But only the romance of it – who else in his generation had been wounded in the war? – made his limp tolerable for Jake. Every late-night movie about Blitz-ridden London fuelled an image he had of himself and his parents. Whenever he felt sorry for himself a certain kind of film-score music played in his head. It had been playing, he realized, while he paced studiously in front of the Rouaults.

Cooney led McKay out into the spacious foyer of the museum's new wing. A staircase spiralled up to the next two floors. Bright sunshine poured through the two-storey-high plate glass window. There was grey wall-to-wall carpeting everywhere, and a Calder mobile, hung from the third-floor balcony, filled the air with colour.

'Another thing I don't like in there,' Cooney said loudly over his shoulder, thumbing back towards the room from which they'd come, 'is you feel like whispering. It's like a damn church.'

'No, no, Ned-boy, you missed the point. It's like a home. It's where they lived. That part was their house.' Jake looked around. 'This is just another museum out here.'

Cooney was already halfway up to the second floor. McKay followed him.

'Catch that,' Cooney said, when in the first gallery McKay joined him in front of a wall-sized oil painting of a native family group by Gauguin. In a lower voice he said, 'Check those boobs.'

'I've seen better in the *National Geographic*.' McKay knew as well as Cooney what attitude to strike, and in fact the sight of those breasts interested him too. He *was* like Cooney. Perhaps he had been foolish to allow himself to be impressed by the room downstairs and its Rouaults. He certainly shouldn't have let it show.

'But these are full-sized, Mac,' Cooney whispered. 'And wait'll you see this!' He darted into the next gallery.

Jake followed, but without hurrying. Cooney was definitely looking less and less like the buddy Jake wanted. Was everything the occasion of a crack to him? When McKay entered the next gallery it was deserted. Cooney had shot through it, apparently ignoring the huge Monet *Poplars* that dominated the stark white room with its soft violet hue. Jake didn't know the painting. The lyrical bright world of Impressionism was new to him. He could not pass that painting without looking at it, without squinting towards its corner to see whose it was. Jake considered himself an educated young man. He'd done well at St Anselm's, a first-rate Benedictine school on the far side of Washington, but he'd skipped art in favour of theatre, and it was coming as a shock to him that here was an entire world he had not noticed before. A world that took his breath away. In *Poplars* the air shimmered

11

between the trees and the light of the sky and the reflecting water seemed, right on the very canvas, to fade slightly. Jake felt that if he stood there long enough night would come in that painting. The flowers would fold and the shades of purple would all drain into black. Jeeze, he said to himself. He stared at it. The thing was just a painting. But it was like a window on another country. Jeeze, he said.

'Psst!' Cooney was motioning at him from the doorway.

Jake left the Monet reluctantly. Cooney brought him to a large canvas on which an undraped bulging woman displayed herself. He offered it to McKay with a sweep of his hand as if he were the artist or the pimp. 'Makes you want to get laid, eh?' Cooney whispered.

Get laid? McKay could not imagine exposing his scarred left leg to such a woman, much less getting into bed with her. He had never been naked with a girl, but he knew better than to indicate that. 'I think she's a little plump, don't you?'

Cooney caught the condescension in McKay's voice. 'Not for a quick fuck, she's not.' But he said it defensively. It was important not to be thought to have bad taste in poon.

McKay shrugged and turned away. The painting embarrassed him. Across the room a small statue caught his eye. It was a girl, a ballerina. She stood with her hands behind her back and her face tilted towards the ceiling. From the distance she seemed about to raise her foot. The colour of her skin and hair and shoes and bodice and tutu was the colour of the metal. Was it bronze? If it was metal, why did she seem alive? McKay approached her.

To his relief he sensed that Cooney was moving on again. It would work better if they cased the place separately.

The statue was familiar to him, and he wondered if he'd seen it reproduced.

He circled her. Sculpture was better than paintings because you could walk around it. He saw the artist's name engraved on the pedestal, Degas.

He noticed that the dancer's skirt was made of a delicate uncast mesh, and he found himself wondering how the artist had done that. In her hair she wore a real ribbon. It might have been yellow once, but it was faded and inert. McKay thought they should give her a new one, or the artist should have done that in bronze too. He stopped circling her and drew closer. She was on a pedestal so that her face was about the level of his. He studied it. Her eyes were open but unfixed and she seemed, given the angle of her

12

head, to be dreaming. Of what? Of whom? He was sure it wasn't permitted to touch her, but he did.

He touched her leg, the stiff one. It was perfect. He ran his forefinger lightly from her ankle wrapped in the ribbons of her toe slippers up along the back of her calf muscle and into the faint hollow behind her knee. At that place on his own leg was a grid of scar tissue. He'd had to have frequent operations to adjust the metal pins in his joints to accommodate his growth. No one had ever touched his scars but the doctors and his mother. For years she had massaged his leg every night with lanolin. Her touch was by far the most intimate and consoling experience he ever had. He could remember as a boy looking at his leg after she had finished and expecting it to be healed. He wasn't sure when exactly she had stopped touching him. His most recent operation had been the year before and she hadn't massaged him after that one. Did that mean he was then a man?

Strangely enough, it wasn't his mother's touch he missed when he got older. It was the touch he'd never had, his father's. Jake and his father played golf together on Sundays. It was the extent of the time they shared, but even that was more than the sons of most men in John McKay's position ever got. He was one of the most powerful men on the quiet side of Washington, and even though Jake was not allowed to tell his friends what his father did, he was acutely aware of his father's status.

Jake loved to be seen with his father at Piney Creek. It was an act of defiance of his to play golf or any sport, and it seemed to him his father was on his side against those drinkers in the clubhouse who, Jake was sure, watched him limp to the eighteenth green and, if they didn't snicker, shook their heads. What he liked about playing golf with his father – actually all Jake did, owing to his disability, was hit medium and short irons and putt – was the feeling it gave him that he was like other sons and not finally a great disappointment to his father. The best moments were those stretches of fairway from the tee to his father's ball – those drives of his went like cannon shot – because his father sat with his gloved left hand resting on Jake's shoulder while Jake drove the cart. John McKay was not an expressive man. Neither he nor Jake acknowledged that habitual casual touch, but Jake took it as his reward for forcing himself to learn how to swing a golf club without falling down. Sometimes he slowed the cart deliberately just to prolong it.

Jake would have prolonged touching the ballerina but he heard

13

someone enter the gallery behind him, and he was afraid it was a guard. He withdrew his hand from the girl's cold skin carefully, so as not to attract attention to it. He began to move around the statue slowly, eyeing it the way he imagined a connoisseur would. But a connoisseur of what? Sculpture? Dance? Or pretty girls?

It was not a guard. Only when Jake had the statue between himself and the person approaching did he look. It was very strange when he did. The person approaching was a young girl.

He continued to move, placing his stick soundlessly, pretending to be oblivious. But because she stared at the dancer he could obliquely stare at her. With her slim, breastless body and her delicate profile and her long hair held by a ribbon, she seemed to him the statue come alive. Of course the dancer's hair would have been blonde! Of course she would fill the air around her with a faint perfume! Of course her skin would be just that shade of pink! The girl was much shorter than McKay, though only perhaps two or three years younger. She held her head at a slight angle to look at the dancer's face, but it was the same angle at which the dancer, in her dreaming state, held hers. With that coincidence, the statue ceased to exist for Jake. He saw only the girl, and now he admitted that she was infinitely more interesting to him than any work of art. He would, like Cooney, prefer the sight of any girl in the flesh to any masterpiece in bronze. He had been pretending to like those paintings while waiting, secretly, for this. You phoney bastard, he thought, and he chuckled, watching the girl carefully.

He continued to move. The statue was still between them. He could feel his heart pumping faster, and he loved it. He wanted to whistle. The girl seemed transfixed by the statue. He knew that if she was aware of him he too would seem spellbound, studious, sophisticated.

The girl drifted away from the statue, having apparently not noticed him at all. Was he invisible? He watched her cross dreamily towards Cooney's nude and suddenly he was seeing her without her saddle shoes, skirt, and sweater, seeing her naked, gliding back to him so that he could trace his finger up and down her perfect legs, her soft luminous skin. She invited him, since he could not paint or sculpt, to touch her everywhere, her feet, her calf muscles, her thighs. Her thighs stopped him; how soft they were inside! He stopped breathing. When he pushed her legs apart she arched back the way women did in magazines, turning slightly to hide her crotch, but that was all right because her thighs

14

were what he wanted, her thighs! He touched them gently, would have happily only touched them, but those thighs drew his fingers up, up, until he felt the first edge of that electrified rough hair and she clamped her legs together on his hand and cried, as if she too had been jolted.

She left the room for the next one and McKay could not bring himself to follow her. He stood where he was, leaning, really leaning now on his stout blackthorn. His erection throbbed in his pants and he felt embarrassed. His prick was an enemy at times. It could inhibit him more even than his leg. Would he have had the nerve to go after her, to speak to her, if he'd worn the silver-headed ebony stick his British uncle had given him? His mother's brother had taught him not to call it a cane and to wear it, not carry it, and to raise it with a gentlemanly flourish when he wanted to underscore a point or attract a lady's attention. The idea was to turn his bum leg to his own advantage, and by and large Jake did. But a sub sandwich in your pants? What can you do with that?

Jake resolved to tell his uncle about the girl, though not about his hard-on, and ask what he'd have done.

She was gone. If she hadn't noticed him, at least that meant – didn't it? – she hadn't pitied him.

He found Cooney sitting on a bench on the balcony that over-looked the Calder mobile and the bright lobby. The mobile was made of orange and red ovals hung on what looked like clipped sections of giant coat hangers. Three storeys below people were passing quietly, singly and in pairs, in and out of the museum.

'How you doing?' Jake said as he joined Cooney, regretting his earlier peevishness. He sat on the bench, but in such a way as to rest his chin simultaneously on the crook of his stick and on the balcony railing. 'I love to watch people who don't know you're watching them,' he said. A guard at the door punched a hand counter with a jerk each time someone entered. Jake turned towards Cooney. 'Don't you?'

Cooney leaned forward too. 'That's a good definition of spying,' he said absently. 'I hear your old man is a spook.'

McKay was surprised it had gotten around. The same thing had happened at St Anselm's. He didn't tell anyone, but people knew. His father was senior enough to be mentioned in the papers now and then. It pleased Jake that Cooney knew. He was aware of the effect the revelation had on his friends. He couldn't tell people

15

what his father did, but he didn't have to deny it. 'Where do you hear that?'

'Why? Is it secret?'

Jake snorted. 'Not much of a secret if you know about it. What's your old man do?'

'He's Secretary of the Cook County Democratic Committee.'

'I thought you were from Michigan. Saginaw, Michigan, you said.'

Cooney shrugged, but he was not quite able to feign indifference when he said, 'My folks split up. We lived in Chicago before. My dad still does.'

'Oh. That's too bad.' Jake wanted to look at Cooney or touch his shoulder, but he was embarrassed for him.

'No, it's not. They hate each other's guts. And I don't blame them.' Cooney leaned along the rail towards McKay, and he said out of the side of his mouth, 'You're looking at a guy who got out in the nick of time. I'll eat all the shit those assholes dish out at Georgetown. I'm just glad to be here.'

'It's stupid, don't you think?' They would both willingly now grouse about freshman hazing. On campus they had to wear beanies and class ties and socks mismatched in the college colours, blue and grey. As they'd been told in the orientation assembly, for a full week, not yet half over, any sophomore could tell any freshman to do anything not forbidden by college rules, civil statute or the natural law. But no sophomore had so far confronted McKay. Obviously his stick and limp threw them. But it was common to see freshmen being paraded around the statue of founder John Carroll backwards, with their books on their heads. 'I'm surprised we put up with it.'

'Did I tell you that guy made me dribble a ball around the Quad while I ate my ice-cream cone?'

'Yes, you did.'

'Was I pissed!'

'But you did it. And next year you'll make some other bugger do it.'

'Damn right I will. Trouble is we'll never get back at the son-of-a-bitch sophomores.'

'If we just ignored them that would get back at them, wouldn't it?'

Cooney looked sharply at McKay. 'That's easy for you to say. They leave you alone.' He paused, a rare sign that he understood

16

an implication, before asking, 'What happened to you anyway? Polio?'

McKay shook his head and smiled. 'Nothing so simple,' he said with calculated breeziness. 'I was born in London during the Blitz.'

'No shit! You got that in the Blitz? You must have been a baby.'

'Because,' Jake sang, 'baby, look at me now.'

'London, eh? So your old man *is* a spook.'

McKay smiled appreciatively. 'You have a mind like a trap, Cooney.'

Cooney grinned.

'A mousetrap.'

'But he is, right?'

'My father flies a desk, Ned. He almost never leaves Washington. Who would he be spying on? Intrigue! Espionage! Danger! That sounds more like the Cook County Democratic Committee, if you ask me.'

'Do you know that kid, Fred Yeats?'

McKay stiffened. Fred Yeats's father was with the CIA too. Though he couldn't have accounted for it, Jake had the impression that Mr Yeats was senior to his own father. Jake had known Fred for years – they'd both gone to St Anselm's – but he squinted. 'Fred Yeats? Is he a sophomore?'

'No, he's a junior. He's the proctor's assistant on our floor. They say his old man is a honcho at the CIA, and they say yours is too.'

'Bob Hope's son is a junior. Did you know that?'

'Shit, McKay, answer my goddamn questions! You can trust me.'

'Hey, Ned, there's nothing to answer. Seriously.' McKay put his hand on Cooney's shoulder. He did like the guy, despite himself. What Cooney'd revealed about his troubled family life made McKay feel sorry for him. No wonder he blustered with such cock and such obvious insecurity. 'I know I can trust you.' McKay looked into Cooney's eyes and suddenly realized they had up to then avoided doing that. 'And I do.'

After a moment they both leaned their forearms and chins on the railing again. 'What are you going to write about?' McKay asked.

Cooney didn't answer.

'I was thinking of stealing your topic.'

'The Crotch on Canvas?'

17

'Sort of.' McKay smiled. 'The Female Form in Art.'

'I call a spade a spade.'

'That's why I like you,' McKay said, but with utter indifference A pair of Daughters of Charity with great flapping white headgear entered the museum below. Seen through the Calder, their white wings seemed to float, and Jake wondered for a moment what their bodies were like under all those robes. Did nuns have thighs? Real thighs? As they passed him, the guard corrected his posture and touched his cap. McKay watched the nuns deposit their capes at the coat-check. 'Take it all off, Sisters!' he wanted to cry down to them. He felt expansive and happy. He felt horny.

Cooney nudged McKay. 'Check that.'

McKay adjusted his blackthorn and leaned forward a bit to see the girl who'd just walked on to the spiral staircase from the second floor below them and begun to descend towards the first. He recognized her even from above as the dancer, the Degas. McKay both thrilled to see her again and resented Cooney for having noticed her.

Cooney expelled air between his teeth in a faint whistle. 'What do you think, Jake?' he whispered. 'What do you think?'

She touched the banister lightly. The pleats of her white skirt and the stream of her yellow hair swayed in synchrony as she took the steps, but it was her ass, her hips, those thighs that he saw.

'What do you think?' Cooney pressed.

McKay nodded. Cooney had taste after all. '*Une jeune fille*,' he said, '*en fleur*.'

Cooney gave him a look.

But Jake didn't take his eyes from her. He knew that within a few seconds he'd lose her forever. This was his last chance to memorize her body so that later when he pictured her he would know exactly what the curves of her legs, waist, and chest revealed. Before it hadn't bothered him that she was unattainable. But now, clutching books, tapping down the stairs, heading off to a yearbook meeting or a pep club, she was clearly a girl whom Jake, if his luck had been better, might have met at Piney Creek, say, or even at the freshman mixer. You hide your hard-on by keeping a hand in your pocket.

At the bottom of the stairs she stopped. She looked down one corridor, and then down another. She started to walk towards the wing of the museum that was the original Phillips mansion. She returned to the centre of the lobby, then twirled around, facing first this way and then that. Jake realized suddenly, and it crushed

18

him to do so, that she was waiting for someone. And at that moment she brightened in such a way – she actually skipped once, charmingly, while breaking into a smile – that he knew that whomever she awaited was coming. He leaned forward to see past a disc of the mobile that was swinging into view. He held his breath and clenched his fist around his stick.

It wasn't a boy. From out of the mansion wing with a sprightly step came a woman whom Jake recognized instantly – the blonde hair, the luminous complexion, the exquisite profile, etched beauty – as her older sister. She was carrying a single long-stemmed red rose. Her younger sister, in her presence, glowed. They took each other's hands and kissed each other's cheeks, and McKay thought there was something European, so formal, yet so affectionate, in the way they greeted each other. Perhaps she *was* French.

'I'll take the one with the rose,' Cooney said. It shocked McKay to remember that his classmate had been watching too and it made him angry when he added, 'She has boobs.' It was one thing to have horny feelings but another to flaunt them crudely.

But his resentment of Cooney was lost in his reaction to what he saw then.

The sisters turned back towards that corridor from which the older one had just come. They turned to greet someone else. A tall, startlingly handsome man in a tailored dark suit approached them with his arms open. He too was carrying a rose, but he made nothing of it as the young girl let him enfold her. She kissed him on the cheek. Jake craned to see the man who then offered her the rose. Just then an oval disc of the Calder blocked the view.

How he wished his view had remained blocked and that he did not see when the disc revolved that the man had indeed given the girl the rose and had put the thumb of his free hand in the pocket of his vest. He diddled his fingers on the gold chain. Jake recognized the gesture, and at that moment Calder's mobile turned away completely so that he could see him clearly. There wasn't any doubt. The man, the flower-giver, stood with his arm around that beautiful woman as if they were married. But they weren't. Jake knew that they weren't.

'Jesus Christ!' he said under his breath.

'What?' Cooney asked.

'That's my father,' Jake said.

CHAPTER TWO

'I mean it looks like my father,' Jake said. Cooney was stretching over the railing, his mouth agape. How Jake regretted having blurted the truth.

'You mean it isn't?' Cooney asked.

Jake shook his head, but he was still staring at his father, who at that moment nodded vigorously at something the older sister said. 'I just thought it was.'

La jeune fille turned abruptly and looked up towards Cooney and McKay. Jake panicked when suddenly she pointed with her rose directly at him. She must have noticed his staring, after all, and now she was pointing him out to his father. That voyeur! Jake had an impulse to shrink back against the bench, but he couldn't move.

'She's pointing at us,' Cooney said.

'No.' Jake saw it then. 'She's showing them the mobile.' His father and the older sister turned and watched the floating discs.

Cooney began to wave at them, and Jake did then shrink back out of sight. 'You asshole,' he muttered, but Cooney didn't hear.

It simply could not be his father down there. Hs father was at work. His father did not go around with blondes. His father was devoted to his mother. His father had no capacity for the massive dishonesty the scene below would have implied. It was Cooney's parents, not his, who betrayed each other and hated each other's guts. It was Cooney's parents who were divorced. The strength of his own parents' relationship was something Jake simply assumed, and so was his father's honour. If Jake's eyes, brain, imagination, the synapses of his nervous system were not in fact deceiving him, then nothing was impossible and nothing could ever be taken for granted again.

He slid forward on the bench and brought his face slowly to the railing, and then he looked over it, down. The wings of a Daughter of Charity caught his eyes. He followed her until she disappeared beneath the overhanging balcony, and then his eyes snapped to the left, automatically, to lock on that man again. That most familiar man.

Jake had last seen him very early the previous Monday. Jake

was in his room packing the last of his things when his father knocked. His knocking was how Jake knew it was he. He was formal like that, and polite. He respected the privacy even of his children. 'I'd hoped to go into Georgetown with you myself, son,' he said when Jake opened the door. 'But I can't.'

'It's OK, Pop.' It never occurred to Jake that his father would be able to take the morning off.

'It's not every day a man's son goes off to college.' With a certain bashfulness his father handed him a large package wrapped in blue paper and grey ribbon, the Georgetown colours. Had he thought of that himself? At that moment Jake's mother, still in her bathrobe, joined her husband in the doorway, slipping her arm around his waist. Jake stared first at his parents, then at the box. It was no disappointment to realize that of course his mother had bought the gift and wrapped it. 'I bought it up,' his father said, 'because Guy is here.' Guy Curtin was his father's driver. He had to go. 'Your mother and I hope you like it.'

Jake opened the package quickly. It was a leather attaché case, a real one. Centred between the snap latches were the gold initials J. B. McK., Jr. 'Jeeze, Pop,' Jake said.

'Your father picked it out, Jake,' his mother said, and she squeezed her husband proudly. His accomplishment, Jake understood implicitly, lay not in having found such a perfect present, but in having shopped. He simply never had the time.

So what was he doing in an art gallery in the middle of a week-day afternoon? And what with that woman and that girl?

His father's glance moved slightly with the Calder, and suddenly his eyes fell, it seemed, upon Jake. Who was most in need then of shelter from the other? Neither moved. What animal is it that routs its predator by staring back? Jake was sure he'd read of one. Why did he suddenly feel sorry for his father? He knew why he felt sick.

'He's looking at you, Mac,' Cooney whispered. 'Wave, why don't you?'

Jake had hugged that attaché case, inappropriately perhaps, somewhat boyishly. 'Thanks a lot, Pop,' he said. 'You too, Mom.' He remembered wanting to kiss them both. But he kissed only his mother, and when he and his father shook hands they looked hard into each other's eyes, like men.

Now Jake's father was the first one to look away, and Jake understood why. Once when Jake missed a putt he'd said 'Fuck!' out loud, and then turned to see if his father'd heard him. His father was staring at him brutally, and Jake knew that the way to manifest his remorse and misery was to avert his glance, sheepishly. His father had just done that.

Now he expected him to at least take his arm from the woman's shoulder. How embarrassed he must be! But he remained relaxed apparently. He did not remove his arm from that woman's shoulder. If anything, he squeezed her.

He turned her so that Jake could only see their backs and then, casually strolling as if they were not adulterers, he led her and *la jeune fille* back into the mansion wing of the museum.

Jake stood abruptly and started to go, but Cooney grabbed his blackthorn. 'It is him, isn't it!' Cooney said nosily. But he intended to convey a measured sympathy. He understood these things.

But McKay was steeled against his sympathy, against the same sympathy, in fact, he'd felt himself towards Cooney only a short time before. Poor bastard from a broken home. 'Get your hand off my stick, Ned.'

'Hey, Jake, I'm on your side, man.'

Jake smiled. 'My side in what, Ned?' The blunt stare with which McKay slugged him was too much for Cooney. He was a flank man himself. There was nothing sly in his classmate then or oblique. Nothing ironic. Jake McKay and Ned Cooney were not friends, were not going to be.

Cooney let go of McKay's cane and, with a gesture, said Feel free, Alphonse.

'See you around school,' Jake said. Then he turned and, with as even a gait as he could manage, walked away.

If his father had taken his ladies to see the Rouaults they were gone by the time Jake got there. The gothic hall seemed like a dirge chapel after the modern rooms with their spare white walls and brightly coloured canvases. The Rouault studies now seemed grimly obsessive to Jake, although he did not pause to take them in as he had before. Instead he went quickly the length of the gallery and up the three stairs that led to the even darker vestibule at the Massachusetts Avenue exit. In those last shadows a guard eyed him as if he thought Jake had slashed something. Jake nodded at him and pushed the heavy oak door, which swung open easily. He expected to see his father and the blonde sisters, but the sunlight blinded him for a moment, and for a moment the sunlight rescued him from the gloom of the Phillips mansion.

How had he found it charming? How had he envied the family whose home it had been? Cooney was right after all. Cooney knew what attitudes to take. One wanted to be forever unimpressed, and just world-weary enough to seem not cynical but older. One has been around. Above all one wanted to convey that it was impossible that he should be – anymore, ever again, by no matter what – surprised. Jake went out into that sunlight to meet his father and his father's – he could never have used the word out loud; it belonged to the French and to painters and to another century – mistress.

Another young man might have chosen to leave the museum by its other door, to pretend he had seen nothing, and resolutely never to mention it to anyone. Cooney for all his bluster would have proceeded that way. But Jake had no choice to make in the matter. He and his father had seen each other. They had looked into each other's eyes. It was deal with it right now or never tell the truth to each other again.

His father's Lincoln was at the kerb and Guy Curtin had just closed the door and was scooting around the car towards the driver's seat. The sight of his father's driver surprised Jake, but also reassured him. Better that this all be happening than that he had lost his mind. Jake's father was already in the car. His window was down and he was waving through it at the woman and her sister.

To Jake's surprise he noticed someone else sitting on the passenger's side of the front seat, a young man, a familiar young man, his father's aide; what was his name? He was pointedly looking straight ahead. Jake should have known his name. His father's aide was only a few years older than he was himself. He was tall and thin like Jake, and like Jake he wore his dark hair close-cropped in the collegiate style, and his wardrobe sported button-down shirts and narrow ties. But there was a difference. His father's aide had two good legs, two perfect legs. That was why, Jake knew, he had trouble with his name. A classic mental block. A case of jealousy, resentment, pseudo-sibling rivalry. If Houseman was his brother he'd have hated him.

Dwight Houseman, that was it. Dwight Houseman was a low-handicap golfer, and several times Jake's father had asked him to join them for their Sunday afternoon round at Piney Creek. Dwight Houseman had never been anything but friendly to Jake. He was invariably affable, good-humoured, and on the green in two. Jake disliked him intensely and felt petty for doing so.

But also he understood why his father valued a bright, cheerful, willing young helper like Houseman. What he did not understand at that moment was why, if his father was going to rendezvous, carrying roses, with his beautiful secret friend in the middle of the day, he would do it with Houseman in the front seat. But perhaps in the Agency adultery was routine. And perhaps not only in the Agency but in the world of male adulthood. Jake felt suddenly foolish and naïve. Of course Houseman would be there. He wasn't a kid anymore. And he had never been a cripple in front of whom one had to watch what one said and how one acted.

It was time to put away the things of a child. Cooney had. So could Jake McKay. He would demonstrate right there that he was not shocked, not the simpleton son one had to avoid or protect. Jake might actually have called out at that moment – 'Hey, Pop! What do you say!' – but what he heard come from his father's mouth stopped him.

'*Auf Wiedersehen, Liebchen,*' his father said.

And both women waved back. '*Auf Wiedersehen.*'

And then as the car pulled away, the older one, flourishing her rose, called something else out, something else in German.

And Jake's father nodded and waved once more before sitting back, disappearing from the window as the car made a U-turn into Dupont Circle traffic.

Jake was standing in the museum doorway perhaps a dozen yards behind the woman and the girl. They were holding hands, staring after John McKay's official car until it disappeared.

He knows I saw him and he left! The son of a bitch, Jake thought. Another woman, and in public. The bastard! And a German at that, a Kraut! Jake McKay, who was never going to be surprised again, had never heard his father speak that language before. That he apparently could seemed to compound the deception. What else had the bastard kept from him? Who was this *Fräulein* and how long had she been his *Liebchen*? Jake was not ordinarily conscious of the fact that it was Germans who had crippled him, but suddenly that aspect of the outrage overwhelmed the others. Not that a husband was betraying a wife, but, for an instant, that America was betraying Britain, an officer his allies, a man his own flesh and blood. If an enemy smashes the bone in your infant son's leg, don't you swear never to forgive them? Aren't you honour-bound never to consort with their women?

Had his father stared at him through the Calder mobile or not?

24

Would he have gone off like that, jauntily, if he had? Would Houseman be sitting in the front seat? Jake was suddenly so confused that he had an impulse after all to go back into the museum, find Cooney, make jokes, and insist to himself that none of this had happened. He could do that, couldn't he? All at once the enemy of his family's survival was not his father's conduct but his own knowledge. What was he going to do? He leaned dizzily against a low iron railing that bordered the four steps down from the entrance.

For a moment he thought he was going to throw up, and he had to press the railing to keep from falling. Wait a minute, where was he? Had someone died, or what? Maybe all the hazing shit and his freshman jitters and the stress of having left home and his panic at all the work had gotten to him. It happens, right? Freshmen flip out right and left, don't they? Maybe he imagined his old man and the broad. But when he looked up he saw her and her sister. They were still holding hands, and had stepped into the street, crossing at an angle. Jake watched them absently. They were apparently unaware of him. On the far side of Massachusetts Avenue they crossed into the shadows of Twenty-first Street, went one short block to P Street. They turned right in the direction of Rock Creek Park, the P Street Bridge, and, beyond it, Georgetown, and they disappeared.

And that was that.

Wasn't it?

Jake shook himself. He should now go back into the Phillips and find a topic for his paper.

'Impressionism and Illusions: Some Effects of the Artist's Rampant Imagination on the Inhibited Beholder.'

'Aesthetics and Ethics: The Collapse of Values in the Post-Modern Era and Its Meaning for Art and Marriage.'

Jake squeezed the iron railing with both hands. 'The Form of Family Life in America.' You will not feel this, he said to himself. Feel what? This confusion? This anger? This first adult dose of disillusion, you asshole! Standing here reciting titles and giving yourself orders is stupid. Either go back inside and find Cooney, or.

He took the stairs quickly and crossed into Massachusetts Avenue without waiting for a proper break in traffic. A taxi honked loudly at him, but slowed down, and Jake waved his stick at the driver, thanks, and then exaggerated his limp as he continued. The avenue was six lanes broad, but other drivers stopped for him too. By the time he got to P Street he was hitting a stride of sorts, and when he saw the woman and the girl a block ahead of him he picked it up.

But not much. He didn't want to close more than half a block on them. He was not overtaking them. He was tailing them. He was surveilling them. He was investigating. He was spying.

The district of Georgetown began on the far side of the bridge, and a broad field, an unwooded fringe of Rock Creek Park, spread across two square blocks on the south side of P Street. The woman and the girl followed a path into that field, cutting diagonally across it, but they still walked purposefully. The grass did not lull them, and Jake wondered if, given the charm of the weather, they were going to meet someone.

Instead of following them into the field he continued along the sidewalk, but he kept them in sight as they angled away from him. On the far side of the field, chatting informally, they each took the seat of a swing. At first they both were content to drift in small circles around their feet. There was a European primness in the way they sat. But then the younger one, as if unable to resist, began to push herself back and forth, slowly at first, then more enthusiastically. Even from across the distance Jake could hear her laughing, as if it embarrassed her to be careening up and down like a child. Her white skirt and her blonde hair flashed the sun back at itself. To Jake there was something intensely sensual in the sight of the spirited girl. He longed to be closer, to see her thighs, her underwear. The thought aroused him, but he checked himself. She was not his sex fantasy, but his suspect. He shifted his focus.

The trees of Rock Creek Park had begun to turn, so there were auburn and crimson highlights in the backdrop of the scene. The field was recently mowed and the green of the grass was crisp and uniform. The two figures, solitary on those acres – not even a dog or a flock of pigeons intruded – were like images of the same person. Was his mind playing tricks after all? Was this a movie? Had he really seen his father? Was his family really in some mortal jeopardy that registered like nausea in his stomach?

How could he ever have described these sensations? How could he explain to his mother any of what he had seen or was feeling now? Not that he would. He never would. But the thought of her confused him. He would be absolute in his loyalty to her, of course. But did that loyalty imply his silence? Or his immediate report? Had his father, with that stare in the museum, been requesting his complicity, or sealing it?

No! Hell, no! The answer surged through him, the very words he'd say. Jake McKay was not going to pimp for his father!

Pimp? Did you say pimp? He shuddered, a crisis of disgust. What had his father to do with zoot-suited dandies jiving up Fourteenth Street, their string of sauntering whores tricked out in gauds, clicking their tongues at schoolboys?

He focused on the two blonde figures in the field. Now, instead of a lyric fantasy, it seemed to him he was watching a blue movie. Girl on a swing, writhing, just out of reach, while he, a drunken sailor, jacked off in rhythm with her pumping. That *Fräulein*. In Hamburg whores display themselves behind plate glass windows. What had his father to do with whores?

Jake rebuked himself for veering again towards sex. He focused and focused, as if his eyes were stubborn lenses. He needed clarity of intention. He already understood that he was not going to deny what he had seen. Forthrightness was, unfortunately, his strongest characteristic, his best quality. It was still possible that he might confront that woman, demand an explanation, brand her for what she was. Perhaps he could arouse her guilt, touch her remorse, make her see that there was a family at stake, two daughters and a son, and another woman whose strengths of character depended utterly on her intact pride.

The knowledge of his mother's fragility rode under all of Jake's reactions like an undulating, unbreaking wave. Not that she was a stranger to adversity – she'd been through the war in London, after all, and with a wounded child – or that her graceful solidity was held somehow tentatively, but that her devotion to her husband transcended all her strengths; no, girded them. Jake's mother would not survive the loss of his father's love.

He would never say that, of course. If the German woman asked him, he would say, My mother masters what she encounters. She will master you. Jake McKay would keep to himself what he knew.

At the corner of P and Twenty-sixth streets, the north-western limit of the field, he stopped, but only for a moment. The sisters had left the swings behind, resumed walking, and were within a few dozen yards of leaving the field. Jake proceeded south on Twenty-sixth at what was for him a brisk clip, so that as they crossed on to the sidewalk he was able simply to fall in behind them. They were conversing softly in German, pleasantly. Why wasn't the younger girl berating the older one? If one of his own sisters . . .

He intended to follow them impudently now. He wanted them to notice him, his stick, his limp. Later he would say, I was right behind you, and they would gasp when they remembered. The young girl would not even cover her mouth when it fell open; You! She would have been eyeing him secretly too and it would crush her when she realized that the sin of her sister made the dream they could have shared impossible.

They went half a block like that, Jake following only feet behind, and turned west at O Street, where he lost his nerve. He made the turn, too, but only after crossing to the opposite side of the street. From that distance, while tracking them, he could take in the wrought-iron railings and the weathered brick façades and the bottle-glass windows and the unpolished fancy door-knockers and the arched transoms of the Georgetown row houses.

The woman stopped and flourished a key. While she applied it to the lock of a dark green door in a particularly narrow house, her sister was distracted for a moment and dropped a book and her rose. When she'd picked them up, she was facing Jake, who, despite himself, admired her again, how the outline of her slender body stood out crisply against the quaint building. It was the pleated skirt that kept trapping him. It draped her hips modestly, but her slightest movement rippled the skirt with an irresistible sensuality. The girl looked in his direction, but only for an instant. For long enough, he thought. They'd been talking about him, surely. Now she knew his face. When she turned away her hair twirled and her skirt. She did move like a dancer.

They went inside and the door closed. Only then did Jake notice that the house was made of faded yellow clapboards, the only one of the block not brick. It would be a cinch to find again.

But hell, now what? His confusion welled again. His anxiety had abated while he tracked the sisters, but now it came back, doubled. He couldn't go back to his dormitory as if nothing had happened. He felt panicked. Georgetown was driving him crazy with loneliness anyway. He wanted to go home. He hated to admit it. Home, he wanted home? Home was where his family was, and his panic was that he had lost them. He moved with flair and daring, but only within the ordered lines of the home life he trusted absolutely. But that home life was what his father had betrayed. And therefore destroyed?

'Hello, Mother!' he called.

He arrived at the house as if he were expected. He had fastened seals on his panic and on his anger at his father, on everything but concern for her. He'd come out to Ridge Road without returning to campus to sign out or to drop his notebook off.

'Whatever are you doing here?' she cried from the second floor, but happily.

Eleanor McKay cherished the composure of her life, its routine and predictability. The great – one might say only – advantage to her husband's rigid schedule was the encouragement it gave her to establish a schedule for herself. She had done so early in their marriage; she'd had to in order to continue her work as a hospital volunteer while seeing to the needs of her new baby. Of course her volunteer work had gone out the window when the roof beam crushed Jakey's leg, but her schedule hadn't. Even now, sixteen years later, mornings were given over to what she called house management and other ladies called shopping and mending and planning menus. She lunched on Tuesdays with her garden club and Fridays with the altar guild at St Stephen's Episcopal Church and on most other days at the kitchen table with Emmaline, their maid. It was those breezy friendly lunches that nurtured and protected the perennial loyalty that made Eleanor the envy of all her friends for having such help. In the afternoon Eleanor napped for half an hour and then went to her daughters' school. She worked in the office at Marymount, where she was often teased about being a Protestant. The first time that happened she'd felt obliged to explain solemnly to an impish young priest that when she'd married her husband she'd been required to vow to raise her children in his religion, which was fine with her so long as she could see to the quality of their education herself. In fact she grew to like the priests and nuns, and now that both Dorothy and Cicely were enrolled at Marymount she quite happily donated ten hours a week of her time. She found the orderliness of the place reassuring.

But the end of the afternoon, the very best part of the day, she gave to herself. For an hour, perhaps two if the girls had activities, she would close the door to her small sitting-room, and there amid her books and needlepoint, she would do what suited her, some days sewing, some reading – if she read Shakespeare or poetry from the Oxford anthology she did so aloud – but most days at her leather-inlaid desk writing the long careful letters to old family friends and relations in Britain that recipients universally treasured. Her brother Giles teased that she had a nineteenth-century gift and claimed that he regretted having been assigned to the embassy in Washington because now instead of getting her letters, he saw her.

It was from a letter to her aunt, in fact, that she immediately tore herself when she heard Jake's voice in the front hall. He'd only been away at school four days, or was it three? But she missed him terribly, and she dashed for the stairs as if to reach him before another thought could form itself: something was wrong. His leg.

'Jakey! Jakey!' She knew that he hated the diminutive of what was already a nickname, but she didn't care. She'd called him Jakey as a child and still did when she was feeling especially fond. If her daughters had taken the stairs as recklessly as she did then she'd have corrected them. When she saw her son leaning rakishly on the balustrade at the bottom of the curved staircase she was charmed. It pleased her enormously that he was so good-looking. It was an advantage to which he had a right.

Jake tried to admire his mother's looks as she came down the stairs towards him. She was dressed in a navy twill skirt and maroon sweater that, with characteristic but not absolute modesty, outlined her figure. A string of pearls swung above her bosom. Her long thick black hair was tightly wound into a bun at the crown of her head, exposing her slender neck. She wore lipstick and rouge and something around her eyes, but the colour in her face, its liveliness, seemed to have nothing to do with make-up. But what Jake was most aware of was the air of vulnerability that clung to her. Her looks and her belief in herself depended on everything, whether the line of her eye shadow or the man she loved, being in its proper place. Jake's heart sank. She would die. She would just fucking die!

Jake could not look at her now without seeing also that blonde woman and his father, his father's arm ever so casually around her shoulder, the rose in the crook of her arm. Would that woman have seemed half as sensual and alluring to Jake if he had seen her by herself on the bus? He had to stifle a flash of resentment at his mother for not being as beautiful as that blonde woman was. Guilt pierced him.

'You missed me, eh?' he said as she came into his arms, but his voice sounded hollow and nervous. He was far taller than she was. So was that woman. Only she made him think of his mother as short.

And she seemed frail to him as he absorbed her weight. He held his balance easily, even swinging her. She felt like Dori to him, and Dori was only thirteen. How weak she seemed, how pathetic.

'Missed you? How on earth could I have missed you?' But that seemed funny to her. 'You've only been gone four days.' And she laughed against his chest.

'Three, love. This is Wednesday.'

Suddenly she assumed a mock severity. 'You aren't sent home, John McKay, Junior? You aren't dismissed?'

Once as a fourth former he'd been sent home from St Anselm's in the middle of the morning because, since it was the Queen's birthday, he'd replaced the American flag with the Union Jack on the school flagpole. Eleanor had thought it, frankly, a spirited thing to do, but she did not let on. Jake was reinstated, but only after being severely caned. Eleanor could not help but reflect that the philistine English rites of corporal punishment were observed at St Anselm's, even if the royal birthday wasn't.

'No, no,' Jake said. 'Nothing of the sort. I've come home for my ebony stick.' Despite his apparent composure he still felt nauseated, and it was only with an effort that he kept a tremble from his voice. He had rehearsed this. He bounced his blackthorn off the polished stone floor like Astaire and caught it. 'There's a dance Friday night and I've decided to go.'

'Oh, good, Jake, good!' Nothing he could have said would have pleased her more. Eleanor worried that the tacky business of boy-meets-girl was going to be especially difficult for him at college, and he knew it.

'I'm so happy, darling,' she said, and she ran her hand lightly along the side of his cheek. 'You'll positively wow them.'

'Yeah. With my trusty box step.' He smiled, but he had to wipe perspiration from his upper lip. He looked away when he saw concern cross her face. He simply would not be able to face her if his father . . . But his father had! His family, like a great wooden structure, was already beginning to crumble. Jake alone knew it. His stick shook under his weight, then he straightened up.

'Uncle Giles says dress the part. I should **have** brought it with me.' His ebony walking stick had a silver **handle and** had been designed for wear with top hat and tails, and it never failed, if only in front of his mirror, to make Jake feel like a million sterling.

But that was irrelevant. He had **not decided** to go to the dance and even now did not consider himself bound to do so. It gave him the excuse he needed for being home. His mother had been cheered at first, but now she was looking at him as if she was going

31

to ask what was wrong. He pulled away. Perspiration was on his forehead, too.

'Are you all right?'

'Sure I am.' He grinned. She wouldn't ask again. His mother did not believe it was her place to pry. The ease with which he could deflect her suddenly made him angry, because his father could do it easily too. Pry, God damn it, he wanted to say. Ask me! Make me tell you! Why aren't you beautiful? Jake clenched inside. It was wrong, *wrong* to be angry at his mother. His father was the shit. He couldn't wait to exchange a look with him. And he dreaded to. But wait! What if his father when he arrived found it easy to greet him and what if he was not wearing his dark blue suit and vest with watch fob?

'Funny you should mention Giles,' his mother said. 'He just called. He's coming to dinner. Something's up, he said. He seemed all afluster. I hope it's Cynthia, that he's asked her. He'll hate to have missed you.'

'Aren't I invited?'

Eleanor had to check herself. Of course she wanted him to stay. But she knew that his going off to college, even if it was only across the river, had been a small but important rite of passage. She'd hated that he'd packed his bags and gone, but she wasn't going to show him that. She was not going to cling and she was not going to encourage him to. 'Isn't there a rule or something, Jake? I had the impression you were expected each night for dinner.'

He looked at his watch. It was five o'clock. 'I'd never make it.'

'Well, did you get permission?'

He shook his head.

'Really, Jake,' she said sternly, 'I don't approve and your father won't, either.'

'I could call my prefect and say I'm stuck.'

She looked at him for a long time before saying, 'I suppose you are.' She touched his cheek again, so softly, just to let him know she understood that he was homesick and it was all right. 'Try not to lie.'

'Jesuits don't call it lying, Mom.' Fuck 'stuck'; he was homesick. That was it exactly.

She started up the stairs. 'Then come up and tell me everything.'

'OK,' he said. And to himself he added, Everything but.

*

Jake sat in the kitchen while his mother saw to his sisters' supper. They ate quickly and then Cicely went off to do her homework and Dori went out to choir practice. Later, while his mother dressed, but before either his uncle or his father had arrived, Jake sat in the window seat of his room on the third floor to watch the sundown. That house on a knoll off Ridge Road in Arlington – the road was named for the same ridge on which Lee's mansion sat two miles to the north – offered a view of Washington, but, except for the third-floor rooms, only when the leaves were off the trees. From his window Jake observed the slow draining of the glistening light, the sharpening of basic shapes – pencils and boxes – the oozing of colour out of the landscape and into the blue runway markers of National Airport and Bolling Air Force Base on opposite sides of the Potomac. Jake tried to imagine his father's car cruising across the Memorial Bridge and past the floodlit monuments. Would his father be staring at the city too? Would it cast its spell on him? The lights in the government buildings shone magically at twilight, especially the beacon at the top of the Capitol dome that announced an evening session of Congress. Jake pictured John Kennedy standing in the well of the Senate proclaiming a new era. Men born in this century; Jake was coming of age just in time. If his family crumbled around him he was just old enough to deal with it. But he would make his father pay! The son of a bitch had no honour! Who needed him? Let the Kraut bimbo have him! Jake would take care of his mother and his sisters. Fuck his father!

He shuddered. What was he saying? He concentrated on the silhouetted shapes of the Georgetown spires at the far edge of the city. Georgetown was where Kennedy lived, and now it was where he lived. Finally something of what he saw from that window was his. He'd grown up enchanted by that city. It was to him at night a silvered German Advent calendar, and if he were pressed to identify the task for which he was being raised, wasn't it to open one at time each of those portals, each illuminated shrine, each office with its shining light, and each secret room in the dark? He was to open them even if their secrets were horrible and the knowledge of them ruined everything. Whoever said growing up was easy?

Georgetown University; since he had first identified those spires – at what age, seven? – he had been resolved to go there. The largest spire was the tower of Healy, and now on the fifth floor of that very building was his room. My room; he mouthed the phrase, but had no feeling for it. That room had yet to seem like his. The thought of it filled him with loneliness. His college room was a garret that looked out away from the city. It had sloping ceilings and a paint-crusted gothic window. Immediately below was the brick-paved quadrangle and in its centre Dalgren Chapel with its cloistered arches. It had seemed to him at first that that window opened on a square in Europe in another age. He could have been the young Abelard looking down on the Sorbonne, or Thomas More on the Tower Yard or, for that matter, Anne Frank – *'Raus, Juden! 'Raus!* – peeking out at Amsterdam. It was a soulful room, in other words, and he wanted to like it. But he didn't. He liked the room he'd been a child in. He didn't want to be a man. He didn't want to know what he knew. He didn't want to pry. Could he pretend after all that he hadn't really laid eyes on his father that day? Hiya, Pop, he'd say. How you doing? He'd shake his hand, say things were great, and scoot.

On the floor below him the telephone rang, and it jolted him out of his reverie. His body snapped alert with alarm.

Not the telephone. He listened and it rang again.

He stood and hitched his trousers, trying to calm himself, and leaned towards the sound. One night the year before when only he was in the house and that phone, the red one in the drawer of the desk in his father's study, had rung he had, as he'd been instructed to, answered it.

A voice had said, 'Hold the line, please.' He had held his breath as well.

He'd listened while a series of phones were answered and each time the voice said, 'Hold the line, please.'

And then the voice had called the roll.

'Mr President?' What the fuck was this? he'd thought!

'Present,' Eisenhower said. Jake knew his voice from television. Holy shit!

And down through Christian Herter, Allen Dulles, Richard Bissell, Frederick Yeats. Each one answered, 'Present.' And then the voice said, 'Mr McKay?'

And as steadily as he could Jake replied as he'd been instructed, 'This is Mr McKay's son. My father is at the residence of Patrick Dixon in Alexandria for the evening.'

'Thank you. Please disconnect.'

When he hung up the phone he pressed it against its cradle and prayed both that he'd done it right and that there wasn't a war.

His mother came home that night alone. The next day he got up very early and went out in his bathrobe to the tube by the mailbox at the end of the driveway. The headline of the *Washington Post* said, 'NASA Weather Plane Shot Down in Russia.'

It rang again, and now he heard his mother's footsteps on the stairway as she dashed down to get it. He went after her. His heart was pounding.

She'd left the door to the study open. She stood with her back to him. He remained in the doorway and listened as she said, 'Mr McKay is not here. This is Mrs McKay. I assume he is at the office or en route.' She paused. 'Indeed I will, of course.'

When she hung up she leaned on the phone the very way Jake had.

When he said, 'What is it?' she jumped and faced him.

'You startled me,' she said harshly.

'I'm sorry.' Jake watched his mother fumble for a cigarette. Had she forgotten he was home? 'Did they say what it is?'

'Of course not.' Eleanor was remembering other times, the bursts of that sound, the night without him and without explanation, the blank look her husband offered whenever she had dared to ask, What is it? 'We don't ask that, Jake,' she said. Having gotten her cigarette going, she jammed it out, and the gold bangles on her wrist made a sound that, though nothing like the red line's peculiar ring, put them both in mind of it.

'It's weird, though,' Jake said.

She looked at him, moved the downpour of hair off her face. She was wearing a floor-length green gown, which, though elegant and formal, suggested a quiet supper at home. 'Why?'

'They should know where he is. He's at the office, right?'

'He may be coming home.' She looked at he ship's clock on the bookshelf. It was after seven. He was rarely home before eight. 'I called him to say Giles was coming.'

'But what about the phone in his car?' The pitch of Jake's voice was unnaturally high. He heard it himself, and that, in addition to everything else, frightened him. He held himself rigid under his mother's worried eyes. If she asked what was wrong this time, he was afraid he might tell her because he couldn't keep it in any longer.

She stared at him for a long time. She wanted to ask, but she couldn't.

She shrugged. 'The phone in his car is not secure.' That word came more naturally to her than it would have to Jake. She straightened and crossed to him at the doorway. She switched the light of her husband's study off and took her son's arm and awkwardly led him out of the threshold so that she could close the door. 'You know the rule, dear heart. We don't ask about what doesn't concern us.'

'It doesn't concern us?' Jake remembered how the crisis had developed that spring. The weather plane turned out to be the U-2. The uproar led to the cancellation of the Paris Summit and to Khrushchev's shoe-pounding at the UN and to his terrifying ultimatum on Berlin. Every daybreak for a week Jake woke and went to his window to see if Washington was there. Ground Zero. The papers talked about bomb shelters and evacuation, and there were air-raid drills in school. Everyone was worried, but it was worse for him. He'd taken that phone call. 'It doesn't concern us?' he repeated, his voice cracking. He'd seen them at the museum. 'World War Three?'

CHAPTER THREE

Soon Giles arrived. Jake knew it was he from the sound of his car kicking up the gravel in the driveway, and by the time his uncle was at the door Jake was waiting for him. Jake was ambushed by an impulse to throw himself into Giles's arms, but he resisted it and as a consequence greeted him more stiffly than usual.

Giles Patterson was a fifty-year-old man of average height, but he was so thin and dressed so trimly that he seemed taller. That evening he was wearing a tweed jacket over a tan chamois vest. When he took Jake's hand he held it longer than their handshake required. 'My God, you!' he said, and his deep eyes stroked Jake.

And Jake blushed. His uncle's spontaneous affection nearly undid him.

'What a hell of a bonus this is!' Giles said. And he hooked his other hand around Jake's neck.

Eleanor came down the stairs just then. Giles went to her and hugged her more warmly even than usual. Jake saw a look of disappointment come into his mother's eyes and he understood only then that Giles had been drinking. That didn't disappoint Jake. 'I've been promoted,' Giles announced. 'Let's celebrate!' He turned and led them into the living-room.

Promoted? But why did his uncle seem morose? Perhaps he knew about Jake's father too.

Once he had a sizeable glass of whisky and soda Giles sat at the baby-grand piano and plucked out an ironic version of 'Over There'. In the middle of it he stopped abruptly and said, 'Regrettably, loves, it means I'm going back to London!'

Eleanor blurted, 'Oh, Giles! No!' and for a moment her distress was palpable. But she reined it and moved to one side of the piano's open sound box. Jake took up a position on the other. He found it hard to concentrate on what his uncle said. Was it possible something was happening that was not related to his father's infidelity?

'But what about Cynthia?' Eleanor asked, foolishly, Jake thought. Even he knew that his uncle's regular companion would not be an issue. Eleanor obviously was channelling her reaction away from her own feelings. She leaned on the piano the way women did in ads, but Jake had to look away from her. Her angular prettiness seemed utterly unsultry and, despite himself, he held that against her.

Giles struck up and sang, 'You ask me how I feel . . .'

'Stop it, Giles,' she said. 'I'm serious.'

Giles took a healthy swallow of his drink. 'Cynthia is neither here nor there.' He continued to play softly. 'What matters at a time of transition, of transfer, of remove, are the perennial virtues, values, commitments.' He leaned back like George Shearing and sang, 'Is our true love real?' drawing out the vowel sound of *real* like a jazz singer. Even his bitter mockery did not obscure his talent. Giles could have been a supper-club singer in New York, though when he sang popular ballads it was always to send them up. He stopped singing abruptly then and brought the cover down on the keys with a slam. 'No!' He stood. 'It isn't real. It wasn't real.' He looked at his sister impatiently. 'I knew it. Cynthia knew it. Why the bloody hell didn't you know it? Did it never occur to you that I don't want to get married again?' He turned to Jake and looked at him helplessly before downing his drink and stalking across the room to the table with the ice and whisky.

The year of Giles's divorce was the year Jake took Giles's name at Confirmation. That had sealed their friendship. Giles had been openly moved by Jake's gesture and he remained the only adult besides his parents to whom Jake felt permanently attached. If the prospect of his uncle's move to London wasn't throwing him the way it was his mother, that was because Jake immediately saw it as an excuse to go to England in the summer.

One of Jake's great memories was roaring through the Winchester countryside in hs uncle's Austin-Healey, his uncle singing the 'Hallelujah Chorus' until Jake joined in. It became a joke with them that Giles was at any time liable to burst out with a phrase from Handel and wait for Jake to match it with the next. It got that summer so that most of the time he could. Jake never thought of the Austin-Healey without a twinge, however. It was in his uncle's car after an entire afternoon's effort that both of them realized that, because of his stiff leg, he was not ever going to be able to drive a stick-shift.

Eleanor joined her brother at the table. 'Will you fix me one while I see to the girls?'

'Certainly, darling.'

She squeezed his elbow. 'It's just that I'll miss you so terribly,' she said softly and then left the room.

Jake listened to the clinking of the silver stirring spoon against the glasses. He said, 'She wishes you'd get married because she can't imagine that you could be happy living alone.'

'Shall I mix one for you, old man?' It was like his uncle to make such an offer – the first to Jake in that house – offhandedly.

'No, thanks, Uncle Giles. I do my drinking at Tehan's.'

'Tehan's! A boisterous undergraduate public with fly-ridden barmaids, doubtless.'

'Exactly.'

Giles winked as he came back to the piano. 'Or fly-riding,' he smirked but more to himself than to Jake. He placed his sister's drink carefully inside the sound box and put his own on the edge of the piano. He lifted the cover and began without fanfare to play a Chopin étude. A lock of his thick hair – Jake's mother's hair, but with grey in it – fell over his eyes each time, with a certain rhythmic flamboyance, he lowered his head, and it fell back each time he raised it. Sometimes his gaunt body seemed more misused than trim. His moustache was tidy and symmetrical, but like everything else about him, it seemed somehow undernourished. In the wrong light his moustache could seem a mere smudge on his lip. His wrists and fingers carried nothing but skin and nerves, but they dazzled those piano keys as he played that master effortlessly.

The year of his divorce and of Jake's Confirmation had also been the year Giles came to Washington as the cultural attaché.

He'd been given the post presumably not only because of his erudition and flair but because of his readiness to underwrite out of his own funds the costs of the exchanges of orchestras and art exhibits it was his pleasure to arrange.

Finally he stopped playing and he slumped over the keys. The classy whisky-ad ambiance of his performance faded. The music had been intended to distract and soothe. It hadn't. 'He who stands fast,' he mumbled, 'stands not alone.' He looked up at Jake sharply. 'Comfort me.'

It's 'ye', Jake thought, but said quickly nevertheless, 'Comfort me my people.' He coudn't touch his uncle's shoulder, but he wanted to. If he was being promoted, why was he so distraught?

Jake sensed a question forming in Giles's mind, but he was surprised when his uncle asked, 'Where is your father?'

'He should be home,' Jake said. It was nearly eight-thirty. John McKay tried always to arrive in time to tuck Cicely in and to check Dori's homework.

'I have to see him,' Giles said matter-of-factly and sipped his drink. He looked up at Jake suddenly as if he'd just been indiscreet.

'Me too,' Jake said.

'What are you doing here anyway? I thought you donned the gown this week.'

Jake nodded. Was there a chance he could confide in Giles? 'I did. Although at Georgetown one wears a beanie, not a scholar's robe.'

'You should have gone to Cambridge. Popping home at your first distress isn't healthy. I should have damn well insisted. Clare College for you. I thought those monks were famous for their cruelty to boys.'

'They're not monks. They're Jesuits.'

Giles shrugged. A Papist distinction. 'But you come and go as you please?'

'I'm at the library until midnight.' Jake opened his arms as if he were an apparition.

'Ahh.' Giles toasted him.

'Working on a paper: "The Female Form in Art." I'm thinking of describing a statue I saw today.'

'What statue?'

'A girl. A ballerina at the Phillips. Do you know it?'

'*La Petite Danseuse de Quatorze Ans.* A beautiful child.' Giles nodded sadly and looked up from his drink. 'There were over a dozen bronzes cast from the original. The original was of painted wax, and Degas is said to have loved it above all that he did. He would never have permitted her to be copied.'

Jake waited with his question: Why was she copied, then?

'Avarice, simple avarice. His agents within three years of his death in 1917 had taken her, that beautiful child, and made her trite. The greedy bastards would have made a thousand if the moulds hadn't split.'

'How do you know about it?' Jake didn't mean his question rudely. He was thinking about his paper.

'Your grandfather, my father, knew Degas in Paris. He knew what the wax *danseuse* meant to him. Later, during the economic collapse after the war' – Giles smiled – 'the *first* war, he was able to acquire three casts.'

'Three statues?'

Giles showed that his nephew's incredulity amused him. 'Yes, three. They made an impression on me because I was fourteen years old at the time. Her age. And of course these had no tulle skirts. She was in a way naked. That made an impression too.'

'I noticed the skirt. I noticed that the hair ribbon was real silk.'

'Satin. On the original so were the shoes and so was the bodice.'

'What happened to the three statues?'

'Your grandfather fell under her spell too, *la petite*. What do you think happened to them?' Giles stared at his nephew. This was a lesson.

'I don't know.' Jake felt suddenly queasy.

'He had them melted down. If he could have acquired all fourteen – he'd have happily spent his fortune doing so – he'd have melted down every bronze so that the wax, even fading, remained unique.'

'Your old man must have been pretty tough.'

Giles laughed. 'Tough? To love a piece of sculpture so much?' He reached across the piano and placed his hand on his nephew's head. 'Jake, the worst enemy of art and, forgive me, the truth, is the cliché. It creeps in on us and we must resist it on every front. Make that the subject of your paper.' He wanted Jake to sense his infinite fondness for him. And his hope. So, despite knowing that he had become pompous, he went on. 'And that is why, too, you must not fail in life. Forgive me my exhortation. Failure in one as bright as you and sensitive, and in one of your extraordinary background, your extraordinary parents, and in one with such opportunity, failure like that has become, I'm afraid, all too common. It is trite. A cliché. Avoid it.'

'Like the plague.' They both laughed. His uncle's affection, when he displayed it like that, always moved Jake even if it did depend on his having had a few drinks. His uncle's ambition for him stoked Jake's own. But his uncle's effusiveness embarrassed him. 'Better I should be melted down, right?'

Giles nodded and withdrew his hand. 'So why aren't you at the library?'

'Can I ask you a question about my father?'

'Of course.'

'I mean in confidence.'

'Isn't everything in confidence?'

'Does he speak German?'

Giles laughed abruptly, but Jake sensed that the question threw him. 'What?'

'Does my father speak German? I never heard him speak German before.'

'And now you did?'

'You were the one who was in Germany. Not him, right? He spent the war in London, right?'

'As did I.'

'But you were in Germany. You told me stories about Berlin. About children who hid in broken tanks. You parachuted in at night.'

'Now, Jake, speaking of confidence, perhaps I watered my discretion to tell you some of that. God, it's years! Whatever did I say? I probably exaggerated for the story's sake.' Giles paused. 'Whatever in the world are you driving at?'

'You'd think a son would know what languages his father speaks.'

'Yes, if the son's father punched tickets on the tram, you would.'

Silence fell between them then, a suspicious silence, the very opposite of their previous intimacy.

Giles, hoping to dispel it, but also hoping to understand, said softly, 'So you've come home three days into term to ask your father what languages he speaks?'

Despite a will to check himself, Jake blurted, 'I can't explain it until . . .' He looked towards the hallway and the stairs; his mother was coming. He said hastily, 'If my father walks in wearing a three-piece blue suit and a crimson tie and his gold

41

watch and chain, then I have to talk to you. I'll have to talk to someone.'

'Your father always wears his watch and chain.' Giles stared at his nephew, but he couldn't read him, and he tried to dismiss the qualm the young man's strange anxiety had stimulated.

Eleanor entered from the hallway with Cicely in tow, come to say goodnight. The girl was in her pink nightie and when she saw Giles she dashed across the room towards him. He stood. Cicely leaped into his arms, and Giles nuzzled her. 'My blossom,' he said, and though he clenched his eyes shut, tears came out of them.

Jake and his mother exchanged a look while Giles clung to Cicely, overclung to her. Jake's mother was embarrassed by her brother's emotional display. Jake was stunned by it. What was going on? Cicely was a sport and she held fast to her uncle's neck and didn't squirm out of his embrace. When he put her down he wiped his eyes quickly and then reached automatically behind her ear and found a quarter there, which he twirled between his fingers and then, while Cicely squealed with pleasure, pocketed without comment. It was well-known that their uncle charged twenty-five cents a hug. In Jake's day he'd charged a dime.

Cicely then kissed Jake goodnight and was about to go upstairs with their mother when headlights flashed through the large living-room windows. 'It's Daddy!' she cried. His arrival was never routine to her. It made all the difference if he was the one to see her to her room. Only he could turn off the lamp by her bed, which meant that if he was late in coming home, she had to go to sleep with her blanket over her face.

Eleanor, Giles, and Jake proceeded single file behind Cicely out into the stone-floored foyer, and they watched John McKay's entrance and his daughter's welcome as if they were scoring them.

McKay arrived like a cavalier, flinging his hat towards a banister post, missing it, but just, scooping Cicely and twirling her.

Jake deliberately tried to overlay the sight with a precise memory of his father's greeting of *la jeune fille* at the Phillips, but he could not summon more than a hazy image of what he'd witnessed. Instead, he saw in detail the discs of the Calder and the roses.

When he focused on it, his father's suit confused him. Three pieces and dark blue all right, but it was pin-striped. Jake hadn't noticed pin-stripes. Pin-stripes were what dominated his perception now, and they completely disoriented him. He was, he would later say, grasping at pin-stripes. But he knew what he had seen, and his father's appearance now only confirmed him. He steeled himself for his father's glance.

'You!' John McKay said. But he was speaking to Giles. 'How are you?' He settled Cicely in the crook of his arm, but he was focused on Giles. He'd asked the question so solemnly and was so intent upon its answer that Giles, instead of having been promoted, might have been recently bereaved.

Giles raised his glass as if that were reply enough.

Only then did Jake's father turn to him. 'I saw your car outside. What gives?'

'He's going to the dance on Friday,' Eleanor said, as if that explained Jake's presence Wednesday.

But McKay was waiting for his son's reply, and while he did so he hooked the thumb of his free hand in his vest pocket and diddled his fingers against his watch chain.

Jake could neither say, 'I saw you today,' nor even look directly at his father. He felt a great shame; the knowledge of his father's unfaithfulness was corrupting him. Once he'd carried a dead auto battery on his shoulder. When he got to the gas station and put it down, feeling quite proud of himself for having gone three blocks without resting, the sleeves and right shoulder of both his cotton windbreaker and his shirt had been shredded, eaten away by leaking acid. The fright that discovery gave him had been momentary but extreme, and he felt a like one now. God knew what acid had been bathing him all day. Jake said, 'I wanted to see Uncle Giles before he left.' A dumb thing to say. He hadn't known about the transfer, and surely his uncle wasn't leaving for weeks. In fact, Giles hadn't said.

'Dwight Houseman called,' Eleanor said, 'an hour and a half ago.'

Jake thought, Why in hell didn't she say it was Houseman?

John McKay nodded, then looked at Giles. 'Pour me a scotch, will you?' And he carried Cicely up to her room.

Eleanor went into the kitchen. Jake followed his uncle back into the living-room: I saw him today. I could just say I saw him with a woman.

While he fussed with the glasses Giles said absently, 'Three-piece blue suit. Crimson tie.'

'Was it crimson? I forgot to notice.'

'The colour of blood.' Giles waited.

'I saw him today. I saw him with a woman.'

'Where?'

'The Phillips Collection. He had his arm around her.'

'And he saw you?'

'I thought he did, but . . .'

Giles was stirring the drinks more than was necessary. He was taking pains not to strike the glass with the spoon. He seemed suddenly obscure, remote, careful, and Jake felt that he had made a mistake. He stopped speaking and waited.

His uncle said, 'You're certain it was him.'

Jake shrugged. 'I saw him from ten yards. I saw his car, his driver, his ADC.'

'And the woman . . . ?'

'Blonde. Very good-looking. They met her sister.'

'At the museum?'

'Yes.'

Giles faced him. 'You saw your father and this woman and her sister at the Phillips?'

'And they spoke to each other in German.'

'You heard them speak in German?'

Jake nodded, but shame welled in him again and he had to look away.

'Your father was apparently intimate with them?'

'Yes. He gave each of them a flower.'

'A rose?'

'Yes. How did you know?'

'And you saw your father leave in his car?'

'Yes.'

'Alone?'

'With his driver and Dwight Houseman.' Jake could not admit he'd followed the woman and her sister to Georgetown.

Giles touched his nephew's sleeve and said quietly, 'I understand. You're afraid he has betrayed us.'

It was Giles's use of the word *us* that moved Jake and relieved him. He fell against his uncle and began to weep. He tried desperately to stifle his sobbing, to keep it secret, but he couldn't. The enormous wave of anxiety that he had stubbornly held back broke now and poured out of him. This was the strongest emotion he'd ever felt. He could not speak. His uncle pressed him and stroked him. His uncle was the only one with whom he could ever have uncovered himself like this.

'You were right to come home. You want to talk to him, don't you?'

Jake shook his head no. He sniffled, like a child, and wiped his face with the back of his hand. Giles gave him his handkerchief.

'But that's why you're here, and you're damn right, old man. Something like this you have to hit face-on. You have to tell him. And when he explains himself you have to believe him.'

'He doesn't owe me an explanation. He won't make one and I don't need one.'

'You know all about it, is that it?'

Jake looked sharply at his uncle. 'I saw them.'

'You saw what? An informal caress in a public place? Was it an intimate little bistro? No. Candlelit dinner for two? No. A posh night spot? Dancing cheek-to-cheek? My boy, a museum! An art gallery! In the middle of the damned day! That's all you saw!'

'When has he ever had your sister, my mother, to an art gallery in the middle of the damn day? When does he give her roses?' Jake gave his uncle's handkerchief back to him.

'I don't know. Let's ask her, shall we?'

'No!' Jake looked nervously out towards the foyer.

'I'm sorry. I didn't mean that. But you'll ask your father.'

Jake shook his head. 'I'm saying nothing. It was stupid of me to come here. I panicked.'

'You must tell him. You must give him a chance to explain.' Giles trembled. He had something at stake in this too.

Jake was unprepared for the rush of his uncle's emotion. 'Uncle Giles, if it was nothing, then it would be wrong of me to let him know what I suspected. If it isn't nothing, then I choose to answer him with my silence.'

'Answer him?'

'He said just now, "What gives?"'

'Ah, he was short with you. His greeting failed your standard. Now you'll punish him. Dear nephew, perhaps there are good reasons for his greeting and for other things. Perhaps the man carries what you know not of.'

'I'm sure he does, Uncle Giles. But I'm just beginning to understand that we all do.'

'We all do what, dear?' Jake's mother asked nervously on her way into the room. She sensed their tension and she watched her brother and her son carefully as she crossed towards them.

'What we can, Mom.' Jake kissed his mother's cheek. 'I have to get my stick,' he said, and left.

From the foyer he heard her say, 'I don't know what's wrong.' When Giles said nothing she told him, with a brightened voice, 'He's going to take the ebony cane you gave him to a dance on Friday.'

'Stick, Ellie,' his uncle said peevishly. 'Stick.'

When Jake returned to the living-room no one was there. On his way to the kitchen he had to pass his father's study and as he did the door opened.

'Come in here, Jake.'

His father stepped aside, but Jake, having stopped in the corridor, didn't move. He had a stick in each hand, and he leaned on them. Both of his legs trembled, but only for a moment. He looked directly at his father. 'Where's Mother?'

'She's in the kitchen.'

Jake still did not move. He had not openly defied his father since he was twelve.

'Come in here, son, please.' His father walked into the room. Jake followed him.

Giles was sitting on a corner of the partner's desk, staring at his drink.

'Close the door, please.'

Jake did so. His mother would wonder what was up. His father indicated a chair and Jake took it.

'Your uncle tells me you have something on your mind.'

Jake did not look at Giles. In confidence, he'd said. In confidence! That Giles had spoken to his father was a blow Jake could not allow himself to feel. 'Yes, sir, I do.' He noticed that the knot of his father's red tie was pulled down from his collar, which was open. Face-on, Giles had said. But Jake, not out of any hope or desire now to avoid the issue, came at him from the side. 'Mr Houseman called you on the red line.'

'I know he did.'

'Did you call him back?'

'No.' McKay had himself strictly reined.

Jake sensed an advantage and pressed it. 'Wasn't it urgent?'

'Did you take the call?'

'No, Mother did. But I gathered it was urgent.'

'It was,' McKay said, as if he were trusting his son with something. 'You can assume that. And you can assume that I am aware

46

of what Mr Houseman wanted . . .' He stared at his son sternly, then turned away and paced the room. 'Now tell me about the Phillips.'

'The Phillips?' Jake panicked. He wanted to deny suddenly that he'd ever heard of the place. He grabbed at the fact of this new betrayal, his uncle's. Tears threatened to come again. 'Didn't Uncle Giles fill you in?'

McKay looked over at Patterson. For reinforcement? The kid was going to flog them with his wounds. Hell, who could blame him? John McKay did not want to mishandle this. But Giles's gaze remained fixed on his glass, even as he raised it and drank from it and lowered it.

'Suppose you tell me, Jake,' McKay said as kindly as he could.

Jake said nothing. He had nothing to be ashamed of, and he had no account to make. And if he opened his mouth he was going to weep again.

'Giles says you saw me.'

Jake nodded. And then he waited. What terrified him was that when his father offered him his excuse he knew he would not believe it.

But McKay did not offer an excuse. He exhaled strenuously and said, 'I saw you too. But then I convinced myself that I was mistaken.'

'I wish you were.' Jake was relieved. If his father had lied to him . . .

'So do I,' his father said, an abject admission. His first ever to his son.

Jake looked over at his uncle and saw, to his horror, tears on *his* cheeks. His father, who had not noticed that, said, 'So what now?'

Jake shrugged. In fact he was in control of himself. He was his father's son. 'So now I go back to school.'

His father nodded and diddled his goddamn fingers in their chain. He turned his back on Jake to say, 'I must know, son, if you intend to tell your mother.'

'Not tonight,' Jake said. Not ever, but fuck him. Let him wonder. His anger welled. By comparison to his earlier panic it was calming.

'I don't blame you for being upset.'

'What I wish, Pop . . .' Jake's anger faded as quickly as it had come. All he felt now was pain. '. . . Is that you could make everything all right again. Like you used to.'

47

His father nodded, but said nothing. Jake looked at his uncle, whose tears had stopped flowing but whose cheeks were wet still. His mother's dear brother was a drunk. Jake had to look away from him to check his disgust.

He stood up. Well, his father hadn't lied to him or said that someday he'd understand.

At the door of his father's study he stopped. 'It's a funny thing, Dad,' he said. His voice cracked but he didn't care. 'I saw her sister as someone for me.'

'Her sister?' McKay said. His confusion was obvious and total. He could not have feigned it, and that was when Jake realized that *la jeune fille* was the *Fräulein*'s daughter.

CHAPTER FOUR

Tehan's was across the street from the School of Foreign Service and next door to the toney shop where alumni bought their blazers and college seals. Tehan's didn't fit. It had the look more of a lunch-room with its counter – not bar – its bright fluorescent lighting, and red Formica booths than a tavern, but it was open until eleven, when underclassmen had to be back in their rooms, and it served beer in small glasses for a dime. By the time Jake arrived at nine-thirty Tehan's was crowded with students who had fled in mock panic – it was always mock this early in the term – from their first assignments.

It was not like Jake to walk into such a place alone. He didn't expect to see anyone he knew and he vaguely intended to sit at the counter by himself. What he needed after Ridge Road was the light, the noise, and an observer's dose of the jovial camaraderie of Hoyas. A jukebox blocked half the door; the Kingston Trio was singing, 'Scotch and soda, mud in your eye.'

There was an open stool at the near end of the narrow counter, but before Jake had slid on to it someone called, 'Mac! Hey, Mac! McKay!'

It was Cooney hailing from a booth in the far corner of the room. He was sitting with two fellows Jake recognized as freshmen, and that surprised him. He had tacitly assumed that his classmates would be too timid yet to venture out on weeknights. Ordinarily he would not have. He approached the booth, conscious of the eyes in the place that fell briefly upon his leg. Cooney's loud call had drawn attention to McKay, but he didn't mind. He moved carefully, erectly, with his stick dramatically, across the crowded room. Cooney grinned goofily at him as he approached and McKay was surprised at the wave of fondness he felt for him.

'Hello, Ned. How goes?'

'Mac, this is Olsen and Barnett.'

McKay shook hands with the two and slid in next to Cooney. Three blue-and-grey freshman beanies were stacked on the table.

'Where'd you disappear to today, anyway?' Cooney whined.

'Me?' McKay looked wounded. 'When I went back up there, you were gone. You could have waited for me.'

Cooney stared at McKay for a moment. What the hell had happened at that museum anyway? Finally he shrugged and indicated the other two. 'Olsen and Barnett are roommates down the hall from me. It was like a tomb on four tonight.' Cooney said to Olsen and Barnett, 'Mac has a single on five. Wish to hell I had a single. My roommate's a fruit-cake. Study, fart. Study, fart. Study, fart.'

'I hear the proctor on five's a real bastard,' Barnett said. 'That so, Mac?'

He shrugged and then said, 'Jake, call me Jake.' McKay smiled, but he had to nip this Mac business in the bud.

'Tell you what,' Cooney said. 'I'll call you Mac; you can call me Coon!' And then he collapsed in laughter.

McKay exchanged a look with the other two. Cooney was a little weird.

'What's it like on five, Jake?' Olsen asked. Make conversation with the new guy. Let him know you're not like Cooney.

'My room would remind you of an artist's garret.' Olsen looked back at McKay blankly. 'Sloping ceilings, you know? Narrow windows? Bohemia.' McKay paused. 'It'd remind you of Anne Frank's hideout in Amsterdam.' Olsen nodded vaguely. The waitress went by and Jake raised a finger at her. Fly-ridden, fly-riding; Giles had imagined a teasing wench, but this girl was heavy and sullen. Without a nod she cruised back towards the counter. Jake said, 'Speaking of Nazis, what do you guys make of this shit?' He indicated the stacked beanies.

'Where's yours?' Cooney asked.

Jake shrugged.

'You'll catch it,' Barnett said.

49

'If they catch me,' Jake smiled. In fact he hadn't intended to defy the hazing regulation. It simply never occurred to him to go back to his room merely for his beanie. He was like a sleepwalker, operating calmly as if the inner turmoil he felt was someone else's.

'The sophomores leave McKay alone,' Cooney said.

Jake refused to take offence at the implication. 'If it's shit, Ned,' he said amiably, 'it's shit for everybody.'

Cooney turned his palms up. 'At Annapolis they make you eat puke.'

'Plebes,' Barnett said. 'They call them plebes. For plebeian.'

And at Eton they are fags. McKay knew better than to refer to the English school, his uncle's school. He unstacked the beanies and arranged them in a row. He poked Cooney. 'At least the Navy calls a spade a spade.' As Jake repeated Cooney's cliché, his uncle's admonition came back to him. Avoid clichés. Avoid failure.

'Call a coon a coon,' Barnett said. He was not a southerner but the racist crack came automatically. He and Olsen laughed.

At that moment the short sophomore with the bad complexion who had presided over the first freshman assembly on Monday walked into Tehan's. He had introduced himself without humorous intent as the orientation marshal. He conducted the assembly as if it were a military briefing, but succeeded – was it his manner, his acne, or the regulations he announced? – in making the freshmen feel like boys at camp. Still the class had listened to him respectfully and so far had meekly observed the inane rituals of hazing.

Jake nudged Cooney. 'As I said, speaking of Nazis . . .'

'George Lincoln Rockwell himself,' Cooney said under his breath. Olsen and Barnett turned to look. The sophomore was standing near the jukebox with a couple of his lackeys. There were no places left in Tehan's, and it amused the freshmen to watch colour rising in the marshal's face as he realized he'd have to leave. In fact he did turn to go, but one of his buddies stopped him and pointed to the freshmen in the booth in the corner.

As he approached, Jake realized that he felt sorry for him. He was even shorter than he'd seemed, and his complexion was worse. The sores on his face glistened. Jake wasn't prepared for it when the sophomore said gruffly, 'Past your bedtime, isn't it, fellows?'

Cooney drained his glass and Barnett reached for his beanie. Jake hadn't reacted yet when the waitress arrived with his beer.

He thanked her, gave her a quarter, indicated she should keep the change, and then squeezed towards Cooney. 'We can make room for a couple of you,' he said to the sophomore.

'That's kind of you,' one of the marshal's flunkies said, 'but we'll need the whole booth.'

The waitress was collecting empties. Jake said to her, 'We'll need another round right away.'

'All four?' She nearly tripped on Jake's leg, which was stiff along the edge of the booth. She stared at it rudely.

'Yes.' Jake faced Olsen. 'We were talking about Annapolis, right?'

He began to drum his fingers animatedly on the table and move his shoulders as if he were a jazz musician.

Olsen wouldn't look at him, but Cooney put in gamely, 'Joe Bellino's going to be unstoppable this year.'

George Lincoln Rockwell leaned over the table and fingered the beanies. The number 64 in blue felt was pasted over the front grey panel. 'Weren't you guys at the assembly?'

'Yes, we were,' Barnett said.

'So you got the run-down.'

'We did.' Cooney smiled ingratiatingly.

'Well?' The sophomore opened his hands and waited for them to stand up.

McKay stopped drumming and sipped his beer. When he spoke it was with a professor's accent. His cockiness served to control a hysteria he felt. 'I believe you said, "All public functions." I believe you said, "On campus." We're not on campus now, and this is a private function.'

'What do you mean not on campus? This is Tehan's.'

'If you get the proprietor to ask us to leave, we will. Right, fellows? Or the D.C. police. But we're not leaving for you.' Jake smiled, and then the waitress arrived with their beers. 'Thank you kindly, miss.' He put a dollar on her tray and waved away her gesture with change. Then he looked up at the marshal. Suddenly he felt great.

'Where's your beanie?' the sophomore asked.

McKay stared at him solemnly for a moment before saying, 'Jesus, man, listen to yourself.'

'What's your name, bud?'

'McKay, John McKay, Junior.' One of the flunkies started to write it down, so McKay spelled it for him. They glared at McKay for a moment. Then they left.

51

'Christ, Mac, now what?'

'Relax, Ned. I was wrong before. They're not Nazis. They're sophomores.' But inside, McKay was saying to himself, I don't believe I did that!

'Oh, brother,' Barnett said, staring wide-eyed at the mirror on the wall behind Cooney and McKay. 'Look who's coming.'

'Shit!' Olsen chugged his beer.

Cooney leaned towards McKay, but with his eye on the student who was approaching. 'Yeats,' he whispered. 'I told you about him. His old man is in the CIA. He's the PA on our floor.'

Fred Yeats was a natty, good-looking young man whose dark-framed glasses gave him the look of an intellectual. 'Hi, Jake,' he said. He ignored the other three.

But Olsen said breezily, 'How you doing, Fred?'

Cooney was staring at McKay; you said you didn't know him!

'Hello, Fred,' Jake said. 'This is Cooney and Barnett and Olsen.' He said to Cooney, 'We went to the same prep school. St Anselm's, right, Fred?'

'Fairy Hill,' Yeats said. It was how their rivals referred to the priory school. Yeats shook hands with each one. 'You guys are on my floor, right?'

'Lucky for you,' Cooney said.

'Not for you,' Yeats replied sternly, and he stared Cooney down. 'Did I see what I think I just saw? Did you guys tell Tracey to shove off?'

'It's all right, Fred,' Jake said. 'He was under the impression we were nearly through.' There had never been such dissonance between how Jake felt and how he was coming across. Inside he was a screeching lunatic. I can't believe I'm doing this! Fuck all sophomores! Fuck them all!

Yeats looked at his watch. 'Well, you are through, right?'

'I thought we didn't have to be in our rooms until eleven,' Cooney said with a hint of a whine.

'For the night, asshole. That gives you forty minutes. If I was you I'd get moving.' Yeats stepped back to let Olsen and Barnett slide out of the booth, but Jake nursed his beer. Cooney had to tap his shoulder to get him to stand up so that he could get out. Both Barnett and Olsen looked at McKay's leg while he stood for Cooney and sat again. 'Nice meeting you, Jake,' Olsen said.

'See you around, fellows.' Jake raised his hand. He wasn't moving. Now suddenly he felt numb. His manic agitation had drained away.

Yeats slid into the booth opposite McKay. The other freshmen stood there awkwardly. Their beanies dangled at the ends of their arms, like fruit.

'What'd you decide to write on, Jake, by the way?' Cooney, like a child sent to bed, was trying to prolong their talk just another minute.

'*La Petite Danseuse*, Ned. The Crotch on Canvas is all yours.'

Jake and Cooney laughed. That they shared the joke made them seem like friends. But Jake felt like a sleepwalker again. Sleepwalkers do amazing things, he'd read.

Cooney turned to Olsen and Barnett. 'Let's hit it, guys. Yeats and Mac got some top secrets to trade.' He winked broadly, and then followed the other two out. Jake watched them go. At the door, as he expected, they turned to look at him once more. Cooney would say, once they were outside, he got that leg in the Blitz. He would say it as if he'd been there. Would he then say that McKay's old man was having an affair with a beautiful blonde?

'What an asshole,' Yeats said.

'How does he know about your old man, Fred? He knows about mine.'

Yeats shrugged. 'Beats the shit out of me. I ignore it. I tell people my father's a lawyer and let it go at that.'

'My father *is* a lawyer, originally.'

Yeats nodded. 'Most of the old guys are. That's because Donovan was. And now Dulles is.'

'Old guys! My father's not fifty yet.'

Yeats did not reply to that. After a silence he said, 'Jake, I wouldn't be saying this but you're a friend of mine. We have a lot in common. Hazing eats it. We all agree with that. But it still goes here. You don't want to buck it. Believe me.'

'I'm not bucking anything, Fred. I just came in for a beer.' Jake would like to have let it go at that, but a new wave of feeling broke in him. 'I didn't come to Georgetown to wear a beanie, Fred. You know what I mean?' Why was he saying shit like that?

Fred nodded sympathetically. 'But, Jake, don't make things tougher on yourself than they already are.'

'What do you mean by that, Fred?'

Yeats dropped his eyes. A leg like McKay's was not to be referred to even obliquely. 'Tracey can make it uncomfortable for you.'

'Can he get me fired?'

Yeats shook his head no. 'The Jesuits stay out of it. But they also let him have a free hand. The theory is that sophomores are being trained to lead.'

'Then why train freshmen to grovel? Why don't they just get some gerbils from Biology and run them through the hoops? They make guys jog backwards around the statue of John Carroll with books on their heads. Now what do you think John Carroll would say about that?'

Fred laughed. 'Probably that we missed his point.'

Jake reached across the table to squeeze Yeats's arm. 'Hey, Fred, don't worry about me.'

'OK. Welcome to Georgetown.' Yeats was uneasy, but he raised one of the glasses and when Jake raised his they clinked.

'By the way, Fred, did I ever tell you I heard your father's voice on the red line last spring?'

'What?' Yeats was shocked.

But so was Jake. Why was he bringing this up? It was weird. He was like two people, one watching, the other performing. 'Relax, relax,' he said. 'I heard him say, "Present."'

'Oh.' Yeats exhaled dramatically. 'I thought you meant you'd listened in.'

'I wish I had. The President was on too. It was the day the U-2 got shot down.'

Yeats looked around; who could hear them?

'Didn't you ever have the urge to listen, Fred?'

'Hey, Jake, Jesus! This isn't funny.'

'I've just been realizing something. I don't know much about the world I grew up in. It bothers me. You've grown up in it, too. How much do you know?'

'My father sells shoes, Jake. Really. For all I know.'

'Do you ever ask him questions?'

'Like what?'

'Like about Berlin. Don't you think we've come pretty close to lighting the candle there lately? Don't you find you want to know? Haven't you ever wanted to flip through the folders he brings home?'

Fred was nervous now. He took his glasses off and began to clean them. 'God, Jake, you're really acting weird. What are you saying?'

'I'm saying you're the only guy I know who might under-stand what it's like to have top-secrets as members of the family.'

'You can be very proud of your father, Jake. I know I am of mine.'

Jake swirled what remained of his beer so that it coated the glass. 'Sure. That wasn't my point.'

'It's the only point there is. Don't think about the other stuff. It takes discipline to do what our fathers do, and it takes discipline to be their sons. Assholes like Cooney sniff around us. Who sniffs around them? You're never sure, Jake. Certain people would love to know what we know.'

'I don't know shit. That's what I'm telling you.'

'You know a lot of stuff, ace.' Yeats leaned forward dramatically. 'Your old man is top-level CIA. So is mine. They know everything there is to know. And we know them. Be careful, Jake. This isn't kid stuff.'

'What'd your father do during the war?'

'Huh?' Yeats leaned back against the booth.

'World War Two. Your father. Where was he?'

'Overseas.'

'The Pacific? Europe? Where?' He pressed like a prosecutor.

'Europe.'

'England?'

'No.'

'Well, hell, Fred, where? The rest of Europe was Nazi.'

'Not Switzerland.'

'He was in Switzerland?' McKay thought about that for a moment, then said, 'So was Dulles.'

'He was in Berne. My father was in Zurich.'

'Near the border.'

'I guess so.'

'Dulles kept in contact with resistance groups, wasn't that it?'

'I don't think we should be talking about this, Jake.'

'Fred, the war's over. The Germans lost.'

'My father never refers to the war. I assume he was working for Dulles, though. He has been ever since. Where was yours?'

'London. He was OSS liaison with SOE.'

'What's that mean?'

'Special Operations Executive. The British equivalent.'

'They call it SIS now.'

Jake nodded. They were strutting their stuff with each other. 'My father's contact was my uncle.'

Yeats looked at him quizzically.

McKay explained. 'The chap my father worked with introduced him to his sister. He claims she was one of the glories of blacked-out London.'

'That's why your mother's English.'

'Now you're getting it, Frederick. I knew that thick-headed peevishness would pass.' Jake smiled and Yeats blushed and nodded. 'Do you think our fathers worked together in those days, Fred? I know that my uncle used to parachute behind the lines on secret missions all the time.'

Yeats stared at him.

'He told me.'

'And your father too?'

Jake shrugged. 'My uncle doesn't talk about my father's stuff. He's not in the biz anymore, but I guess he respects the fact that Dad still is. My uncle used to bring cash and forged papers to resistance fighters. If that's what Dulles was doing, too, maybe your old man and my uncle hooked up. I'll bet they did.'

'I don't think the British and the Americans did that much together. It's still pretty cut-throat between them, I gather.'

'Oh? Between CIA and SIS? Where do you gather that?'

Yeats stared at McKay. 'Ian Fleming, Jake,' he said finally. 'Where else?'

'How many languages does your father speak?'

'French. He speaks French.'

'Not German? Most Swiss speak German, I thought.'

'Most Swiss are bilingual, Jake.' Yeats paused, then added, 'Maybe he speaks German. I don't know.'

'How could you not know whether your father speaks German?'

'What's eating you, Jake?'

'I just found out my old man speaks it, and it bothers me that I didn't know it.'

'He probably speaks Russian too.' Yeats added condescendingly, 'I'd say it's certain that he *reads* it.'

Jake tried to check the anger that was welling in him again. His feelings, the way they kept rolling in on him, alternately anger, worry, grief, were keeping him off balance, lightheaded. Why should he be angry at Yeats? 'That doesn't bother you? Your ignorance of your father's life doesn't bother you?'

'It's none of my business.' He looked around Tehan's again. 'We shouldn't be talking about it here.' Students were heading back to their dorms for curfew. Yeats stood up. 'We shouldn't be talking about it period.'

56

'You mean, don't buck it.'

'That's just what I mean.'

'Don't make things tougher for myself than they already are, eh?'

'I didn't mean anything by that. I've got to go. I have to tuck your classmates in.'

'Wait a minute, Fred.' Jake stood up. It took him a second to retrieve his blackthorn from under the booth. When he was upright he leaned towards Yeats. 'I didn't intend to press you. I know what you're thinking: I have a chip on my shoulder. I wear a stick. I, as they say, carry a cane. But that has nothing to do with this.'

'With what, Jake?'

'I'm not eating puke for anybody, get it?'

'Who said anything about eating puke? Christ!' Yeats turned and started to go, but McKay grabbed his sleeve.

'Your sophomore friends will think it's them I'm bucking. But it won't be. I'll be bucking something I can't quite name because where I come from the goddamn names of everything that matters, including this feeling I have, are all classified. And, Fred, I think you know what I'm talking about.'

'McKay, I haven't a clue what you're talking about.' He jerked his arm away. 'You're on your own.'

'*That* is what I'm talking about.'

'I always thought you were on the team.'

'How can I be on the team when nobody tells me what we're playing?'

A faint curtain of rain had closed on the street. The water, a first dull sheet of it, glistened up from the pavement and from the brick sidewalk. Jake stood in the entrance to Tehan's to turn up his collar and then crossed the street to his car, a five-year-old pale blue Ford convertible parked illegally in front of the Foreign Service School. He'd intended to move it to the student lot, but, with the rain, decided the hell with it. He got his books and his ebony stick and locked the car. He turned to go back across the street, but a strange light from inside the Foreign Service School building caught his eye and he approached it.

The most striking feature of the building's exterior was the two-storey-high plate glass window. Protruding from the top of it was an overhang that sheltered him from the drizzle. Inside, the huge bronze globe that dominated the lobby was illuminated, but softly, and the light that had attracted his attention was the eerie brown glow of that giant sphere. It shone exotically, like the oiled skin of a mulatto fighter. Encircling it, a staircase not unlike the one at the Phillips spiraled up to the second and third floors. The stairway, he thought, to heaven. Suddenly Jake imagined a line of dancers in sailor suits and doughboy outfits tripping gingerly down those stairs, saluting and singing and then falling away as Fred Astaire came tap-tap-tapping down, then up, then down again, with his top hat and cane and a song about the wonderful, wonderful world.

Jake cupped his hand against the glass and peered in. He'd walked past that bronze globe a dozen times already – half his classes were in that building – but only then did he notice, because the beams of light rippled across the surface, that it was turning. A motor drove it. The Western Hemisphere was just sliding into view. Once he focused on it he could see the globe clearly. He easily picked out Europe – the box of Iberia was always the great clue – and he found himself, as the unmarked continent rolled slowly away, trying to picture the borders of Germany. Where was Zurich? Where was Berlin?

'What do you see, old man?'

The quiet voice from behind startled Jake, but instead of turning abruptly he brought his face back from the window slowly. In its reflection he saw the vague but familiar figure. 'Uncle Giles,' he said. For a moment he felt truly frightened. In the glass against the drizzle his uncle, always gaunt and ascetic, seemed ghostly, and Jake's mind could not work quickly enough to account for his presence there.

Giles sensed his nephew's shock and he explained by saying simply, nodding over his shoulder, 'Tehan's, you told me Tehan's. A snap to find. I thought you might come here.'

'I didn't intend to.'

'And now you're' – Giles craned to look through the window – 'what, thinking of breaking in?'

'I was looking at the globe,' Jake said dully. His uncle had grievously betrayed him only hours before, and he remembered.

Giles joined him at the window and peered in. 'Ah, yes,' he muttered. '*Vera Totius Expeditionis Nauticae.*' It was the inscription on top of a sixteenth-century Portuguese chart that had hung in his father's library. What had happened to it? he wondered. 'The world of man. Enchanted Balloon.'

Jake and Giles stood side by side for some moments, watching

58

the globe turning. The demarcation of land and water and the levels of topography were indicated abstractly, by the contrast between shining polished surfaces and rough-hewn textures in the bronze.

Jake was thinking that without the pastel patches of a Rand-McNally map he would be hard put to identify nations, much less cities. He had a lot to learn.

Giles said absently, 'One sixth of its surface, good Lord!' He watched the globe turning in silence again before saying, 'Do you notice that every nation disappears from view but one? It never completely goes away.'

Jake had not noticed that, and he still could not have defined its borders, but he could guess. 'Russia,' he said.

'The Soviet Union, more precisely.' Giles peered. 'Bloody waste of the earth's surface.' He paused again, then recited, 'From Poland to the Pacific. From Persia to Alaska.'

'We could be looking down from the U-2, I guess, eh?'

Giles laughed. 'Not me, my boy. Too high for comfort, but not so high they can't smoke you.'

Jake stepped back from the window before his tipsy uncle could throw an arm around him. 'Why did you come here?'

Giles faced his nephew and leaned wearily against the window. A sober man in daylight would not have tested the glass like that. 'Jake, I rather owe you an explanation. Don't you agree?'

'Because I spoke to you in confidence?'

Giles nodded once, barely.

And then neither spoke. Jake looked out at the rain, but Giles did not take his eyes off his nephew's face.

'Jake,' he said softly, 'I'd be dearly grateful if you'd look at me.' But his nephew would not.

'I told your father, Jake, because my loyalty to him runs as deep as mine to you.' Giles waited. He expected a remark about John's loyalty to Eleanor, but Jake said nothing. 'If I hadn't told him, don't you see, it would have breached a lifetime.'

'I never thought of you as that close to my father. I thought you were closer to my mother.' And to me, he added to himself.

'Your father and I are brothers, Jake. What we've been through together has made it so. Between brothers it's not the expression that counts, but the bond itself. Your secret would have ruined that. I'm sorry I couldn't explain it to you at the time.'

'Did you know already?'

'About Anna-Lise?'

That name, the nuance of it, its specificity, the biography implied in it, and the ease with which his uncle spoke it made Jake's fear concrete. He looked at him.

'Yes, I've known.'

'For how long?'

Giles did not answer him.

'Uncle Giles' – the calm in Jake's voice was counterfeit – 'why are you on my father's side against your sister?'

'Old man.' Giles put his hand on his nephew's shoulder now. 'It is so infinitely more complex than you imagine.'

'What? Life?'

'I don't blame you for feeling condescended to . . .'

'Don't shit me!' Jake jerked out of his uncle's grasp. 'It's not my feelings that matter! What about my mother? Would you like to explain how infinitely complex it is that her husband of nineteen years has been stretching the point with *schöne* Anna-Lise?'

'No, I wouldn't.' Giles lapsed into silence. Jake's vehemence stunned him.

'Of course you wouldn't. She would be shattered. What holds Mother together is her absolute trust in him. You know that.'

'You mustn't underestimate her. Your mother has her strengths.'

'I'm telling you, Uncle Giles, this will break her apart. She worships him. She gave up her world for him, except you. She thrives on the little he gives her, but only because she believes she gets everything he has to give. Tell her now that she has been sharing him, not only with the noble fight for freedom but with an Anna-Lise, and she will crack before your eyes. I know her.' What really enraged him and shamed him was that he was himself every bit as dependent on his father as his mother was. *He* was cracking before his own eyes.

'I'm not telling her,' Giles said absently. He had withdrawn apparently into a vacuous contemplation, a tangible melancholy.

'And my father knows her. That's why all he asked me was if I was telling. As if I could do such a thing to her.'

'You might credit your father with some feeling for her situation.'

'I don't,' Jake said fiercely.

'I gather.'

Jake looked at his watch. 'I have to go,' he said, but he didn't move.

'I see you have your ebony stick.' Giles indicated the cane under Jake's arm. 'I don't think I told you about it, did I?'

'You said it was yours when you were my age. You wore it with your tails.'

'I was a perfect Oscar Wilde at school. I loved nothing so much as going in full evening dress with white gloves clutched in one hand, that silver-topped stick in the other, to the Alhambra for the Ballet Russe de Sergei Diaghilev.' Giles took Jake's stick and looked closely at the finely engraved handle. 'We were younger than you are. We were insufferable dandies. My father was positively horrified by my frivolity. Which was of course its point. He considered my stick' – here Giles held the ebony up to see it better – 'an affectation. Which is what it was until I gave it to you. Don't you see, old man, this stick did not acquire its dignity, or for that matter its true beauty, until you began to use it?'

'Beauty is in the hand of the holder.'

'Precisely.' Giles offered the cane back and Jake took it somewhat solemnly.

'That stick has its secrets, my boy. Believe me.'

Jake nodded. Didn't everything? 'I really have to go, Uncle Giles.'

'I tracked you down tonight, unforgivably, because I simply couldn't go off with the evening's hash being our last . . . Jake, my hearty, I may not see you again.'

'Don't be crazy.'

'I'm leaving soon.'

'When?'

'Soon. I had hoped we might . . . Oh, Jake, my heart sinks to see you and your father at swords' points. You're the two I love most in the world. I wanted to help you see . . . Jake, you mustn't turn your back on him. I could help you understand. It's what uncles are for.'

'I want to understand.'

'See me tomorrow then. We'll talk tomorrow. Let's meet.' The boy hesitated. 'I'm leaving, Jake. I'm going away.'

'I was thinking I could come and see you in the summer.'

'And tomorrow?'

'Will you tell me what you know?'

'I'll tell you what I can.'

'It's been a while since we went up the Monument together. We could meet at three.'

'Perfect. I'll see you at the top.'

CHAPTER FIVE

Jake McKay dressed carefully the next morning, his blazer and flannels, his loafers, a striped shirt, and a grey silk tie, his best. At his mirror he considered his appearance. He had slept badly and looked slightly haggard, but haggardness was considered an asset on a lean, modern young man like him and he knew it. Jake was aware of his own vanity. That morning, with the image fresh in his mind of his uncle outraging and amusing London as one of its precious young flits, it made him uneasy. Jake had tried to suppress what hints of Britishness in speech and manner he'd inherited from his mother because at St Anselm's the most foppish boys had imitated the English monks slavishly. Even in the English, English accents, and for that matter their wit and literateness, seemed pompous and effeminate. Jake had cultivated an American style of manliness with the peculiar elegance of its slightly coarse language and feigned indifference to the good opinion of authority. He had, only partly consciously, begun to model himself after his father, whose understated but always meticulous dress was an image of that American brilliance which achieved its effect by refusing to draw attention to itself. In point of fact Jake had yet to meet a man who matched his father for strength of presence or for the ease with which he established his superiority. The form of Jake's ambition had yet to be defined, but the content had been implicit for years in the awe in which he held his father. It was important that morning that he get his version of that quality of appearance just right not because he was a dandy – he wasn't – but because he was afraid that if he did not maintain a rigorous hold on himself now that his confidence in his father was destroyed he would be destroyed too. The night before he had impulsively repudiated the rites of hazing. He had no stomach for the conflict that implied, but now he had things to prove if only to himself. He had decided to go downstairs dressed like a man instead of a muff.

He sensed as he entered the dining-room that the only other students not wearing the beanie, the tie, and the mismatched socks were upperclassmen. He crossed the hall carefully, with as little jerk to his gait as possible, and he let his blackthorn jig a bit with each step. The morning light filtered dully through the large gothic windows. The rain of the night before had become a grey clotting mist, which seemed to have seeped into the huge dark-panelled room itself and now clung to the vaulted ceiling, damping the chatter and the spirits of the breakfasters.

He took his place in the cafeteria line behind a string of fresh-men whom he did not know but who were tricked out in their goofy attire. They stepped aside, expecting Jake to go ahead of them, as would have been his privilege were he indeed an upper-classman. Obviously they assumed he was not a fellow freshman. He smiled and indicated that he was happy to stand in line. What else could they do but turn back to their conversation and ignore him?

Just as Jake was about to take a tray from the stack a committee of sophomores, led by the short fellow who'd confronted him in Tehan's, approached him. George Lincoln Rockwell, Cooney'd called him. That Cooney had a gift for the apt insult. Yeats had called him Tracey. At that first assembly the kid had called himself the orientation marshal.

'McKay, you seem to have forgotten something.'

'Hello, marshal,' Jake said amiably, but inside he trembled. How would his uncle carry this off? Equal measures of warmth and panache, that's how. 'Did you sleep well?'

'You want a special exemption, is that it? You're used to getting special treatment?'

'Not particularly, no.'

'So we should handle you the way we'd handle anyone else?'

'Of course.'

Tracey hesitated, but whatever qualm he had, he mastered. He stepped back and his companions – Tracey disdained the physical enforcement himself – simply picked McKay up and carried him out of the dining-room.

It happened too quickly for Jake to take in any but the crudest impression. During the cacophonous burst of hooting and whistling, the exit chorus, he realized that his fellow freshmen were as entertained by his humiliation as the others were.

The sophomores carried him briskly upstairs to the nearest lavatory, put him into a shower, and turned on the water.

Jake simply leaned against the cold tile wall under the blast of frigid water. Instantly he was soaked, but he did not move. The stream was hitting him at the base of his neck, a yoke, a rabbit punch.

One of the sophomores said, 'Next time wear your duds, asshole.'

As they left Jake heard one of them say to another, 'I think he started to cry.'

He hadn't, but he wanted to. He felt desolate and alone. He was afraid. But he had begun something he simply could not stop.

He waited until he was certain they were gone, and then he went as quickly as he could to his room. He changed clothes and he combed his hair so that the school photographer could have focused his lens on its part. With his hair glistening and slicked back, with his twill trousers and English tweed coat, he looked more the dashing figure from another age than ever. Instead of his blackthorn he wore his uncle's silver-headed ebony, and he went back to the dining-room.

Everyone was seated by now. Jake was aware that the noise level fell as he entered. He saw Cooney at a nearby table and waved at him as he made for the serving line. When half a dozen sophomores met him at the now diminished stack of trays, the room grew absolutely silent.

Tracey said to him quietly, 'I thought you didn't want special treatment.'

Jake took the two steps that separated them. He wanted to be as close to Tracey as possible so that the sophomore would have to crane his neck to look up at him. 'Look, Tracey, I'm sure you're a very nice fellow and someday perhaps we'll be fast friends. For this morning let it be enough for us to treat each other like grown-ups. What do you say?'

Unfortunately even Jake heard the pleading in his voice, the note of false bravado. No wonder they weren't intimidated. When Tracey didn't respond, McKay started to go around him. He walked unsteadily now. Perspiration had already dampened his fresh shirt. The sophomores stopped him. They picked him up again quickly and more roughly. This time he wasn't ready for them and he dropped his stick. The clattering noise it made when it hit the floor underscored the absence now of hooting and whistling. The room's silence bathed the scene like stage light. But McKay knew as he was carried out that his fellow Hoyas were regarding him suspiciously. Hazing was a harmless ritual. The freshmen did not consider themselves above it and neither, in their time, had the others. It was good fun, sport, a rite of autumn. Who the hell did this guy think he was?

They took McKay to the same shower. This time they stood

over him while the water ran. He let it soak him as it had before.

Then the sophomores left.

McKay couldn't move even to turn the water off. What had he begun? Would he spend the day, the week, his entire career in wet clothes, in that tiled booth, in the cold corner against which he pressed himself and pressed himself and pressed himself? For the first time in his life he felt utter despair. He was trapped. He couldn't quit and he couldn't go on. He couldn't go home but he couldn't stay here. He wanted his father, Pop, to come and save him. But Pop was gone. Pop didn't exist anymore. Pop was a stranger now who betrayed his family and ruined it. Jake leaned against the tiles and realized that the water pounding him obscured his tears. He wept like a child.

He would not have moved – the paralysis offered a kind of comfort – but even through the noise of the shower he heard someone come into the lavatory. He turned the water off, and tried to pull himself together.

'I thought you might need this.' The voice met itself coming and going off the room's flat hard surfaces, but McKay recognized it.

Fred Yeats was holding his ebony stick out to him. 'Thank you, Fred. I appreciate it.' He stepped out of the stall, wiping the water from his face as if it were only shower water, and took the stick. 'My uncle gave it to me.' He leaned on the cane as if testing it. 'It's my best stick. I only bring it out on special occasions.'

'I'll say this for you, Jake.' Yeats smiled at him. 'You're a stubborn son of a bitch.'

'That's true, Fred.' McKay started past him.

Yeats reached an arm out tentatively. 'I just talked to Tracey. I told him you were a friend of mine. I told him to lay off.'

'I'll outlast him, Fred.' He had a hold on himself now, but not nearly so firmly as he pretended.

Yeats shook his head. 'Check the bulletin board.'

'Why?'

'He's extending hazing period. For every day you don't cooperate, your classmates have to eat the crap an extra day.'

'You're kidding.' Jake was shocked. The fuckers took their shit seriously.

'He told me to tell you you don't have to wear the socks, if that's your problem.'

'Do you think it is?'

'I told him it wasn't.'

'Can he do that, extend hazing?'

Fred nodded.

'He'll have to keep it up through Christmas.'

'He's counting on your friends to lean on you.'

My friends? Jake tried to imagine to whom that phrase could possibly refer. Ordinarily he was not given to feelings of self-pity, but all at once it seemed to him not merely that he had no friends but, more drastically, that he had been raised by strangers to live alone. He swallowed hard to keep his tears at bay.

'He has to make it work, Jake. Some people got really pissed off when they carried you out the second time, and now it's getting around about your leg. Tracey's afraid you could start something.'

'Tell him to relax, Fred. I'm not starting anything. I'm just not wearing that shit, any of it. And I'm not walking backwards around statues. Hazing doesn't belong at Georgetown.'

Fred Yeats hadn't become the commander of the Dowd Rifles by going around insulting people. But Jake McKay was known as a friend of his, and if this flap worsened it would reflect on him. 'Maybe you don't either, Jake.'

McKay stared at him. 'You mean I could still get the tuition back if I withdrew.'

'As a matter of fact, you could.'

'And you're only saying this because you're my friend.' Jake's despair evaporated before his bitterness.

'That's right, Jake.'

McKay breathed in sharply. It was as if, having believed himself to be riding one fast horse, he realized when they veered away from each other, he was riding two.

'Let's slow this thing down a minute, Fred.' Jake's mind raced on, though. Maybe I should back off, he thought. 'I didn't mean to make a big deal. Hell, if I'd known . . .'

'You should have known.'

'Well, I didn't, damn it! Tell Tracey I didn't understand.'

'You understand now, though, right?'

Jake dropped his eyes shamefully. 'Yeah, I guess I do.'

'Then shape up, OK?'

It was the direct order that did it, as if Yeats was Jake's father. No one talked to him like that *except* his father. And now not even his father would dare to. Jake's anger blasted him again, and stiffened him. 'Shape up? Christ, you're right. I nearly gave in there, didn't I?' Jake stared at Yeats defiantly.

'Don't make a fool of yourself, buddy. The sophomores can be stubborn when their backs get up.'

66

'My back is up too, Fred.' Why? Because of Yeats's refusal to soften? His refusal to indicate sympathy? The counterfeit of his affection insulted McKay. The suggestion that he leave George-town infuriated him, and, despite himself, he felt that emotion building. 'My back is up too,' he repeated, lifting his cane. 'You tell them that, friend.' He shook the cane in Yeats's face. Yeats flinched and backed off. When he described this later he would say McKay had seemed insane and violent, perhaps the way cripples were when their rage at life's unfairness overtook them. 'You tell the next son of a bitch who touches me is going to get this stick across his face!'

L'Enfant laid Washington out according to a plan that anticipated the invasion of the city by a great army of foot soldiers. The broad avenues – spokes on a wheel – intersected at circles that were strategically placed so that batteries of cannon could be mounted to command access to the heart of the city. If invaders pressed, the defenders could fall back to successive positions until taking up in the centre of the mammoth concentric grid the best one from which to resist because it was on the hill, and the building which dominated it, the Capitol, would also serve through a long siege as the bastion.

Jake McKay could see L'Enfant's plan clearly. He was more than five hundred feet above it, inside the Washington Monument, and he was seeing the city whole, the way officers see their battlefields on maps. It was easy to picture an army – suppose Napoleon had defeated Wellington and held Moscow; wouldn't he have moved against America? – storming down from the hazel Maryland hills, the puffs of cannon smoke, the trains of bayonet-, kit-bag-, canteen-bearing men, the troops of horses, the carriages and buckboards, the fires marking like red pins the places on the outskirts where the armies were engaged. He could hear the artillery open up as the Frenchmen made their first foray into range and then once they attacked the steady boom of the defenders' guns from what are now known as Logan Circle and Dupont Circle and Sheridan Circle and Thomas Circle. And Jake could hear the cries of women and children in root cellars and closets and slave holes. Their husbands and fathers were in the streets taking shot in the face, falling from horses, getting run through with pikes, and having their legs cut off at the thigh by the molten shrapnel of the enemy's vicious new cannon shells. A scene of such carnage. But it was the children he heard, not

67

the fathers. The wives, not the husbands.

From the bunkerlike observation deck – cement floor and walls, barred narrow window – Jake looked down on Washington and saw it as a city not of powerful men but of powerful men's children.

Congressmen and senators, generals and cabinet officers, economists and analysts, chiefs of staff and directors and lawyers and speech writers and ambassadors and administrators all had at homes in Bethesda, Alexandria, Spring Valley, Chevy Chase, Arlington, McLean, and Silver Spring children whose first names they sometimes could not think of and whose birthdays they remembered because their secretaries told them to.

The city was besieged by thousands of – not French soldiers – children, boys and girls and sons and daughters and nephews and nieces, two centuries' worth of them, boring down the avenues without weapons, rushing blindly at the city of their fathers and finding them, those fathers and uncles, behind their – not desks – cannon, saying Ready, aim, go to your room. Don't make things worse for yourself than they are. The guns roared.

Jake stepped back from the small window, from the chill but also from the light. The day, a cold one for September, was over-cast but clear. The cubicle of the Monument observation deck was on the other hand ill lit and still damp from the rain. A pair of tourists excused themselves and squeezed in front of him. He had an impulse to volunteer as their guide. He knew more about the city than anyone. He had considered running his own sightseeing service in the summer. He could tell these tourists, say, about the time his British relatives stormed Washington and burned the White House to the ground.

He moved to the west window. A solitary old man was blocking it. When the old man looked around at Jake, Jake smiled at him. No hurry. But the old man moved away. Jake took his place. Now he could look more directly down to see the Monument's sharp reflection in the long thin unrippled pool. The symmetry of that shaft matted in black, framed in white, laid out on green felt, soothed him. The mall at that point was bordered on both sides by lines of tempos, the low flat-roofed unornamented buildings that had been slated to be torn down after – not the Second, ladies and gentlemen – the First World War. The bushy red-tinged trees, which looked like the heads of broccoli plants, caulked the space between each two tiers of buildings. Jake ran his eye to the very foot of the Monument to see the bright crescent of American flags, and he thought he heard those flags snapping.

He let his eye drift west again to Lincoln, that mammoth bronze father of the people, for the people. And his son? His son died in the White House. Of neglect? Jake tried to picture a sick child in the bronze arms of the Great Emancipator and couldn't.

He tried to picture himself as a child in his father's arms and unfortunately could do so all too easily. It wasn't that his father was made of bronze at all. This pain that kept him on edge, continually nauseated, on the verge of crying all the time, revealed acutely how much Jake had loved his father and trusted him.

Jake let his gaze drift across Constitution Avenue and up the sharp incline to the yellow acropolis which, because of its position at the very foot of the city's axis and its remove behind stucco walls from the avenue, tourists never noticed and natives rarely inquired about. Not one building, but several, all the colour of parchment, the compound had served since the war as the head-quarters of OSS, then the CIA. It was what Jake was waiting to look at but not wanting to.

Jake picked out L-Building. He knew better than to try to see his father's window; it faced north. But automatically he conjured up the building's corridors with gleamng, white-flecked black linoleum slightly undulating underfoot because it was laid over ancient wooden floors. On the walls at intervals – he'd paced them out when his father brought him in on Saturdays – of fifteen yards were hung huge prints in the style of *Army Magazine* illustrations: tank battles seen from the air, truck convoys on jungle roads, Sabre jets and MiGs dogfighting over mountainous terrain. What Jake remembered best about his father's office was the leather couch – the smell of it, the cold suppleness against the back of his neck, on which he habitually lay to look up at the huge map of the world that covered the wall behind it. Korea and Peking, Moscow and Berlin; it had soothed Jake's acute fears of the coming war to focus on the places where the enemy lived. They had houses too, right? With children they loved and tucked in at night and took to the office on weekends? Jake said to his father once that the Russians didn't want to be blown to smithereens any more than we did, and his father explained sadly that Communists were different from us. They sent their children off to be raised in communes and they believed that the end justified the means.

Jake focused on the tiny white guardhouse at the compound entrance on Twenty-third Street. Perhaps he'd see his father's car coming or going. Twenty-four hours before, that car with Mr Curtin at the wheel and his father tucked under the lamp in the right rear corner had left the compound for the Phillips Collection. Dwight Houseman was with him. Did Dwight Houseman always wait outside while his father went to be with blonde Germans? Where had he met her today?

'My son saw us,' he would say to her. 'But he'll never tell.'

'Still, my darling, *ve* must be careful.' From now on they would meet only at her house on O Street in Georgetown, scrupulously discreet as they'd been in the beginning.

Jake closed his eyes and leaned against the cold stone wall, gripped the iron bar that kept loonies from jumping and let the wind massage his face. It was a feeling, this disappointment, that he had to get used to.

A hand closed on the small of his back, gently. Jake could smell his uncle's cologne.

'How beautiful . . .' Giles said.

'Are the feet . . .' Jake replied.

'Of them that preach the gospel of peace . . .'

'And bring glad tidings of good things.' Jake faced him. 'Alleluia.' He said it ironically. His pensive melancholy held.

Giles bowed, looked pointedly through the window. 'We are risen indeed.'

They stood side by side gazing out at Washington. Jake said, 'It used to seem to me that one saw everything from up here. But actually all one sees are roofs.'

'Churchill gave speeches to us when we were crouched in our basement shelters during the air raids. It was the tops of the buildings that went on fire, not the cellars. "To the roofs, London!" he would cry. We had to put the fires out. "To the roofs!"'

'And did they?'

'Of course.'

'That's where I am now, Uncle Giles. On the roof.'

'You've had a shock, lad, haven't you?'

Jake nodded. After a few minutes he said carefully, 'You said last night that you could help me understand.'

'Do you know how theologians define faith?'

'As a virtue?'

'Faith is the acceptance of revelation not on its intrinsic merit but on the authority of the One who gives it. I've thought about what I'm going to say to you, Jake, and I want you to accept it on my authority. Do you understand?'

70

'I'm not sure.'

'No matter.' Giles looked over his shoulder, a show of seeing that no one else was there. 'I know what I can tell you and what I can't. What I have to say is very simple, and you will either accept it because I am its source or you won't.' He paused, but Jake did not comment. 'Your father is not romantically enmeshed with Anna-Lise. She works as a translator – she is proficient in eight languages – and she performs on occasion special services for your father's office. If they met at the Phillips yesterday, it was so that she could deliver to him, discreetly, her most recent work.'

'Discreetly!' Jake blurted. 'In broad daylight? In a public place?'

Giles nodded, and said firmly, 'Yes, discreetly. The openness of their meeting was the essence of its discretion. Obviously they accomplished the exchange of matter surreptitiously, but the public nature of their encounter was essential, and so was its apparently romantic character. We can assume that the matter involved is one of an extremely sensitive nature. Your father was not in a position to explain that to you last night and neither was I. I would not dare speak of it to you now unless I was sober as the stone spire of a church.'

'To be sure you don't say too much?'

'My prince, I have said too much already.'

'How do you know about it?'

'The roses. The key lies in the roses. He gave her roses, you said. Do you know the meaning of *sub rosa*?'

'Sure. Secret.'

'Well then.'

Jake stared at his uncle. He was not in a mood to be toyed with.

'*Sub rosa*,' Patterson went on. 'Literally, under the rose; from the ancient custom of hanging a rose over the council table to indicate that all present were sworn to secrecy, and probably connected with the legend that Cupid gave a rose to the god of silence, Harpocrates, to keep him from revealing the indiscretions of Venus. The *Oxford English Dictionary*, more or less.' Patterson grinned.

Jake waited.

'*Sub Rosa* is the designation of Anna-Lise's function. The rose is like her code symbol. Nothing more. At least as far as your father is concerned.' He raised his bony shoulders and dropped them. 'As for me . . . I introduced Anna-Lise to your father. She has worked for certain offices in the Embassy, offices with which

I have nothing to do, but I'd seen her coming and going and I confess myself to have been somewhat smitten by her cool Nordic detachment and I arranged to meet her. If anyone has been inappropriately enmeshed with that woman, it is I.' Giles bowed.

'What's inappropriate if it's you?'

'The indiscretions of Venus. Anna-Lise is married.'

'And that was her daughter?'

'Magda. She would be' – he thought for a moment – 'sixteen.'

Jake stared down at the parchment-coloured buildings. Not to believe his uncle was unthinkable, and yet he didn't feel nearly the relief he'd have expected to. If his father's treason had evaporated, why hadn't the weight of it? Because Jake's own righteousness had evaporated, to be replaced by guilt. 'I guess,' he admitted, 'I don't mind adultery so much if it's wrecking someone else's family.'

'Adultery, Jake, is what Irish bartenders do when they put water in the whisky.'

The two of them stared out at the horizon – not a discernible line that day, but a finger smudge of grey above the hills – and, unconsciously mimicking each other, they took flesh between their teeth, Giles a crooked forefinger, Jake his lower lip. Finally, Jake said, 'Why do I still feel lousy?'

'Because life is bloody awful and now you know it.'

'Not so awful if my father's not a liar.'

'It *is* awful, Jake. What if *I* was?'

'If you were what?'

'A liar.'

'When?'

'Just now.'

Jake faced his uncle.

'What I've explained to you, old boy, *could* be the truth. And if it was, wouldn't that redeem things somewhat? "How beautiful the feet" and all that. It was not my purpose to deceive or provide excuses for your father. It is only my purpose to suggest to you that there *may* be other explanations than the most obvious, and I conjured one. *Sub Rosa*: a code! It might account for the roses, mightn't it? Perhaps your father deserves the benefit of the doubt.'

'You mean she isn't a translator?'

'I mean who knows for certain what anyone is? Life *is* awful, Jake. All we have are these small fondnesses. Don't squander the love of your father. *That* is what I mean. I did. My entire generation did. And it ruined us. Cling to your father no matter what.'

'Wait a minute. You just made that up, that stuff about the rose?'

'You're not listening to me. What difference if I made it up? The fact that you were prepared to accept it *as* fact suggests that you were premature in your judgement of him.'

'But now *you've* deceived me!'

'No, no, no, Jake. If I wanted to deceive you I would simply deceive you.'

'Well, Christ . . .' Jake stopped; he tried to see his uncle's point. '. . . You deceived me for a moment.'

'That's true but not important. An uncle's prerogative. I'm teaching you something new. We know almost nothing about each other. We are a sequence of surprises and disappointments and, now and then, delights. What matters is that we hold on to each other through everything. Don't you see?'

'I do see that, and I appreciate it. But I also think there are consequences to behaviour.'

'You speak with such assurance. Such a young man's rigour. I would love you no matter what you did.'

'My father wouldn't, and you know it.'

Giles shrugged and stared out at Washington, not daring, apparently, to look at Jake as he asked, 'Could you say as much to me?'

'That I . . .' Jake hesitated. This was soft ground. '. . . Would love you no matter what?'

'No matter what I did.'

What, an axe murder? 'Uncle Giles, you're my godfather. What could change that?'

Giles remained immobile, his gaze fixed.

'When are you leaving, anyway?' Perhaps Giles was afraid that once he went back to England Jake would forget him.

'Within the fortnight.'

'Can I come over in the summer?'

'Of course.'

Why won't he look at me? 'You can take me up to Cambridge.'

'Indeed so.'

What was he staring at? The National Cathedral, so Anglican, its medieval tower dominating the city's north-west hill? In the shadow of that church sat the tidy enclave of the British Embassy, but from the Washington Monument the Embassy's Tudor manor

73

house and its glass-and-steel chancellery were hidden in the trees of Rock Creek Park. 'We can't quite see your office.'

Giles looked at his watch. 'Good Lord, I must be off.' He smiled at Jake. 'To the roofs, London, to the roofs.'

'So I guess Mom will have a farewell dinner for you, and I'll see you there?'

'With any luck.'

'She's going to miss you, Uncle Giles. A lot.'

Giles nodded but he held his nephew's eyes.

'And I am too.' Jake's hurt at what Giles had done was gone, replaced by the old reassurance of affection. It was a relief to discover that he still could trust someone and love him.

He expected his uncle to embrace him. Giles often embraced you, coming and going, but now an emotion had overtaken him too, one Jake could not plumb, but which stripped his uncle of his customary glibness. Giles's eyes had filled.

Jake wanted to repeat himself – I'm going to miss you, too – but couldn't. He too was stripped.

Comfort ye. Jake wanted him to say Comfort ye, so that he could reply, Comfort ye my people.

They took the elevator to the ground in silence and then parted, having said only. '*Ciao*, your lordship,' and 'Toodles, Jake.'

CHAPTER SIX

Ned Cooney had been waiting at the near end of the long corridor outside the dining-room. The evening meal was already half over, and he had begun to think that McKay wasn't coming.

'Hey, Ned-boy,' Jake said as Cooney fell into step with him.

'Jake, I gotta talk to you before you go in to eat. I went up to your room a dozen times this afternoon, but you weren't there.'

Jake stopped. The raucous sounds, forks on plates and clinking glasses and boisterous conversation, filtered out from behind the frosted glass doors. 'What did you want to talk to me about, Ned?'

Cooney fingered his beanie and he said shamefacedly, 'God, you know.'

Jake was wearing a lightweight madras-pouch sport coat and chinos, a knit tie, brown socks, penny loafers, and no beanie. He was wearing his blackthorn. 'Look, Ned, I got myself in a little bind, right? If I'd known it was such a big deal I wouldn't have started it, but what can I do?'

'Nobody would think you were a jerk.'

'Who asked you to talk to me? Tracey?'

Ned shook his head. 'Some of us had a meeting. Frosh. We agree with you in a way, but we don't think it's that important. We just want it over with. Already it goes until next Tuesday now, instead of Sunday, because of you. We think you should cool it.'

'And they asked you to talk to me because you're my buddy, right?'

'I guess so.'

After a silence Jake asked, 'Ned, why can't you look at me?'

'Because I'm embarrassed. I think you're right and I admire you. I wish I had your guts.' He looked up sharply. 'But I don't. None of us do. We just want it over with. You know?'

'It doesn't take guts, Ned.'

'Damn it, McKay, it could have been fun! Hell, college is supposed to be fun. What's a little beanie, for Christ's sake? Who does that hurt? And hell, I like the tie. "Class of '64", that's nice.'

'I like the tie, too, Ned.'

'Well, shit, Mac! What'd you have to go and make it an issue for, then? Now everybody puts it on, it's a moral commitment, for crying out loud. Who the fuck needs that first thing in the morning? It could have been like, you know, a lark. It still could. Come off it, all right?'

Jake looked away from him.

'What do you say?'

'Ned . . .' McKay faced Cooney. If he were composed, sure of himself at last, it was because that afternoon he'd felt his uncle's love. 'It started small, but it got big fast, and I'm stuck with it now, and, I guess, so are you. I made a gut decision for myself. Not for anybody else. If the sophomores try to keep hazing going past Sunday, then maybe you guys will have to make some kind of decision too. Your mistake is in thinking that I'm the problem. The problem is Tracey. You should be talking to him, not me.'

'But, what? You go in there now, and they're just going to haul your ass out again.'

'Maybe. But this time they're going to know they did it.'

'Shit, Jake! How can you expect your classmates to just sit there while you get your ass whipped?'

'I don't expect anything of my classmates, Ned.'

Cooney could not account for the intensity of his attraction to this guy. If I was smart, he thought, I'd stay the hell away from you. 'Well, you're ruining our dinner. We wanted you to quit it, but we also don't think it's funny when they gang up on you. Or I don't, anyway.'

'I don't think it's funny either, Ned. I'm scared.'

The simple admission surprised them both. 'Well, fuck,' Cooney said, but to himself. He twirled the demeaning child's hat between his hands. All it needed was a propeller. Who were they, characters in comic books, Archie and Veronica? Suddenly he crushed the beanie and stuffed it in his pocket. He looked up at McKay. 'You want company or what?'

Jake hesitated.

'I'm not taking the tie off, though. I like the fucking tie.'

Jake laughed out loud. Affection and relief surged through him. But he checked those feelings. Are you doing this because of my leg? Because you feel sorry for me? Those were his questions, but he didn't ask them. The affection of his friends could seem to him to be mere kindness, but that defensiveness of his was self-indulgent and he knew it. He decided his first intuition about Cooney had been right. They would be friends. They were friends already. 'Sure, I want company. Jeeze, are you kidding?'

'Well,' Cooney said with a determined intake of breath, 'you got it.'

They entered the dining-room without swagger.

The noise fell off dramatically.

Perhaps it was that the two were late or that there *were* two or that Tracey had already planned his next move. The sophomores did not confront them. McKay and Cooney moved promptly through the cafeteria chute and took places at a table without incident. The noise returned to normal. The other fellows at their table included McKay and Cooney with special enthusiasm in the circular conversation about baseball, the geography quizzes, Kennedy's campaign, and, it seemed, everything but hazing.

To breakfast the next morning Cooney wore the tie still, but not the socks, and several others, including Barnett, showed up without beanies. Barnett pulled up an extra chair to sit at the table with Jake and Ned, who greeted him as if he were just returned from a trip. Their enthusiasm, a modest good humour really, radiated from their table. Other freshmen took notice, could be *seen* to take notice, of their energetic satisfaction with themselves. Naturally, Tracey had to do something to salvage his authority.

He stood on a chair and announced that before first period there would be a special orientation assembly for the freshman class. In Gaston Hall in the Healy Building, where the ghosts of a century and a half would be on his side.

McKay sat in an aisle seat towards the rear so that his stiff leg would not obstruct passage. Every freshman had arrived promptly, and upperclassmen were hovering out of curiosity by the large doors and along the rear walls. A pair of middle-aged Jesuits entered the hall and the bustle fell off for a moment until it was clear that, taking a pair of the rearmost seats, they too had come as spectators. Cowpunchers hooking their legs over the slatted fences of the OK Corral.

Out of nervousness McKay had an inclination to lean over and talk to the fellow in the next seat, a freshman whom he hadn't met, but the guy struck up with the fellow on his other side. Getting his distance?

McKay studied the room. It was the hall in which the requirements for hazing had first been laid out for them. The docility with which students always took their orders there was tangible. Jake had to stifle a feeling of repugnance at the sight of all the beanies, hundreds of them, on those bobbing puerile heads. They should have been fixed with pins on girls at St Doreen's in Peter Pan collars and plaid skirts.

Jake looked for Cooney but didn't see him. Cooney had claimed he had to go to the bathroom after breakfast, but he hadn't reappeared. None of the few who'd left their beanies off in the dining-room were visible now, and Jake felt more isolated than ever. He recognized his feeling of separateness for the self-justification it was. He knew better than to credit his sense of superiority. The kid next to him was expounding on Henry James. Jake had to stifle an urge to say that once you discover Proust you won't ever go back to James.

He leaned forward to listen to the students in front of him. One was telling another that he had seen Jackie Kennedy coming out of her house on O Street the day before, and she was so beautiful he had decided to volunteer for the campaign. The other kid gave him a Kennedy button to wear.

The lines of the room, in the dark panelling on the side walls, in the moulded lintels of the doorways, of the pillars and arches that supported the balcony, and over the front platform itself, were inspired by the pointed gothic archways of the cloister outside the hall. It led to the enclosed monastic quadrangle outdoors and, in its centre, to the medieval chapel. The setting induced awe and simultaneously a sense of artificiality, as if what was about to occur, like an event of theatre, had infinite meaning and no real meaning at once. In its original design and in the crests it featured of Jesuit saints, the room had been intended to evoke the past; now, of course, it was over a century old. More a lyceum than a theatre, despite its theatricality, the hall had little colour and that was concentrated in the faded purple drapes which framed the proscenium arch. They were not a complete curtain any more than the platform was a true stage. On the wall behind the podium was mounted in a niche a bust of Dante, whom Jake took to be some Greek philosopher. This university aspired to greatness. Jake did too. He could not believe the Jesuits would regard him as a misfit. Surely they encouraged in students initiative and assertiveness. But presumably Jesuits had designed this rigid auditorium, which encouraged anything but.

Cooney entered with Barnett. They were wearing their beanies and ties. They had the grace at least to display their embarrassment in the high colour of their cheeks. They split up meekly to find single seats, pointedly not looking around. Only on seeing them did Jake realize he was not surprised. It was easy to imagine the scene in their room, the agony of it, as they fluttered this way, then that, choosing. Jake didn't blame them. Their problem wasn't Tracey or the sophomores. It was him. He had failed to make it possible for them to join him.

Tracey entered the hall through the ornate doorway that bisected the left wall, crossed briskly to the centre aisle, followed by his committee of six, and strode down the incline. The talk and laughter ceased at once, so that when Tracey took the four stairs up to the platform the sound of his shoes on the wood was audible even back where McKay sat. The sight of the hazing committee and the effect of their entrance made Jake realize how afraid he was. What was going to happen? How could he get out of this? What if he threw up?

Tracey called the assembly to order with some tentativeness, but everyone rose and he led the throng in reciting the Hail Mary. He asked the blessing of the Holy Ghost.

As Tracey began his remarks it was obvious that he lacked the qualities usually associated with status in school: a certain manly esprit, an ability to amuse, an ironic intelligence, a disarming friendliness.

'We obviously,' he said, 'ah, have a snag, have *hit* a snag with the programme this week.' He fumbled with index cards on which he'd written his speech.

Despite his own nausea and fear, Jake felt sorry for the guy. Obviously his position as chairman was his crack at leadership in his own class. He was probably orientation marshal by default; who would want it? He had no knack for public speaking, and he stammered through a paragraph about the importance of tradition at Georgetown. But then he did something that surprised Jake. He apologized. He regretted that he'd violated the fellowship of the college by enforcing perhaps a bit too vigorously the traditional customs of hazing, which, he read, 'are essentially good-humoured in intent, not punitive'.

He looked up from the card and squinted at the crowd. 'Of course I'm talking about you, McKay.'

The students, including those clustered in the doorways and spilling out into the corridor, were absolutely still. Tracey waited, apparently expecting a response of some kind, a waved hand, a holler.

Jake waited too, not breathing. His heart pounded loudly enough, he was sure, for others to hear.

'I mean,' he said, 'about, you know . . .' He referred to his cards again. 'We were out of bounds,' he read, 'at Tehan's. Tehan's is free territory. I was wrong. The rules of Orientation Week don't apply there.' This was the perennial college applause line about beer. Tracey waited while the students clapped formally. He grinned out at them – wasn't the applause a point for him? – but even his relief lacked vitality.

Jake realized that Tracey was displaying the flip side of the despot's swagger, and that involved not merely this awkwardness and insecurity but a deliberate show of it. He hoped to bolster his authority with their pity. Politicians often tried the ploy, and it never worked because pity undermines authority absolutely. Feel sorry for your father and forget it. But Tracey was only chairman for the week, and he was desperate. Please let me do this, fellows. Look how short I am; look at my skin. And watch, I can't even talk to you without stammering.

'Your class hat and your class tie,' he read, 'are symbols of the fellowship into which you seek entrance. They are to be worn proudly. But McKay has his reasons too, and we recognize that.' Tracey looked up from his card and recited, 'We admire it.'

Applause scattered across the room.

'Therefore the Orientation Council has decided that McKay is exempt from the requirement to wear the class socks.' Tracey looked up again, expecting to be interrupted, but the room was silent. Don't refer to his leg, you s.o.b.! 'And the Orientation Council has furthermore voted to give McKay the privilege of choosing to wear either the hat or the tie, one or the other, as a symbol of his solidarity not with us sophomores but with his own stalwart class of 1964 and dear old Georgetown.' Tracey held out a beanie and a tie then, over the podium; come on up, McKay, and choose.

Jake's classmates began to applaud and they turned in their seats towards him. Everyone knew exactly where he was. He could sense their relief. A compromise! If he and Tracey came to terms they were off the hook. Who wants to begin college by choosing sides? Who wants to have his nose rubbed in the fact that he suffers the indignities of hazing willingly? Jake's classmates were applauding Tracey's generous spirit and they were applauding because no way could McKay refuse his offer.

Jake got up from his seat and the applause quickened. He buttoned his sport coat. Inanely he worried that the perspiration that had soaked his shirt by then would show through his jacket. He was under control but just barely. His stick felt slippery in his sweaty hand. As he walked down the aisle his classmates began to stand up. For a crippled kid he had guts.

He took the stairs to the platform one at a time. The applause died down, but there were whispers. *He got that leg in the Blitz!*

At the podium Tracey offered him his hand and Jake shook it. Tracey's hand was sweaty too. They were a pair of terrified kids. When Tracey offered the beanie and the necktie, McKay surprised him; putting his stick under his arm, he took both. His classmates applauded again. *That McKay was all right.* Tracey yielded his place at the podium. When McKay had received the History Award at St Anselm's, it wasn't like this.

He arranged the beanie and the necktie carefully on the walnut lectern so that they were visible. He took the blackthorn from under his arm and stared at it while the room grew quiet. It was like preparing to hit a golf shot on the first tee, with the clubhouse watching.

Golf. He'd forced himself to play that game to win his father's approval, but his father wouldn't approve of this. You take yourself too seriously, son. I know it, Dad. Jake McKay decided that approval was not the most important thing.

'I have wanted . . .' he began. Then he stopped. Already he'd forgotten what he was going to say. Perspiration beaded on his lip. The room grew even more tense as some students wondered if McKay was ever going to pick up the sentence. 'I have wanted,' he began again, 'to be a student at Georgetown since I was a child.' He stopped again. Was he still a child? He hung on to his flimsy thought as if it were a log to float with. 'We lived across the river in Virginia. I used to stare out my window at the spire of this very building. I began thinking of myself as a Georgetown man' – he gave it two beats – 'when I was six.'

That he'd made a joke surprised them all, no one more than Jake. It released their tension. They laughed more loudly than it deserved, but their reaction, their support, reassured him. Suddenly he felt himself relax some.

'Unlike many of you, I grew up in this city. You perhaps appreciate more than I do what Georgetown represents to people in New York or Illinois or Massachusetts. But I know what Georgetown represents here.' Jake saw in a flash what he had to do. He had to let them see that he was strong. He had to make them understand that something important was at stake here. He had to tell them how he really felt. He had to tell them the truth.

'Georgetown is like the mind of this city. Maybe the soul of it.' His voice grew calm, and he began to speak more slowly, more certainly. 'This college has been here since George Washington, and every President and every senator and every general has been aware of it. I think they have been, anyway. And maybe – who knows? – they took some comfort from the sight of our spire here.' What comfort had Jake taken all those years? The words came easily, still slowly. 'Georgetown, seen from a distance, represents a kind of dignity, if you ask me. It represents democracy. And also, well, you know. Excellence under God.'

Jake fell silent for a moment. Such rhetoric was rare to him. Only the purity of his feeling justified the use of such words. His audience was absolutely silent. He had pointedly ignored up to then the beanie and the tie, and he continued to do so.

'And now there is a new reason to be proud to be at Georgetown. As you know, only a few blocks from here, from this very room, is the house where . . .' He paused, to let them wonder what he was going to say. His voice went up in pitch suddenly as if he were at a convention. '. . . the next President of the United States lives.'

There was a burst of applause, but it died quickly. McKay's

81

reference to Kennedy took them by surprise.

He stepped from behind the podium, but held on to it so that he could gesture freely with his stick. He felt release and power, and suddenly his speech took on a life of its own.

'In November, when this country elects as its President the first man who, like us, was born in this century and the first man who, like us, is a Catholic and the first man who, like us, has an entirely new vision of what the world needs from America – well, when that happens, I want to be part of it. John Kennedy is our neighbour. And some would say he's our brother. He's one of us.'

Jake stopped. He smiled at them knowingly and added, 'And he has one heck of a classy wife.' While they hooted, he picked up the beanie. When they fell quiet again he said, 'And I ask myself, with all due respect to you and to the traditions of our school, would John Kennedy wear this thing?'

No one laughed.

'When he was our age he was practically on his way to the Pacific to fight the Japanese. Would John Kennedy wear this tie? Maybe he would. But not, with all due respect, because some sophomore told him to. They tell us that hazing is all in good fun. I'm sure it used to be. They tell us that hazing is a sign of solidarity with the past. It is indeed. If we reject it, we do so not out of disrespect or because we don't love fun – of course we love fun! – but because we believe something new is happening this year. It is the future we associate ourselves with, not the past; the responsibilities of adulthood, not the frivolities of childhood. Senator Kennedy means no insult to his elders; we all know better than to squander the love of our fathers. We cling to them no matter what.' Jake knew even as he said them where those words came from; an image of his forlorn uncle – that streaked face in the glass two nights before – flashed before him.

'But we do so as men! Don't you agree?' He stopped. The eyes of every member of his class were riveted on him. No one moved. 'We came to Georgetown to do something serious. We claim our places here as members of the new generation. It is a new decade. It is our decade. John Fitzgerald Kennedy says that we are responsible for the world. He does not speak to us like children or expect us to act like children. Well, why in God's name should we dress like children?'

Abruptly he sailed the beanie out into the audience. His impulse triggered theirs. Dozens of freshmen took their beanies off, and most burst into conversation. *Christ, he's right! This guy is right!*

But before the hall broke into pandemonium McKay slammed his stout blackthorn on the podium, jarring the microphone and silencing the room. 'I move the question,' he shouted. 'All in favour of ending hazing here and now, for our class and for all future classes, say, "Aye!"'

'Aye!' some shouted, but not all.

'I didn't hear you!'

'Aye!' they answered, this time resoundingly. And several hundred beanies were hurled spontaneously into the air.

The black-robed Jesuits on the margins of the auditorium exchanged glances. Here was a lad to make something of. Here was a class at last.

McKay turned around. Poor Tracey behind him was dumb-founded. McKay intended to give the tie back, but thought better of it. Leave the bugger alone. Jake would keep the tie as a souvenir of his first triumph as a man.

The pent-up schoolboy nervousness of the class was released. McKay walked out of Healy Hall and they followed him exuberantly, but at his pace. Cooney shoved forward to grab his arm. 'You were right, Mac! You were right! You were right!'

'Ned, do me a favour,' McKay said. He had to speak loudly to be heard.

'Anything, Mac! Anything!'

'Call me Jake.' McKay slapped Cooney's back affectionately. Cooney grinned and nodded.

His classmates hailed him as they careened, a throng, out into the balmy September morning.

Those who were free during first period headed across the Quadrangle for the Ryan Lounge to buy coffee and thump each other. *Did you see the fucking look on that asshole's face?*

In the basement room with the eye-level gothic windows an upperclassman was sprawled on the tattered couch reading the *Washington Post*. He held the paper above him so that, as McKay carefully took the four steps down, it was as if the front page were floating on the dust in the narrow morning sunbeam just for him. He had no choice, in other words, but to read the sixty-point headline and see the photograph.

'British Diplomat Defects,' it said, above the picture of his uncle.

CHAPTER SEVEN

The storey-high globe revolved slowly on the far side of the polished lobby. Jake watched it through the anarchic traffic of students changing classes from the phone booth in the corner of the entrance foyer of the Foreign Service School. It was late morning. He had just come from geography class – the catalogue called the course 'The World of Man'. He had spent the entire fifty-minute period deciding what to do.

'The Central Intelligence Agency,' an operator said.

The topic of the professor's lecture had been cultural diffusion. There are three ways in which innovation spreads around the world: migration, trade, and conquest.

'Mr McKay's office, please,' he said.

In the classroom one wall was covered with a map of the world that reminded Jake of the one in his father's office. But the classroom's other walls held other maps of the world, which jarred the eye because at their centres lay not the North American continent but, in the case of the German map, Europe, and in the case of the Russian, the Soviet Union.

A second voice, also a woman's, said, 'Room five hundred.'

Jake could picture it. When you went through the door with those numerals on its frosted glass you entered not a room exactly but another broad corridor along one wall of which desks were arranged in neat rows and secretaries sat working their typewriters with playback plugs attached to their ears. Spread along the other wall were closed doors, behind which, presumably, men in shirt-sleeves and narrow ties were speaking into their dictaphones. At the end of that corridor was a panelled double door which opened on his father's outer office, a room carpeted in blue and anchored by a stout leather couch, a weighted chrome floor-model ashtray and the desk of his father's secretary. Miss Kirby had been with him for more than ten years. Above her desk was the only picture to be seen in those rooms, an oil painting of the quays along the River Liffey in Dublin. Miss Kirby made more of her Irish lineage than her boss did of his, but it was he who'd given her the painting for Christmas one year. It hadn't occurred to him that she'd want to hang it in her office, but she lived alone in a studio apartment and rarely had visitors. On each of the eight or ten occasions that Jake had come to the office, Miss Kirby invariably pointed to the painting, identified the scene as Dublin, and confided that his father had given it to her personally and when she retired she was taking it with her.

'Mr McKay, please,' Jake said. The palms of his hands were perspiring, the phone receiver was clammy, and his own voice, resonating strangely in the booth, sounded unfamiliar to him. What was he going to ask his father, exactly?

A man, not his father, came on the line and said, 'May I help you?'

I saw Giles yesterday. He told me to cling to you.

'I'm calling to speak to Mr McKay. This is personal.' He noted the exasperation in his own voice as if it were someone else's. *Keep yourself in check.* He sat up straight while waiting for the man to answer and he stared at the bronze sphere across the lobby. *Migration, trade, and conquest, eh? What about espionage?* The globe's turning seemed more dignified than it had the other night. *Every nation disappears from view,* his uncle'd said, *but one. Bloody waste of the earth's surface!* His uncle had bitterly clenched his fist at a mere topographic abstraction of Russia and now he'd fled to the country itself? Jake's mind veered away from that. He remembered how ghostly pale, preoccupied, and unhappy he'd seemed that night. *'Old man, it is so infinitely more complex than you imagine.'* In his anguish Jake clung to a perverse hope, that his uncle had been kidnapped by the KGB.

'Who's calling, please?'

Make up a name quick, he thought. *But why? This was our side.* 'This is Mr McKay's son.'

The man paused again. Jake imagined him in his shirt-sleeves with his laminated identity card hanging from a chain around his neck, in his small office behind one of those seven doors, covering the mouthpiece of the phone with his hand and whispering to another man, but this one in a suitcoat, 'His son, Patterson's nephew.'

'One moment, I'll connect you.'

Jake's premonition had been that they would refuse to put him through to his father. *At a time like this, talk to a kid? What if his father demanded, What in hell are you calling here for? Because the KGB might get me too, Dad!*

'Jake? Is that you?'

'Hi, Miss Kirby. Yes, it is.'

She would be leaning forward on the very lip of her chair with a pencil in her hand and a steno book ready. A frail woman of fifty, she wore her eyeglasses on a shoelace and she had a round gold watch the size of a quarter pinned to her blouse. Nuns wore such timepieces under their wimples. When Miss Kirby took a phone call she always began by pulling that watch down on its tightly-wound cord, noting the time and letting it snap back up to its pin.

'Your father isn't available just now, Jake. I'm sorry.'

'Is he there though?'

'Not right here, no.'

'Where is he?'

'He's in conference.'

'But he's there, right? I mean he's not in Moscow or someplace.' Jake closed his eyes and leaned his head against the phone booth wall. His remark was flippant and cruel, but he didn't regret it. They had better not ignore him, was his point.

'Where are you, Jake?'

'I'm at school.'

'I'll have him call you. I know he wants to talk to you.'

'You do? Did he say so?'

'I'm sure he wants to, Jake.'

'Have you seen him, Miss Kirby? Have you seen him this morning?'

'No, Jake, I haven't.'

Jake sat up again. 'Then you don't know where he is, do you?'

Jake heard a man's voice speak sharply in the background, the man with the suitcoat. The senior men always kept their suitcoats on. He would have come from upstairs.

Jake's father had taken him up to the Director's office one Saturday. Allen Dulles had risen from his thronelike leather chair and bellowed a hearty welcome. 'So this is Mac Junior!' Jake liked him instantly, with his great white moustache and his warm handshake. Not an athletic-looking man like Jake's father, and not a hero either; more a professor with his pipe and tweed sport coat over an open-necked plaid shirt. But no matter what he looked like, the exploits of his undercover operation during the war were legendary. Mr Dulles pulled a flashy gold penknife out of his pocket and cleaned the bowl of his pipe. 'Your father and I go way back, son. He's my right-hand man.' How far back? To that medieval house in Berne where you met secretly with Admiral Canaris? Did my dad help you infiltrate the *Abwehr*?

And then Allen Dulles had become the Ivanhoe of the Cold War, the KGB nemesis, the overturner of governments, the best spy in the world. Jake had read about him in *Saturday Evening Post* and *U.S. News and World Report*. It never occurred to him to wonder why if he was the keeper of such secrets he was so well known. Imagine what the public did *not* know! And imagine, if Jake's father went back to the beginning, what adventures he'd had too! Since his father's exploits were unsung, they were even more heroic than Dulles's.

'And listen, son' – Mr Dulles had put his hand on Jake's shoulder – 'we can use smart young fellows like you in the service. Keep us in mind.' Jake had looked at his father. How should he react to this? His father had never encouraged him to even consider . . . Involuntarily Jake's eyes must have dropped to his stick because Dulles said, tapping his head, 'What counts is what's here' – and he tapped his breast – 'and here. Any son of John McKay . . .' Dulles leaned towards Jake confidentially. 'Your dad is the only man I know whose heart is as large as his brain, and his brain is the size . . .' He winked at Jake grandly. Both were aware that his father was blushing at the praise. '. . . Of an acorn.'

'I'll have him get in touch with you, Jake,' Miss Kirby said, but her voice shook. 'I have to go. Really. I have to go.'

'Wait a minute, Miss Kirby. What's going on? Tell me what's going on. Is it true?' Should he ask for Mr Dulles?

'Jake, you know I can't say anything.'

'Oh, Miss Kirby, don't tell me that.' What was in her voice? 'Just say yes or no; is it true? What's happened to my uncle?'

A long silence, but he could hear her breathing. Fear. It was fear. 'Miss Kirby? Miss Kirby?'

He heard the click when he was switched to another line. A man's voice said, with a familiarity that made Jake angry, 'Son, your father will get back to you this afternoon, OK?'

'OK. Thanks.' He hung up. What's happened to my uncle? he repeated to himself. He pictured Giles bound hand and foot and gagged. The image made him feel faint, and he shook it off.

He remained leaning against the cool wall of the booth, and he closed his eyes again. Surely his father would rescue Giles. The CIA would. The CIA was, like the Church, an institution whose mysteries he had been taught to revere, and he did. His father's position as a custodian of those mysteries had always seemed to him a kind of sacred office. By the light of its aura Jake had learned to read; he'd learned to conjure details of a world other boys knew nothing of. A mammoth struggle between titans was even now under way just beyond the margins of ordinary consciousness, and its outcome was in doubt. Lulled citizens were blind both to the struggle and to the ramifications of defeat, but Jake was not. This was the battle against the dark. Jake's father was a prince of our protection and his colleagues were swordsmen, Knights Templars, self-sacrificers. The compound of parchment-coloured buildings on the edge of Foggy Bottom was the citadel, and the Agency itself was holy.

Then why was Miss Kirby afraid? And why was Jake shaking inside with fear of his own? With terror?

He channelled his emotion into the act of carefully taking from his pocket the clipping he had with like care folded earlier. He opened it on the metal shelf, then looked out at the lobby to be sure no one was waiting for the booth. Students had scattered. The next period had begun. He was going to miss theology; fuck it. Two young Jesuits leaned on the brass railing across the lobby, smoking and talking, indifferent to the revolving bronze sphere that dwarfed them.

Jake looked at his uncle's photograph, a face-on picture that showed Giles smiling. It had been taken outdoors. The collar of his tweed overcoat was turned up and a plaid scarf draped his neck, partly obscuring his perfectly knotted tie and a buttoned cardigan sweater. His rich hair, showing less grey than he had now, fell across the right side of his forehead. The left side of his face was in shadow so that half his thin moustache was invisible, but both eyes gleamed brightly out at the picture-taker. This man liked whomever he was looking at very much. This was not the photograph of a traitor.

'British Diplomat Defects.'

Despite the prominence given the headline and the photograph, the story was short. It was datelined London; obviously the official announcement had come just before the edition went to press and was simply reported without elaboration.

'Sir Giles Patterson, a prominent English social figure and the Cultural Attaché to the British Embassy in Washington since 1954, has defected to the Soviet Union, according to a statement issued early this morning by the Foreign Office here.

'Patterson is known to have flown yesterday from Washington's National Airport to New York's Idlewild International Airport where, using a false passport and posing as a German national named Alfred Berger, he boarded a Lufthansa flight to Frankfurt, West Germany. He then proceeded on a connecting BOAC flight to West Berlin, where he is presumed to have crossed by routine means into East Berlin. Patterson left Washington, according to the Foreign Office statement, only moments before he would have been arrested by agents of the Federal Bureau of Investigation whose warrant, obtained with information supplied by the British Secret Intelligence Service, charged him with espionage.

'Patterson is the scion of a leading family, based in Worcester, whose members have since the seventeenth century achieved prominence in industry, politics and the world of art. His grandfather was F. E. Patterson, a well-known lawyer and orator who served as Secretary of State for India from 1892 to 1897. His father, Colonel Sir Lawrence Patterson, VC, OBE, was a hero of Château Thierry in World War I and a famous early collector of Impressionist Art.

'Patterson, himself an honours graduate of both Eton and Trinity College, Cambridge, served in the army with distinction during World War Two, earning among other commendations the Distinguished Service Order. At the end of the war he entered the Foreign Service and served before being posted to Washington at the British Embassy in Bonn, West Germany. According to the Foreign Office statement, Patterson's diplomatic functions have always been limited to the administration of cultural exchanges between Commonwealth nations and the host country. He did not have top-level security clearance and is not regarded as having had access to sensitive military or diplomatic information.'

And that was all the story said. Jake fastidiously folded the clipping and put it back in his pocket. Had he expected it to read differently this time? Tell him more? Why, he wondered, hadn't they mentioned his mother? Patterson's sister, the Honourable Mrs Eleanor McKay, who worships her brother and who will never believe reports of his defection, makes her home in Arlington, Virginia, with her three children and her husband, whose occupation could not be ascertained.

The call home was the one he dreaded making. He fumbled in his pockets for a dime, found one, deposited it, and dialled. The phone rang once and was picked up.

'Hello?' Yet another man's voice, not his father, not his uncle, but not quite a stranger either.

'Who is this?' Jake demanded.

'Jake? Jake McKay? This is Dwight Houseman, Jake.'

'Oh,' Jake said. Now that he was in college perhaps he should call his father's aide by his first name. Had he just been invited to? 'Mr Houseman, Christ, what's going on? They won't tell me where Dad is. Is he there? Is my mother OK?' Despite his enormous ambivalence towards his father's aide, Jake suddenly hoped that Houseman would tell him what was what.

'Jake, your mother is resting. She's had a rough morning.'

'What's going on?'

'A couple of dozen reporters are camped outside. I guess she was sort of defenceless here for a while when the news first broke. The reporters frightened her. But it's under control or will be soon. Their editors will have gotten the word to call them off. Damn press.'

'Is my dad there?'

'No, he's not.'

'Where is he?'

'I haven't seen him, Jake. He must be at the compound now.'

'Miss Kirby says he's not.'

'Oh.'

'He's not in Moscow or something?'

'Come on, buddy.' Dwight Houseman's tone, despite its rebuke or because of it, brought Jake back, like a tether. Sarcasm wasn't going to win anyone over. But how could he display his feelings, his confusion and anxiety, to the only rival he had? Why should Houseman know more about his father's situation than Jake did?

'Maybe,' Jake said, 'they kidnapped my dad too.'

'Jake,' Houseman asked confidentially, 'what's your information?'

'I read the *Post*. There's nothing in the *Times-Herald*.'

'The *Post* has it more or less the way it is. Beyond that, don't believe what anybody tells you. In fact, it would be best if you didn't talk to anybody.'

'I'm coming home.'

'I wouldn't recommend that, Jake, until these reporters are gone. That's liable to take a few hours. I'll be here. Your mother's OK, and the girls are too.'

'Are they there?'

'Your mother kept them home from school.'

'Let me talk to Dori, would you?'

90

'Sure. Hang on.'

Dori impressed adults as assertive and self-confident, particularly for a thirteen-year-old, but Jake knew that she was more like their mother than not.

'Is that you, Jake? Really?'

'Hi, Hunky. It sure is.' He should have asked Houseman how much his sisters knew. 'I'm just calling to make sure everything's hunky-dory.'

'Ja-ake, you promised!'

He wasn't to call her Hunky because it rhymed with *chunky* and if her schoolmates ever heard it she might as well . . .

'You're right. I'm sorry. Mr Houseman said Mother's lying down.'

'All these men are here. There's a TV truck in the driveway.'

'Don't go out there, sweetie, OK? What's with Mother?'

'She's in a bad mood. I guess she's asleep now. Uncle Giles is sick. He went back to England.'

'Was she crying, Dori, or what?'

It took Dori a moment to answer. 'This morning? Early?'

'Yes.'

'She screamed really loud for a long time. Somebody called on the phone and she really screamed. It woke me up and Sissy up. I was scared, Jake. Are you coming home?'

'I am, Dori, a little later. Mr Houseman will be there until I come. He'll do anything you want, OK?'

'Will he call Sister Angela?'

'Sure he will. You put him back on and I'll tell him to. Sister won't mind you missing a day.'

'Tell him to ask Sister Angela to get the nuns to pray for Uncle Giles.'

'Good idea, Dori. You take care of Sissy now, OK? And when Mother wakes up you tell her I'll be home this afternoon. We have to stick together, you know?'

'Like a family.'

'That's right, Dori. All of us and Dad.'

'Jake, I don't think Dad's going to be here much.' Dori was crying now. 'Something's wrong with him too.'

'We'll have the sisters pray for all of us, Dori. OK?'

'OK,' she said and then for a moment sobbed into the phone. Houseman came back on.

'Was she finished?' Jake asked sharply. 'I wasn't finished talking to her.'

'I've got her here, Jake. I'm holding her.'

Why should the image of Dwight Houseman holding his sister, consoling her, have infuriated Jake? His resentment at such a moment shamed him. 'Look,' he said, 'they're worried about school.'

'I know. I'll call the nuns as soon as you hang up. Is there anything else you think I should do?'

'Can you level with me?'

'Jake, I don't know any more than you do.'

'Why would my uncle defect?'

'I don't know, Jake. Honest to God.'

'What does *Sub Rosa* mean, do you know?'

'Private. Confidential.'

'I mean as a code.'

'I never heard of it as a code, Jake.'

Jake fell silent. It soothed him, he admitted, to be on the phone, even with Houseman.

Houseman said after a moment, 'Dori's got a hold of herself now. You want to say goodbye to her?'

'Sure . . . That you, Dori?'

'Yeah.'

'I love you, Dori. Take care of Sissy and Mother, all right?'

Dori said she would, and then she asked Jake if he wanted to talk to Mr Houseman again. He said no.

Jake was coming out of Dalgren Chapel against traffic when someone called him. Students were crowding in for the noon Mass – a First Friday observance – but Jake had gone there half an hour before to be alone, to sit in the lofty silence, stare at the flickering blue votive candles and try to take in what was happening to his family. He could not. His mind had simply refused to settle for more than an instant on anything. Finally, in fact, he'd given up trying even to recall with precision the previous days' events beginning with the scene at the art gallery. His recollection had kept drifting into the hassle over hazing, which now seemed absurd. He'd begun, as Dori suggested, to pray. But that quickly seemed phoney to him. He had to *do* something. But what? When the other students began filing in, the chapel seemed stuffy and airless. He wanted to go home, but he couldn't. There was no place to go but his room. The thought of that lonely cell made his heart sink. Then he thought of the girl in the pleated skirt. If he found her, would she talk to him? Would she know something? Her mother, he saw suddenly, was a link between his uncle and his father. And now a link with him.

'Mr McKay!' someone called again.

After the shadowy chapel the bright noon sun made it hard to focus. Jake looked quickly around, but didn't see anyone. The day had turned out to be a late summer masterpiece. Jake kept walking, not to elude whoever was calling him, but to get away from the throng at the entranceway.

'Hey, wait a minute, will you!'

Jake turned to see a man rudely shoving through students, a portly middle-aged man who was holding the stub of his cigar above his head to avoid singeing anyone. A GI holding his carbine high while wading across a river. By the time he joined Jake in the centre of the Quadrangle he was perspiring heavily. 'Look, I had the courtesy not to interrupt you while you were in church.'

'You were in there?'

'I just came out, didn't I?'

'Watching me?' The hand with which he held his cane shook involuntarily as he asked that. He was being observed? Tailed? Spied upon? 'You were watching me in church?'

'I was waiting for you.' The man mopped his forehead with a soiled red engineer's kerchief. He was wearing a rumpled serge suit. 'Look, I apologize, all right?' He shoved the kerchief back into his pocket and offered his right hand to shake. 'I apologize for coming up on you like this. I would have called ahead, but, hey, who gets notice on something like this?'

Jake shifted his stick and shook hands with the man. 'Who are you?'

'Marty Carlo, the *Times-Herald*, nice to meet you, Mr McKay.' He laughed abruptly but held on to Jake's hand. 'Hey, I'm old enough to be your father. Can I call you John?'

'Nobody calls me John.'

'John McKay, Junior, right? That's you?'

Jake withdrew his hand.

'You have a nice firm handshake, son. That's very important when you're meeting the public. And I like the way you look a guy in the eye.'

'Thanks, Mr Carlo.' Jake smiled, but he felt quite desperate. 'Look, I have to go, I'm afraid. I'm late already.'

'I wanted to buy you lunch. What are you late for?'

Nothing. He'd just cut his last class of the day. And that girl wouldn't be home from school yet. He had time to kill. How wonderful it had seemed early in the week to have Friday after-noons free, but now he'd have gladly registered for every period and he'd have arrived at each class early. Carlo's direct question threw him. Even as a child Jake had been unable to lie convincingly, and that still seemed a failing to him. 'I'm just late, OK?' He immediately regretted his show of defensiveness. It gave him away.

'But you gotta eat lunch, right?' The reporter struck a match and touched it to his cigar, even though his cigar was still lit. He waved the match out flamboyantly, and Jake realized it was for that gesture he had struck it. 'Where's a good place to eat around here, son?'

'Would you mind not calling me "son"? You can call me Jake, all right?'

Carlo grinned. 'Now we're getting somewhere, Jake.'

'But I really have to go.'

The portly man shrugged, apparently resigned. 'Where should I eat lunch, though?'

'Try the Neptune down on M Street.' Jake had never been in the place, which was why he recommended it. He'd noticed the neon mermaid in the window.

'Sounds good. What time?'

'You don't seem to understand. I'm tied up.'

'No, you're not, Jake. You can't kid me. Look' – I'm only thinking of you, bud – 'I gotta write this story whether you help me or not. Now I can turn in this: "The boy, obviously defensive and hiding something, refused to be interviewed by the *Times-Herald*, thus adding weight to the suspicions mentioned above." My editor will love it. Or you can sit down with me for half an hour and tell me what you want me to write.'

'I don't know anything. This has nothing to do with me.'

'Jake, lad, I should explain. I'm not on the political beat, or the criminal. I'm a feature writer. My piece is about your family. Just background. I know you don't know anything about your uncle or your old man, what they're up to. I just want to know, like what schools you kids went to and how'd it feel growing up with an English mom, that sort of thing.'

'"Suspicions mentioned above." What's that?'

'You tell me,' the reporter replied quickly.

'You suspect my father?'

'Of what?'

Jake barely checked himself in time. Treason, that's what. The word rang in his head.

No, that was a bell tolling, the first gong of the Angelus. Jake and the reporter stood like peasants in a field, suspended above their labour, staring at each other while the bell tower of Dalgren Chapel reverberated. *We fly to Thee.* Conversation was impossible for some moments. When the ringing stopped and the echo faded, Jake said, 'I don't suspect my father of anything.'

'I wouldn't think so. What about your uncle?'

'You mean what schools did he go to?'

Carlo smiled. 'I guess he went to good ones, huh? I went to Fordham.' The reporter let his gaze drift around the Quadrangle, the brick paving stones, the porticoed ambulatory between Healy and Ryan, the arched windows. 'We always felt a little inferior to Georgetown.'

'I know what you mean. We feel a little inferior to Harvard.'

The barb missed. 'Are you an American citizen, Jake?'

'What do you mean?'

'You were born in England, right? Your mother was English.'

'Is English.'

Carlo shrugged. 'You could be an English citizen.'

'When I turn twenty-one I'm supposed to declare myself. It's not a big deal.'

'I see.'

'I'd have thought you'd have known that.'

'I told you. I'm a feature writer. Human interest. I don't know about immigration rules.' Carlo smiled likeably, then dropped his eyes to Jake's stick. 'How's your leg?'

'My leg is fine,' Jake said smoothly. He was catching on to the reporter's technique: thrust, lay off, and thrust. Any reaction, even the lack of one, was a revelation. 'Why do you ask?'

Carlo drew his notepad out of the inside pocket of his coat and made a show of referring to it. 'I understand you were injured in London during the Blitz.'

'Technically it wasn't the Blitz, but afterwards. Who told you that?'

'Let's see . . .' He flipped pages and found it. 'Cooney. Fellow by the name of Cooney.' He looked up. 'Friend of yours.'

'You talked to Cooney?'

'We had a cup of coffee a little while ago. A place called Tehan's. He thinks the world of you. Said you were something of a class leader.'

'I wouldn't know about that.'

'He told me . . .' He turned a page and studied it. Then slowly, absently he said, '. . . About the Phillips Art Gallery.' He looked up at Jake and watched him.

Jake went rigid inside, clamped down on his emotion and for once did not, or so it seemed to him, betray himself. 'The Phillips? What about it?'

'You spotted your father there a couple of days ago. Cooney seemed to think you were surprised.'

Jake laughed. 'Ned's a dramatizer. That wasn't my father, and I told him it wasn't. He was crushed because the guy was with his wife and daughter. Cooney panted after that girl all over the museum. If it'd been my father she'd have been my sister and Cooney could have met her.'

Carlo nodded, smiling. 'He said she was a knock-out.'

'Cooney's a little hard up, if you know what I mean. Dream city.'

'As long as I have my pad out' – the reporter fished in his pocket for his stub of a pencil and found it – 'do you mind? When was the last time you saw your uncle?'

Jake shrugged easily and said, 'Two, three weeks ago. I forget.' He would be a maestro of deceit now. The man's mistake had been his reference to Jake's leg. For years Jake had known how to lead away from that.

'Was he a visitor at your home?'

'We played golf, he, my dad, my mother, and I.'

'Oh.' He wrote. 'I notice you call him "Dad" and her "Mother".'

'He's a Yank and she's British. If it were reversed I'd call him "Pater" and her "Ma".'

'You play golf, do you?'

'Wickedly.'

'What was your first thought when you heard the news?'

'That he was a traitor.'

Carlo looked up sharply. Here was a headline.

'Ned Cooney, I mean,' Jake said. 'For talking to you.'

'I mean your uncle. Do you think he had a nervous breakdown or what?'

'You obviously know more about it than I do.'

'Do you believe what they're saying, that he's in Moscow already?'

Before Jake could answer, the Dowd Rifles, the ROTC drill team, began to file out of the armoury in the basement of Ryan.

They assembled on the far side of the Quadrangle in five ranks of four; their prompt synchrony and their M-1 rifles with fixed chrome-plated bayonets were the more startling for the cadets' being dressed in mufti. A practice session. The reporter and Jake watched while they dressed their rows and came to attention. An officer gave the cadets their orders. Jake recognized him: Fred Yeats. Even from across the courtyard he impressed with his panache. The team began to march directly towards McKay and Carlo, who moved automatically out of their path. Carlo seemed stunned by the sight. McKay had watched them from his room.

As the squad approached, Yeats barked out a command and the unit split into two columns, which immediately began to criss-cross each other with exact precision. At another order the columns fell in with each other again and each man began to twirl his rifle. The bayonets flashed dangerously. Suddenly each cadet threw his rifle over his shoulder to the man behind him, while those of the last rank hurled theirs forward above the entire team to the men in front. No one missed in the rapid exchange, and they hadn't broken step.

Jake was dazzled. All at once those cadets with their close hair-cuts and their perfect posture and their tangible sense of their own skill represented to him the perfect alternative to this life of tension and anxiety. Those cadets didn't have terrible truths gnawing at their guts. They didn't have uncles to worry about or fathers. They weren't terrified inside. Ordinarily such display of conformity, of the obliteration of individual will, left him cold. But now he admired it enormously and envied it. If he were not 4-F, Jake McKay, the Sam Adams of the Beanie Revolt, would have signed up on the spot for the permanent hazing of martial life. Why? Because those bright young men with dancers' grace and athletes' rigour could throw blades at each other and not flinch. They were not lonely and they didn't have to think. And they had no secrets. Fred Yeats thought Jake should get on the team. How Jake wanted to.

'Those boys are liable to hurt somebody,' Marty Carlo said finally, as the team marched out of the Quadrangle through an archway that led to an open lot by the gym. 'I wouldn't want to catch one of those bayonets in the eye.'

Jake faced the reporter and assessed him anew. Rumpled, ill-shaven, dissolute, jowly, overweight, he was the antithesis of the strong youthful men on parade. Marty Carlo made a living by bullying people into indiscretions that he then served up as news.

Get away from me, you flea, Jake thought, mystified suddenly that this defeated man had intimidated him. This man was nothing compared to Jake's father. Nothing compared, traitor or no, to his uncle!

Jake looked at his watch. 'Like I said, Mr Curvo, I'm late.'

'*Carlo*, Jake. Marty *Carlo*.'

Jake began to walk away.

'What about lunch? You said the Neptune, right?'

'Right, Marty. I'll see you there in an hour.' Jake entered the Healy portico and called over his shoulder, 'Get a booth, OK? I like a booth.'

'It's on me. Don't forget.'

'No, no.' Jake waved his blackthorn from the door. 'I pay my way.'

'I insist! I insist, son! Son?'

CHAPTER EIGHT

Pierre Salinger came to the door of the townhouse. 'Gentlemen,' he said.

The reporters, a dozen of them, crowded in around Salinger, who, on the top step, was visible above them. Jake was watching from across the street. He leaned against the side of a car as if it were his.

'Mrs Kennedy asked me to convey her regrets, gentlemen. We're going to have to cancel.'

The reporters groaned. 'Aw, come on, Pierre,' one called. 'We've been out here for an hour and a half.'

'This session's been scheduled for a week!' another complained.

Salinger gestured with his hands, Take it easy, boys. 'She's very sorry. She's just not up to it.'

'Oh, yeah? What if it was TV?'

'That's not the point, fellows. The networks weren't invited. This interview was just for you guys, but she's not well.'

'Don't give us that!' A lanky reporter jabbed a finger at Salinger. 'Tell her we got a job to do, will you? Fifteen minutes. How about fifteen minutes?'

'Nothing.' Salinger's face reddened. 'Nothing for the weekend.'

The reporters groaned again.

'Look, guys, I'm sorry. Go back to headquarters. Have a beer on me.'

'Tell her next time, Pierre, she gets the Inquiring Photographer!'

'For Christ's sake, Hal,' Salinger said angrily, 'the lady's pregnant!' He glared at them all. 'The lady is pregnant!'

'She's also the nominee's wife!'

Salinger stared at him. 'You are a son of a bitch, Arnie. You're all sons of bitches!' Salinger turned and went back into the house, slamming the door behind him. The reporters whistled and hooted, but only for a moment. They began to drift away.

But then a hot red Triumph lurched to a halt in front of the house. The sports car seemed more to display the couple riding in it than simply transport them. Jake recognized at the wheel Kennedy's youngest brother, recognized the characteristic vigour. Each of them possessed the qualities of youth but in a way that enhanced the impression of mature responsibility they made, as if the Kennedys knew better than the rest of us how to strike that mythic balance between the grave and the merry. At his side was a blonde woman whose beauty, next to Kennedy's, staggered Jake. Those splendid lads. Their golden women. Born in this century. The future is theirs. Jake stared at her as she followed the young Kennedy out of the car and skipped across the sidewalk to the door of the house. They took each other's hands and waved at the cluster of reporters as if they'd been the objects of such attention all their lives.

'Ted,' one called, 'what do you think of France's atom bomb?'

'*Vive la différence!*' he shot back, and then disappeared with the blonde into the house.

Jake waited for a few minutes, but nothing else was going to happen. Soon the reporters were gone and only the policeman standing a few yards from the door indicated that the house was special. When the policeman looked in Jake's direction – Move along, fellow – he straightened up and sauntered along O Street. To the cop he was a college kid with a limp, but to himself he was an anxious cluster of wants which all seemed, despite their radical disproportion, equally intense. He wanted a left leg with which he could double-clutch and downshift; he wanted a sports car. He wanted a blonde, brainy woman. He wanted the wit it took to cry *Vive!* and the nerve to tell reporters who hound mothers that they are all sons of bitches.

At Wisconsin Avenue in the Little Tavern on the corner he ate three dime hamburgers, sitting on a shiny green stool next to an old man who'd slept in his clothes. When the old man saw Jake's cane propped between them he said, 'What's a matter with you?'

'Bad sprain,' Jake replied.

'Win some, lose some.' Despite the balmy sunshine outside, the geezer was wearing an overcoat. The weather turned bad on you only if you weren't ready for it.

'How about it?' Jake said as he was paying up. 'Let me buy your coffee.'

'If you insist.'

Marty Carlo had insisted. A son of a bitch, yes. But also a sad sack trying to keep his bosses off his back.

'I insist.' Jake gave the old man a smile and stood up.

'What are you running for? I'll vote for you.'

'Vote for Senator Kennedy,' Jake said from the door.

'I knew his old man in Boston!'

Jake waved and headed down O Street. He felt lightheaded now and detached, sleepwalking again. He was heading for that faded yellow clapboard house, but without thinking what he was going to do there. The blonde woman was his link. That was all. He had to connect with her. How or why he didn't know. But right then he didn't need to. He found that, as long as he was moving, he could keep his mind more or less empty and his desperation more or less at bay.

Because of his sleepwalking mood, it didn't surprise him when he saw at the next corner, alighting from a school bus on which were stencilled the words 'Dunbarton Academy', *la petite danseuse*. She stood at the kerb and waved at the bus as it gunned away. But from behind their windows the other girls seemed to ignore her. Jake focused on them. They seemed so young. Not too young for the middle-aged geniuses of Paris, perhaps, but too young for a sophisticated worldly freshman at Georgetown University. If her chums were children, what was that blonde girl? She looked in sweater, plaid skirt, saddle shoes – although with nylon stockings, not bobby socks – the perfect teenager. Her blonde pony-tail registered every movement of her head. Her hair was tied with a dark ribbon, but he could not tell if it was satin.

She tarried at the corner until the bus disappeared, then, slinging her leather satchel over her shoulder, she began to walk down O Street towards her house. Jake fell into step behind her about thirty yards back. He had three, perhaps four, minutes to think of a way to stop her.

At the corner of the last block before the park, the one on which she lived, he called out to her, 'Excuse me, miss! Excuse me!'

She stopped and faced him, and as he closed the distance between them he exaggerated his limp. He knew what impression he was making on her as he approached. Not merely that he was crippled but that on a well-groomed handsome young man like him – he was not immodest, only conscious – his Harris tweed, his rep tie, his pressed chinos, the articulate features of his face all underscored the outrage that anyone should be. He wanted her to be shocked by the contrast between his robust, masculine self-confidence and the infinite humiliation of his physical condition.

'Thank you for stopping. I'm in a bit of a jam, or I'd never be so rude.'

'What is the matter?' He'd forgotten that she was German, not French, and her accent, light as it was, surprised him.

'Cooney is in the park across the way and I can't quite nab him. I can't move fast enough.' He indicated his leg. 'He thinks I want to play.'

'Cooney?'

'My Irish setter. Will you help me catch him?'

She looked off towards the park, hesitated, but only for a moment. 'Of course.'

'Thanks, thanks a lot.'

She left her books on the stoop of her house and they continued down the block to the park. The field was empty. 'He went through that hedge when I lost him.'

She ran on ahead. At a break in the hedge she looked back, then disappeared. Jake had no idea what was behind the row of shrubs, and as he stalked along towards it he chided himself. This wasn't what he'd had in mind.

At the hedge he called her, but there was no answer. He flamboyantly began to call his dog: 'Here, Cooney!' He began to laugh. 'Come on, Cooney!'

Beyond the hedge the plateau fell off in a steep bramble-covered slope to the heavily trafficked roadway that ran parallel to Rock Creek. Jake tried to follow the girl down the hill, but the footing was impossible. He stayed where he was, but continued to call.

When she re-emerged from the thicket she wore a look of real anxiety. 'There's a road down there! Do you think he's . . . ?'

'No, no, no! He hates cars. He stays away from roads. I think he'll find us if we stay in the open. Let's go back out to the field. There are some swings.' Jake remembered the arc she'd cut while her mother watched. 'Do you know the swings?' he asked ingenuously. What the hell, he wasn't *that* sophisticated.

'Sure.' She set off again and led the way through the hedge and out into the field, but then waited awkwardly for him. 'I'm sorry,' she said when he'd caught up with her.

'You're very kind. I appreciate it.'

They walked together in silence to the swings, and each took one, sitting idly. He'd hoped that she would let it fly again as she had the other day, but she twirled the seat slowly in place, bracing her arms against the taut helix of the chains. Jake pretended to keep an eye peeled for the dog. 'When he sees me here he'll come quickly.'

'How old is he?'

'Pretty old.'

They fell silent again. The girl, staring off, conveyed her expectation that at any moment Cooney, luxuriant red mane flashing in the warm sun, was going to come bounding across at them, barking irrepressibly at the joy of his own return. Jake felt awash suddenly in shame. Had he ever so cynically abused someone's trust before? Someone's innocence? Was this taking advantage of a virgin?

'How old are you?' he asked abruptly. The question had popped open in his head like a flashlight rolling out of the glove compartment.

'Sixteen,' she said, staring down at her feet.

'I'm eighteen. What's your name?'

'Magda.'

Jake remembered his uncle. Adultery is what Irish bartenders do when they put water in the whisky. What if Giles had told him the truth? Magda, he'd said. Sixteen, he'd said. That older woman was not her sister but her mother, not an adulteress, but a translator.

'Magda. That's a pretty name.' From Magdalen, he thought. Let him who is without sin cast the first stone. 'My name is Jake.'

She looked up sharply. 'From Jacob?'

Was she asking if he was Jewish? 'No, John. A nickname for

John.' Her stare embarrassed him. He let his gaze drift around the field again. In the distance a woman with two children had just come off the P Street bridge. The children suddenly began to run ahead of her towards the swings. One fell. It would take them several minutes to cross the field.

'No sign of Cooney yet.' Jake wanted to imply concern but no worry. He smiled at Magda. 'If you want to swing go ahead. I won't think it's unsophisticated.'

She wound her chains down out of their spiral and looked at him coolly. I am not a child, her manner said. Still, she pushed off a little and began to swing slightly. Her plaid skirt flared at a corner.

The sight of her knee caught him by surprise. He wanted to see her thighs. Immediately he felt his erection coming. I'll push you, he wanted to say! Anything to touch you. A burst of sexual feeling cracked through him. Through her sweater he could see the outline of her breasts. She wasn't flat-chested after all. He realized he was staring at her and he blushed.

She looked away from him, but she was not embarrassed. He saw suddenly that she was much more worldly than he was.

Magda said, 'I still don't see your dog.'

Jake almost told her the truth right then. That he had no dog. That he wanted to see her naked. That he had never felt such lust before.

The children approached ahead of their sitter and Magda called to them. 'Come, come! You can!' She hopped off her swing and gracefully picked the little girl up and put her in the seat and carefully began to push her. The other child watched shyly for a few moments, while their babysitter hung back. Jake admired Magda. The child trusted her. Magda seemed not only beautiful to him but good. Finally the second child climbed on to a swing too. The babysitter took over from Magda. Magda and Jake drifted off a distance and turned to watch.

'Children are so innocent,' Magda said.

Her statement seemed unnaturally sophisticated to Jake, but also pointed, as if she knew he had deceived her. He could think of nothing to say. It took all his nerve just to look at her. He noticed the small green flecks in her blue irises, but he resisted the charm of her eyes. He had to rein his runaway sexual impulses. 'Magda what?' he asked, trying to deflect his unease. He had stopped her with a purpose and it was time to pursue it.

'Magda Dettke.' She paused before adding, 'I'm German.'

'Dettke . . . Dettke,' Jake pretended to mull. 'Is your sister a translator, by any chance?'

'My mother is!'

'And her name is Anna-Lise?'

'How did you know?' She stared at Jake, mouth agape, her sophistication obliterated by her surprise.

'I think my uncle has spoken of her. I think perhaps she has done work for him at the embassy. Doesn't she work for the British Embassy? So does my uncle. He admires her.'

'He *speaks* of her?'

'Yes. Why shouldn't he?'

'Because my mother works at home. She receives her work and returns it in the mail.'

'But she goes out. I'm sure she does. To the museum, for example.'

Recognition crossed her face: the museum! 'I saw you there,' she whispered. Her hand went to her mouth while her eye fell involuntarily to Jake's stick.

'I go to Georgetown,' he said quickly. 'I wanted to meet you. I pass here all the time. I'm sorry.'

Magda turned and began to run.

'Don't go! Please!' She ignored him. 'Please, wait!' Jake began to canter after her as best he could, but she opened up the distance easily. He'd blown it. Jeeze, had he blown it!

He almost never tried to run like that, was strictly forbidden to do so. The trick was to keep his weight on his right leg for as long as possible, and then to really lean into the blackthorn. Still, every time he swung his rigid left leg around, the jolt registered on the pins in his ankle and knee, and a sharp pain shot from his heel to the lower underside of his thigh. The pins wouldn't break, but the cartilage into which they were set could tear easily. He'd been warned. 'Magda, wait!'

He had to get altitude – *up* and down, *up* and down! – by doubling the force with which he shoved off from his right foot. 'Magda, please!' What if she simply disappeared around a corner or slammed that door in his face? The afternoon gaped up at him like the bottomless canyon he would fall into without her. Not that *she* was so awful. Life is bloody awful, old boy, and now you know it. 'Magda!' If he lost her like this, before he explained himself – he'd deceived her and frightened her like a pick-up artist or a pimp – then not only would he have sullied a dream – he had seen for a moment what his grandfather saw in Degas's statue; he'd seen what Degas saw! – but also, and worse, he would have destroyed his access to the single clue to the double mystery of his father's apparent infidelity and his uncle's apparent treason.

He waved his stick at her. Even he could forget his disability. When he came down on his left leg he crashed to the ground, not a mere stumble but a radical collapse. The unforgiving earth slammed back at him. He bounced like a stone.

He lay with his face against the grass, teeth gritted, and remained motionless for what seemed a long time.

'Jake?'

He was dreaming it.

'Jake, are you hurt?'

He felt her hand on his shoulder. She was a statue come alive. None of this was happening except in fancy. He was asleep in his room on the third floor with the view of Washington. His father and mother were snug in each other's arms, and his uncle would be coming over in the afternoon for dinner.

'I'm sorry I made you run.'

He opened his eyes and squinted up at her. The sun was behind her and it blinded him. He hid his face in the crook of his arm. Jeeze, it was no dream.

He wasn't hurt. His chinos would be wrecked. Screw his chinos. Abruptly he sat up and looked at her. 'I'm all right. Thanks very much.'

She sat down next to him, primly arranging her skirt and tucking her legs in close. 'I noticed you in the museum.'

'I followed you home. That's how I knew where to find you today.'

'What about your dog?'

'No dog.'

Magda began to laugh. She laughed and laughed until, when she touched his arm, he began to laugh too.

'I looked for your dog!'

'My dog Cooney!' Jake screeched.

They were like school chums at recess. Having surrendered to their silliness, there was nothing to do but indulge the thrill of it. Jake became even more hysterical than she was. The past days' tension poured out of him. He laughed, crazily, and the relief he felt was bliss.

When he finally stopped laughing he realized that she had stopped well before him. He said, 'I knew you would be kind.'

He felt much calmer, and it was clearer to him now what he had to learn.

Magda fixed her eyes on her hands in her lap.

'So that *was* your mother.'

'We go to a museum every Wednesday.'

'Always the Phillips?'

'Different ones.'

'Your mother seems nice.'

Magda nodded.

'And that man you met, the one who gave you roses, he was your father?'

'My father is dead.'

Her sharp green-flecked eyes snagged him. 'I'm sorry,' he said. Hadn't Giles said her father was alive?

'He died in the war. I don't remember him.' She began to knit and unknit her fingers. 'He died in Berlin.'

'Is that where you're from?'

She nodded. 'My grandfather was a professor at a famous university. It's in East Berlin now.'

'How long have you been in Washington?'

'Six years.'

Jake nodded casually, but an alarm went off in him. Six years? *. . . the Cultural Attaché to the British Embassy in Washington since 1954 . . .*

In 1954 Jake knelt with Giles before the bishop; he was taking Giles's name. The sacrament of Confirmation made Jake a soldier of Christ. The bishop struck him lightly on the cheek. Later Giles explained that that ritual gesture came from the ceremony of knighthood, the tap with the sword. Everything seemed grander, more charged, when Giles explained it. Jake remembered how glad he was that his mother's brother had been sent to Washington.

'And before Washington?' he asked carefully. 'Where did you live before?'

'Germany.'

. . . served before being posted to Washington at the British Embassy in Bonn . . .

'In Bonn?' Jake asked.

Magda shook her head. '*Köln.* Cologne.'

Jake stared at her. He knew that Bonn and Cologne were adjacent cities. He'd drawn close to something secret here, but he didn't know what to ask. Paranoia surged in him. He had to resist an impulse to look around.

After a moment, to pull back, Jake said, 'Not many kids of our generation remember the war.'

'I don't remember it.'

'But it killed your father. You can't forget that.' Jake looked briefly at his own leg. It would have been shameless of him to invoke the melodrama of the Blitz. He said sombrely, 'Our parents were against each other.'

'No. My parents were against Hitler. All Germans claim that now, I know. But with them it was true. My grandfather and my father were heroes. Hitler killed them.'

Did that make them, also, traitors? 'I admire that a lot, Magda.' Jake was conscious of the stilted sincerity in his voice. 'Really, I admire that.'

'Here people think badly of Germans. Of all Germans.'

Jake remembered how tentatively she had waved at her school-mates. He imagined her standing on the edge of countless clusters. He touched her arm. 'I don't think badly of Germans. Certainly not of you.'

'Ah, but you are different. You can be infatuated' – she paused coyly before adding, with a worldly toss of her head – 'with Degas.'

'That's a terrific statue, isn't it? Did yo᠎ know that the original was made of painted wax, and the bronze casts were done only after Degas was dead?'

'No, I didn't.' Magda smiled at his impulsive display of the arcane. It was meant to impress and it did.

They fell silent again.

Then Jake said casually, 'I thought it might be your father in the museum because I heard him speak to you in German.'

Magda shrugged and smiled. 'Many educated persons speak German. Even some Americans.' Her tone implied that the man was either not important to them or too important to discuss lightly with a stranger. She stood up, brushed her skirt, then offered her hand to Jake.

His impulse would ordinarily have been to get up without her help but her hand was irresistible.

She took more of his weight than he expected and he got to his feet easily, almost gracefully. 'Thanks,' he said, and when he pressed her hand slightly before letting go of it she pressed back.

He was conscious of her body only inches away. Now, perhaps because of the queer intimacy they'd shared or because of the strength with which she'd hoisted him or because of that slight pressure from her fingers, it seemed a more womanly body than before. He smelled her perfume, a modest scent, but it had the effect of an electric shock, a pulse from her private parts to his. To his horror his prick stirred and he was sure she would see it bulging in his pants. But he didn't turn away. She was a woman to him, not a girl. And his acute lust made him feel, not ridiculous for once, but like a man.

'You have mud on your face,' she said.

Jake's hand went to his cheek, and then he looked down at himself. Yes, his erection was visible, but he didn't care. In fact, he wanted her to see it. His chinos and the left sleeve of his jacket were badly stained. 'God, I'm a wreck.'

'Would you like to wash? You should wash.'

'What a jerk, eh?'

'I mean at my house. You could get the mud off, at any rate.'

'Your house?' Jake let her see his surprise, as if this wasn't what he'd hoped for. 'But your mother would be there.'

'Yes. Perhaps she would like to meet you. If, as you think, she has worked for your uncle.'

Jesus Christ! Jake thought. The girl does not get it! She believes me! He found it impossible to comprehend that the week's devastating events had no significance whatsoever to her. 'Thank you,' he said. He made a show of rubbing the dirt off his hands. 'I'd like very much to wash up.'

Anna-Lise at the door, frowning and with her golden hair drawn tightly back from a stern part in the centre of her head, intimidated Jake.

'Mama,' Magda said shyly, 'this is Jake. He fell.'

'Good afternoon, ma'am.'

Anna-Lise stared at him without moving back from the door to let him enter.

'Mama, I invited him to wash his face.' Magda pushed by her mother and held the door back for Jake, but he did not move.

'Jake McKay,' he said, and he held his hand out to Magda's mother.

Anna-Lise took his hand. Her expression and her silence conveyed to Jake that she knew everything. That she could stand there subdued, in control of herself, as if her only question was, What kind of creep has my daughter brought home? relieved Jake somewhat. She stepped aside for him.

A small hallway from which a staircase led up to the left opened to the right on a tidy parlour and then led beyond to a dining-room. In the parlour a pair of pale blue love seats faced each other on either side of a fireplace. Scraps of paper and pieces of kindling on the floor indicated that Magda's mother had been preparing a fire. Jake thought that strange on such a warm day. The walls of the room were painted white. They were bare. No carpet or rug covered the old undulating polished floorboards. On the mantel above the fireplace was a bud vase holding two red roses.

Anna-Lise said, 'Give me your jacket.'

Jake took it off and gave it to her, and she walked away from him down the short hall to the dining-room. Magda pointed to a narrow door in the corner. 'That's the WC,' she announced.

Jake went into the tiny bathroom – it filled the angled dead space below the stairs – and washed his hands and face. He hadn't cut himself, but a faint red bruise showed on his left cheekbone. He cupped his face with both hands and tried to learn by staring into his own eyes what was happening. He had no plan. He had no idea what to make of Magda's mother or what use to make of her. But what the hell, what was there to lose?

He walked through the dining-room to the doorway of the small kitchen, which jutted back in its own ell. Magda's mother was at the sink, her back to the room, rubbing at the sleeve of his jacket with a cloth. Magda was next to her.

Magda said, 'She does know your uncle.'

'I thought you might.'

Anna-Lise half-faced him. 'That is why you came, isn't it?'

'Yes.'

'Why did he come, Mama? I don't understand.'

Anna-Lise looked sharply at Magda: You have been raised not to ask such questions. Then she turned back to the sink, rubbed the jacket vigorously for a moment, held it up, then shook it. Satisfied, she crossed to Jake and held it open for him. He put it on a sleeve at a time and then thanked her.

'Now you must go.'

'I was hoping you might . . .' Jake looked peripherally at Magda. A wave of his previous desperation was breaking on him. '. . . talk to me.'

Anna-Lise shook her head slowly.

How can you not talk to me? You know everything! I won't tell anyone, not even Dad! Just talk to me! 'You won't?'

Magda interrupted again. 'Talk about what?'

109

Anna-Lise faced her. 'Be still,' she said. Magda dropped her eyes.

Anna-Lise softened, but only enough to say, 'Jake, I am sorry, very sorry.'

Jake turned and led the way through the dining-room. Through the green door he saw the fireplace in the parlour. Light your fucking fire, he thought. At the front door he turned back. Magda was behind him. Her mother had not followed. 'Listen . . .' he began.

But she interrupted, 'I don't understand what's happening. Do you know my mother?'

Jake shook his head. 'Believe me, I'm more confused than you are. Anyway, I really appreciate how kind you were.'

'It wasn't kind. I wanted to.' She looked away from him.

'Anyway, thanks.'

He opened the door.

A car jolted to a halt right in front of him, and Jake McKay jumped. A long black car, a familiar car. Jake's eyes flicked first to the driver – it was Mr Curtin staring straight ahead – and then to the passenger's door just as it opened. For once surprise was on Jake's side.

'Hi, Dad,' he said.

If John McKay had been slugged he'd have reacted as he did then. Jake thought for a moment his father was going to pass out. Colour drained from his face and his mouth fell open. But he recovered quickly. 'Back inside, Jake,' he said.

He was carrying a Pan-Am flight bag. With his free hand he gestured Jake into the house. Magda and her mother were standing in the hallway. Jake's father handed the bag to Anna-Lise. Otherwise he ignored her. He crooked a finger at Jake and Magda. 'Come along.' He led them into the dining-room. 'Sit down.'

Magda and Jake sat at the table.

'Listen to me carefully. I'm closing the door now and you are staying here until I come back in from the other room.' He concentrated his gaze on Jake. 'You saved me a trip, son. I was going from here to your dorm. We're going home.'

'Today?'

'In a few minutes. We have to take care of your mother.'

'Did he do it, Dad?'

McKay nodded. A curve of feeling swept across his grim face.

Then he turned and crossed into the parlour, closing the door behind him, but not before Jake heard Anna-Lise's fire crackling to life.

Jake and Magda sat in silence, listening. With the door closed they could hear nothing from the other room.

Magda stood. 'He is your father?'

'Yes. I apologize. I should have told you.'

Magda stared at him for a moment, then said, 'Is it that you think I am a child or a fool?' She stood and crossed into the kitchen. She went to the stove and lit the ring under the kettle, then returned to the dining-room, to the corner cupboard.

Jake watched her taking down cups and saucers. He couldn't help but admire the lines of her body. Was there no limit to his capacity for sexual distraction?

'Nice dishes,' Jake said as she placed a cup and saucer before him. An inane comment, but he wanted to channel his nervousness and his awkwardness into small talk. The dishes' rich blue and amber pattern had its appeal. He picked up the cup. Even he could tell from the feel of that china, the way the light shone through it, that it was special. He turned the cup over. A crown was stamped above the word *Meissen*, and above the crown was the word *Isenberg*.

'Isenberg was my mother's name,' Magda explained. 'Her family made porcelain. You should be careful. Real Meissen is impossible to get now.'

'Meissen is behind the Iron Curtain?'

'Yes. But the factories were all destroyed by . . . .' She looked away.

'Us.'

She shrugged. 'My mother's father had left the factory anyway. He was against his father. He was against capitalism. He preferred the university in Berlin.' Magda studied her own cup.

'Why do they call it china?' Jake asked. 'They should call it Germany.' He smiled ingenuously, but he shot his gaze at the parlour door for an instant. What were they doing in there?

'In Germany we never did call it china. We used a word that translates "hard-paste". But of course the Chinese invented the process of firing porcelain and all of the great designs are Chinese. This one, for example. The "Chinese bird" was introduced to Saxony in the eighteenth century, but a version of it has been found on ware in China dating to the fourteenth.'

'Jeeze, you know your stuff.' When his father came out of the parlour would he explain things to him?

'My great-grandfather probably supervised the firing of this setting. Surely he handled each piece. Nothing left the factory that he hadn't touched. He was a huge man. He had a great drooping moustache on which my mother, as a child, tugged and tugged, but he never protested.' Magda laughed because at this point in the telling her mother always laughed. 'She thought she could make his whiskers come off.' She put the cup down. 'My mother thinks I should know everything about my family. Her father was a Communist. And so was my father.'

Even that revelation seemed from this demure, formal girl almost routine. Jake sensed that she was trying to shock him, but he seemed to have as little capacity now for surprise as she had. 'Is your mother a Communist? Are you?'

Magda shook her head. 'In those days being Communist was just a way of being against Hitler. My mother says that my father would have nothing to do with them now.'

'Do you know what my father does?'

She shook her head.

And Jake said, 'Neither do I.'

He stood and crossed the few feet to the parlour door. An old-fashioned thumb-latch held it shut, but not securely. By pressing against the worn pine just slightly Jake was able to open it a crack. A sliver of light cut in from the other room, and shamelessly he put his eye to it. What did he expect to see? His father and Magda's mother making love on the floor, his trousers at his ankles, her skirt at her throat?

His father was kneeling in front of the fireplace with his back to the dining-room. Anna-Lise was at his side. It took Jake a moment to realize what they were doing because the room itself, despite the fire, was darker than it had been. The curtains had been drawn. Anna-Lise was removing pages from a binder and handing them to him one at a time while he fed them into the fire. The scene seemed liturgical. The priest and deacon huddle over the thurible while the altar boy watches from a corner. Burnt offering. Jake remembered the Greek word from Religion class: holocaust.

Jake was aware suddenly that Magda was right behind him. He looked at her.

'May I see?' she whispered.

He stepped aside and she took his place at the cracked door, but at that moment the doorbell sounded. Jake pushed Magda aside, to look.

John McKay quickly shoved the Pan-Am bag under the love seat and replaced the screen in front of the fire. He removed his suit coat, loosened his tie. Anna-Lise removed her barrettes so that her hair poured down over her shoulders. She unbuttoned her blouse, exposing her brassiere. The doorbell rang again.

Anna-Lise began to rebutton her blouse as she went to the parlour door that opened on the front hallway. Jake's father was crossing towards him. Jake backed away from the door. When it opened, his father gestured towards the kitchen and said, 'In there.' Jake and Magda quickly obeyed him, taking up a position just out of sight in the galley-style kitchen. The last thing Jake saw was his father closing the door on the parlour and taking a seat at the dining-room table.

Jake and Magda stood close together by the stove, listening. They heard Anna-Lise lead several people into the dining-room.

'Hello, Mac,' one said.

'What the fuck are you doing here, Fred?'

Jake had never heard his father use the word before.

The man didn't answer.

'This is an outrage, Fred,' John McKay said. 'I insist that you leave here at once.'

'Look, Mac, you know the score as well as I do. It makes everybody jumpy when you disappear like that.'

'Disappear? God damn it, even file clerks get off for lunch.'

'Lunch!' The man laughed, and so did the others. 'Look, Mac, you'll have plenty of time later to prove you like girls. Today you have another priority.'

'You and your goons can go back to the compound, Fred. I'll be right along. Who's so jumpy about me, anyway? Jim?'

'Among others, frankly.'

'You?'

The other man didn't reply. Jake was paralysed, listening to them, but he understood suddenly that it was infinitely important that the man not enter the parlour and notice the fire, the scraps that hadn't burned. His father would never convince them he'd wanted a fire for the romance of it.

'Come on, Mac. Get your hat.'

What was familiar about that man's voice?

'How'd you know to come here?' A pause. 'Of course, Houseman. My loyal ADC. Fuck!'

'Look, McKay, where and when you get your tail is your business . . .'

'Please!' Anna-Lise broke in. You are not to refer to me in this way! was implicit in her voice. But the man ignored her.

'. . . But not today. Now let's go. I have the authority of the Director.'

'I'm calling him.'

There was a commotion. The telephone crashed to the floor. Jake craned around the edge of the door to watch them. He was exposed slightly, but the four men were so intent upon his father that they didn't notice him. Two of the men were holding his father, each by an arm. He was angrily leaning towards the leader, and now Jake realized that there was something familiar about that man's appearance. 'You've been waiting for this, you shit!' Jake's father said.

'Damn right, Mac. I've lost twenty good men to that bastard, and God knows what else. You'd better convince me that he pulled it off alone!'

'He burned me more than you, Yeats.'

Yeats! Jake had met him after the solemn Mass when the new chapel at St Anselm's was dedicated in his third-form year. Fred Yeats. The name rang in his head. You can be proud of your father, Fred Yeats, Jr., had said. I know I am of mine.

'Convince me, Mac. You convince me.' Then, more quietly, he said, 'Go ahead, Jerry.'

Jake saw one of the men holding his father jab his shoulder and within seconds his father slumped.

At that exact moment Jake heard grotesque screeching right behind him and he jumped with fright while pulling back from the door. He and Magda grabbed each other as if they were about to be killed.

But the screeching was the whistle of the tea-kettle exploding with steam.

Before Jake could react, Magda pulled him into the narrow space between the refrigerator and the wall. They crouched together while the terrifying whistle continued, and they held each other.

Had he just seen his father stabbed with a hypodermic needle? What was this, a forties melodrama? Hitchcock? Jake clung to Magda with his face buried in her. He had never been more frightened in his life. But even now her perfume stung him and he was more intensely aware of her flesh than he'd ever been of

114

anything. His forearms were pressing against her breasts.

All at once the screeching stopped as the kettle was removed from its flame. Someone had come into the kitchen. 'Just a teapot!' he called. He was only inches away.

Then from the other room Yeats could be heard saying, 'We're not through with you, *Mädchen*.'

Then there were the sounds of the men leaving. The front door slammed behind them.

Anna-Lise ran back through the house to the kitchen. 'Magda!' she called.

Jake backed out of the cramped space ahead of Magda, but he clung to her. He would never let go of her.

'Are you all right?' Anna-Lise demanded.

Magda nodded, and pulled away from Jake, who wanted to yell, 'Fuck, no! How could we be all right!' But he said nothing. He stood there trembling. Magda was trembling too.

But Anna-Lise dashed away from them. She returned to the front door, to lock it. Then she went into the parlour through the far door, which she closed behind her. Jake, as if hypnotized, limped to the near door and applied his eye to the crack.

Anna-Lise had retrieved the flight bag from under the love seat and was coolly feeding its remaining pages into the fire.

CHAPTER NINE

The pale man in the three-piece suit was describing Giles Patterson as a probable victim of Soviet blackmail. He was Douglas Edwards and this was the evening news. Jake was alone in the den, watching with the volume very low, but unknown to him, Dori had been listening from the threshold.

'What does that mean?'

Jake snapped the set off and faced her. 'What, Dori?'

'Sexual . . . I don't know the other word.'

'Proclivity. It means there's gossip about Uncle Giles.'

'What kind of gossip?'

Jake's sister stood in the doorway with the light of the hall behind her. She was tight-lipped and fierce. Now that she had finally dared to put a question to Jake, he felt obliged to answer her. He had to protect her from the full weight of the implications, but he was himself too frustrated by the ineluctable mysteries to flaunt them at her. It wasn't as if she were Sissy's age. Dori was five years younger than he was, but only three years younger than Magda. Magda had stood in the doorway of her house to say goodbye to him. What was so captivating about a girl framed in such a way? Jake looked warmly at his sister, but for a moment he saw her as Magda. 'Be careful,' she'd whispered, as he was leaving. 'Will you call me?' She'd thrust into his hands a piece of paper with her phone number on it. Then, quick as a darting bird, she'd kissed him.

The thought of Magda made Jake resent Dori's intrusion. That was the trouble with sisters. They always intruded. But it wasn't Dori's fault. He had to be patient. 'Come in here and sit with me.'

When she sat on the arm of his easy chair, he took her hand. 'You know how at school there are two kinds of kids? The ones who do everything pretty much the way everybody else does? They wear the same clothes and use the same slang and like the same records. You know the ones I mean?'

Dori laughed. 'You mean me.'

'Me too.' Jake rubbed her head. 'But then there are the other kids who don't quite fit in. Maybe they dress differently or something.'

'Nonconformists?'

'Yeah, sort of. When you grow up, being a little different may or may not be a bad thing. Crooks are a little different, and that's bad. But geniuses are, too, and what would we do without them? Either way, people tend to wonder about you if you don't fit in. I guess it turns out that Uncle Giles hasn't been fitting in as well as it seemed. What they're saying about him now is that he's a homosexual. Do you know what that is?'

'Of course I know,' she said peevishly.

Her tone warned Jake not to condescend, and he had to stifle his impatience again. He nodded. 'It's not necessarily their fault, but people generally give them a bad time. I guess you know that.'

'People call them names.' Dori paused, then with a catch in her voice, asked, 'Is Uncle Giles a queer?'

'They're saying he is, Dori. I guess if he was, he was ashamed of it. They're saying that the Russians found out about it, and that if he didn't come over to their side they would tell.'

'But he went over and they told anyway?'

'Maybe they did. You can't trust the Russians. See, he wouldn't have been any good as a spy for them, even though he worked at the Embassy, because all he did was set up concerts and exhibits and like that. So what they did was make him defect so that everybody would be embarrassed and maybe the English and the Americans would have an argument because they'd all worry a lot about whether he was a spy.'

'Is he?'

Jake shrugged. 'The main thing is, it probably wasn't his fault. Maybe they kidnapped him. We don't know. Maybe he had a nervous breakdown.'

'Is that what you think?'

Jake didn't answer immediately. Then he said, 'I don't know what to think, Dori. I'm as confused as you are.'

'What happens if a nervous breakdown comes?'

'Are you worried about Mother?'

Dori nodded. 'Why won't she come out of her room?'

'This is probably the worst thing that ever happened to her, Dori. Uncle Giles was her big brother, right? Like I am to you. Wouldn't it just knock you for a loop if I . . .'

'But you wouldn't, Jake!' Dori burst into tears. 'You wouldn't!'

Jake wanted to hug her, to rock her, but the mode of their affection, brother and sister, didn't permit it. 'Of course I wouldn't,' he said. 'But if something almost as bad happened in a family you were the mother of, then your kids would have to take special care of you, wouldn't they?'

Dori nodded.

'And that's us, right? Is Sissy still with Emmaline?'

'Yes. They're playing dominoes.'

'Well, why don't you and I go up and see Mother, then? Maybe she's awake. We'll take her some dinner, OK?'

Eleanor McKay wasn't in the bedroom but in her sitting-room. At the door Jake heard the radio. A newscaster was droning. When Jake knocked, his mother turned it off. After a moment she called with false cheer, 'Come!'

Dori went in first with the tray.

'Oh, you dears! You absolute dears!'

Jake was pleased to see that she was dressed. She was wearing a sweater and skirt, but also slippers still. She was putting a last pin in her hair.

'I was just coming down.'

She's been surreptitiously listening to the news as he had. Jake felt a rush of the anxiety they had in common.

'But, well,' she said, taking the tray from Dori, 'let's just sit here, shall we? Where it's cosy.'

Eleanor sat at her desk with the tray, which held a plate of tuna salad arranged on lettuce, and a dish of fruit and cheese. Dori sat on an edge of the wing chair and Jake slid in beside her.

'How are you, Mother?' he asked. How to be solicitous without making her feel even more inadequate?

'Oh, Jake, I'm sorry I've been such a mope. What would I do without you? When did you come home?'

'A couple of hours ago. Everything's under control. The newspapermen are gone. Mr Houseman says they won't be back.' It was an effort to pretend that the issue was newspapermen and not the kidnapping of his father. Jake knew he couldn't tell her what he'd seen.

'Dwight's so nice.' She stared at the plate of fruit and cheese, but her attention had drifted.

Dori and Jake watched her carefully.

After a few minutes she looked up and smiled. 'Your father is lucky to have him.'

But Houseman had betrayed their father. Jake had never liked the son of a bitch. 'I saw Dad today, Mother. He told me to tell you everything's all right.'

Eleanor was shocked. 'You saw him? Where?'

'At school.' It was the answer he'd rehearsed. 'He came by in the car. He only had a minute. Campus isn't that far from the compound, you know.'

'What did he say?'

'That everything's going to be all right.'

She smiled quickly. 'I'm sure it is.' She picked up a wedge of apple and took a dainty bite, then touched the napkin to her lips. 'Do you think I could have a bit of tea?' She looked at Dori, whose face, in Jake's opinion, warned of a coming panic. *Is my own mother asking my permission? Or is she announcing an errand she wants me to run?* Eleanor resolved the problem by adding, 'Would you, dear?'

'Sure, Mommy!' Dori chirped. She hopped up and promptly left the room.

Jake's mother looked directly at him then. 'Have you explained to them?'

'To Dori, yes. Sissy's content to leave it alone. There are no newspapers in the house, but Dori came into the den while I was watching the news. They never mentioned Dad.'

118

'Who warned Giles? That's what the radio says everybody's asking.'

'Who *warned* Giles?'

'He was going to be arrested. Somebody warned him. That's why he got away.'

'*I* would have warned him, Mother.'

They stared at each other. They both knew. The warning had come two nights before, when John McKay and Giles had had their long talk in the den. Was that possible? Wouldn't that mean that Jake's father was capable of a personal – no, *familial* – loyalty more intense than his loyalties to his country and to his oath? Unthinkable. But how else account for Yeats's behaviour towards his father this afternoon?

'Did your father say when he was coming home?' Jake heard the other question in her voice: *Am I going to lose him, too?*

Jake had to look away from her.

She said, 'Do you remember last year when people were afraid that the Russians were going to blockade Berlin again, and the President said he'd use nuclear weapons?'

'Sure, Mother. How could I forget?'

Eleanor folded and unfolded her napkin while she spoke. 'Your father didn't come home for a week. Do you remember? It's so unfair that we lose him just when everything gets so' – she shuddered – 'frightening.'

Life is awful. Jake thought of his uncle. Bloody awful.

'I was obsessed, positively obsessed by . . . I had no idea what your father was dealing with. It was worse than the war. In the war one knew. One knew, Jake!'

He wanted to close the small space between them, but he couldn't.

'I had only one clue. I always knew that as long as he was still in Washington things were under control, and I could tell.'

'How could you, Mother?'

'The helicopters.' She smiled. Then she leaned to the lower left-hand drawer of her desk, opened it, and withdrew a pair of olive-drab army field glasses. 'These are your father's. He never missed them because I left the case in his trunk. I know where the helicopters for evacuating Washington are. Helicopters will take the senior people – not VIPs necessarily, but the men who will manage the war – to that underground headquarters in the mountains. As long as they're in Washington, then it's all right. As long as the helicopters are still there.'

Jake took the binoculars from her. 'Where are they, Mother? The helicopters.'

'Lined up at Bolling, in front of a big hangar. When the alert is on, they move them out on to a corner of the runway. A general's wife told me. I could see them from a hill near Saint Elizabeth's.'

'You would go over to Saint Elizabeth's with these?'

She nodded. 'Every day. Twice, perhaps three times. I know it sounds crazy, but only to someone who doesn't understand. Other wives I know have done as much. Berlin was much worse than people thought, much closer to . . . No one ever knew we were on full alert. People aren't afraid enough, Jake.'

'You should have told me, Mother.'

'I couldn't tell you, Jake. You understand that. I shouldn't be telling you now. It's all secret.'

'But if Dad goes off to a cave in a mountain, I have to take his place, right? What's a son for?' He raised the binoculars and looked at her through them. 'I feel real close to you.'

'Oh, Jake.' She opened her arms.

He put the binoculars down, crossed to her, and knelt, somewhat clumsily, to let her hug him. Their custom required that even at that moment he be inside her embrace, not she in his.

'You are so strong,' she said.

And that pleased him. Also, it was true. Suddenly he felt stronger than ever.

When he pulled back she caught his face in her hands. He saw her eyes snag on something. 'What is this?' she asked. She was staring at his cheekbone. He pulled back, but she held him. 'You're bruised.'

'No, I'm not.'

'What happened?' she demanded, much too loudly.

'Nothing happened, Mother. I fell.'

'You fell! You never fall!'

'Sometimes I fall, Mother.' He freed himself and got to his feet.

'You fall? And you don't tell me?'

'Sometimes,' he said softly. He fidgeted with his stick. He sensed how volatile she was. He had to be very careful. 'But if I was hurt I'd tell you.'

'You didn't fall! You didn't fall!' She shook her head, but eyed him steadily. Her lips trembled.

He tried to soften her gaze with his own. 'I fell, Mother. Really.'

'Someone hit you.'

'No, Mother.'

'Who? Who?' She stood up. 'I demand to know! I will not have you deceiving me! I forbid it! Now who hit you? Who hit you?'

He dropped his stick, grabbed her shoulders, and shook her. She was so light, so frail. He kept forgetting that. 'I'm telling you the truth, Mother. No one hit me. I was crossing a field in Georgetown. There was no path. I tripped. I landed on my cheek. I did not hurt my leg, and it wasn't my leg's fault. You'd have tripped in that field. Anyone would have. You may chastise me because I wasn't careful. You may feel disappointed that I was clumsy. But you mustn't think I'm not telling you the truth.'

She looked at him helplessly. 'Are you telling me everything?'

'Yes, Mother. Everything.' He would remember that statement as another lie to her. He'd lied to her once earlier in the week, hadn't he?

He should now have taken her inside his embrace. She'd have allowed it. An embrace would have been gracious and loving at that moment, but only in principle. In the doing it would have been, like tears for once, glib and therefore false. Another lie. He would not tell it. He let go of her shoulders.

They remained where they were, only inches apart, but each carried aspects of the burden the other did not know of. It may have been the same burden, but the difference between the effects it had on the mother and the son was vast. He had a vague set of fears which, however dreadful, engaged him, and as each one came to pass it seemed to leave him more stupefied, yes, but also more alive. She, on the other hand, had only one fear, a worse fear. Not about her brother or husband, but about herself. She was having to hold on to an oiled surface.

'What time is it?' she asked suddenly.

'Seven-thirty, maybe.'

'Goodness, Jake!' Eleanor's hands fluttered to her face. 'And you're not dressed!'

'What do you mean?'

'The dance! Tonight's your dance! You're going to the dance!'

That was the lie he'd told her; he'd come home for his ebony stick. 'I'm not going, Mother,' Jake said evenly. 'I'm staying here.'

'Don't be silly. You have a date, don't you?'

Magda Dettke. Jake pictured her on that swing, arching back towards him. *Would you like to go to a dance with me? Why, certainly, when is it? Well, actually, it's tonight.* 'Mother, after what's happened I'm not going to any dance.'

'But you love to dance.'

'I'm staying here with you and the girls.'

'Please, Jake, you make me feel like an invalid. Honestly, I'm perfectly capable of taking care of them, and if I need anything, I have Emmaline. Who is your date?'

'Jeeze, Mother, you don't give a guy a choice.'

'Darling Jake' – she gave him her weightiest and sanest look – 'you came home to see what you could do for me, right?'

He nodded.

'I'm telling you now it would mean so much to me if you went. All week the thought of you at your first college dance has made me very happy. If you don't go, then . . . I'll know that things are as bad as . . . well . . . they seem. If you go, then perhaps . . . Oh, Jake, do you understand?'

'I guess I do, yes.'

'Then you're going?'

'I will if you insist.'

'Oh, good! I do insist! It will make all the difference to me, Jake, really. Now, who's your date?'

'I haven't got one. But that's OK. There'll be girls from Trinity there, and Goucher.'

'Girls without escorts?' Eleanor feigned a loss of breath.

'They arrive without escorts, Mother. But they don't leave that way.'

The Class of 1963 Presents Les Brown and His Band of Renown and the All-College Kick-off Mixer. MacDonough Field House. Eight to One, Tonight.

Jake looked at his watch. It was nearly ten. Strains of '"A" Train' drifted from inside the gym out to the deserted vestibule where he was standing. He tried to imagine anyone dancing to that number and couldn't. The dance poster was mounted behind glass, and he let his focus shift so that instead of seeing the sign he saw his own reflection. His hair, still wet from the shower, was slicked back as if he were a European. He was wearing a brilliant red vest with brass buttons, his navy blazer, and tan slacks, sharply creased. In his left hand he carried his ebony stick. It had so put him in mind of his uncle that he'd almost been unable to bring it. But hell, he said, he'd wear if *for* Giles, and for Giles he wore his most dandified item, a blue silk cravat. That was what made him look European, he decided. He was a prince, a young lord, a viscount, a baron. He was John Barrow McKay, Jr., the traitor's nephew. The first guy who makes a crack gets an ebony stick in the eye.

Jake had not come to the mixer for his mother's sake, and he certainly wasn't there to dance. He had his reason.

He cocked his sleeves, let his gaze linger for an instant on the reflection of his own face in the display case. Then he went through the double door to the inner vestibule and paid his admission. Then he entered the gym itself.

He stood for a moment letting his eyes adjust to the dim light and taking in the spectacle of the decked-out hall. Blue and grey crepe paper hung everywhere and hundreds of lovely young men and women were indeed dancing with verve and skill to the now-blaring brass music. The band was on a spotlit stage at the far end of the gym. A beam of purple light swirled randomly across the ceiling and through the darkened upper level of eerily empty bleachers. Jake wondered what they'd done with the basketball hoops, then recognized them as the girders of the elaborate blue-grey crepe paper waterfalls that gave the dance its aquatic motif.

'If it isn't Fee-Dell McKay!'

Jake turned to find Ned Cooney standing behind him with a cup of punch in each hand and a broad grin on his face. 'Hi, Ned.' Jake was surprised to discover that the sight of his classmate assuaged something in him. It was an awkward thing to walk into a party alone.

'Where the hell did you get off to today? You cut Theology.'

'I went to chapel instead.'

'A bunch of us wanted to take you out to lunch to celebrate. We hung out at Tehan's waiting for you and boy, did I get bombed. I been flyin' all day.'

Was that only this morning, that speech? That victory? Jake only dimly recalled what the issue was: beanies? Was it possible that Cooney, that Georgetown, did not know about his uncle? But how could they? The news had yet to mention Jake's father.

'And they're writing an article about you in the paper! I talked to a reporter, built you up like you were running for Congress. And, by the way, we think you should run for class president, and I want to be your campaign manager and I got your slogan already; want to hear it?'

Jake laughed. 'Ned-boy, what's in that punch? You're shit-faced!'

Cooney grinned proudly and began to weave slightly. 'Walk softly, but carry a big stick! What do you think?'

'*Talk* softly, Ned. *Talk*.'

'I can't talk softly. It's too fucking loud in here. Where are you sitting?'

'Nowhere. I'm just cruising around.'

'Well, come with me, laddy. We got a tableful.' He indicated the two cups of punch he was carrying. 'I am about to ring the bell and after that the lights begin to flash, and then . . .' His eyes flared dramatically and his voice shot up in pitch and volume. '. . . Tilt! Tilt! Tilt!'

Cooney started to lead the way, but Jake grabbed his arm. 'Why did you tell that reporter about the museum?'

Ned's eyes widened. 'He asked me about it.'

'He asked you about the Phillips, just out of the blue?'

'He asked me about your family, if I knew your family.'

'So you told him you knew my father?'

'I told him I'd seen him. What the hell's wrong with that?'

'What else did you tell him?' Even in that noise Jake's voice was louder than it needed to be and had the effect of sobering Cooney.

When he jerked his arm free of Jake's grasp he spilled some of the punch. 'Shit!' he said. 'I told him what a terrific guy you are. What an asshole that makes me, eh?'

'Look, Ned, you don't mean any harm. But you really screwed me up. I told you that wasn't my father.'

'Right. It was Santa Claus. I'm not stupid. I got the picture. I didn't tell the guy your old man is stuffing the broad. Who cares if he is? But I didn't tell the guy, see? All I did was build you up and this is the thanks I get. Look, so your old man is getting some through the fence. Everybody's old man is, Mac. Wise up. We got to get all the ass we can. Starting tonight. You coming?'

'No, thanks, Ned. But do me a favour, will you? Don't talk about it again, OK?'

Cooney started off without replying. Jake grabbed his arm again. 'I mean it, Cooney.' Cooney blinked. 'This is very serious. I need your promise. Don't talk about it again.'

'OK, Jake. I won't.'

Jake let go of his arm and touched his cheek. 'Thanks, Ned. I appreciate it.'

Cooney nodded and moved off.

It took Jake fifteen minutes of sidling through the gala maze, scrutinizing each cluster of revellers, each pair of dancers, each young god – who'd have understood why the legion of pretty girls held so little interest for him? – to find Fred Yeats. He was sitting at the head of an ROTC table. The raucous cadets were wearing their issue blues, but with crisp white shirts and black bow ties. Jake could not decipher Fred's rank insignia, but an implicit deference in the attitude of the others suggested that he was the senior cadet at the table. He was lounging rakishly between two stunners who seemed to compete for his attention. For a long time he failed to notice Jake.

One of the cadets leaned over to Yeats. 'Here's that freshman.'

When Yeats looked up, Jake said, 'May I have this dance?' And he slapped his friend's shoulder cockily. 'How you going?'

'Jake McKay, I'll be damned. Look here, fellows,' Yeats announced. 'The man who killed hazing!'

The cadets, on cue, applauded, half-mockingly. Jake was amazed to realize that no even Fred Yeats had made the connection between him and the defector.

The band was only a couple of dozen yards away and had just begun its swooning rendition of 'Blue Moon'.

'Pull up a chair.' Yeats leaned back to haul an empty metal folding chair up to the table. Jake took it and then shook hands all around. Yeats flung an arm around Jake. He was feeling no pain. 'I was damn proud of you today. You guys and dolls should have been there.' He turned to the girl next to him and said confidentially, 'This fellow's only been in school a week, and already he's done it a big favour. He's got a future.' He turned back to Jake. 'I hear you're running for President.'

'Not me, Fred. That's Kennedy.'

Yeats laughed disproportionately and slapped the table. 'You should join Rot-see.'

Jake simply touched his cane to his forehead.

Fred blushed for an instant and the others squirmed, but he recovered by saying solemnly, 'That 4-F stuff is a crock, if you ask me. A guy with your guts could make the difference when the crunch came. You've got what it takes.'

'I appreciate that, Fred.' He took the lapel of Yeats's blue jacket between his fingers. 'Nice uniform. I'd love to try it on, though. This may be my only chance.' He grinned at Yeats and then winked at one of the girls.

'What, right now?'

'Why not?'

Yeats shrugged. They both stood. Yeats slipped out of his

125

jacket while Jake took his blazer off.

'"Blouse", we call it,' Yeats said while holding his jacket for Jake. Jake slipped it on and snapped the lapels across his shoulder blades. The effect of the silver-studded uniform in combination with the blue cravat at his throat was to make Jake look like the CO of a crack honour guard. The girls' eyes brightened, and Jake felt a moment's resentment that he could never wear such a thing.

'What's this?' he asked, fingering the braided blue rope at the shoulder.

'Dowd Rifles,' Yeats said.

'I saw you guys today. Those damn bayonets, man! Amazing!'

'A question of timing. It's simple if the timing's right. Like yours was today, Jake. I don't mind admitting you were right.'

'That's big of you, Fred. Us St Anselm's boys have to stick together, right?'

'*Damn* right.'

As Jake took the ROTC jacket off, he stumbled clumsily, and it fell to the floor. He sensed the rush of the girls' pity, but he didn't mind. He bent over from the waist with a surprising agility. While he appeared merely to be retrieving the jacket, he was also sliding Yeats's billfold out of its inside pocket. When he straightened up he took his blazer back and hid the billfold under it. Yeats donned his own jacket, buttoned it foppishly, and sat down again. Jake remained in his shirt-sleeves. 'Nice to meet you all,' he said. Inwardly his heart pounded. He was amazed at himself, that he was pulling this shit off.

'Before you go, Jake,' Yeats teased, 'say something in British.' To the table he explained, 'McKay does a wicked accent. He's half British.'

'Does that make him half Russian?' one of the cadets cracked.

Yeats whipped around. 'That, Heffernan, is exactly the kind of shit the Russians would like to start. Can it.'

'Sorry.' Heffernan's girl wouldn't look at him. She was mortified.

Yeats said with that solemnity of his, 'That must have been something for you today, Jake.'

Jake watched him carefully. What, that my father was drugged and kidnapped by yours? He checked his feeling before it surfaced. He had to remind himself they were talking about his uncle. But they didn't know it. He didn't care what they knew, but still he maintained his phoney cool. 'Because he's British? Like my mother?'

126

Yeats nodded.

'It was, Fred. A wretched day.' But he bounced his ebony stick off the floor and caught it. 'My favourite Brit uncle gave me this stick; did I tell you?' He winked at Heffernan. 'Us bloody blokes aren't all bad, chum. Cheerio.'

He limped off, conscious in particular of the way the girls' eyes lingered on him.

In a cubicle in the men's room he opened the billfold, found his friend's driver's licence and on it what he'd come for: Frederick Yeats, Jr. 1411 Colesville Rd., Silver Spring, Md.

As he left the fieldhouse he handed the billfold to the guard, saying, 'Someone must have dropped this.'

Outside he looked up at the night sky, feeling exhilarated and relieved. 'God damn, McKay,' he said aloud. 'You did it!'

CHAPTER TEN

Jake hadn't slept anyway, so it was no burden to be out before dawn. The streets of Washington were deserted, but even as the city woke up, the streets would fill slowly, since it was Saturday. The wide-open thoroughfares, especially downtown, made it impossible not to drive too fast. As he sped past the White House and turned north on New York Avenue he longed again for a peppy sports car that could take such corners properly. The old Ford Fairlane that his parents had given him lumbered through the streets. Still, it was a convertible. At a stoplight he put the top down despite the chill.

He knew the way to Silver Spring, and once there, he pulled into an all-night gas station and went to the phone. It was six o'clock, but what choice did he have? He called his mother. She answered groggily. He apologized for the hour, told her what a great time he'd had at the dance, and then asked to speak to his father. But his father had not come home. That was what he had to be sure of. He told his mother to go back to sleep, and she hung up without even asking why he was calling. Now he knew what he had to do. He was flying on automatic pilot.

The station attendant directed him to Colesville Road, and by the time Jake found 1411 the sun was above the far hills. In daylight he couldn't just sit across the street in his baby blue convertible and wait for Fred Yeats's father to come out. How did one do this? How, for example, could one confirm that Mr Yeats was even home or, if he was, that he would simply get in his car and lead Jake to his father? One could ring up the Yeats household and see if he answered. But wouldn't that make him suspicious? Remember with whom you are dealing, lad. The CIA knows more about this shit than you do.

One block up Colesville, on the opposite side of the street, was a Catholic church with a large parking lot into which a few cars were even then pulling; the daily communicants on their way to the early Mass. Jake had slowed his car, but not stopped it, and so now he continued up the block to the church, turned into the lot, and parked so that he had a clear view of the Yeatses' house. He pressed the button that put the car's top back up, and he waited. Once the Mass-goers had disappeared into the church he picked up his mother's binoculars and focused on 1411.

The house, like the others on the street, was situated on a hill well up from the road. A cement driveway shot steeply up to the attached garage. The house was a large red-brick colonial. Stately elms overarched it. Shades were drawn in all of the windows. Did Fred Yeats have brothers or sisters? Jake scanned what part of the yard was visible, but saw nothing.

He was conscious of the binoculars, their weight, the texture of the snug hide cover, the feel of the lenses against his eyes. Those lenses had pressed against his mother's eyes. He pictured her on that hill, picking out helicopters, studying their markings, memorizing their numbers, noting their positions, looking like some spy for signs of the scramble! scramble! scramble! Had she taken her brother to that hill with her? Had he memorized markings, too? Oh, Giles, Uncle Giles, you bastard!

Jake lowered the binoculars and examined them. On each side was a metal ring to which once, no doubt, had been attached a leather cord for the user's neck. His father's neck. Jake pictured him standing on the roof of a building in London watching for the Luftwaffe, trying to match up the sight of silver-edged black crosses with the foop! foop! foop! of the distant explosions. 'To the roofs, London! To the roofs!' Jake could hear Churchill on the wireless exhorting his countrymen, could see those bent Limeys climbing the rickety exterior stairs with their fire buckets. 'To the roofs!'

He put the binoculars to his eyes again, but saw no sign of life. He settled to wait.

Was this absurd? A cloak-and-dagger fantasy? Teenage silliness? He had to fight off his second thoughts. If he did not follow his most powerful impulse, despite its bizarre melodrama, what exactly would he do? He focused on his father, on what had happened to him. The memory reconfirmed him.

Eventually the Mass-goers came out of the church, got into their cars, and drove away. Jake would say, if someone asked, that he was waiting for his mother, who was in the sacristy ironing altar linens.

Shortly after eight o'clock, Jake snapped his head alert. Had he been dozing? When he focused on the Yeatses' garage, the panelled white door was rolling up into the gutter, and then a grey sedan backed slowly out. A hunter's rush pumped through him as he watched the car – a 1960 Buick – angle down the steep driveway and then swing out, tail first, into Colesville Road. Though a major four-lane, the road was still empty of traffic. The Buick curled around to face the church, and in the instant it took the driver to put the car in forward, Jake found him. Even from that distance, through the windshields and with binoculars, Jake recognized that face, the hawkish nose, the pointed chin, the fixed stare.

The sight of Mr Yeats alone in his car coming towards him frightened Jake. *OK, hotshot, here he is; now what?* Could he let the hulking grey Buick roar past the church parking lot and call it good enough? He'd made his decision already. To the roofs, London!

He put the binoculars down, started his car, waited for the Buick to pass, then pulled out into Colesville Road after it. What's the trick to following a car without attracting attention, particularly if traffic is sparse? For one thing, if you're driving a convertible, you keep the top up and hope they think, when they see you in the mirror, that you're a different car each time.

Having started out too close, he hung back. But then he nearly lost him when Yeats turned on to the relatively well travelled Military Road. Better to risk being noticed, Jake decided, than have him disappear around a bend. He stayed within a dozen car-lengths of the Buick when there was other traffic to melt into. When traffic grew sparse again as Yeats headed out into farm country north-west of Washington, Jake gave him more leeway. The Buick roared steadily along, its worldly-wise driver apparently oblivious to the college kid resolutely on his tail.

Forty-five minutes out of Silver Spring the terrain became hilly and the road was suddenly narrower and banked on both sides by large trees. They'd left tobacco fields and dairy farms behind, and only when they were driving through dark autumn woods did Jake realize that the sun had, in the open country, warmed the morning considerably.

Jake came around a curve to find the Buick just ahead of him slowed nearly to a stop, and he panicked. It was everything he could do to keep from hitting the brakes with all his might, but he slowed the way any driver would. Was Mr Yeats going to make him get out of the car and then jab him in the shoulder with a hypodermic? Jake prepared to pull out into the other lane as he closed on the Buick, but it was not necessary. The Buick turned. Jake kept going, but out of the side of his eyes as he drove by he saw that Mr Yeats had entered a narrow private road, paved and marked on either side by stone pillars, but no sign.

Perhaps a thousand yards farther along Jake slowed and pulled off into the high grass of a small meadow He shut the engine off and leaned heavily on the steering wheel. Driving gloves. He needed driving gloves if his hands were going to perspire like this. One did not wear driving gloves, of course, unless one drove a stick-shift.

He leaned his forehead on the upper edge of the wheel, between his fists. Now what?

Now listen to the birds chirping, asshole.

Let's review, he said. Your father was taken against his will to this place in the woods by bad-man Yeats. Or is bad-man Yeats the good guy? Whose side are you on, anyway? How can I be on the team, Fred, when no one tells me what we're playing?

So what's to lose? Just go in there and say you want to see your dad. What can they do? Maybe they'll let you see him. Then what? Then you say, 'Hey, Pop, Uncle Giles told me to cling to you, so here I am.' And then see what he says.

Jake drummed the fingers of his right hand against his ear, a gesture his uncle used to make, which meant, 'Play it by ear, kiddo!'

If he went on foot and then didn't like what he saw maybe he could get out without having been noticed. He got out of the car, closing the door quietly, but then, on second thought, opened it again and reached in for the binoculars.

The road turned out to be about a quarter of a mile long. For

Jake, marking each step with his blackthorn, that was a long walk. By the time the house came into view, a sprawling four-storey white mansion with great pillars supporting the canopy of a grand porticoed entrance, he was relieved. The house was stately but also welcoming, utterly unsinister. The grounds, a walled garden to the left and a rolling lawn to the right, were well kept and implied that people lived here who liked visitors. Jake studied the place while approaching it slowly. No bars on the windows. In the gracious curving driveway Mr Yeats's Buick was parked behind a black Lincoln. It looked like his father's car. On the trimmed lawn immediately in front of the house were arranged in good order a set of croquet hoops. From the garden side of the house a fountain gurgled faintly, though Jake couldn't see it. The sound of water drew him. He was already too close to have any use for the binoculars, and suddenly he felt foolish carrying them. Jeeze, what was he going to say?

In counterpoint to the gurgling fountain he heard voices from the garden and crossed the lawn to the serpentine brick wall that enclosed it. The pungent scent of clipped boxwoods refreshed his sense of smell and reminded him of the formal gardens of Mount Vernon. What image could have been more benign or more reassuring?

At the wall he had to stretch only slightly to see over. The garden, a maze of shrubs with a pair of fountains at opposite ends of a white gravel path and an arbourway arched over with roses – roses! he emphasized to himself – was simply beautiful and would have transfixed him, but his eyes were drawn by a voice. He saw the terrace. A familiar voice. He saw the table and the man sitting at it with a newspaper open in front of him. The man was calling over his shoulder to someone in the house, calling, Jake realized, for coffee or juice or pastry, calling a servant, calling from the complacency of a Saturday morning breakfast in the garden. The man, lord of the manor, country gentleman, privileged guest, was his father.

And then Dwight Houseman came out of the house carrying a dish which he placed carefully in front of Jake's father, who nodded his thanks and resumed reading his paper.

A dozen paces along the wall was a wooden gate. Jake crossed to it and without hesitating put his hand on the latch. Even before he depressed it, however, an alarm went off. Loudspeakers mounted either in trees or on top of the house began to whoop! whoop! whoop!, sending the piercing awful noise out across the forest, terrifying not only rabbits, squirrels, deer, crows, and orioles, but also Jake, who alone of those creatures did not bolt.

Not that he bravely held his ground. He was paralysed. The siren screeched away as if it were never going to stop. It was a sound calculated to fill the mind with images – scramble! scramble! scramble! – of men on the fly, flying after him.

No point running. No point standing there either. He opened the booby-trapped gate and went through, thinking his father would make Mr Yeats and his henchmen leave him alone. But his father was gone. There was no one in sight. The terrace was deserted.

Still Jake approached it. When he had climbed the four flag-stone steps up to the patio the siren stopped whooping. Jake saw the half-full coffee cup and an untouched plate of strawberries and cream on the white wrought-iron table. That morning's *Washington Post* was draped across the matching iron chair where it had been dropped. By turning his head slightly he could read the headlines of the entire front page. *Nixon Endorses Javits Plan. Kennedy Calls on Truman. Film of Soviet Dog in Orbit Released. Bunche to Leave Congo.* And, in smaller print in the corner, *Nats Bow Again to Yanks.*

Nothing about the British defector. Nothing about the kidnapping of John Barrow McKay. Nothing about McKay's wife, the traitor's sister, or his son at Georgetown, who snubbed the press.

Jake took a step towards the house but hesitated. Where the hell was his father? The elaborate french doors were ajar, but screen doors prevented his seeing into the house. He stared dumbly for some moments until he realized that someone was standing behind those screens. 'Dad?'

The door opened and Mr Yeats stepped out. 'Who the hell are you?' he asked gruffly, but he looked uncertain. Jake started to go to him. He had the bizarre impulse to treat the encounter like a college interview. Good clear eye-contact, nice firm handshake. But he stopped. Someone else was watching from behind that screen. 'I'm a friend of Fred's, Mr Yeats.' Jake's statement caught Yeats off guard, as Jake had intended. He was shifting the ground under him. Yeats eyed him warily, but Jake pressed, infusing his voice with earnest cheer. 'We went to St Anselm's together. I met you there once, at the dedication? And now we're both at Georgetown. I saw him last night. He said to say hello, if I saw you.'

Yeats looked pointedly at Jake's stick. 'Who are you?'

'I came to see my dad. I'm Jake McKay.'

'You're who?' Yeats's surprise unfurled itself with a snap.

'Mr McKay's son. I'm sorry about the alarm. But I'd like to see him, please.'

Yeats turned slightly towards the door and Dwight Houseman came out. Yeats looked at him quizzically and Houseman nodded.

'Hi, Mr Houseman,' Jake said.

'Hello, Jake. How are you?'

Yeats said sternly, 'I'll have Mr Houseman escort you home now. You've overstepped the line quite a lot, son, by coming here.'

'I'm not going until I see my father. My mother's not doing so hot, and I have to talk to him.'

'Your father isn't here,' Yeats said.

'That's right, Jake. He isn't.'

Jake laughed. 'I just saw him.' He pointed at the cup on the table. 'That's his coffee, and you just brought him those straw-berries, Mr Houseman. I saw you.' He raised the binoculars inanely.

Houseman and Yeats exchanged a glance, then Yeats said, 'It doesn't matter. You're leaving now and Mr Houseman is taking you.' Yeats nodded at Houseman, who took a step towards Jake.

'Hold it,' Jake said. He took a step back, nervously. 'You better let me see my father. There's a reporter who wants my story, and my dad has to tell me what to say.'

'You don't say anything, Jake,' his father said from inside the house. The sharp familiar authority of his father's voice, but dis-embodied in that way, stung Jake. Worried affection rose in him and threatened to break the perfect tension in which he'd held himself now without rest for twenty-four hours. Dad, help!

His father stepped through the screen door. He looked all right. He was clean-shaven and wearing a fresh white shirt, but no tie, and the trousers of his blue suit. It was as if he hadn't quite finished dressing for the office. When he looked at Jake, however, his face was impassive, impossible to read. Was his father angry to see him? Or relieved? Or indifferent? Jake had no idea.

His father turned to Yeats. 'I think I should talk to him, don't you?'

Was his father asking Yeats's permission?

Yeats nodded and flicked his head at Houseman. The two of them went into the house.

John McKay watched them disappear behind the screens and

133

then he crossed to the french doors to close them.

When he and Jake were seated at the white garden table he said, 'You know, son . . .' But then he stopped and only stared at him.

Jake sensed that a quiet, morose rebuke was coming. His father's disapproval now would crush him.

But then his father said, '. . . You are a very brave young man.'
Jake blushed.

'And it moves me that you've come here.'

Jake had to avert his eyes from his father's stare.

'It's just what I would have done,' he said. He was speaking with some effort and little inflection. 'How did you find us?'

'I followed Mr Yeats.' He raised the binoculars. 'I used these.'

It took a moment for the field glasses to register with McKay, but then he reached across to take them. 'My God, I haven't seen these in years.'

'You used them in the war, I guess.'

'I certainly did.' McKay fondled the glasses, then tried them out.

'You and Uncle Giles,' Jake said quietly. He fingered the grain in the knobby head of his blackthorn. At first he thought his father, who seemed to be tracking a bird, hadn't heard him.

But he lowered the binoculars and looked at Jake. 'That's right, son. He and I were a team.'

'And after the war too?'

McKay nodded. 'He came to Washington as head of MI-6. Do you know what that is?'

Jake nodded.

'The attaché job was just his cover. He was the link between British Intelligence and us.'

'The news says he didn't know that much.'

McKay snorted and sat up, showing more life. 'That's what we want the news to say. Fact is, son, Giles knows everything I know. It's a disaster.'

'The news said he's a queer.'

Jake's father flinched. 'I'd rather you didn't use that word about him.'

'Is he?'

McKay shrugged, but he said very carefully, 'He is a homosexual, yes.' Jake's father put the binoculars to his eyes again for a moment, then lowered them. 'The press goes berserk about this stuff.'

'They're saying someone warned him.'

'I know that.'

'Did someone?'

Jake's father smiled. 'You're good at this, you know?'

'Please tell me, Dad.'

McKay leaned back in his chair. 'All right, I will. The warning came from Moscow. Your uncle's cover was blown, as we say, because rival factions in the Soviet equivalent of CIA . . .'

'KGB?'

McKay smiled and nodded. 'Yes. Rival factions in the KGB are at each other's throats. One faction believed, unfortunately mistakenly, that Giles is a double agent working for the West, not a trustworthy Russian spy. They informed the British as a way of getting rid of him. But the other faction found out almost immediately. It happens that they are the more powerful, and so did two things. They eliminated their rivals – violently, we can presume. And they warned Giles in the nick of time. Obviously we can't explain that to *Newsweek*, or the Senate, for that matter. We can't alert the KGB as to how much we know about their inner workings.' McKay shrugged. '*Newsweek* and the Senate would rather believe it was one of us, anyway. You know Washington. Commies everywhere.'

'And homos.'

'That's right. About your uncle, the horror is not that he is homosexual. The horror is that he betrayed us.'

'You and Mother?'

'Yes. And you. His family, Jake. His family. And his country. You will never know what damage he has done. Perhaps no one will.'

'You don't seem that angry at him.'

'I'm beyond anger, Jake. I had convinced myself that Giles wasn't like the rest of his generation. They had a terrible loss of faith in themselves. They turned against everything. I'd hoped Giles was different.'

'If he loved you, Dad,' Jake began with a crack in his voice, 'how could he have . . . ?'

'That's a very good question.' McKay looked stonily at his son. 'Perhaps there's a lesson in there somewhere.'

'About homosexuality?'

McKay shook his head. 'About what happens when political conviction goes one way and personal commitment goes another.'

'Couldn't he have just had a nervous breakdown?'

135

'If he did, it's lasted twenty years.'

'I can't believe he lied to me, Dad. I just can't believe it. Any more than you would lie to me.'

McKay nodded: I know what you mean.

Jake asked, 'Will I see him again? Will I ever see him again?'

'No, son, you won't. You should think of your uncle as having died.'

Jake refused to look away, even as his mind refused to register fully what his father had just said. His uncle *wasn't* dead. And his father? Suddenly the boy felt an uncharacteristic surge of worry for *him*. 'What about you, Pop?'

McKay fiddled with the binoculars for the distraction. He said quietly, 'After my time here, I'm afraid it's over for me, Jake. After things have cooled a bit, I'll have to resign.'

'Resign! Why?' McKay didn't answer right away and Jake blurted, 'Are you under suspicion?'

His father shook his head. 'What, of warning Giles? Heavens, no.'

'Then why?'

'Because I trusted him.'

'So what! Everybody trusted him.'

'Not like I did, son. I made a terrible mistake. I have to pay for it. That's all.'

'But what will you do, Dad? What will Mom say?'

'Look, I understand how you feel, but right now those aren't the most important questions.'

'If they're making you resign, why don't you just come home with me now? The hell with them!'

'Control yourself, son.' As if to show him how, McKay picked up the binoculars, spotted a bird, and followed it.

Jake reined his anxiety, his anger, but he still did not understand. 'If you're not under suspicion why did Mr Yeats take you off like that? Why are they keeping you here?'

'The KGB isn't the only intelligence agency with its rival factions.' He lowered the binoculars to look at Jake. 'Mr Yeats got carried away yesterday. But it's understandable. His job is to keep the KGB from getting inside our shop. He's paid to be a little paranoid. He didn't know yesterday what he knows now.'

'So you can leave if you want?'

'Of course. But what we're doing here is infinitely important. We have to put together piece by piece everything your uncle might have had access to since 1954. And since I was in charge of relating our outfit to his, that's mainly up to me. We have to figure out how much damage he has done us and what we have to change to limit it. It's called debriefing.'

'Mr Yeats is in charge?'

'Well' – Jake's father smiled thinly – 'we're working together. Anyway, I'm afraid your being here won't help. And I'd be grateful if you'd go with Mr Houseman.'

'Why him?'

'Because I'm asking you to, Jake.'

'He betrayed you, though.'

'How do you know that?'

'I heard you say it.'

'That was yesterday. He was just doing his job, son. None of us knew what we know now.'

'I still don't know it.'

John McKay shook his head. 'Jake, don't press me.'

But Jake wanted to press him, was desperate to. Not about his uncle now, but about Houseman. Tell me, Dad, he wanted to say, if you like me more than him. Why can't you confide in me if you confide in that guy? Is it his legs? Will you make him beat me up if I refuse to go? And if I ditch him, is he allowed to shoot?

'He doesn't have to take me. I have my car.'

'They'll feel better if he follows you. OK?'

Jake nodded.

'Tell me how your mother is.'

'Not so hot. Can't you call her?'

'Now I can. And I will. I want you to take care of her, though. I'm counting on you. What we're doing here is going to take some time.'

'I don't understand why you can't come home at night. Mother needs you, Dad.'

'What we're doing is tricky and urgent. I'm afraid it has to come first, Jake. I'm sure you can understand that without my using big words.'

Like 'political conviction' and 'personal commitment'? How much did Jake dare ask him? 'Maybe I should take a leave from school. I could still get my tuition back.'

'Don't be ridiculous. You can still go to school. But maybe you should live at home. Would you be willing to do that?'

'Sure.'

'Son, I appreciate it.' McKay reached across the table to grasp

Jake's forearm. 'You're really something; you know it?'

Jake stared at the red jewel of his father's class ring. *Columbiensis Universitas*. 'Can I ask one other thing?'

'Sure. Why not? You've already joined me in Top Secret City.'

Jake lowered his voice. 'What were those papers you and that woman burned yesterday?'

McKay coolly picked up the stale cup of coffee and sipped it. He looked at his son over the rim. When he spoke his voice was barely above a whisper. 'I didn't know that you saw that.'

'I couldn't help it, Dad.'

'Jake, that's one I'm going to have to ask you to give me.' He turned slightly in his chair and threw a glance towards the door.

'Also, Dad, what was Uncle Giles doing at our house that night?' Jake couldn't help himself now. The question tumbled out. 'And are you having an affair with her?'

McKay leaned into his son. 'The stuff about Giles and about those papers you have to drop. You are never to ask me about that again. Understand?'

Jake nodded. He welcomed his father's authority. It had been the lack of it that threatened.

'And you are never to discuss any of this with anyone. Not the press. Not Mr Yeats. Not Mr Houseman. Not even your mother. And in particular those papers I burned; it did not happen. Right?'

'Right.'

'As for that woman, I will tell you once and then I will never refer to it again, nor will you. Her name is Anna-Lise Dettke. She is from East Germany. She is an agent of mine. She has been an agent of mine since the war. Understand, Jake? She is a spy for our side. Not even Yeats knows that. Now I have just entrusted her life to you. Do you understand?'

Jake nodded. *Sub rosa*. Relief surged through him. He would believe his father on his father's authority, but also he noted that what his father was telling him squared with what Giles had said and Magda, too, for that matter.

His father continued. 'And I have told you because I love you, and because I love your mother. I have never been unfaithful to her, Jake. Not with Anna-Lise. Not with anyone. It is important that you believe that because you may have to help your mother believe it. You know what it would do to her if she didn't.'

'I'll take care of her,' Jake said, 'and the girls too.'

'I'm depending on you, son.'

Jake stood up. He planted his stick firmly and said, as if he had forever imagined that such a moment with his father was possible, 'It's about time, Dad.'

CHAPTER ELEVEN

The next day was brilliant and warm and they all went to Mass together, even their mother, who usually went to Episcopal services alone. On the way home Jake's sisters cheered when he proposed that they all drive out to Great Falls for the afternoon, and his mother responded with her first enthusiasm since the news about Giles had broken. She proposed packing a picnic lunch, and when the girls cheered again, Jake joined them.

Dwight Houseman arrived just as they were all piling back into Jake's car. In chinos and tennis shoes he looked like a classmate of Jake's, instead of their father's assistant.

'We're going for a picnic, Mr Houseman!' Dori announced.

Houseman leaned into the open car. Jake had already put the roof down. 'That's great,' the young officer said. 'Am I invited?' He grinned ingenuously.

'Certainly you are,' Eleanor McKay replied. She was as fond of him as the girls were.

Jake stiffened, but managed to grin up at him. 'They make you work on Sundays?'

'A picnic wouldn't be work. It'd be a picnic. Where shall we go?' Houseman hopped into the back seat between Sissy and Dori.

Jake started the car, stifling his resentment. 'Great Falls,' he intoned, 'all aboard!'

As he swung out of the driveway, his mother reached across to touch his leg, a modest, affectionate gesture. When Jake looked at her she withdrew her hand to tie a kerchief around her hair, and for a moment he saw her as the high-spirited girl his father had fallen for. Her deep green eyes held his. She wanted him to know how grateful she was, and how relieved.

The ride to Great Falls up the Virginia side of the Potomac was a release for all of them. Houseman made Jake regret his reticence by leading the girls in rousing renditions of campfire favourites. They used 'A Hundred Bottles of Beer on the Wall' like a ram, battering it against the wind, verse by oaken verse, right down to '*No* bottles of beer on the wall!' Sissy wanted to begin it again, but Dori insisted on 'Row, Row, Row Your Boat'. And in the front seat, whenever Jake looked at his mother she was sitting sideways gazing fondly back at her daughters or happily over at him. The blue kerchief flapped in the wind but framed her face serenely, as if she were lounging in the bow of an Oxford punt. Perhaps he underestimated her. In those moments, given those glimpses of the girl she'd been – after all, she lived through the Blitz – he marvelled at her resilience and the power of a family to heal itself even of grievous wounds.

At Great Falls Jake was left behind when Houseman, his mother, and his sisters scampered down across the boulders to the edge of the river. Despite the bright sun, a damp haze, actually a cloud of spray, hung over the rapids, which at that point fell forty or fifty feet in a few hundred yards. The steady roar of the river was so loud that it filled the park.

Perched on the edge of a picnic table and poking absently in the dirt with his stick, Jake found himself benignly mulling over the events of the week.

Houseman came back alone. 'I said we'd get the sandwiches ready.'

'Good idea,' Jake said.

They spread the cloth in silence. While Jake laid out the food, his father's assistant fished the napkins, glasses, and utensils out of the basket.

'Your mother seems better, Jake.'

'Dad called her yesterday. That helped. I think she'd begun to be afraid that . . .' Jake stopped and looked at Houseman. 'Her brother dropping off the edge of the world like that really confused her.'

'It would confuse anybody.'

'Why aren't you with my father, Dwight?' It was the first time he'd called him by his first name.

'Because I can do more good here.'

'What, keeping an eye on me?' When Houseman looked at him quizzically, Jake said, 'You know what I mean.'

Houseman smiled. 'You shocked hell out of them yesterday, that's for sure.'

'I still don't like the idea of that place.'

'Routine, Jake. Really. Isolation is part of the technique. They have to try to remember every detail. Your dad knows that. I don't find the salt.'

'Probably isn't any. Emmaline claims salt is bad for you. She never fills the shakers at home either.' Jake opened a Coke and handed it to Houseman. 'So where are we, Dwight? Are you on my tail from now on?'

'They don't want you back out there, Jake.'

'What, they haven't moved him to another place?'

Houseman stared at him. Of course they had.

'They're afraid I'll talk to someone, aren't they?'

'Don't be silly. Who would you talk to?'

'The press.'

Houseman shook his head. 'The press won't touch this.'

'Oh, really? I talked to a reporter Friday.'

'That was Friday. You may have noticed nothing was in the paper yesterday or today.'

'Maybe I've been approached by Senate investigators, Dwight. Wouldn't your bosses be afraid of that?'

Houseman studied Jake, evidently trying to decide if he was bluffing. 'I would have guessed your father impressed upon you the importance of keeping the lid on this stuff.'

'He did.' Jake opened his own Coke. 'I'm just thinking out loud, trying to imagine why Mr Yeats would have you on my case today.'

'You're getting a little paranoid, aren't you?'

'I guess I am, Dwight. I should get a hold of myself, eh?' Jake grinned at Houseman.

'Besides, I don't work for Yeats. I work for your father.'

'That's not what my father says. You put Yeats on to him the other day.'

Houseman stared at his Coke.

Jake regretted his thrust, but, having made it, he pushed again. 'Right?'

Houseman shrugged, but he was not blasé about this. 'When the Director asks a question, you answer it.'

'But when a man's in trouble I should think you'd stick by him.'

Houseman looked up sharply. 'Your father's not in trouble.'

'Who are you kidding, Dwight? Me or yourself? My uncle and my father have been together since 1940. Now my uncle's in Moscow. My father's under house arrest. His career is over. How the hell do you spell *trouble*?'

'What do you mean, "over"?' Houseman asked sharply.

'He has to resign. He told me so. You didn't know that?'

Dwight dropped his eyes. 'I was hoping he could avoid it.'

'Maybe he could have if you'd kept your mouth shut.'

'That isn't so!' Houseman said emotionally. Then he checked himself. 'Look, Jake, you and I could work together on this thing. It would be easier for everybody.'

'Fine, Dwight. But I think we should be clear about where our loyalties lie. I only have one loyalty and it's to my old man.' Suddenly Jake realized the difference between himself and Houseman, and, realizing it, he relaxed. Houseman was not his rival, and not even, perhaps, his enemy. 'Your loyalties are more complicated than that. I understand,' Jake said, as if he were absolving Houseman, 'and I'm sure my father does too.'

'I'm sure he does.'

'It's the difference between a son and an ADC.'

The two young men stared at each other in silence. The girls arrived then, breathlessly. Each had a fistful of polished round pebbles.

When Eleanor came she praised the girls lavishly for their finds and she praised the young men for having spread the lunch. Her buoyant mood dominated the table as the five of them took their places on the benches and hungrily dug in.

By the time they returned in late afternoon to Ridge Road, no one had a barrier raised against the surprise that awaited them.

Dori was the first to see it. 'It's Daddy!' she called, as Jake swung the Ford into the driveway. 'It's Daddy!' John McKay's limousine was parked in front of the house.

Sissy began to yell too, 'Daddy! Daddy!'

'Hush, girls,' Eleanor said, but she was riveted to the sight of the Lincoln, and her youngest daughter ignored her. Bouncing on the seat, Sissy kept it up: 'Daddy! Daddy! Daddy!'

Eleanor whipped around and screamed, 'Be quiet!' and Sissy burst instantly into tears.

Jake stopped the car behind the limousine and got out, leaving the engine on and not thinking even to take his cane. He loped awkwardly to the front door. In the stone-floored hallway Emmaline and Mr Curtin were standing together waiting for him to ask his question. But Jake simply stopped in the doorway, bracing himself.

Mr Curtin began, 'Is Mrs McKay . . . ?'

Eleanor came slowly in after Jake.

Emmaline brought the frayed corner of her apron to her mouth.

Mr Curtin said, 'Mrs McKay, your husband has been taken ill and I've come to bring you to the hospital.'

Eleanor leaned into Jake's back. He turned towards her, but she straightened, a ruthless act of will. 'Where is he?' she asked.

'The Naval Medical Centre in Bethesda.'

'What happened?' Jake asked.

'Tell us later,' Eleanor ordered abruptly, and then she swivelled and stooped in one motion to intercept her daughters, who were just barrelling through the door. She scooped them both into her arms and hugged them. After a moment she said, 'Daddy's sick, dear hearts. Jake and I are going to the hospital. You're going to stay with Emmaline, and if you've done all your homework you can watch the World of Disney.'

The girls numbly took in what she said. When she released them, having kissed each, they took their places on either side of Emmaline, each holding firmly to a hand, and they watched from the hallway while their mother and their brother left in the limousine with Curtin and Houseman.

'A stroke,' Mr Curtin answered as they pulled on to Ridge Road. 'He's had a stroke.'

'Eleanor!' the white-haired man with the great moustache said, coming towards her with his soft hands out.

Jake recognized Allen Dulles, but otherwise barely registered his presence. He and his mother arrived with Houseman and Curtin taking up the rear. Jake was looking beyond Dulles through the open door behind him. White drapery floated just inside the darkened room.

A doctor and a nurse were on opposite sides of the bed in which McKay was lying. Jake hadn't imagined that his father would have tubes protruding from his nose or bandages around his skull, but such evidence of illness would have shocked him less than what he saw. His father seemed only to be sleeping. His hair was mussed, but only slightly. There was colour in his cheeks. Still, Jake felt on seeing him a terrified wave of grief, as if he were dead. Tears filled his eyes.

He turned to receive his mother as she followed him into the room. *Mom, yesterday he made everything all right again!* Jake wanted to collapse into her arms. *And now he's sick! Pop's sick!*

Eleanor was staring at her husband. She was so dumbfounded

that Jake was filled suddenly with terror that he would lose her too. *Mom, Mom!* He wanted her to hold him.

I can't handle this! I'm in over my fucking head! Jake leaned against the door frame and watched his mother approach the bed. Where had his strength gone? Just yesterday his father had made him feel ready for anything. But not this.

He shut his eyes against his tears. He had to fight this off. He had to help his mother. She needed him now.

He forced himself to join her at the foot of the bed and he took her arm. 'He looks OK, Mom.'

When she faced him Jake saw her tears. 'I love him very much,' she whispered.

Jake nodded. His tears overflowed. He put his arm around her. They stood like that in silence for some moments.

Jake realized that the doctor was staring at him. Under his white physician's coat he was wearing a Navy uniform. The doctor looked from Jake and Eleanor to Mr Dulles in the doorway. Mr Dulles raised a finger and the doctor went to him. They left the room.

Eleanor slid out of Jake's grasp and into the doctor's place at her husband's bedside, opposite the nurse who was checking his pulse.

Eleanor took his limp hand into both of hers, and that simple gesture devastated Jake. How often had she done exactly that for him! How perfectly had she dedicated herself to his recovery! He had come to long for it as much for her sake as for his own. He had recovered and she had blossomed. Now she would do that again, but with his father instead of him.

Jake went out into the corridor. He blinked his eyes against the bright lights and against his tears. Before the doctor with his studied solicitude could touch him, he demanded briskly, 'Why does he look all right?'

The doctor and Dulles exchanged a look.

The doctor said simply, 'Your father had a stroke, son. A stroke brings blood to the head, and stroke victims often have good colour.'

'What is that, a stroke?' Jake had heard the word hundreds of times but only now realized he had no idea what it meant. Golf stroke? Oar stroke? A heart attack of the brain?

'I understand your father has been under rather exceptional stress. A stroke is one of those unpredictable ways the body, even in an apparently healthy person, registers such stress.'

'But I mean what is it? What is a stroke?'

'An embolism in an artery in your father's brain. An embolism is what we call it when an embolus lodges in a canal too small to permit its passage.'

Jake shook his head. 'An embolus. I don't know what that is.' Jake realized as he asked them that his questions had no relationship to his feelings, which were panic and fear.

'The main thing is that your father is going to pull through.'

'Will he be paralysed?'

'Yes, he will be. His entire left side is affected. But that may well improve with time. We can't say yet what his permanent condition will be.'

Allen Dulles said then, 'We'll take care of him, Jake. Don't you worry.'

Jake looked at the Director and felt a rush of gratitude that he was there. 'Hi, Mr Dulles.' His tears overflowed again, but he didn't care.

Mr Dulles put his hand on Jake's shoulder.

Jake nodded at him and for a moment was afraid again that he would fall to pieces. But the strength, the simple authority of Mr Dulles's presence shored him up. Dulles could make things all right. Jake said unsteadily, 'You won't make him resign now, will you?'

'I guess that's up to the doctors, Jake.'

When Dulles glanced at him, the doctor said, 'It's likely that his functions will be impaired. He will require nursing care. I'm afraid retirement is a likelihood.'

'I'm not talking about retirement.' Jake stared at Dulles. 'You were going to make him resign.' He felt suddenly an overpowering sense of menace. Whose side was Mr Dulles on? He pulled out from under his arm.

The doctor said, 'It will depend. We know there's been some trauma.'

Jake looked at him. 'You mean in his brain?' *I can't handle this*, he added to himself. *How can I even ask this stuff?* His brain!

'Yes.'

Jake thought he would faint. Brain damage? His father? He couldn't handle this alone. 'Mr Dulles, maybe you don't know everything that happened! They were holding Dad in a house out in Maryland. I think someone did something to him. I saw Mr Yeats stab him with a needle.'

145

'Now, now, Jake, calm down,' Dulles said. 'No one did anything.'

'Embolus!' Jake gunned his question at the doctor. 'What's an embolus?'

The doctor looked quickly at the Director for guidance, but got none. 'An embolus' – a page of a text could be seen to fall open in his mind – 'is a foreign or abnormal particle circulating in the blood, as a bubble of air, a blood clot, and so on.'

'A bubble of air!' It was all the explanation Jake required. He turned to Dulles. 'Where's Mr Yeats?'

This was not the doctor's business. He excused himself.

Allen Dulles said calmly, 'Son, I don't blame you for being upset.'

Jake grabbed Dulles's arm. 'Listen, Mr Dulles, I think somebody *did* it. A bubble of air, he said. You can make that with a hypodermic needle, and they had one. I saw it!'

'Jake.' Dwight Houseman came up behind him and put his arm around Jake's shoulder.

Jake shook him off. 'You did it!' he cried. 'You all did it!'

Allen Dulles said, 'Son, I've been with your father for twenty years. I consider him a dear friend.'

'So did my uncle. My uncle *loved* him.' Jake began to sob. And he did not resist when Dulles took him into his arms.

It couldn't be. The CIA kill his father? Or try to? No! Impossible. But maybe his father wasn't co-operating. Maybe they thought he was a traitor too. Maybe they wanted him to commit suicide, but he wouldn't. Maybe they couldn't trust him anymore.

I don't trust any of you, Jake thought, even while Dulles held him. I'm in over my head and no one can help but my old man, and you've done something to him. I *know* you have!

He began, while stifling his sobs, to shut lids on his feelings, a cauterizing of emotion to survive it.

Dulles noticed that he'd gone limp and he held Jake at arm's length. Jake was inert. Dulles said, 'I'm sorry about your father.' Then he turned to Houseman. 'Stay here. Take care of them.'

Dulles let go of Jake and walked away.

Houseman took Jake's arm, but Jake didn't notice. Houseman watched Dulles go and said, 'He has a son of his own, a bright fellow who had a great career at Princeton. But then in Korea he took a Chinese bullet in the head and never recovered. But he didn't die, either. He lives with him in their house in Georgetown. It's his deepest secret, Jake. He knows what you're feeling.'

146

Jake looked at Houseman, having barely heard what he'd said, and without any consciousness that he was about to make a statement himself, 'I'm in over my head, Dwight.' What should I think? What should I do?

But what could Houseman say?

Jake freed himself from his grasp and walked away.

At the end of the corridor was a window, to which Jake walked slowly. Night had already fallen. He was on the fifteenth floor of the hospital that dominated one of the hills north of the city, and from that vantage the distant view of Washington was not unlike the view from his room in Virginia. But from this side the familiar landmarks, the illuminated Capitol dome and the Monument obelisk, were reversed, as if they'd do-si-doed, and the towers of Georgetown were blocked by the near hills. For the life of him he couldn't remember what the college looked like or who his friends there were or what courses he'd chosen or why he'd cared one way or the other what kind of clothes they made freshmen wear.

This was Bethesda Naval Hospital. His mind tossed up, as if it were a coin, a fact he hadn't known he knew. James Forrestal died here. He killed himself. He jumped from a window like this one. Was that what they wanted his father to do? Was that what they wanted *him* to do? And who were they? Who were *they*? There were secrets everywhere in this damn city, secrets behind every façade and every face. He would never believe, simply believe, anyone again.

His uncle might as well have held a rose over the whole city when they'd stood at the top of the Monument together. How theologians define faith. How beautiful are the feet. To the roofs, to the roofs! Comfort ye.

Oh, Giles, I would love you no matter what you did – provided you do not destroy my father and my family. Since you have done that now, I will never forgive you. It was a vow he made solemnly – I will never forgive you – with his eyes, like a hand on the Good Book, resting on the city he had until then worshipped.

What the fingers of his right hand found, since they were in his pocket and not on some Bible, was a piece of paper. He took it out and looked at it. A telephone number.

He looked back towards the room where his parents were, looked back guiltily. He should go to help his mother. No, he should go ask *her* for help. He should *run*. But he didn't.

147

Near the elevators was a phone booth. He closed the door quietly. Perhaps he would believe Magda Dettke. Perhaps he would even love her. Why not? This was like a dream. He was like a sleepwalker.

He dialled the number carefully. This was the beginning of the next part of his life. The phone rang once and to his great relief was answered. It was as if an embolus had passed through the ventricle of his heart successfully.

But the operator said, 'I'm sorry. This number has been disconnected.'

And he wondered, Had he made her up? Was he crazy now?

LONDON/BERLIN

1945

CHAPTER TWELVE

Group Captain Patterson drove with his left arm stiff, a strut between his shoulder and the wheel, while his right hand rarely left the polished knob of the gearshift. It had been months since he'd got out of the city and, in tracing the serpentine country roads, he was taking full advantage of the bright afternoon. It was the last day of March. Patterson had not noticed the return of colour, a range of greens really, to the tips of the trees, hedges, and to faint patches on the hillsides which promised grass. Spring had come as a complete surprise every year now for six.

An observer might have thought him reckless for throwing his roadster much too quickly into turn after turn, but Patterson knew these roads as well as he knew the lines around his eyes. He had been driving them this way since he was twenty. He was thirty-five now and weary of everything but the thought of Callow's End.

He was not on leave and it was curious that he should be going to the ancient seat of his own family on an official matter, a matter, in point of fact, as the Baker Street argot had it, of urgent priority. How, exactly, had this untidy mingling of his personal life and his military duty developed? And how, for God's sake, had he allowed himself that fatal indiscretion – this was the millionth time he asked the question – for which his sister's husband would simply not forgive him?

The were huddled together in a doorway off Piccadilly into which they had dashed when the thundershower began. It was a year ago. They had both just been promoted and assigned the joint command over Jedburgh, the British-American project of supplying the Maquis. Everyone knew that the Allied invasion of France was only weeks away, and it was going to be up to Jedburgh – the so-called Jed-teams were named after the base in Scotland where they did their training – to see that the French Resistance had what it needed to impede the Nazi counterthrusts from the interior. For Patterson and McKay, group captain and colonel respectively now, the assignment was the culmination not only of the work they'd done together, nurturing resistance movements throughout Europe, since the early days of the war, but also of their friendship. They'd just celebrated with dinner – four courses with a proper wine for each – at Giles's club. Patterson did not hold his liquor as well as McKay did. He could admit that now. That's why he'd made his mistake. Giles laughed bitterly. It had been callow of him.

Callow's End. What great-great-uncle, he loved to ask, had named it that? In fact, as Giles knew full well, the name of the estate predated by centuries the Patterson family's ownership of it, and did not refer to the people at all. Owing to the thin soil in that portion of the county, the land was sparsely forested. The *land* was callow, or underdeveloped. But Giles had applied the notion to himself as a schoolboy and had cultivated behaviour to reflect it. *He* was callow, naïve, unfeathered. Unfortunately, it was a mode those years – and give us music, music, music! – had reinforced. The fact that his father had devoted himself to collecting art instead of to a proper business or public service didn't help. Everyone had assumed Giles's father was pissing away the family fortune instead, as it turned out, of protecting it with his shrewd acquisitions against the Depression. Consequently there was very little pressure on Giles to abandon his studied ingenuousness even after university. He was not the only member of his class or generation to be saved from frivolity by the war.

The house at Callow's End dominated a hill and consisted of two portions. The original, dating to the twelfth century, was a crenellated Norman keep about fifty feet square and four storeys high. Giles's great-grandfather, the industrialist who'd made the fortune and acquired the estate, had renovated the keep, but it had not been maintained and was now in disuse. The main part of the house was a Georgian masterpiece built of old brick and local stone around a great hall whose oversized leaded windows faced on both sides broad terraces which swept down east and west away from the house towards the most beautiful scenery in Worcestershire. Until the war the grounds had been perfectly cared for, but now, even though a dozen more people were in residence – his mother's cousins could not tolerate London; who could blame them? – the gardens were gone to seed and the fields were mowed only in late summer.

It had been so for some years now, but still Giles was shocked at the condition of the lawn as he approached the house. Ripley would immediately offer the obvious excuses: 'No petrol for the tractor, Mr Giles, and the scythe hasn't edge enough to sharpen anymore.' Ripley would not mention that the horses were all gone or dead.

When Patterson used to draw within sight of the house he'd always given Oscar Wilde his head and his cherished horse would gallop furiously the last two hundred yards, so he did that now in his automobile, gunning around the curved gravel driveway and utterly destroying the tranquillity of the scene. Another time it would have bothered him that the decline of Callow's End had yet to be stemmed even now that his practical and efficient sister was there. Did Ripley make his excuses to her? The decline was inexorable. Another time he'd have wondered, as he often did about England herself, was it the war doing this to us, or had we simply turned, like meat past its time? But on this day he roared towards the house without such thoughts, as if he were on horseback, as if his father, who was always pleased by Giles's rambunctiousness, were waiting with his counterfeit rebuke for kicking up the gravel, as if nothing since those golden days had changed, or, if it had, as if only for the better and he was the one – hence this haste – to bring the news. How beautiful the feet of him . . .

The roadster fishtailed with a flourish when he hit the brakes. He killed the engine and hopped out without even removing his gloves. He was home.

'Hello, Mr Giles,' the Irish servant said at the door. 'A pleasant journey up, then?'

Patterson was stunned. He recognized her as Mary O'Connor, his beloved nanny, but hadn't she died three years before? 'You're . . . ?' He stared at her. She was wearing the familiar white dress like Mary's, starched like a nun's. Giles could smell that dress, that starch.

'Mary O'Connor's Kate.'

'Kate?' She and Giles had been infants at her mother's breasts together. They'd played in the mud along the river together.

Kate nodded. 'I came back for the funeral and then, well . . .' She shrugged. 'I stayed.'

'So you did, Kate.' Giles put his hand out and they shook. 'No one tells me anything.'

Kate curtsied.

And Giles nodded as she left. She looked old to him and ill-used. If there'd been a mirror on the wall just there he'd have looked at himself, at the lines around his eyes. Was it the war? Or would this be happening anyway?

'Kate,' he called, just as she disappeared through the door that led to the kitchen wing.

Her head reappeared. 'Sir?'

'Am I correct in thinking Colonel McKay is here?'

'Indeed he is, sir.'

'The child is well recovered, I trust?'

'It'll break your heart, sir, that thing he's wearing. No child should have to suffer so. It's a sure sign of sin in the world.'

'No doubt you're right, Kate.' Giles had seen his nephew only once since the incident and that through a window in the hospital shortly before Eleanor took him out of London. At that point the doctors had still expected to amputate. He did not therefore expect to be heartbroken at the sight of the baby in a plaster cast, but Kate's remark reminded him that this was the day not of his own homecoming, but of his nephew's. It was only to bring his son home from the Worcester hospital that John McKay had come up from London. The child had been in one hospital or another since his leg was crushed in June, almost a year ago.

That the V-2 bomb had hit his sister's house in Knightsbridge, demolishing it, nearly killing the boy, had been a shock to Giles for all the obvious reasons. But the shock doubled when his sister's husband had become so uneasy when Giles offered his consolation that he could not acknowledge it. Giles had never imagined that Mac could be immobilized by his embarrassment.

'Where are they?'

'In the nursery, sir.' Kate lowered her eyes and blushed. 'The same as you used, Mr Giles.'

Giles nodded and she disappeared again.

Before going up the stairs Giles crossed to the large double doors that led to the great hall, the two-storey-high room around which the rest of the house was arranged. Although far from his favourite room – the hall was anything but cosy – it had left the sharpest impression on him.

At Christmas, his father in white tie and tails, stepping on to the platform, glass in hand, jazz band including Negroes poised behind him, to say in his strong round voice, 'Let the festivities begin!' And then the dancers, penguins leading flappers through the latest American steps, Giles watching from the balcony. By the time he knew how to dance like that there were breadlines in Worcester and his father said the festivities would not be seemly.

Giles opened the huge oaken doors. Perfectly balanced, they still swung on their hinges easily. The hall was decked out, but not for a ball. Wooden folding chairs were arranged neatly on either side of a centre aisle at the head of which stood a table and a lectern. The table was dressed with linen candles and a small crucifix, obviously for services.

His father's paintings were all removed. Giles had seen to that early in the war, but it still surprised him. The hall seemed naked without its Picassos and Braques and Mirós. The family crest above the huge fireplace and the boar's head and the antlers mounted along the balcony seemed altogether pagan suddenly. The small cross on the makeshift altar rebuked the room. Beware religion, Giles thought. He hoped his mother hadn't taken to it. Or Eleanor.

Giles remembered then that Eleanor had written him about it. The Catholics in the village hadn't a place to worship since their church burned, an accidental fire, curiously enough, having nothing to do with the war. So now they had the hall. The war makes us generous, he thought, and them receptive.

'Not Chartres exactly, eh?'

Giles turned slowly. 'Hello, Mac.'

McKay was standing on the step just inside the doors. Like Patterson he was in uniform. Why were the Cousins able to look handsome and resolute at the same time? That was one of the great questions to emerge from the war in England. British officers whose resolution was past proving by now still invariably looked foppish. Giles's own moustache, standard issue, just like Monty's, case in point. McKay was clean-shaven and tan, though God knew how. He'd been at Baker Street all winter too. Giles's elegant slim physique, the *beau idéal*, paled beside McKay's solid build. The American was a full six inches taller. His thatch of black hair parted just off the centre of his head was like him; it barely seemed to have been combed, much less fussed over, but not a strand seemed out of place. On McKay's shoulders those flashing silver eagles perched nonchalantly. Royal Air Force insignia of equivalent rank managed somehow to seem apologetic by comparison. Had Patterson always been tempted in this way to feel inferior to John McKay?

That night at Giles's club it had been Mac who confessed to feeling outclassed. The club reminded him, with its cracked

155

leather wing chairs and its permanent cauldron of steaming punch by the fireplace and its newspapers on rods and its Beardsley-like caricatures of old members on the walls and its French drawings in the loo, of the club in Newport, Rhode Island, where he had worked in the kitchen as a boy.

It had been like an admission when McKay, looking around Giles's club, said, 'My father never set foot in such a place. He was a teller in a local bank.'

'He must be proud of you, Mac,' Giles said.

McKay laughed briefly, but a small sadness was what communicated. 'It confused him when I won scholarships, first to a college in Providence, then to law school at Columbia. My father had accepted his place as a change-maker for the rich. He thought I should be what he was. A servant of some kind.' McKay fell silent, watching the other men in the dining-room.

Giles realized he would never have befriended a bank teller's son if he were English.

McKay smiled and said, 'He was suspicious of all my achievements until, when I was admitted to the bar in '38, I got an appointment as law clerk to Bill Donovan. Clerk! He liked that, a fitting title for a teller's son. And he admired Donovan, of course.' McKay laughed warmly now. 'Not because he was a hero of the Great War or because he was the bull of Wall Street, but because he was Irish!'

Giles had long understood that Irishmen, even assimilated ones, were never more than an inch away from their feelings of inferiority. He'd learned that night at the club and after it that they are within an inch also of their resentment.

Looking at Mac now, on that step above him, a towering man, his black Irish features, his dark Gaelic eyes, Giles thought, No wonder Eleanor loves him.

'How's the tyke?' Patterson asked.

'Forgive me, Giles,' McKay said. He seemed weary and unhappy. 'But is that why you came out here?'

Giles sensed that if he answered yes to that question Mac would forgive him everything. 'No,' he said. 'It isn't. But I'm concerned nevertheless.'

'He's asleep finally. He fought us tooth and nail. He didn't want to come home.'

'Eleanor wrote that the doctors were pleased.'

'They're hopeful. He'll never walk. The knee joint's ruined. But he'll keep the leg.'

Giles wanted to ask, Why can't we ever talk about this at Baker Street? Their offices were within two floors of each other. They met at staff briefing three times a week.

'And Eleanor? How's Eleanor?'

'Strong.' McKay let his admiration for her show. 'Very strong. She's with Jake constantly. When he sleeps, she studies. By the time the cast comes off she'll have her certificate as a nurse.'

'That's Eleanor.'

'What does bring you?'

'Home?' Giles cocked his brow. Both men were aware of the irony. Who was John McKay to ask Giles Patterson to justify his coming to Callow's End? Yet both men accepted his right to do so.

'I had to talk to you, old boy.'

'I'm returning to London Monday. You know that or could have learned it.'

'It couldn't wait.'

'Giles, really.' McKay shook his head.

Once when they were hiding from the Gestapo in a shuttered bistro in Biarritz waiting for the Basque mountaineer who would lead them through the Pyrenees to Spain, they drank wine until they were blotto. Patterson went down to the cellar to piss, but came up flourishing two magnums of champagne and McKay, in a fit of sobriety, shook his head in exactly that way and said, 'Giles, really.'

But that night during the thunderstorm in the doorway off Piccadilly he had not done that. He had simply bolted.

Giles could still remember each instant, each word of their fatal encounter.

They'd been on their way home from Giles's club when the downpour started and they were waiting in the doorway for it to ease off.

'That was a hell of a dinner, Giles. Thanks.'

Giles bowed with mock solemnity, but he was the one to feel grateful. McKay had gone on from talking about his father to reveal more of himself than he ever had before, and Giles had never felt so close to him.

They each leaned against a wall of the alcove. McKay watched the rain. Giles watched him. He realized how drunk he was when his impulse to express himself began to grow. He resisted it at first. Mac was his sister's husband, after all. But the damn rain didn't let up. They were too close to each other for too long. Giles couldn't help himself.

'Mac . . .' he began tentatively.

McKay continued to stare out at the rain.

'. . . don't you think when two men have survived what we have, it is banal in the extreme to apply to them ordinary standards of expression? What a bond there is between us now!'

McKay had faced Patterson at that point. His expression was still benignly drunken. He was trying to understand what his best friend was saying. He put his hand on Patterson's shoulder, partly to steady himself, but partly too to express his feeling.

'What a love,' Patterson said nervously. 'Don't you agree?'

Mac's eyes snapped. Love? Had he said love? Mac stiffened. During the war men seemed to develop a knack for bringing themselves back from the edge of stupor to alertness.

'The valorous love of men for men,' Giles said.

And McKay pulled back, actually pressed himself against the wall of the alcove.

'At least let me declare myself, old boy.'

Patterson would have happily heard McKay say, 'Giles, really.' If McKay had only known how to brush him aside, how to put him off lightly, then Patterson would have stopped right here, having found the limit of their friendship without having fouled it. But Mac only stared at him, with shock, yes, but with an acute anticipation too, which, unfortunately, misled.

'I love you, Mac.'

Now in the great hall of his father's house – a house like that never belonged to the master of it until he was dead – Patterson had to resist the urge to ask McKay what the bloody hell he thought he was going to do to him in a doorway off Piccadilly? Why not think of it as an undergraduate faux pas? A mere lapse? Do you always run from poofs? Are you afraid you'll want to thrash them? Or kiss them? Patterson ran his finger along the ridge of one of the wooden chairs. It was dusty. Whom should he resent? Mary? Kate? The parish priest? He knew McKay was staring at him. He raised his eyes. 'Yes, Mac, *really*,' he said. 'It wouldn't wait.'

'What wouldn't?' Mac hadn't moved, and suddenly his looming, curveless, stolid American *staying* infuriated Giles.

'Your orders wouldn't, colonel,' he said sharply. 'You're coming back with me to London, and now.'

'Like hell. You go back and tell Baker Street to frig itself.'

158

Giles laughed at McKay's Puritanism. 'Frig' was the sort of thing a man said around his family. If McKay felt free to put Eleanor and the boy first now, it was only because Jedburgh had just been rendered obsolete by its success. Eisenhower had crossed the Rhine and the Maquis, no longer an underground army for the Americans and British to control, was now de Gaulle's.

'Not Baker Street, colonel.' Giles enjoyed himself when he said this, as he'd imagined he would. 'Downing Street.'

They went to the nursery hoping to find Eleanor, but when they opened the door quietly she was gone. The shutters were drawn against the afternoon and the room was dark but for a few bars of light where slats were missing. McKay stepped aside as Patterson approached the crib, his own crib. The room itself held no special meaning for Patterson. His memories of it had more to do with Eleanor's infancy than his own. But the crib. As he rested his hand on the railing he felt the rough gashes in the wood, his gashes. He had gnawed the railing endlessly with his new teeth – had he hoped to eat his way out? – and now for an instant he could taste the varnish and the wood.

'Oh, Christ, Mac,' he whispered. The child seemed to be sleeping with a large white log, the cast that entubed his left leg from hip to toe. He was wearing a faded blue flannel gown, but it was bunched at his waist where both his hands clutched it.

McKay reached down and freed the gown from the child's grasp and drew it down to his feet, then whispered, 'He's forever uncovering himself. He won't tolerate blankets either.'

Gnaw the thing, Giles thought. He said quietly, 'He's of an age, I suppose, when he knows something's wrong.'

McKay shrugged. 'Twenty-six months. My hunch is he thinks everybody wears one starting out.'

The two men stared at the boy in silence. How had this happened? Not all the buildings they had seen blown, nor all the nights in shelters, nor the familiar high-pitched squeal of incomers would answer them. They had been given their joint command in March. They had stopped being friends in April. In June the Allied invasion of France was launched and they began working around the clock. They had hardly noticed that the Germans, as if in retribution, had launched that same week the V-2 campaign, rockets aimed to fall at random over London, hitting with any luck the houses in which the wives and sisters of the invaders huddled over babies. True, the Nazis hadn't set out to maim this particular child, but given his Yank-Brit blood, they'd have rejoiced if they knew they'd done so. And better to maim a child than kill it. How else, since the war was clearly lost, have your vengeance on the future?

'Bastards!' Giles whispered. 'Bloody fucking bastards!'

'Them?' McKay asked. 'Or us?'

Giles looked at him sharply and for the first time saw guilt in his brother-in-law's eyes. At the moment the rocket had hit the house, dislodging the crucial beam, McKay had been in the forward gunner's bubble of an Avro-Lancaster supervising a massive night-drop of arms and supplies near Rouen. Eleanor had not been able to reach him for three days and by then the child's leg was infected. The doctors were about to amputate. McKay had raged against them – civilian incompetents! – and had the boy transferred immediately to an American army hospital. Unfortunately his emotion, the greatest anger of his life, had spilled over on Eleanor, too, which he regretted. He had not seen how she was wounded until too late.

Giles thought that Mac's self-hating question was typical. McKay refused to allow himself to be angry at the enemy until the enemy was defeated. Anger interfered with waging war. Meanwhile, let anger reduce utterly to ruin what waging war was intended to protect. 'Them, Mac. You should be clear on that. They did this. Not you. And certainly not Eleanor.'

'I know that, Giles. I . . .' McKay checked himself, but his pain was evident.

Giles wanted to scream at him, Don't stop, Mac! Talk to me! Talk to me! I know what a flippant, callow thing I did! You must forgive me! Instead he said calmly, 'You've got yourself in the dock over this, and you shouldn't.'

'Have you been talking to Eleanor?'

Giles read the distrust in McKay's question, and responded to it. 'It's you I want to talk to.'

McKay blushed and turned. He looked down at his son. 'I feel as if I . . .' He stopped again. He simply did not know how to speak now.

Giles hoped that he wasn't like this with Eleanor too, but he feared he was. 'Don't go rigid on them, colonel.' It used to be that they'd addressed each other by rank as a sign of affection, but now it implied Patterson's complaint that Mac had gone rigid on him. Giles had made a mistake, but Mac was making it permanent. Giles had sullied their friendship. All right. But Mac was the one who made recovery impossible.

'I don't mean to,' McKay said. He was intent upon the child now. 'I want to do all right by him.'

Giles said, 'You will.' Once he would have touched him too. But now he couldn't.

Giles never remembered vividly enough how beautiful his sister was. When he and McKay found her she had just turned on the wireless in the library and was sitting on the arm of a leather couch, leaning towards the speaker. He saw her in profile. Her dark hair was combed long, against the fashion, and poured over her shoulders like Guinevere's. The radio chimes announced the four o'clock afternoon report. It was impossible for senior officers whose access to the news was unrestricted to appreciate what that broadcast meant to civilians everywhere in the realm, especially now that each day's reprise described the retreat of the Nazis.

'Lady of the Manor,' Giles called, crossing to her quickly.

She stood and faced him. Her composure held for an instant, then exploded. She was wearing a high-necked naval sweater and woollen trousers, and was like a roustabout when she flew at him. 'Giles! Giles!' She fell with her full weight upon his neck and shoulders. The blow he took to his throat rendered him speechless for a moment. Conceivably his emotion could have done that. He never remembered vividly enough how fond he was of her.

Once, after a night of dancing at the Metropole, within a few weeks of his having introduced her to McKay, she asked him when they were alone, 'Are you jealous?'

And he'd frozen. He'd never discussed his homosexuality with Eleanor. He couldn't imagine that she'd approve. He'd had no idea his infatuation with the American was so evident, and it mortified him to have his sister speak of it. Of course he was jealous. McKay was obviously head over heels for her. Patterson regretted ever introducing them.

'Jealous! Don't be ridiculous!'

'But' – and here she'd toyed coyly with her handkerchief – 'he's taking me from you.'

'You!' Giles said despite himself. Jealous over you! And he'd laughed. 'Of course I'm jealous.' He hugged his sister and kissed her cheek. 'I'm sorry I ever introduced you.'

Now, in the library, she brought her head back to look at him. 'Oh, we've missed you! Does Mother know you're here?'

'No, and you mustn't tell her!' Giles had her wrists and was unlocking her grip on his neck. 'I have to go straight off.'

Eleanor's mouth fell. 'You can't. You must see Mother! You must see Jake!'

'Oh, Eleanor,' Giles said breezily, 'not you too. Don't call the helpless creature that awful name.'

'He's not a helpless creature!'

'Of course he's not. I only meant . . .' He looked at McKay. 'You people and your nicknames.'

McKay laughed. 'Who? Us Yanks? Us Micks? Or us Papists?'

'You're not going really!' Eleanor said.

'I'm sorry, love. I must. And so must John. That's why I came.'

Eleanor faced McKay, disbelieving. Behind her the radio announcer was describing the collapse of German defences around Mainz. 'But listen,' she said, indicating the radio, 'we're winning at last. They can do without you for a weekend.' She looked at Giles as if he'd uttered an obscenity. 'Get out of here! You can't have come for him! This is his first time home in months. Our baby is here now. Our baby needs him!' She pushed against Giles's chest. 'I need him!'

McKay took his wife by the shoulders and turned her. 'Darling, darling . . .' He expected her to come into his arms, weeping.

But she jerked away from him. 'Don't "darling" me! For weeks I've counted on you for this. You know how important it is that we do this right for him. I'd never have asked the doctors to release him if I'd known you were leaving.'

'I didn't know! It's as much a surprise to me . . .'

'Then don't go! Don't go, John. Stay till Monday. Stay through the night. I can't face the night listening to him screaming.'

'He won't be screaming, dearest. That was before.' He held her. 'He won't be screaming now.'

Giles watched his sister sob uncontrollably in Mac's arms, and he thought because he loved them both, here was yet another reason to want the war over. But who needed yet another?

CHAPTER THIRTEEN

The room in which Patterson and McKay were asked to wait was in the cellar of 10 Downing Street. Apparently it served during daylight hours as an office for typists. Now, eight o'clock on a Saturday evening, it was empty and ill lit. In the shadows the half-dozen covered typewriters loomed eerily, like unfinished, therefore draped, works of sculpture, or like the shrouded corpses of babies.

McKay had yet to ask Patterson if he knew what the Prime Minister's summons could mean. Patterson marvelled at the man's self-possession, and he admitted at last that he was no match for it. 'What the hell is up, do you think?'

McKay looked up from his clasped hands. 'Having to do with de Gaulle, I'd say. He wants the ciphers.' When Jedburgh had transferred command of the Maquis to the general, they had withheld the communications codes that he'd have needed to control the airlift. He still had to go through Baker Street for supply. It would not do to have a Frenchman giving orders to the RAF or the Air Corps.

Patterson shook his head. 'Not the Prime Minister. Not his sort of flap.'

That was the extent of the speculation they shared. They waited for nearly an hour. The silence between them grew to seem normal.

Finally the door snapped open. A sleek-looking naval officer put his head in. 'Gentlemen?'

They followed him down a narrow corridor, but instead of going upstairs to the book-lined carpeted study they'd both imagined, they descended yet another flight of stairs. They were meeting in raid-secure quarters, though V-2s had stopped falling in London when the mobile launch sites were all overrun in Brittany the previous autumn.

The fact that Churchill'd summoned them to his bomb shelter heightened the tension Patterson felt. He wanted to roll his eyes at McKay, even as they wound through the dank sub-basement corridors.

Finally their escort opened a metal door and deftly stepped aside. McKay had to duck in order to enter. He and Patterson found themselves in a spacious, carpeted, if windowless, room, which reeked of cigar smoke. Two men were rising at their places at a broad trestle table: Churchill and a stout American general whom neither Patterson nor McKay recognized. While saluting sharply, both newcomers took in the details of the room. A map of Europe covered the wall to the left. The facing wall, behind the table, was covered by a large soiled map of France. Fingers had been poking at it for over a year now. Against the other wall were arranged a cipher machine with keyboard and tickertape, a standard console wireless, and a small table, which held an announcer's microphone. Patterson realized – To the roofs, my arse! – that from this womb Churchill had dispatched his fellow Londoners to the tops of their burning houses.

The Prime Minister held his hand out across the table. 'Good to see you, Patterson.'

'Prime Minister,' Giles said, and they shook hands warmly.

'Seen Randy?' Churchill asked, then stabbed his teeth with his cigar.

'No, sir. Not since the bash at Christmas.'

'Ah, you were there, were you? Did we greet each other?'

Patterson laughed. 'Indeed we did, sir.'

Churchill smiled impishly, '*Beaucoup de Noël*.' He squeezed Patterson's hand once more and he said earnestly through his cigar, 'Damn good to see you, Patterson. I wish your father'd lived to see your service.'

'Thank you, sir.'

'And this is McKay.'

'Yes, sir.' Giles stepped aside and swept an arm towards Mac. 'Colonel John McKay.'

Churchill grasped McKay's hand. 'How's your son?'

McKay flinched. It was the last question he expected the Prime Minister to ask. 'Better, sir. Thank you. He's home now.'

'Good.' Churchill took them both in with a glance. 'Your Jedboys have done superbly. That's why you're here.' He nodded towards the general at his side and then sat wearily. 'Know each other? Of course not. This is General Groves. McKay and Patterson, general. Headed up Jedburgh.'

While shaking hands with them General Groves said, 'Can't say I know Jedburgh.' He took his seat and leaned towards Churchill. 'Top secret, eh?' And then he laughed – stupidly, Patterson thought. The man wore the crenellated insignia of the Corps of Engineers on his breast.

'Take your seats, gentlemen,' Churchill said. When they had, he continued, 'Bedell Smith was going to be here, but he's stuck in Mainz. I wanted Strong to come in anyway, but Groves here tells me no one else. Imagine that? Not trusting Strong?'

Groves straightened in his chair. 'It's not a matter of trust, Prime Minister. Not at all.'

Churchill waved at his smoke. 'I know. I know. Irrelevant anyway.' He fixed McKay and Patterson with his famous stare. 'General Groves is here on the authority of the President. Mr Roosevelt and I attach no higher priority to anything than to what we are about to discuss. Is that understood?'

McKay and Patterson both nodded.

'To the point then, to the point. How up to date are you on SHAEF, Patterson?'

'Eisenhower is at Remagen. As of this morning the front extends a dozen miles up and down the Rhine from Cologne. The Ninth and First Armies have crossed the river. Monty's bridgehead at the Ruhr is secure, and Patton is preparing to break out for Kassel. I'd say the Hun has had it, sir.'

'Aye, which is when he's dangerous. Point number one here is that Eisenhower decided two days ago not to take Berlin.'

Neither Patterson nor McKay reacted.

'Not my decision, not Roosevelt's. Eisenhower's. Military decision for military reasons.' He grunted.

Patterson understood that Churchill was anticipating with them the storm this news would cause. The Russians had demanded at Yalta that Germany east of the Elbe be left to them. Churchill had said fiddlesticks. He and every other Englishman wanted the prize. Churchill wanted to go to Berlin himself. But the Americans needed Russian help to finish the war against Japan. The Americans couldn't see the soup for the fog. If Roosevelt had been himself at Yalta he'd have said fiddles too.

'You know about the Redoubt,' Churchill said.

'The National Redoubt, yes, sir,' McKay said promptly, and as if he were a quizzed briefing officer he defined it: 'The Bavarian stronghold to which the Nazi forces will retire for their last stand.'

'Impregnable Alpine fortress, I believe,' Churchill said. He eyed McKay steadily. 'Labyrinthine tunnels, facilities for hundreds of thousands of elite troops, mountain fighters, werewolves, food for a decade, underground factories capable of turning out tanks and Messerschmitts.'

McKay, sensing the curve in Churchill's remarks, backed off. 'I gather the reports have included some exaggeration.'

'You should know, colonel. They emanate, as far as I can ascertain – but who tells me? – from a single source, from your man in Switzerland.'

'Yes, sir,' McKay said, although Allen Dulles was his man only in the sense that they were both OSS. McKay knew that Dulles had for some months been warning of the Redoubt strategy, but

G-2 detected no movement in numbers of German troops towards Bavaria which would have lent it credence. Was Churchill implying now that Eisenhower had decided not to commit his army to the drive for Berlin out of fear that Dulles was right?

'And your man's sources,' Churchill went on. 'Do you know them?'

'Well-placed sources in the German command, I gather, sir.' That was all McKay felt free to say, even to the Prime Minister.

Churchill nodded, but not because McKay's answer had been accurate. Both men knew that Dulles's source in the *Abwehr* had been executed by the Gestapo after the July assassination attempt. He blew a cloud of smoke towards McKay, then waved at it impatiently and sat forward. 'The Red Orchestra, heard of it?'

'Yes, sir,' McKay said.

'The Berlin anti-Nazi underground.' Now Churchill briefed the others, Groves and Patterson. 'They're convinced the Redoubt is real and that Hitler is planning to go there. A mountain lair, a last glorious defiance of the world, worthy of Wagner.'

'The Red "O",' McKay said, pretending to address himself to Groves and using the familiar form of the code name, 'has provided extremely useful intelligence on previous occasions. Among other things they have accurately reported to us throughout the war the comings and goings to and from Berlin of Hitler, Goebbels, Himmler, and the dozen other senior Nazis, despite elaborate ruses to keep their whereabouts secret.'

'So you're inclined to take these so-called Red "O" reports at face value.' Churchill eyed him carefully.

'Yes, sir.' McKay knew that both Dulles and General Donovan did.

'Good,' Churchill said, sitting back as if he'd scored one.

General Groves said, 'If there is a Redoubt, then Ike is right.'

Churchill looked sharply at the engineer. His expression said, This is not the conversation to which you have a contribution to make. When he spoke, however, it was to say, 'If there were a Redoubt then of course Hitler must never be allowed to reach it.' He faced McKay and Patterson. 'These "Orchestra" people claim, I gather, to have uncovered the old boy's planned route out of Berlin, an airplane hidden in the Tiergarten, a stretch of road that crews are constantly repairing to serve as his airstrip, etcetera. If there were a Redoubt it would behoove us, I suppose,

166

to impede somewhat the proper functioning of that aircraft. That's the urgent recommendation of the "Orchestra". Do you agree, gentlemen?'

'Indeed so, sir,' Patterson said promptly.

'What you need, sir,' McKay offered, 'is a small raiding party trained to operate inside the enemy's territory, making its assault at exactly the right moment.'

'By "right moment" you mean . . . ?'

'Soon enough to prevent the Führer's escape, but late enough that he is unable to devise an alternative.'

'You wouldn't have such a small raiding party in mind, colonel, would you?'

'Of course I do, sir. As I presume you do. Jedburgh.'

Churchill said aside to Groves, 'They've dropped a hundred teams into France since D-Day.' To McKay he said, 'We'd need your best.'

'You'd have them,' McKay said. 'I'd go myself.'

'And I, sir,' Patterson said. Then, anticipating Churchill's objection, he added quickly, 'Now that the Maquis is on its own, our command is geared down anyway.' Unable to restrain himself, Patterson poked McKay. 'Christ, Mac, one last lick!'

Churchill stared at the tip of his cigar. At last he nodded solemnly. 'So you regard it as a worthy mission?'

'Yes, sir,' both officers responded. A shot at Hitler himself?

Churchill wagged his head. 'You're bloody fools.' He looked at Groves. 'But that's what we're counting on, isn't it?'

McKay and Patterson exchanged a quick look.

General Groves stood, fussed with his tie, and fingered the table. Ordinarily at his briefings he used a pointer. 'Men, what the Prime Minister has outlined up to now has been what you might call the stated purpose of your mission, your cover story if you will, what you tell your own support people as well as this underground group in Berlin. I gather they are Reds?'

'The only organized resistance that has survived in Germany, general,' McKay said, 'are Marxists. They are as intent upon Hitler's defeat as we are. Even more so.'

Groves looked down at Churchill. 'You didn't explain that to me. Our whole purpose is to keep the Reds out of it.'

'Outline your project, general,' Churchill ordered.

Groves cleared his throat. 'Well, if they're Reds, they wouldn't help you anyway unless you gave them the cover story.'

'Help us in what?' Patterson asked.

Groves looked briefly at Churchill. He didn't like having to explain himself to operations people. 'Your true mission will be to deliver one of my men into the Ministry for Armaments and Munitions. You won't need to know what his purpose is.'

'Of course they will, general,' Churchill barked. 'Elaborate.'

Groves blushed but there was something steady in his eyes. He was a man who knew when to yield and when not to. 'Obviously, we're talking about weapons research. We have reason to believe the Germans have mastered the theoretical problems associated with the production of what you might call for want of a better term a super-weapon. We are not concerned that they have actually built it or that its use threatens us now. But their research could prove invaluable, and not only to us. Our forces have just captured the main, shall I call it, research facility in a remote part of Germany, but records there indicate that all data is collated and analysed in Berlin itself, in the Ministry, where there is also apparently a small laboratory in which auxiliary experiments are carried out. Our need is twofold. First, to establish that the Ministry is indeed the collating centre where the Nazi scientists have stored the data they have accumulated. Second, to prevent that data and whatever primitive construction they might have begun from falling into Russian hands. Point two, naturally, must receive top priority. That's why you can't let your Commie friends know what's up.'

'Forgive me, sir.' Patterson addressed himself to Churchill. 'Then the National Redoubt is not the issue?'

'My dear Patterson, in my humble opinion the National Redoubt is a gothic fantasy, whether German or American one cannot be sure. The fact that this Berlin "Orchestra" – where *do* Secret Service people get these silly code names? – fears such a development is what has come to matter. Undoubtedly General Groves is right. They would not be inclined to help you deprive the Russians of a war prize, potentially, by the way, a war prize of historic proportions. They must at all cost be kept at arm's length from it. They must not even suspect what you are doing.'

'Therefore, as part of the cover, we carry out the sabotage of Hitler's airplane?'

'Blow up the Funkturm if you have to, man, to convince them you're playing their programme. But you also get to the Ministry for Armaments. Discreetly! It would be a catastrophe, a political disaster, even if your mission were otherwise successful, if Dr Stalin learned after the fact what we had done. Far better,

168

I'm afraid, that your collaborators should . . .' Churchill let the thought hang.

But McKay was an officer who wanted to know what was expected of him, and to make it explicit said, '. . . Become casualties.'

Churchill nodded.

McKay looked at Patterson. They regarded these German resisters as the true heroes of the war. Had they just been ordered to kill them?

McKay, addressing Groves now, said, 'Preventing this . . . material . . . from falling into Russian hands implies what, sir?'

'Destroying it. Possibly the air raids will have done that for us, although the work I'm talking about is conducted, according to our information, in bomb-secure quarters below ground level in large rooms that once served as the building's stables. We must in any case have confirmation, and we can't get that from the air. The Nazis may be farther along in this than we think. We must be absolutely certain that the Russians find nothing.'

'Yet another reason,' Churchill mused, 'to let Patton take the damn city. Ah, well, unlike the rest of us, generals are paid to fight one war at a time.' He winked at Patterson. 'Right, Group Captain Patterson?'

Patterson remained discreetly silent, and the cramped stuffy room seemed suddenly inhospitable. Groves seemed inclined to sit, but he sensed an expectation from Churchill and shuffled in place awkwardly. Both Patterson and McKay understood that the briefing was incomplete. They waited.

Finally the Prime Minister said, 'Well, general?'

'Sir?' Groves couldn't have been more ill at ease.

'Oh, really, my man!' Churchill snapped. 'Hadn't you better indicate the risks? That is the custom in the service when you are dealing with volunteers.'

Churchill's rebuke unsettled Groves utterly.

McKay said, implicitly in Groves's defence, 'I believe, sir, the risks are clear enough.'

Groves cleared his throat. 'Radiation. The Prime Minister is referring to radiation.'

Patterson leaned forward. He had assumed the secret weapon had to do with rocketry. The V-2s had already demonstrated the Germans' edge in that. But radiation; the word suggested the mythical death rays about which periodic rumours had spread in London throughout the war. Patterson was no physicist, but he

169

knew that radiation was a danger associated with uranium research.

'Even in primitive stages,' Groves was saying, 'components of this process emit radiant energy which in extreme dosages can be fatal. The risk to you, but more particularly to my man . . .'

'Forgive my interrupting, general,' Churchill said, 'but I take exception to your referring to Professor Neisen as your man. He is an eminent British scientist, the head of the Clarendon Laboratory, a former colleague of Einstein, Nagel, and Otto Hahn, as well as an old personal friend of mine. He happens at the moment to be on loan to your project in New Mexico. He is anything but your man.'

'I beg *your* pardon, sir. It is indiscreet of you to refer by name to his colleagues or to geography in connection with my project, and I object!' Groves's anger fed his authority, and he went on more confidently. 'Dr Neisen is all that you suggest. He is a brilliant scientist. The fact that he studied physics in Berlin qualifies him superbly for this mission. For our purposes, with all due respect, he *is* my man. I was attempting to describe the potential risks to him and to these men.'

'Do proceed.' Churchill looked at his watch.

Patterson was trying to recall what he'd read of Hahn and Nagel. The German physicists had received enormous publicity in 1938 or '39 when they claimed to have split in two the nucleus of the uranium atom. At the time Hitler's propaganda machine had made much of the fact that a pair of Berliners had discovered nuclear fission. Nothing, however, had been made of it since. Indeed, uranium research had been a common topic in popular news about science, but since 1939 no mention had ever been made of it in the press, and now Patterson guessed why.

Groves lectured on. 'The degree of risk to you, and, as I was saying, in particular to him, depends on the level of sophistication of the German research. The hazard of radiation can be minimized through simple procedures, but only if the exact nature of the process is understood. We do not know, frankly, what to expect to find in Berlin. A primitive construction at most, but one which could be very instructive to the Russians and very dangerous to you. Even if the proper safeguards have been established, they may have been upset by air raids or –'

McKay cut in, 'They may be upset by us when we attempt to destroy the thing.'

'Correct, colonel. Dr Neisen, of course, will be in authority at

170

that point. He understands these things better than any of us.'

Patterson said blithely, 'The worst it can do is kill one, I suppose.'

Groves answered, but slowly – why introduce a discussion of sterility or leukaemia? – 'That's true.'

Patterson shrugged, 'Well, then.'

Churchill had to avert his eyes. Young Englishmen had been shrugging like that for too long now.

'What's the timetable?' McKay asked.

'Fluid,' Churchill said. 'There will be a moment, perhaps literally a moment, between the time the Nazis leave the last Berlin ditch in panic and the time the Russian horde sweeps over that ditch after them. That moment of chaos and collapse will be the only one you have. It could occur in weeks, or perhaps not for months.'

'Neisen can't be spared,' Groves said, 'until just before it happens.'

'Has the man ever jumped out of an airplane, general?'

'I doubt it, colonel.' Groves laughed. 'He's probably sixty.'

'Then we have to have him immediately,' Patterson said. 'He has to be made fit and he has to be trained. Or did you think we'd send him parcel post?' Patterson looked at Churchill. 'We need him immediately.'

'You have him. Old Eric is "your" man now. Agreed, general?'

Groves's assent, however begrudging, was evident.

'And he's not sixty,' Churchill said, rubbing his cigar out on a tin plate and standing. 'He's sixty-five. But he's as fit as a Bengal Lancer. You'll do damn well to stay up with him.'

Patterson and McKay shook hands with Groves, then followed Churchill to the door. The Prime Minister flicked his head towards Groves and whispered, 'He built the Pentagon. He's spent the war building the Pentagon.' He raised his eyebrows in disbelief.

As Patterson and McKay were about to leave he stopped them. 'Which of you is in command, by the way?'

'Held jointly, sir,' Patterson answered.

'Well, there were reasons for that in Jedburgh, I suppose, but not in this.' Churchill took McKay's arm. 'Any objection to serving under the Crown, colonel?'

McKay looked at Patterson, who felt his first fear of the evening.

But McKay said, 'Not in this case, sir. None at all.'

171

'Good. Which of you has German?'

'I do, sir,' McKay answered. '*Ein wenig.*'

Churchill squeezed Patterson's arm. 'Then *you'd* better brush up your Russian.'

'Indeed, sir.'

'What will you call it?' Churchill asked boyishly. 'The operation?'

'You have a suggestion, sir?' Patterson asked.

Churchill smiled. 'Your code names are so dreadful. "Tiger" this, "Barracuda" that. I have given it a moment's thought, in point of fact. These Red "O" people have a symbol, I understand.'

'The rose.'

Churchill gestured with a new cigar. 'So call yourselves "Sub Rosa".' The Prime Minister looked back at Groves. 'That should please the general, if he knows the expression.'

'Sub Rosa it is, sir.'

Churchill beamed. 'When you have the plan, get back to me. I want to bless it.' He tousled Patterson's hair as if he were Patterson's uncle. 'And you, your Lordship, and you.'

'I knew Neisen at Cambridge. Well, I didn't know him precisely. Now and again I saw him. His study was across a courtyard from my tutor's, and I often watched him reading. He read with his nose to the paper as if he were smelling the words.'

'I'd have thought physics required sharp eyes.'

Patterson laughed. 'You're thinking of fly-tying. Physics is an act of abstraction nowadays. Or atomic physics is, at any rate.' Patterson let the clutch out and the roadster shot forward, nearly hitting the taxi in front of them. The same taxi had been impeding their progress since Charing Cross. The great advantage to the air raids had been that they eliminated London's traffic jams at night.

As they inched across the city, each man was influenced subliminally by the constant shifting from first to second, rarely to third, then down again: stopping, starting, a series of jolts. Neither man had yet taken in fully what this new mission would entail, but certainly it would require shifting, a series of jolts. They had been desk-bound for nearly two years, administering the largest commando project of the war in Europe. For three years prior to Jedburgh, however, each had made numerous jumps into enemy-held territory. France mainly, but also Yugoslavia and, in Patterson's case once, Greece. It had never occurred to either that they would drop into Germany, much less Berlin, and the prospect, coming from nowhere just as the end had seemed at hand, required a return to a discipline of mind and will that had, as victory approached, lapsed utterly.

But that night both were aware that the most profound shift required by this last mission would be a personal one. That awareness was what kept them silent during the drive back to the small hotel near Baker Street where McKay had quarters.

Patterson was afraid it was up to him to acknowledge the freeze in their relationship, since he had caused it. But what if McKay took his remarks as yet another overture? At an intersection, waiting for traffic to move again, he said, 'Mac, I appreciate the vote of confidence back there. Just because Winnie needs a C-in-C doesn't mean we do.'

'I meant what I said, Patterson. I don't object to your authority.'

'We've operated well enough, you and I, without . . .'

'You know as well as I do, it's different in the field. In Jed all we've done is draw up charts and fill in the blanks and write the widows. Baker Street is one thing. Berlin's another. The Prime Minister is right. You needn't worry about me.'

'If I gave you an order you disagreed with, you'd still follow it?'

'Certainly.'

'I can't imagine giving such an order, of course.'

Traffic picked up again and they fell silent, but Patterson was determined to break through McKay's reserve. He found it easier to speak while staring through the windscreen or at the rear-view mirror. 'Why am I the one whose soft middle is always on display?'

'Soft middle? Christ, what are you talking about?'

'Goddamnit, McKay, you know what I'm talking about. You're the only person to whom I've ever exposed myself in this way. What an imbecile I am! Exposing myself to you, the only person in the world who has never lost control. Do you know what I hate? The goddamn part in the middle of your hair. Even your fucking hair is perfect! I want to reach across and mess it! Do you hear? Mess it!'

McKay's face was turned away, but he said softly, 'You misunderstand me, Giles. I don't judge you. I don't think ill of you. But my hair, since you choose it as your metaphor, is *my* hair.' He faced him. 'And you don't touch it. As long as that is clear, we have no problems. None in Berlin, none in Callow's End.'

173

Giles forced himself to focus on his driving, but he could hardly breathe. Metaphor? What metaphor? He'd been talking about the bastard's hair! McKay *had* misunderstood him. Or had he? Even Giles was unsure now what the intensity of his permanent emotion revealed, where it came from, what purpose it served, what exactly it proposed. It did not matter that McKay was causing anger in him now, not fondness. All of his responses to the man were extreme. He said carefully, 'Look, Mac, we have to pull this one off together. In this instance, you don't stay in your office and I in mine. We don't co-ordinate this time through our execs or through memos or weekly worksheets. You remember how it is . . .'

Giles looked over at him quickly. Once they had lain together under a tarp in the back of a truck all the way across the Alps. They'd hugged each other for warmth.

'. . . We have to trust each other absolutely.'

McKay shook his head, somewhat impatiently. 'We have to conduct ourselves like military men, that's all.'

'Of course. That's all I meant.' Suddenly Giles remembered how Mac had held Eleanor that afternoon, patting her back, promising her that their child would not be screaming. How the hell did he know the child wouldn't scream? No son of a McKay would scream, that was how! But that child was a Patterson too. Who had a right to scream – scream at God – if that baby didn't?

Giles stopped the car in front of McKay's hotel, shut the engine off, and turned in his seat. The forlorn look on McKay's face surprised him. Were his feelings about the bastard overly harsh? Ordinarily Patterson could admit that once he was angry or hurt he exaggerated. Maybe McKay had not turned to stone. But the son of a bitch said nothing to make things better. He just sat there. All right, Giles thought, we'll do this your way. I will not let you see how you frighten me. 'All out, old boy. First stop, but not the last.'

'Where are you going? We should be at Baker Street. We have work to do.'

'Not tonight, my friend. Peace has come to London with the spring and one must celebrate. *A demain!*'

McKay stared at Patterson. 'Giles, you're not serious.'

'Not only serious, colonel, but, as of now, in charge. I just gave myself the night off.' Patterson smirked inwardly. I do not judge you, McKay had said. I do not think ill of you. But now if he deigned to speak it would certainly have been to say, 'You choose a strange time to indulge yourself, group captain. I, for example, have a crippled son, to whom, for reasons of what war remains, I do not go.'

Patterson was determined not to be stared down. Let him wonder when I get laid and drunk, which it is I do first. Let him wonder, if he cares, with whom.

CHAPTER FOURTEEN

April, 1945, would have been memorable if only for the magnificent spring weather that brought the most brilliant greens in years to the fields and hedgerows, and the sharpest reds and yellows to the flowering shrubs and perennial beds, and the calmest, most soothing blues to skies all over Europe. But nature deceived. Events were anything but tranquil.

In the second week of April Franklin Roosevelt died. In that week the Russians took up positions close enough to Berlin to launch a massive artillery barrage, the noise of which, when joined to that of non-stop British and American air raids, deafened some children for life. In that week the Minister of Propaganda, Herr Doktor Joseph Goebbels, announced that the Führer would remain in Berlin to direct her defence and share the fate of her citizens whom he loved. Those few Berliners who believed the announcement were enraged at Hitler for conducting his senseless last stand in their midst. Officers, including generals, and common soldiers alike stripped off their uniforms and hid in the cellars of their houses with their terrified families if they lived in Berlin, or took to the roads leading out of the city to the west if they did not. A Berliner's fondest dream at that moment was to be captured by the Americans, who, it was hoped by many, would at the last moment join forces with the remnant *Wehrmacht* against the Mongol horde from Russia.

April 20 was Adolf Hitler's fifty-sixth birthday. He celebrated with a party in his bunker headquarters beneath the *Reichskanzlei* just off the Tiergarten. While the Nazi high command savoured Russian caviar and French champagne in those dank, dispirited quarters, Marshal Zhukov's tank corps achieved its great break-through, leading the advance from Lausitz to the Berlin suburbs of Spreewald and Oranienburg. No sooner had Hitler's birthday festivities ended than his senior generals, Himmler, Göring, and most of what remained of the Reich's administration joined the populace in flight. For the next days the roads west of Berlin were clogged with a desperate throng of people walking alongside or pushing or pulling or riding in every imaginable conveyance. Roads to the east, on the other hand, were utterly deserted except for the sites here and there of hastily constructed tank barriers manned by poorly armed units of the Hitler Youth, or the aged soldiers of the *Volkssturm*. The Reich had turned in its last hour to the very old and the very young, not because they alone now believed, although they did, but because they alone did not understand what was coming.

And all the while the sun shone benignly.

But in the centre of Berlin one might not have seen the sun at all as the end of April approached because so many fires poured smoke into the sky. Even if there had been men organized to fight them, there was no water. The systems of the city were completely broken down, including the massive subway, which was just as well, perhaps, because its tunnels and stations were jammed with the wounded and the old, with pregnant women and invalids who, unable to flee, had crammed into those concrete tubes to escape the ever-worsening fires and explosions and collapses caused by the relentless bombardment. Hell was, for once, above.

On April 26 Hitler, fearing that these tunnels would offer the advancing Russians direct and easy access to the area of the *Reichskanzlei*, ordered them flooded. It was one of his last orders and certainly one of the last to be carried out. When the water, diverted from the nearby Spree River, gushed into the tunnels south of the Alexanderplatz, thousands of the most desperate of his beloved Berliners, whose fate he had remained to share, drowned like rats.

On April 28 the advance guard of Zhukov's army crossed into the city proper, expecting to engage dispirited remnant German troops. But on the Wilhelmstrasse and at the Alexanderplatz near Hitler's headquarters, they were met with surprisingly fierce resistance and were forced to rejoin the main body of the army outside of the city. Elite units of the SS had remained to protect the Führer. They were charged with guarding not only the bunker, but the secret tunnel that led from it to the flak tower near the East-West Axis in the Tiergarten. Several hundred yards of that roadway were being meticulously maintained even while the air raids continued.

176

When the anti-aircraft battery atop a second flak tower on the opposite side of the Tiergarten was abandoned, Jörg Dettke sent a one-word message on the wireless the OSS had supplied him five years before and which he kept hidden in the garret of a convent in Schöneberg. The OSS did not know that the Red Orchestra headquarters was a Catholic convent. If they had they'd have perhaps misunderstood Dettke's word – *Nun!* – as some kind of code. As it was they read it correctly, as the German word for 'Now!'

On the night of April 28 an extra B-24 Liberator joined the Mars Squadron when it took off from Tempsford Airfield. It seemed to be one more RAF heavy bomber like the others, but it carried in addition to its crew of six a contingent of five parachutists. They were Patterson and McKay; a Sergeant-Major Cooper, an ordnance expert who, though he had never jumped, had headed up a detonation team in London for three years – the only NCO to do so – and had then supervised all Jedburgh training in explosives; an American warrant officer, Billy Nichols, who though only twenty-two years old had already gone into the hole, as Jed-boys called their missions, more than thirty times. Nichols was regarded by McKay and Patterson alike as the best Jed member to have survived the campaign in France. These four sat on their packs – the parachutes curved under them like chaises longues – in the cramped steel chamber above the main bomb bay. The fifth man was apart somewhat, hunched over a small bucket, vomiting, while the plane pitched and yawed its way across the North Sea towards Bremerhaven.

Giles Patterson watched Neisen sadly. The image of the professor in his study bent over his reading matter came back to him. The absurd juxtapositions of the war had come to seem commonplace, but this one – the gentlemanly scientist who lived in a pristine world of abstraction, against the pathetic wretch over his slop bucket – was in a way the cruelest. Neisen was a dignified and reserved man, and Patterson had not presumed to tell him they had shared a courtyard at Trinity. He tried to imagine him working on a weapons project directed by the crude-featured Groves, but couldn't. Even at Cambridge Neisen had been regarded as one set apart. Nothing obliterated such distinction, however, like an extreme and public case of nausea.

Patterson exchanged a look with McKay. They were both worried about the scientist. They had seen what North Sea airsickness could do to the stoutest soldier. At best it left him exhausted and dehydrated, physically spent and mentally drained at just the moment when his faculties had to be at peak. Patterson grabbed hold of the girder above his head and hoisted himself. He made his way past Nichols and Cooper, stooped and moving sideways because his parachute bulked behind him. He nearly fell twice as the plane dropped in the fierce winds. It wouldn't do to recall that they were flying in close formation with three hundred other aircraft, all blacked out. It was not unheard of for planes to collide in such conditions.

Patterson crouched by Neisen, braced himself against the scientist's shoulder, and put his mouth to his ear. Ordinarily one did not even attempt conversation in such noise as the unmuffled four engines made. For many men the noise itself was by far the most unsettling aspect of the experience, and compared to it a blind fall even into the flak-ridden sky was a relief. Patterson said at the top of his voice, yet with a convincing nonchalance, 'This is the worst of it, doctor, I promise you.'

Dr Neisen forced a smile, then wiped his mouth with his handkerchief. His spectacles, of which he was carrying two extra pairs, were spattered with droplets of vomit, but he seemed not to notice. His face was more aged looking than it had been up to then. The ordeal was eroding his habitual resolution. During the weeks at the training site on the Jed River, he had put himself through the paces with vigour and good humour. He had successfully completed half a dozen parachute jumps without any sign of a novice's stress. Before the war he'd been a world-class singlehanded sailor, twice the winner of the Ireland-to-Wales, and it was ironic that his stomach should so betray him now. He had always taken for granted the subservience of his body. Being at its mercy unnerved him, and it showed. But when he put his mouth to Patterson's ear, he spoke with his old confidence. I have more to draw on *in extremis*, he seemed to say, than young men like you begin to suspect. 'I was just reviewing in my mind the procedures!'

Patterson nodded vigorously; yes, dwell on something else. 'You go out after the colonel and ahead of me. We'll be your *parens*.'

'As in parenthesis? Or as in Mum and Dad?'

Patterson missed the scientist's try at humour. 'Hand on the bit,' he continued. 'Steady count of three. And pull for all you're worth.'

'Don't I . . .' The rest of Neisen's question was lost in the noise. Patterson put his ear to his mouth. Neisen repeated himself. 'Don't I say, "Geronimo!"?'

Patterson laughed. 'If you like. Count three *or* cry out "Geronimo!" Either way you'll be clear of the plane before your silks open. But don't do both. You'll have a few hundred feet on us if you do, and we like to stay close by as we descend.'

'I make it one hundred and forty-eight feet, to be precise, with all due respect, group captain. We fall, like apples, at thirty-two feet per second per second.'

'I stand corrected.' With a familiarity that would once have seemed inconceivable to both of them, Patterson clutched the older man's neck as if he were a schoolboy and Patterson the coach. 'Or rather, fall.'

Neisen laughed gratefully. The plane lurched and he braced himself. 'I'm all right now, Group Captain Patterson.'

Patterson made his way back to his place next to McKay, nearly falling on him. 'Rough fucking crossing. I may lose it myself.'

'How's he holding up?' McKay asked.

'Valiant old bugger.'

'He can't hit the DZ sick. The Red Orchestra has to think he's been at bat before.'

'They will, don't worry. He knows what he has to do.' Patterson settled back against the curved metal of the fuselage frame. McKay habitually dealt with tension by being rigid, somewhat mean, but Patterson was the master of a counterfeit nonchalance – he leaned back now and closed his eyes as if to catch a little sleep – that had nothing to do with the terror he felt. He had never conquered his fear of the entire process, the night flights, the jumping, the in-close combat. He had learned simply to ignore it and to disguise his reaction to it. He and McKay were the perfect pair to lead such raids because Mac reassured the party by a manner that suggested he could master the most awful turn of events, while Patterson did so by a manner that insisted nothing untoward was going to happen.

Over the Netherlands the air turbulence died and the Liberator began to make its gradual descent. Anti-aircraft batteries weren't encountered until east of the Elbe, but they seemed less threatening – a sequence of distant fooping sounds – than the North Sea winds had. In fact, since their aircraft had dropped well to the rear of the bomber formation for the sake of the parachute drop, the hazard from gunners who had had three hundred previous planes to sight by was intense. The fooping sounds grew less distant, but the airplane never lurched or veered from its course. Sergeant-Major Cooper stared at the ceiling of the fuselage as if he were still in a London bomb shelter, and the explosions were going off above instead of below. Soon the fooping sound was replaced altogether by the constant dull roar, a surf, of the bombs landing. If there'd been windows to look out they could have seen the city ahead, brightly lit.

The pilot's task was to pick out amid all those burning buildings the one large blot in the very centre of Berlin, the 630-acre park, in which no light shone and no fire roared. It was the opposite of normal procedure, when the dropping zone was pinpointed from the ground by set patterns of flashes from Aldis lamps or flashlights or burning haystacks. But in Berlin that night only the absence of fire would indicate. The wave of bombers that were just sweeping away now had all been targeted south of the Tiergarten. Red, green, and white flares had been dropped at ten thousand feet to illuminate the district from Tempelhof Airport to the Teltow Canal. It had worked. The Tiergarten itself loomed up from several thousand feet as a black hole in the middle of the burning city. The pilot descended to a thousand feet while the radio operator began his broadcast on the prearranged frequency. Within moments he had the response he sought and signalled both the pilot and the crew chief. The pilot took the plane down to seven hundred while the crew chief went back to prepare the parachutists.

Now the navigator and pilot *were* looking for lights, the headlights of four automobiles set to flash every five seconds beginning with the radio signal and arranged in a quadrangle on the southwest corner of the Tiergarten, but north of the Zoo and the Zoo flak tower. The plane circled until the flashing lights were seen. The pilot corrected his course to narrow the circle to its smallest possible circumference directly above the signalling autos, and he ordered the bombardier to open the bay.

Cooper leaned over the bomb bay as the doors whirred open, but Nichols grabbed his arm and said, 'Don't look!' The trick was never to look.

Cooper shook Nichols off. He had defused unexploded bombs for three years; he always looked. He expected to see a city aflame below him. He was prepared for a vision of hell. But all he saw was a black hole, because the plane was circling so low over the park that no fires were visible. That black hole roared up at

Cooper like an animal. As a child once he had fallen into a well. The memory, unrecalled in years, nearly paralysed him. He grabbed Nichols's arm back. 'Christ!' he said.

The crew chief, according to procedure, slapped Nichols's shoulder and hollered, 'Joe!' But Nichols, having recognized Cooper's state, pushed him out first. The crew chief hollered 'Joe!' again, and Nichols went, followed by McKay, Neisen, and Patterson. Each one dropped into the pitch void like so much metal.

Nothing reassured Giles Patterson like the violence – whump! – of the jolt his body took when his parachute opened. He quickly took his bearings. Laid out before him was a scene a pale shade of which one could never have imagined. Fires raged in every direction to the very horizon, with the exception of the area directly below him. He strained first to spot the flashing head-lights, saw them, and resolved to recommend his pilot for the DFC. Next he looked for the other chutes, to count them. He was aware that Cooper had panicked at the last moment. He wouldn't have been the first to have failed to have pulled his rip-cord. But there were four chutes staggered below Patterson, billowing in a common wind. The wind would carry them south of the DZ if they didn't ride it by manipulating the lines. The leaders were well on target. Nichols would take care of Cooper. Neisen's silk was the easiest to identify from above because it bore phosphorescent markings exactly so that Patterson could track it. Neisen was drifting fast. The old sailor wasn't reading the breeze tonight. Perhaps his nausea had done him in. McKay was trying to stay with him, but from below it was difficult at best. Patterson eased in his main lines, drew sharply down on two of them, and went after Neisen.

Only the flashes of the artillery pieces and the tracers of the arching shells distracted Patterson. Zhukov's tanks and ordnance, especially the rapid-firing 'Stalin guns', had been booming away for two days now from Oranienburg, where the main body of his army was massing. Patterson was surprised at how close they seemed. Berlin was a city of 350 square miles, one of the largest in the world. On the maps he'd memorized, Oranienburg read as a distant suburb, but from his floating perch it seemed just beyond the district of Pankow. Or else the Russian guns had taken up new positions since G-2's report. The steady barrage seemed aimed at him and close enough to burn his skin with powder.

Neisen was at the wind's mercy. Patterson swivelled to orient himself in relation to the DZ. He could see now that the Tiergarten, like Hyde Park, was not forested, exactly, but had many trees. He'd read that it served as an arboretum and its half-dozen small lakes had been stocked before the war with specimens of every kind of fresh-water fish found in Germany. In the centre of the Tiergarten was the Victory Column, a nineteenth-century tiered monument suitable for a wedding cake, and even through the haze he could see the gaudy *Viktoria* atop it. Her gilded wings reflected the fires of the city. Patterson noted the column because it sat astride the East-West Axis, Hitler's take-off strip. At its far end was the Brandenburg Gate, the silhouette of which stood out against the glowing city. Near the gate, he knew, was the reinforced hangar in which a fuelled Fieseler Storch, a fast, light, fabric-covered reconnaissance plane, was waiting. That plane would take Hitler to the mammoth Rechlin *Luftwaffe* base ninety miles outside Berlin, and from there in a Junker 390, an aircraft which had already proved capable of flying non-stop from Germany to Japan, Hitler could transfer his headquarters to Bavaria. Or he could – and wasn't this more likely? – flee to Spain or Greenland or to any nation in Latin America. And preventing that, Patterson thought suddenly, is one's *cover* mission?

When he looked down again for Neisen he was gone. Patterson was within a few seconds of landing himself. Once he drifted below the level of the trees he was blind. He concentrated on making his body limp, every part of it except his jaw, which he tightly clenched shut. Better to break a leg on impact than to bite one's tongue off.

He hit the ground before he saw it. Instinctively he rolled. He was up, and even while he hauled in his silk he felt the exhilaration that came with having survived the jump. But his mind clamped on to the task at hand. It had been his responsibility to stay with Neisen, and he had lost him. By the time he had his parachute rolled his eyes were adjusted to the dark, but he still couldn't make out where he was. The earth underfoot was bare and hard-packed; he'd expected grass. Perhaps it was a playing field of some kind. Wasn't that a fence about forty yards away? Yes, a white-washed fence all around. He was in the centre of a circular field.

'Don't move, Patterson!' a voice commanded with crisp

authority from out of the darkness. It was Neisen, and Patterson started towards him.

'I say, man, don't move!'

Patterson froze and listened. Only then did he pick up the sound, a low hissing. Was someone signalling? The other chutists were at the DZ hundreds of yards away. 'What is it?' Patterson whispered.

'Cobra,' Neisen replied coolly. 'On me.'

Patterson involuntarily looked at the dirt at his feet. There was nothing on the ground before him, but now he understood. They'd landed inside the Tiergarten Zoo. It wasn't a playing field fence all around; it was a wall. They'd landed – you will not react to this, he commanded himself – inside the snake pit.

He did not move a muscle, but stood where he was, straining to see. After a moment he could make out the rigid silhouette of Neisen stretched on the ground thirty yards away from him. Would the cobra be upright, poised to strike, hood spread? If he assumed a prone position would he be able to see the outline of the snake, a black target against the pale wall? Patterson lowered himself as slowly as he could. Do not think about the other snakes. Do not think about what you might lie on, you might touch.

By the time he was on his knees he had his sidearm drawn. Do not think. See. Aim. Do not think. He was prone now, his face two inches from the dirt. He drew his arms together ahead, supported his gun hand, and took aim. He could see clearly the form of Neisen's body. What else? If the snake was not erect or if it was lost against the background of Neisen's bulk, then he could do nothing. The gunshot, if it missed, was going to cause the cobra to strike.

He saw it. He was sure he saw it. The broadest part of the huge snake was facing him. He closed an eye and aimed.

And something moved against his own leg.

Ignore it!

But the thing went over his leg, on to it, began sliding up it.

Ignore! he ordered, ignore!

But from behind him, from no farther away than his own waist, he heard it begin very softly to hiss.

He could picture it. Hooded. Erect. Tongue whipping towards the nape of his neck.

What was the worst that could happen?

When he fired at Neisen's cobra, his own would strike.

183

Well, then.

Good luck, boys, he thought.

He cocked an eye again. Softly, softly, he began to squeeze the trigger.

But before the trigger engaged, a voice some yards, not many, behind him said slowly and quietly, 'Together now. One. Two . . .'

And their two gunshots sounded like one.

McKay was at Patterson's side, then passing him by in the dash towards Neisen. Patterson, as he got up, couldn't resist looking back at the snake writhing, headless, behind him.

Patterson must have aimed as truly as McKay had because Neisen wasn't dead. He was up, kicking madly and screaming, 'Get them off me! Get them off me!' His previous rigid calm was gone completely, replaced now by panic at this new terror. Something was at his feet. Was he kicking at vipers?

Only McKay's example enabled Patterson to stifle his own panic. 'Alley-oop!' McKay cried. 'Let's go!' And he grabbed the scientist by the shoulders, leaving the legs for Patterson. But Neisen was kicking madly. 'Get them off me! Get them off me!' It was like trying to grab the legs of a Russian dancer. Vipers? Copperheads? Patterson refused to think. He clamped the old man's legs, swept him off the ground, and ran.

Only once they were all over the wall did Patterson realize they had carried out as well what Neisen had kicked at in such terror, not snakes but the tangled shrouds of his parachute. They all realized it and they laughed hysterically. *Willkommen im Dritten Reich!*

As they recovered, Patterson looked at McKay, who, for the first time in a year, did not look away.

'Good work, Giles,' he said.

Though Patterson was feeling that Mac had done it all.

CHAPTER FIFTEEN

The horn of an automobile, at five-second intervals, a steady series of short blasts.

Patterson and McKay approached from opposite sides with their weapons ready. Neisen hung back. In the darkness it was impossible to tell how many men waited in the car.

On signal Patterson jerked the right rear door open while McKay thrust his pistol through the left front window, expecting to jam its muzzle against the driver's cheek. But there was no one there. And no one was in the rear.

Yet the horn of that very automobile sounded again. The other three automobiles that had illuminated the dropping zone were gone.

McKay and Patterson looked at each other across the seat back. Then Patterson saw the glimmer of string running from the chrome ring of the horn to the doorpost.

And McKay felt cold metal press into the flesh below his own jaw-bone, not the blunt muzzle of an automatic, but the finger-thin snout of a Luger.

'Get in, my friends,' the voice said.

They obeyed. The man kept his pistol against McKay's cheek. 'Now call your third member.'

Patterson spoke softly into the dark. 'Brigadier Bard!' Neisen appeared and got into the rear seat beside him.

'I am Jörg Dettke,' the man said. He was a lean blond whose face seemed the face of a friendly boy, but whose eyes lit the shadows with harsh wariness. After a moment in which no one moved, he held the Luger up and said, 'This is not necessary. We are comrades, no?'

'*Gewiss*,' McKay said, rubbing his jowl.

'Speak in English, if you like.' Dettke put the Luger in the pocket of his worn suitcoat. He coiled the string and untied the end of it from the horn ring and put it in another pocket.

McKay said, 'You should be as cautious in all things. It was foolish to bring us down so near the zoo.'

Dettke looked sharply. It had been a while since he'd been

rebuked. 'The animals are all dead. The keepers killed them out of mercy.'

'Not all of them,' Patterson said from the rear. He detested snakes.

Dettke started the car engine. 'If you think a few creatures in a zoo are what threaten here' – he looked at each man in turn, obviously judging them – 'then it was a mistake for you to come.'

McKay offered Dettke his hand. 'I'm Colonel John McKay.' They shook. 'And this is Group Captain Patterson, who is in command.'

Dettke turned to shake hands with Patterson, who said, 'Deferring to you, of course, where appropriate.'

'Of course,' Dettke said, and for the first time smiled. He looked at Neisen. 'And you are Brigadier . . . ?' The question was implicit. Why was the man of senior rank not in command?

'I am Brigadier Peter Bard,' Neisen said easily, as if it were commonplace for an officer of his rank and age to parachute into such a situation. 'My purpose is to represent the Prime Minister at the ceremonies of surrender when they occur.'

'The ceremonies?' Dettke repeated the word dully.

'Indeed so.' Neisen smiled.

Dettke faced forward but he found Neisen's face in the rear-view mirror and stared at him.

Patterson asked, 'Herr Dettke, where are Nichols and Cooper?'

'Waiting for us,' Dettke said. He put the car in gear and without snapping on the headlights drove slowly forward. Obviously he thought the arrival of 'Brigadier Bard' ridiculous, but in Patterson's judgement he'd accepted the explanation. Ceremonies! The absurd British sense of form. Tea in the jungle!

McKay turned in his seat a few centimetres at a time so that finally he was able to cast his eyes quickly back at Patterson. Patterson nodded. They agreed. Dettke would do.

Patterson watched him while he drove. His sharp profile stood out in silhouette against the pitch-black background of the park. His blond hair was cut very short, suggesting the Prussian style, and that perhaps was what gave him his certain boyishness. Under his dark suitcoat he wore a white shirt open at the neck. The collar of the shirt was clean and that seemed remarkable to Patterson. His movements in driving – they were crossing a field – were decisive and exact. In the mirror Patterson saw that he had intelligent eyes, but they were quick, he sensed, to disbelieve. Those qualities – intelligence, disbelief – were no doubt what had saved him. This was not a man whose hatred of Hitler dated to the heartbreaking loss at Ardennes or to the generals' ill-fated plot or even to the routing of Rommel in North Africa; not a man, that is, for whom Hitler's greatest crime was this defeat. Patterson knew that Dettke had been actively opposing the madness from inside it since 1936. He had refused either to rationalize the regime's evil as mere excess or, for the sake of his own safety and his own innocence, to repudiate it grandly by moving to America. If all Germans had done as Dettke, then Hitler would have been a mere embarrassment, a momentary lapse in Germany's movement from empire towards democracy.

Well, towards socialism. Patterson reminded himself that the man was a Communist. But so had Patterson himself been at Cambridge. What was Communism in the young if not the political froth of all that bubbling love of man? It was a rare adult who kept faith with his first ideals even when those who shared them didn't. Patterson realized that if he were a German he'd be a Marxist still. He was disposed, in sum, to admire Dettke. It was difficult to contemplate – though as they drove slowly through the eerie park he did – that he and Mac might have to kill him.

Dettke brought the car to a stop, but he let it idle. 'There,' he said, pointing through the windshield. Patterson, McKay and Neisen strained to see.

A concrete fortress more than ten storeys high and equally broad loomed before them. The outlines of dozens of steel-shuttered portals were just visible. Nothing stirred in the place or near it.

'The Zoo Bunker,' Dettke said. 'On top are the flak towers from which the gun crews fled only two days ago. They had no more shells to fire. When we confirmed that, we knew we could bring you in.'

'So it's deserted?' McKay asked.

'On the contrary, the tower itself is jammed with Berliners, thousands of them, one upon the other, floor upon floor of them. They think that if the steel doors are bolted the fires will not find them. The defeat will not find them.'

'But it's so quiet.'

'Those walls are five feet thick. Inside I suppose it is not quiet. Women and children, many wounded. Imagine.'

They stared at the hulking building in silence.

'The twin of this tower,' Dettke said at last, 'is at the far end of the Tiergarten. But with three differences. It is joined to the Führer-bunker beneath the *Reichskanzlei* by a tunnel nearly a thousand metres long. Instead of a barracks hall on its first level, that one has the hangar in which the airplane is secured behind large steel doors. And that one is still guarded by a force of several hundred members of the *Schutzstaffel*.'

'Is it crammed with civilians like this one?'

Dettke shook his head. 'The uppermost batteries are still manned. And in the floors below is a *Luftwaffe* hospital. As of some weeks ago the doctors were treating the wounded members of important families, but otherwise the patients are soldiers.'

Neisen said without a hint that he knew he was out of turn, 'Do you mean to say the attack on Hitler's airplane implies an attack on a hospital?'

McKay and Patterson exchanged a look. Their first problem with Dettke's report had nothing to do with concern for the wounded. They'd had no idea the airplane would be secured in such a fortress. It was a monster building, worthy of pharaohs. With an SS guard in place at the other bunker, it was impossible to conceive of penetrating it.

No one answered Neisen.

Dettke put the car in reverse and slowly backed away. He swung the car around and drove over the field they'd crossed, but now more swiftly.

They left the darkness and relative tranquillity of the Tiergarten behind for the lit chaos of the freshly bombed city.

Neisen, McKay, and Patterson had all been in London through the Blitz. It was impossible not to recall – though this was never referred to in England anymore – that the Germans had launched their air raids on London in 1940 only after British airplanes bombed Berlin. The *Luftwaffe* had been pounding RAF bases mercilessly and Churchill had ordered Berlin attacked in order to provoke the Germans into attacking London. The strategy had worked – the RAF bases were spared – but London was brutally bombed.

But what the two Englishmen and the Yank were seeing now in Berlin was different from London. On both sides of the deserted streets through which Dettke sped, fires raged out of control and their flames, furious, brilliant, crackling, dwarfed the buildings they devoured. The streets themselves were littered with concrete debris and burning vehicles and whole pieces of furniture, once-prized bureaus, sofas, bedsteads that desperate residents had pushed from their windows in mindless frenzy. Yet Dettke drove those streets skilfully, having let the heavy auto out full, drifting through turns at high speed without ever losing control.

In London, once the *Luftwaffe* had come and gone, the streets came to life with the noises of reaction: all-clear signals, ambulance sirens, water-truck Klaxons. And with citizens oozing up from shelters like bubbles from under the lid of a boiling pot; fire fighters and home-guard members and mounted police and medics and nurses and even children, all pitching in to limit the damage, to douse the flames and clear the rubble from throughways and search for survivors and, later, to pull out the dead. But here no one stirred. Dettke's was the only automobile on the street. No police, no medics, no sirens. The only sounds were the deafening roar of the fires, storeys high, around them, and the more remote but more menacing booming of heavy cannon. The bombers came in waves with breaks of an hour or more between them, but the baleful Russian artillery kept up its barrage unceasingly as if a thunderstorm hovered permanently on the horizon. Now and then the ground trembled even under their speeding auto as a round landed nearby.

Just as Dettke wheeled out of a narrow street into a broad square, the clouds overhead opened to reveal a nearly full moon, which illuminated in a ghostly pale wash an entire section of the city where no fires burned. The buildings had been reduced to ruins, mere rock upon smouldering rock, and were past combustion. Yet the heat was intense as ever. The air seared their mouths and lungs as they breathed, and in their car, frantically, almost aimlessly, racing around corners, the image that occurred to Patterson was that of a kitchen mouse caught suddenly in a heating oven.

All at once Dettke stopped the car and cursed. It took a moment for the others to see what he saw: a unit of marching soldiers. Twenty ranks of five men abreast, their familiar German helmets in silhouette against the glowing sky, clipped at double time out of a side street. They carried their rifles at an angle across their chests, a precise angle, all the same angle, and that alone seemed in the context of Berlin's destruction an achievement in discipline to rank with Caesar's marches. But that soldierly esprit seemed also an instance of pure madness. To whom were these men loyal now? To what? These were the warders of hell. They adhered absolutely to discipline for its own sake. They were loyal now to loyalty and dedicated only to defiance unto death. They crossed in front of Dettke's automobile, ignoring it. But Dettke, Patterson, McKay, and Neisen watched them carefully until they disappeared. This was an enemy, each thought, still worthy of the word. An enemy! Eisenhower had chosen to bypass Berlin in part because in taking the city he expected to lose fifty thousand of his own men's lives. In fact, by the end of the battle underway that night more than twice that many Russians would die. If remnant German soldiers could still carry their weapons at an angle while marching double time, one could see why.

Dettke said, sadly, without rancour, 'The *Schutzstaffel*. If you asked them they would tell you they are the last defence of civilization.'

Patterson from his place in the rear tapped McKay's shoulder. 'I'd rather hoped we'd be dancing with the *Volkssturm*.'

McKay said to Dettke, 'He means we hoped the SS would all be in Bavaria by now.'

Dettke laughed. 'They are. All but the very best.'

An artillery shell landed across the square, a safe distance, but a ball of fire rose from the rubble, then quickly extinguished itself. The ground under the car rose and fell and the four men instinctively covered their eyes. When they looked again the SS unit had scattered.

'How much farther?' McKay asked.

Dettke put the car in gear. 'We would be there now, but tank barriers block the main streets.'

He drove slowly across the square and entered a narrow lane, but half a block down, a building had collapsed across it. He backed into the square again, but now a hatless soldier stepped out from a doorway with his pistol drawn, an officer.

'Herr Oberst!' Dettke called and waved for him to come. Under his breath he said to his passengers, 'He wants the car.' The German approached unsteadily. He was either wounded or drunk.

Patterson tried to make out his rank insignia.

'*Grüss Gott und Heil Hitler!*' Dettke called.

Patterson could see that the man's leathers were highly polished and the high Prussian collar of his tunic was properly closed. But with every step he grimaced and his pale face displayed his knowledge of catastrophe. This one, at least, unlike the zealots who had just passed, knew what was happening in

Berlin. As he approached, Patterson could see the trappings of his grey uniform. At his throat he wore the silver-edged *Ritterkreuz*, on his collar were the bars of the *Luftwaffe*, and on his shoulders the braided insignia of a colonel-general.

He waved his pistol at them with uneven, jerky motions. ''*Raus! 'Raus!*' he said, and then he steadied himself at a distance of only six feet to aim at Dettke.

Patterson shot him from the back seat. Surprise crossed the officer's face as he fell, not the surprise of his being overtaken by death so much as surprise that someone would shoot him through a closed window.

Dettke hopped out of the car and began to strip him of his tunic and the cross at his throat. When he threw them into the car, McKay barked, 'Let's go, Dettke!' But the German ignored him and went back to the corpse to remove his boots.

'Good Lord,' Neisen muttered. Weren't the Nazis the ones who looted the dead? The Nazis would cut off your finger to get your wedding ring.

'Dettke!' Patterson shouted through the shattered rear window.

Dettke had the man's boots off and was unbuckling his trousers.

Patterson got out of the car, his pistol in hand. He looked across the square, expecting the SS unit to be closing on them, but there was no one.

Dettke had the man's trousers off and was bundling them when he looked up at Patterson.

Patterson lowered his gun. The intensity of Dettke's stare surprised him.

Dettke said, 'You should have aimed at his face. We need this uniform.' He stood, threw the boots and trousers into the car, and then climbed in behind the wheel.

Even before Patterson had his own door closed the automobile shot forward, and the lurch threw him back against the seat. He let his head stay where it fell on the thick upholstery. He closed his eyes. The German general was the seventh man Patterson had killed. Two guards at an ammunition dump in Vesoul, both, it turned out, young boys; a garlic-chewing *Abwehr* agent at the railroad station in Toulouse; a motorcyclist who'd surprised them laying mines on a mountain road near Delphi; the Vichy mayor of St-Jean de Luz, who'd reported Martin Géraud to the Gestapo; the Gestapo captain who'd killed Martin. Patterson could picture each one exactly, and if he'd exchanged words with him, could hear his voice. He could think of none, save the Gestapo captain, without feeling a swell of regret. He had concluded when he'd been assigned to Jedburgh the year before that he would never be in the position to kill again, and that had relieved him profoundly. He was neither ignorant of nor indifferent to the effects on, well, the soul of such repeated callous acts. So it came as something of a shock now to find that he had done it again. The familiar afternumbness was settling over him, but he was seeing that frightened general still, and he was thinking, no, it is right that I aimed at his breast. A man is entitled not to be shot in the face.

Dettke found an open street and drove it wildly. They climbed a hill and soon were passing buildings still more or less intact. It was a residential neighbourhood with once-ornate old apartment houses and faded Victorian mansions that had been divided into flats. Finally, at the top of the hill, Dettke pulled the car through an archway in the middle of a large grey building into a courtyard paved with cobblestones. Patterson craned to look up at the building. It was made of granite blocks, was seven storeys high and crowned by a gabled roofline, the eight peaks of which resembled a rough-edged saw. From windows on several floors, thin white curtains billowed eerily in the breeze, giving the place a ghostly aspect. The glass of the windows had been covered with blackout paper. That the windows were open like that in the night was a sure sign the rooms were empty. From behind the auto came the creaking of the courtyard's huge wooden doors being closed against the street. Dettke shut the hot engine off, and the four men sat motionless for a moment. It was as if they had driven through the worst dream of someone else's sleep.

Patterson glimpsed the shadowy forms of the persons who had closed the oaken doors. Were they robed? He turned to examine them, but they disappeared into the building.

Dettke faced his passengers, smiling. 'Do you know why there are these spacious courtyards within all the large buildings of Europe?'

McKay and Neisen stared at him, unimpressed. Patterson let his eyes float around the courtyard. It was tranquil, safe, a sanctuary. 'Why, because,' he said casually, matching Dettke's incongruous nonchalance, 'of the influence of monastic design. Here we have the inner cloister.' Were those robed figures monks?

Dettke shook his head. 'The answer is always practical, my friends, *practical*!' He got out of the car and the others followed him. In the courtyard, an area more than two hundred yards square, were parked several other vehicles, three automobiles, a medium-sized army truck with a canvas-covered bed, and an ambulance with a dramatic black cross on its side. It was to the ambulance that Dettke led them. 'In courtyards the horse and cart could turn around.' Dettke laughed quietly. He saw the humour if no one else did. 'Horses have no reverse gear, so we have courtyards!' He opened the rear door of the ambulance. A pair of stretchers running the length of the interior lay side by side. He moved one on to the other, exposing a bench, and lifted its lid. Then he stepped aside. '*Voilà!*'

McKay and Patterson moved forward. Neatly stacked inside the metal bench were dozens of dynamite sticks.

'How many?' McKay asked.

'Four hundred and seventy.' Dettke indicated that the bench below the other stretcher was loaded with sticks also. 'Where are the percussion caps?'

'It only takes one,' McKay answered. 'Cooper has it. Where is he?'

Dettke closed the bench carefully and replaced the stretcher. He returned to the car to retrieve the general's uniform and then led McKay, Patterson, and Neisen into the cellar of the grey stone building.

Nichols and Cooper were waiting for them in the lit corner of an otherwise dark, cavernous room. They and three others were huddled in the light provided by a pair of oil lamps on a sturdy old table. A tattered sofa, a canvas cot, and several high-backed wooden chairs were the only furniture. The walls of the room were made of the same large rough-hewn blocks of granite, but these were stained with watermarks and gave a dank musty air to the room.

Cooper, ordinarily a taciturn man, gave an animated account of their ride from the dropping zone. He had been at Coventry, had seen the worst of London's raids, had thought himself beyond horror, but the streets of Berlin had unhinged him. He clutched his olive-drab knit hat in both fists and refused to stop talking. Patterson had to rebuke him sharply to swamp his manic agitation.

The three others in that circle of light were an old man, as old as Neisen, whose bald pate glistened with perspiration, but who seemed otherwise calm; a short man whose face was a shade of green, whose eyes were sunken behind wire-rimmed spectacles, whose hands trembled as he smoked nervously, who impressed, in other words, as seriously ill. The third was a young woman, perhaps twenty, whose hair, pulled tightly from her temples, fell away behind in a golden braid, which set off, by contrast, the delicate pink colour of her complexion on her arms, at her throat, and on her cheeks. She seemed to be blushing under the gaze of these strangers.

Dettke made the introductions. They were Professor Isenberg, his daughter, Anna-Lise, and the sick man, Karl Schott. 'Gentlemen,' Dettke said with a sweep of his arm, 'I give you the Red Orchestra.'

John McKay blurted, 'You mean this is all?'

At that moment a single soft knock could be heard coming from a door in the shadows. It creaked open. A figure crossed the cellar soundlessly and entered the circle of light, a large person garbed from the shoulders in flowing white robes, her head covered in a crisply shaped black veil, the train of which flowed behind. A nun.

She was carrying a bundle of linen as if she'd come to freshen beds.

She went to Anna-Lise and handed her the linen, which the girl deftly undraped to expose the head of an infant, whom she kissed and held up to Dettke. He stooped gracefully and kissed the child too.

Anna-Lise opened her shirt, exposing for a moment her breast, which disappeared as the infant took it.

Dettke watched the feeding of his daughter solemnly. He nodded at the nun as she withdrew. Then he faced McKay. 'Yes. This is all. Unless you count the Sisters.'

'Of course you count the Sisters,' Karl Schott said. Despite his appearance his voice was strong, and in that cavern it resonated.

'What is this place?' McKay asked.

'The Dominican Convent of Saint Magdalene,' Dettke answered. 'An orphanage and school.'

'Twenty-two men,' Patterson said. 'Your network is comprised of twenty-two men, skilled and experienced operatives, you reported.'

'I never said "men". My reports were accurate.'

'Nuns?' Patterson was incredulous and angry. 'This girl, a nursing mother? An old man? A man who's obviously sick?'

Karl Schott stood up abruptly. Sick? He approached Patterson, but instead of speaking to him he held out a pack of cigarettes.

Patterson stared at him.

'Nothing wrong with me,' Schott said amiably, 'that the sun and sleep and the end of Hitler won't repair. Is that what you say? Repair?'

'Cure.' Patterson took a cigarette. 'I apologize. One shouldn't go by first impressions. But we did expect more of you.'

McKay said, 'Group captain, don't you think Sergeant-Major Cooper should have a look at the dynamite?'

Cooper stood up and then Nichols did.

Patterson nodded. McKay was right. Hadn't they learned long before not to be surprised at the exaggerated claims resisters always made for themselves? But in five years of regular reports this man had never exaggerated his accomplishments. Large-scale underground activity had naturally been impossible in Berlin. Dettke had been satisfied to forgo sabotage and attempts at mass organizing in favour of modest but efficient espionage.

Karl Schott went out with Cooper and Nichols.

'I should be congratulating you,' Patterson said, 'not upbraiding you. Forgive me. We knew you'd done the impossible, but we didn't think you'd done it so . . . inexpensively.'

'Inexpensively?' Dettke seemed genuinely puzzled. 'There have been more, many more than twenty-two of us. One could not have counted them. They are dead now or in the camps.'

Professor Isenberg gestured angrily. 'Nuns! You say with contempt "nuns". Mere "nuns"! They have sheltered Jews by the score! You know nothing of Berlin! You know nothing of what we . . .' He began to cough and his daughter reached out to him and stroked him.

She looked steadily at Patterson and spoke in a clean, strong voice. 'You take your comforts for granted. We have none. My father has not been out of these cellars in daylight since July. None of the men have.'

Patterson seemed unmoved, but was not. He said, 'In any case, we have a task before us, no?' He looked at his watch. It was after midnight. 'Immediately before us.' He looked at Dettke. 'We defer to you.'

Dettke withdrew a tattered sheet of paper from his coat pocket and unfolded it. 'You saw the flak tower. This is a plan of its twin.'

McKay and Patterson gathered at the table with Dettke and Isenberg while the girl remained on the couch with her baby.

On the sheet of paper were precisely drawn diagrams of the flak tower, a vertical cross-section of it, front and rear views, and the floor plans of the first two storeys. 'Here you see the anti-aircraft battery' – Dettke traced his finger across the drawings – 'the SS barracks, three floors of the *Luftwaffe* hospital, and here the hangar on the first stage. All entrances to the hospital and barracks and for the supply of the guns are on the west side. Only the hangar opens on the east. The doors are of four-inch steel plate, double thickness, and twenty SS guards are on duty behind them. There is no access from within the bunker between the hospital and the hangar. It is impossible to penetrate. One has to be admitted.' He paused when he realized that Anna-Lise had joined them at the table. She stared down at the drawing. The child sucked at her breast still. Anna-Lise looked up to meet Dettke's eyes. She was afraid. Dettke forced himself to focus on the drawing once more. 'So . . . we will enter with our ambulance here. Notice the ramp brings us in on the second level. The ambulance dock is immediately above the Führer's airplane. The plan is simple; when we are at the dock we detonate our explosives. The floor will collapse on the Fieseler Storch. Herr Hitler will learn within moments that his airplane is destroyed and he will kill himself.'

No one spoke.

'Questions?'

Patterson leaned closer. 'They will simply let us drive inside this place?'

'If we are carrying a wounded *Luftwaffe* general, yes. And a major.'

Patterson straightened up. The uniform they'd needed. 'What were you going to use before we happened on that fellow?'

'Two majors. A general, of course, is better. A *Luftwaffe* general, one of their own. We have a radio in the ambulance. They will be waiting to admit us.'

Patterson looked at McKay, but McKay gave no sign of his reaction.

Patterson said, 'So there are two of us posing as wounded officers . . .'

'Yes, Herr Schott and Professor Isenberg.' Dettke put his arm on Isenberg's shoulder. '*Mein General!*' And then to Patterson he said, 'And I am driving. I will be a sergeant. Would you like to see the uniforms?'

'I'm sorry, Herr Dettke, but you've lost me. What's the plan for your escape?'

'Our escape is not possible.'

Anna-Lise drew her breath in so sharply that she made an involuntary sound, like a squeal. She spoke to Dettke in German, and Patterson surmised that she had not been informed of this aspect of the plan.

Dettke didn't reply to her.

Anne-Lise's eyes filled, but she said nothing further.

Cooper returned at that moment, leading Nichols and Schott. 'It's first-class stuff, group captain. First-class. Enough, placed right, to take down the dome of St Paul's Cathedral.' He nodded at Dettke. 'Just the thing, sir. Where'd you get it?'

'The quarries. One of our members was a foreman in the quarries near Potsdam. He came out with a stick in each sleeve and each leg most nights for two years. "Inexpensively", you said. He was caught in December, the week of Christmas. They blew him up with the dynamic they found on him.'

'Did he know what it was for?'

'To strike a blow only. A futile one, we all supposed. We thought until three months ago that Hitler would win. You surprised us.'

McKay looked at Dettke now. 'Why did you call us in on this? The three of you, blowing yourselves up. What do you need us for?'

Dettke stared back at him. 'We don't need you. We need one percussion cap so that we can control the detonation. Our friend was never able to get the percussion caps.'

Professor Isenberg said, 'That's only half the reason, Jörg. Tell him the other half.'

Dettke pointedly refused to speak.

Karl Schott said, 'We need you to report for us that not everyone acquiesced. Thousands of us said no to him. We are what remains. We must enshrine that resistance, the mrmory of it. You must report for us to the world.' Schott spoke with a rhetorical flair.

McKay said, 'You misunderstand, Herr Schott. We are not correspondents, nor are we acolytes.' McKay glanced at Patterson, then walked out of the light through the shadows to the far side of the room. Patterson followed him. Their footfalls clacked on the stone floor. When they stopped walking, silence engulfed the room. When they began to whisper to each other, the whistle of their sibilants carried extraordinarily.

'We simply cannot permit this, Giles . . . Number one, we can't let them blow up a hospital.'

'They're probably right about the plane, though. If you were Hitler, wouldn't you use it?'

'These people aren't like us. They're in love with the idea of suicide. They all think this damn war is an opera. What else do you do in the last act? Hell, that man has a new baby!' McKay stared back at Anna-Lise. McKay had a young child too. Did that account for his uncharacteristic outburst?

'So what are you proposing?'

'That we attack the airplane, not the hospital. We get in and get out.'

'Wonderful. How?'

He stared back at the cluster in the bright corner. After a moment he said, 'Our friend Dettke goes as the general in the car, not the ambulance. *Ich spreche*, so I'm his driver. You're his ADC. Just the three of us. We go boldly up to the thing. Dettke demands to be admitted, says the Führer's right behind . . . I don't know. He plays that his way. He can do it. They admit us. We pull into the hangar. We drop a grenade. One grenade. We get out. You know how it goes.'

'What about the others?'

'Cooper and Nichols stay here with Neisen. If we don't make it they can still get to the ministry. I'd like to save that ambulance-bomb for the Research Centre anyway.'

'I meant what about the professor and the other one? They're counting on this, Mac. What do we do, say forget it? They want their shot on goal.'

'You're the C-in-C, group captain. You tell them you understand how they feel, but you simply can't permit it. The objective is to destroy an airplane, not to have a catharsis.'

Patterson grunted. 'I'm the C-in-C. That's right. I forgot.'

'So do it.' McKay squeezed Patterson's arm, conveying the rush of his excitement. Patterson felt it too. They grinned at each other. Their old camaraderie!

'Yes, sir,' Patterson said facetiously and led the way back to the illuminated corner.

Patterson outlined McKay's plan, then waited for the Germans to object. When they remained silent, he asked Dettke, 'You can do that? Convince the guards you are this general?'

'Of course I can. I need only speak to them with contempt. I will claim to be General Kreuzer.'

'Then you agree?'

Dettke faced Isenberg and spoke to him in German. Isenberg reacted angrily. He said to Patterson, 'Hans Hoffman was executed for that dynamite. And not only him, but his wife and children.'

'I appreciate that, professor.' Patterson spoke quietly. 'His sacrifice is what honours him. Not whether we use those sticks or not.'

Anna-Lise crossed to her father and, with her child nestled in one arm, embraced him. He slumped with disappointment. She found Patterson's eyes and mouthed the words '*Danke schön.*'

Dettke said, 'Karl Schott will come with us. I insist on it. We have the uniform.'

Schott sat passively in a straight-backed chair staring at his hands. His hands trembled.

Patterson said, 'I'm glad you insist on it, Herr Dettke, because the sooner we establish the line of authority the better. If anyone else were to accompany us it would be one of my men. This is no reflection on Herr Schott. Our experience suggests that guards are alarmed by full automobiles. It is helpful for our purposes, therefore, if the passenger's seat in the front is empty. I am making my decisions on the basis of military judgement. From this point forward I will offer no further explanations and I will expect you to submit to my authority absolutely. Is that clear?'

'Not to me,' Karl Schott said softly. 'Who are you to come here and change this? We have been waiting ten years.'

'What, for a chance to kill yourselves? You don't have to come with us to do that. Why don't you stay here, Herr Schott, and see to the nuns and children?'

Schott exhaled cigarette smoke, then dropped his cigarette and ground it out. He turned and walked out of the room.

After a moment's silence Dettke said, 'He has always remained behind to see to the nuns and children. This was to be his first mission. He arrived at the decision to accompany us only with difficulty.'

'Why? Is he afraid?'

Before Dettke responded the child began to cry; he crossed to Anna-Lise and took his daughter into his arms and rocked her. He offered her the tip of his little finger and she hungrily sucked it.

McKay seemed transfixed by the sight of Dettke and his child, and Patterson realized for the first time that for John McKay the pain of the past year had much more to do with the plight of his son than with the peculiar abrupt suspension of their friendship. The realization relieved Patterson. Perhaps he was not the source of all tension after all. But it made him feel ashamed too. He had been awfully hard on Mac. And his thoughtless overture in the first place had been incredibly insensitive. Why hadn't he just come out since and said, Forgive me, Mac? But he knew why. If his impulse was at all emotional and involved McKay, Giles didn't trust it.

Dettke said finally, 'It is clear.' He looked at Patterson. 'I accept it.'

Professor Isenberg sat heavily on the sofa next to Neisen. Neisen touched him on the arm, affectionately, as if they were a pair of neglected pensioners on a bench. Isenberg covered Neisen's hand with his own and said, 'That's very kind of you.'

Neisen nodded and said, 'We must hold on.'

'Herr Brigadier.' The professor leaned into Neisen. 'When is Zhukov coming?'

Neisen looked at Patterson. It was the great question. But it was McKay who answered. 'According to our reports, professor, the Russians will be here within twenty-four hours.'

'Thank God!' Isenberg said. He pressed the heels of his hands against his eyes, and he repeated himself. '*Gott sei Dank*.'

CHAPTER SIXTEEN

Berlin was a minor outpost on the northern fringe of the Holy Roman Empire. It prospered only when the Hohenzollerns, Electors of Brandenburg, made it their seat of government in the sixteenth century, and its population grew when Spanish Jews fleeing the Inquisition found refuge there. They, together with French Huguenot refugees and with artists and writers and architects who found patrons in the Hohenzollerns, transformed Berlin into a city of culture and learning. By the early nineteenth century its universities, libraries, scientific institutes, opera houses, its Philharmonic Orchestra, its thriving commerce and industry made it the centre of the fledgeling nation, Germany.

Berlin was Bismarck's capital, and when the twentieth century began it had a population of nearly four million and was one of the most enlightened, progressive, and beautiful cities in the world.

As is well known, that changed. Berlin became the world capital first of imperial adventurism, then of cultural decadence, then of racist militarism, and in each of the phases her citizens readily learned the language of the new age. The largest Nazi rallies were held in her stadia, and in Berlin the symbol of German democracy, the Reichstag, burned. Berlin resounded with the cry 'Sieg Heil!' And Berliners were honoured when the Austrian leader made their city his headquarters. In January of 1943 the Allies began their systematic bombing of Berlin, and Berliners moved their carpets and cupboards into their cellars. By the last week of the war the air raids were coming in regular waves, separated most often by intervals of two hours or less.

But that night the bombing runs scheduled between midnight and dawn were cancelled. Berliners, braced as usual in their cellars against the shock of countless blockbusters and firebombs, would begin to think, because of the relative peace – the distant booming of Russian artillery was nothing compared to a full-scale air raid – that something was wrong. In the silence they would not be able to sleep.

Jörg Dettke drove as far as the Victory Column in the Tiergarten. The broad boulevard that bisected the park was completely deserted. To the west of the monument piles of rubble could be seen in the roadway, but to the east the road was clear and the ornamental bronze lamppost had been removed. This was Hitler's take-off strip.

The night sky was clear now and the moon bathed the area around the column in pale light. The adjacent acres in every direction were pocked with craters and the scarred shafts of trees stabbed at the sky grotesquely.

Dettke and McKay got out of the car to switch places, and Patterson, watching from his seat in the rear, had to remind himself it was no dream. Dettke with his peaked hat and McKay with his dull Nazi helmet made a startling pair in silhouette, and when Patterson looked down at himself, at the grey-green of his own tunic, at the rows of ribbons on his left breast, at the Nazi eagle on his right, the garlanded swastika in its talons, he shuddered.

When Mac had taken his place at the wheel, Patterson cracked, 'Mach' schnell, Korporal!'

'*Jawohl, Herr Oberbannführer!*' McKay replied.

And from then on no one spoke.

Each was aware as they gunned east towards the Brandenburg Gate that this was the boulevard from which Hitler would lift off if they failed. Why not, Patterson thought, just hide in the woods until the airplane motor revs, then drive into its path? Kill the bastard. But the answer was obvious. The Russian bear is at the door. The next war won't wait for us to finish this one.

The Brandenburg Gate loomed over the nightmare landscape eight storeys high on six pairs of battered but intact Doric columns, a defiance, Patterson thought, not only of bombs, but of the century. As the staff car drove towards it the massive stone archway seemed to lean towards them, as if it was falling, but that was an optical effect of the thin cloud of dust and ash that billowed up behind from Unter den Linden and Friedrichstrasse.

At that point where a small road intersected the Axis fifty yards short of the gate McKay slowed for a roadblock. They expected it.

As the car coasted slowly into the cluster of black-uniformed soldiers Dettke rolled his window down and inclined out slightly, holding up his *Personalausweis* and displaying his rank insignia. The SS sergeant squinted at him, then snapped upright and saluted sharply. Dettke addressed him curtly. Why wasn't there a roadblock at the far end of the Axis? How do you expect me to fly the Führer out if the strip is not secure? See to it at once! Tonight is the night! Don't you know you can be shot for dereliction?

The sergeant saluted again and the others remained at attention as McKay drove past them.

Patterson stared at Dettke. He was perfect as a *Luftwaffe* pilot on preflight inspection. It had not occurred to Patterson that he would pose as Hitler's pilot. The man was good.

Dettke said, 'Now he will call the hangar and alert them that I am coming.'

They angled off the boulevard towards the concrete flak tower that sat lumpishly on the edge of the Tiergarten. Beyond it, a mere block away, could be seen the rectangular lines of the government buildings on Wilhelmstrasse, the massive Bauhaus offices of the Propaganda Ministry, the H-shaped monstrosity in which both the Gestapo and the SS had their headquarters, the Air Ministry and the graceful former palace of the last Hohenzollern, which served now as the Ministry of Armaments and Munitions. One of the buildings in that cluster, impossible to see from the Tiergarten because it rose to a height of only three storeys, was the L-shaped ochre-coloured *Reichskanzlei*. From its ornate balcony overlooking the Potsdamer Platz, Adolf Hitler had reviewed his troops, received the frenzied homage of the Third Reich, and ranted for a decade now at the world. But it had been some time since he had appeared there. In fact he had not been above ground since April 20, the day he turned fifty-six.

Directly below the *Reichskanzlei* and spreading out from it like the intricate chambers of a tribe of moles was the tunnel complex know as the Führer-bunker. Hitler and his new wife and his most trusted aides and his personal pilot, his doctor, his valet, and his chauffeur, together with a sizeable guard of crack SS, as well as Joseph Goebbels, his wife, and six young children, watched American movies while the city smouldered above them. Hitler's rooms were furnished with fine carpets, oil paintings, and vintage furniture. In total the complex consisted of more than twenty-five rooms, including an infirmary, a wine cellar, a conference room, several apartments, servants' quarters, a communications centre, and a pair of kitchens. Passageways led to the Foreign Office and up to the Chancellery. But its most secret corridor behind a sealed door in Hitler's bedroom shot off like a solitary mutant root towards the north-east for hundreds of metres and ended at the stairway that led to the hangar floor of the massive concrete structure that Dettke, McKay, and Patterson were approaching now.

A pair of Tiger tanks, terrible-looking, but also looking in that setting somewhat domesticated, like stone lions guarding any municipal building, sat on either edge of the paved apron that led to the huge steel doors. Dettke had claimed in his briefing that those tanks would be unmanned. Because of the lack of gasoline most of the tanks in Berlin had been abandoned. Working tanks were on the outskirts, waiting for the Russians. McKay drove between those two as if he did not see them.

Apparently Dettke was right, but Patterson thought he saw a hatch cover lift and quickly drop. They left the tanks behind and he shuddered. He closed his hand around the single grenade he carried. It was the size of a lemon and bulked slightly from the flapped side pocket of his tunic. It was short-fused, set to go within three seconds of the pin's being pulled. The feel of the metal reassured him despite his closely reined anxiety about what was coming. It was bad military practice to go into an operation depending to a substantial degree on good luck. They were depending even more on Jörg Dettke. What really did they know of him? They were depending first on the accuracy of his information. Was there really an airplane behind those doors? And now they were depending on his ability to quickly convince the hair-trigger guards that they owed him immediate and absolute subservience. Even if they accepted his pose, would SS men of whatever rank defer to the *Luftwaffe*?

Patterson had to remind himself that it was in the nature of resistance work to depend completely on such men as Dettke. And Dettke seemed all right.

He was staring straight ahead. The profile he presented in that hat, in that brisk collar, together with the fierce set of his face, would have convinced Patterson, were he a guard. Patterson understood that Dettke was drawing for his impersonation on an inner reservoir of personal authority which, however misapplied here, was by no means counterfeit. Patterson had known men like this before. For a time he'd thought that he was like that himself. When had he discovered his own soft middle? Early in the war? No, in those days of derring-do he'd fooled himself. If one can jump out of an airplane, if one can coolly engage an enemy in combat, if one's comrades look to one for inspiration, can't one dismiss as mere phantom the profoundest image one has of oneself as a man of no true substance?

He was no coward, that was clear. Nor was his attachment to McKay, however unfortunately expressed that time, the issue. Patterson was not worried in some adolescent or, for that matter, in some American way about his masculinity. He was simply conscious of an essential softness he sensed in himself. One of Patterson's strongest memories was of the time, he was perhaps twelve, when he cut open one of his father's golf balls, those resilient little globes, tough as the earth, and discovered it had a liquid centre which oozed away in his hands. At about the same time he had taken to mashing grapes for the pleasure of finding the nut-like little seeds in their centres.

Patterson was certain, in other words, that at some point a pressure would be brought to bear on him, and he would break under it. Or rather, leak, melt, ooze away.

Tonight? Now? He purposefully slid his forefinger into the ring of the grenade pin. It was simple, what he had to do. The hangar was lined with drums of aviation fuel, the most explosive liquid there is. If the Germans only opened the doors, then Patterson knew he could destroy that airplane. As to their escape . . . . well, he could afford to be fatalistic going into action because his partner had no capacity for fatalism. McKay believed in escape and Patterson was alive because he did.

At times Patterson thought that his 'soft middle' was characteristic of Englishmen of his class and generation. If McKay and Dettke had a substance of character he lacked, wasn't it that they were American and German? The Americans had a shocking knack for making present choices without reference to the past, and that gave them, together with their stolidity, an imbecile innocence. How else account for McKay's desire that night to spare a *Luftwaffe* hospital? To him it was full, in that phrase from hagiography, of the wounded and the dying. To Patterson it was full of the bastards who had bombed London. The past was a weight Patterson carried. In his view there were no innocent Germans, had been none since the Somme. The inner core of each Kraut was a stone; Hitler, that stone-heart, embodied his people perfectly.

But the Somme had revealed there were no innocent Englishmen either. Stone-hearts, indeed! Patterson's father's generation had sprinted down that trail to mass brutality too. So Patterson had grown up with contempt for his own people. Only the outbreak of a new war with Germany had allowed him to lay it aside. Now the war was drawing to a close; would he reclaim it? Would he don those old attitudes like a Cambridge robe? They were bitter, chilling attitudes – there are no differences between Germans and Englishmen; and Americans, innocent lugs, are good for their jazz music and their chewing gum. But such attitudes rescued one, if only for the evening, from the certain knowledge that, unlike one's fathers and one's enemies and one's allies, one had at one's very centre a core of nothing.

McKay brought the car to a halt without actually touching the giant steel doors, but a man could not have passed through the space between the front bumper and those doors.

Dettke quietly spoke a few words in German to McKay. Patterson guessed that he told him to keep the engine running and stay behind the wheel. Dettke opened his door and got out.

At that moment a bank of spotlights high above them was switched on and they found themselves illuminated like circus performers. Patterson remained in the car, but he took the grenade out of his pocket and nestled it inside his cupped hand with his middle finger through the pin-ring. He watched Dettke.

Dettke stared up at the lights as if he were an impresario

inspecting them before the show. He carried a riding crop – where had that come from? As he slowly walked along the steel doors, now eyeing the threshold, now a small pothole in the concrete ramp, now the lights again, he absently swatted at his leg. He walked to the far left edge of the massive door.

And nothing happened.

Patterson tried to find McKay's eyes in the rear-view mirror, but McKay was staring at the door. What if nothing happened? Was there a code, a password? Had the SS men already checked with the Führer-bunker? Was Hitler's pilot well known to them? What could Dettke do once he'd pretended to check the door?

He could check the other half of it.

With what to Patterson was a stunning calm, he crossed behind their automobile and paced slowly towards the right edge of the door, swatting his leg all the while.

A panel in the door about a foot square and immediately in front of the car opened without warning. A head wearing the black peaked hat of an SS officer appeared, lit from behind. An intimidating voice barked a phrase in German.

Dettke ignored it. He completed his thirty-metre stroll to the edge of the door, touched the line where the metal frame was joined to the concrete wall, and then turned to walk to a point well back of and directly behind his automobile. Patterson picked him up in the mirror. Dettke had walked to the edge of the glaring lit circle, then faced the hangar with his riding crop linking his hands behind him. For the first time in his inspection he took in the door in its entirety.

The voice spoke again, but now there was an inflection in it, a question.

Dettke said quietly, 'Guten Abend, Herr Oberbannführer. Sie heissen Faupel, nicht?'

McKay was so amazed he whispered, 'Dettke knows his name!'

The voice did not answer. The panel closed.

And slowly the great door, like a curtain at a play's opening, began to rise.

Instead of focusing on the brightly lit concrete hall that the rolling up of the door revealed, Patterson kept his eyes fixed in the mirror on Dettke. Dettke had not moved a muscle. He was standing with his feet slightly spread. A light glistened off the leather of his boots and the metal of the cross at his throat. Patterson tried to read the expression on his face; was there an airplane before them or not?

Patterson let his eyes move the fraction of an inch it required to see the thing, squat in the floodlit bunker, as on a stage: a coal-black single-engine propeller-snout airplane. Its tail was lower than its nose, which gave it a dynamic lifting quality as if already it was airborne, climbing through Berlin's permanent cloud of ash. Because the airplane was black and because the wingspread, perhaps thirty feet on either side of the stubby, square fuselage, was so disproportionate to its length, the machine resembled a giant insect. Like an insect it seemed invulnerable, and all at once Patterson felt a rush of panic. We can't destroy that airplane! That airplane is Hitler's! He felt what he hadn't consciously experienced since the early days of the war, and even then he had never admitted feeling it. He felt that Hitler was invulnerable, invincible. If this was his airplane they were fools to try destroying it.

Patterson checked himself.

The airplane was made of wood struts covered with fabric. Its black colour made it appear more solid than it was. This was a mere reconnaissance plane, built light, designed to carry only two people, and capable of taking off in a short distance. Its purpose was only to shuttle Hitler to Rechlin. If they'd had to destroy an armoured Junker Three-Ninety, then they would have had a problem. But the Fieseler Storch, once that fuel went up, would ignite like straw. They *could* destroy it. They would.

Dettke had begun walking slowly forward.

McKay depressed the clutch and put the car into gear. As Dettke walked into the hangar, Patterson expected that McKay would drive in behind him until they were next to the airplane. But how in hell would they get out? Three seconds. They would have three seconds.

Dettke walked past the car. He ignored it. He was pressing his left hand against his side, just below his heart, as if he had a pain.

He entered the hangar.

But McKay did not drive in after him.

The SS major raised his arm briskly; '*Sieg Heil!*'

Dettke wearily raised his riding crop to the level of his face and dropped it.

Patterson counted six other SS guards at attention around the airplane, all uniformed obsessively in black. The colour did for them what it did for the airplane. They seemed strong, larger than they were. They would have seemed formidable even if they were not carrying automatic rifles.

Why wasn't Mac following Dettke in?

A distance of perhaps fifteen yards separated the nose of the craft from the hangar threshold. One of the guards stood with his back to the propeller, his machine gun at the ready angle across his chest. Patterson could see that his finger was on the trigger. The guard was staring, it seemed to Patterson, directly at him.

Dettke walked to the far tip of the left wing. The major accompanied him. Dettke was still holding his side, massaging it slightly. Patterson realized with a shock that Dettke was covering the bullet hole in his tunic.

Dettke touched the wing flap with his crop and peered at the hinge.

Then he turned to the major and spoke to him.

The major barked an order across the room. A motor whirred and slowly the hangar door began to slide down.

Dettke walked towards the rear of the airplane, even deeper into the hangar.

'Mac!' Patterson whispered.

McKay flicked the mirror with his eyes. If that was a signal, Patterson missed it.

The guard at the plane's nose was problem one. He could cut any move Patterson made with a burst of fire. If McKay had only angled the car in.

The black door was a quarter of the way down.

Dettke was chatting amiably with the major as they both walked forward along the fuselage. Dettke absently touched his crop to the white cross, the plane's only marking. Then he craned to look into the cockpit.

In seconds Patterson was going to lose sight of Dettke, but also, in even less time, the line of vision of the near guard was going to be blocked by the falling door. Yet at that point the door would still be several feet from the floor.

Patterson tried to estimate its rate of closing, but his mind refused to calculate. It was closing slowly.

Patterson stared at the guard.

Dettke stooped to cross under the wing. Patterson lost sight of him.

The door fell. The guard's helmet disappeared, and then his eyes disappeared.

Patterson opened his door and prepared to throw the grenade.

But he waited, an act of instinct. He counted off three seconds. Only later would he understand, consciously, why he did so. In those three seconds Dettke had time to approach the hangar door. In those three seconds the door went down enough so that when, three seconds later, the blast occurred, the door was closed and Patterson and McKay were protected from it. Patterson's hesitation was perfect, also, because when he finally pulled the pin and rolled the grenade under the door, there were still the two feet of space Dettke needed to roll out. The grenade and Dettke passed each other.

A burst of machine-gun fire rattled the door.

And then the explosion, a muffled slap which, without open air across which to rumble, died instantly. The floodlights sputtered out. From under the threshold of the hangar door, along the length of it, smoke rolled down the concrete apron and curled away.

Patterson was hauling Dettke into the car when McKay popped the clutch. The car was already in reverse. He swung it around in an arc, stopped abruptly, shifted gears and shot forward towards the pair of guardian tanks.

Unmanned? Had Dettke said unmanned?

Patterson saw the rear hatch of the right tank, the nearest one, being lifted. He leaned out of the car window, aimed his pistol, and waited. He had to squint against the wind as the car picked up speed. The hatch cover flopped back. A head appeared, no helmet. Patterson fired. The face whipped back. Blood shot out of a hole in its forehead, the hole Patterson had made. He saw the man's face – not a man's; a boy's. Mouth twisted, eyes staring, body wrenched against the metal. It was a boy no more than ten years old.

The car flashed by the tank. Patterson turned to keep his gun aimed back at it. He remained like that, hanging half out the window, aiming at the tank long after they had left it behind in the dark. As the car roared through the Tiergarten it seemed to Patterson he could still see that face. Pimples, the boy had pimples.

Boys that age were supposed to be cutting open golf balls and mashing grapes, devising melodramatic metaphors for their insecurity. At the Somme, at least it wasn't children. Our fathers gave us the technique of mass killing and we have gone them one better by applying it to children.

What was a boy that age doing inside a tank? Patterson's mind tossed up the word that answered him: *Kellerkinder*. The boy was a *Kellerkind*. The orphans of Berlin, thousands of them after two years of terror-bombing, had made the maze of cellars, abandoned buildings, and now, apparently, abandoned tanks, into their homes and playgrounds.

Patterson slumped with his head out the window and he explained into the wind, we were destroying Hitler's airplane, sealing the bastard's fate. We were sparing the sick and dying in the *Luftwaffe* hospital. We were saving noble resisters from their own suicides. We were escaping so that we could get on with our real mission, our important one. That is how it happened that I killed a boy his age.

CHAPTER SEVENTEEN

'Chirpy fellow, aren't you?' Patterson said.

'I said good morning.' McKay made room for Patterson on the tattered sofa.

Patterson sat. He inhaled smoke from his cigarette and sipped his coffee. He had only moments before awakened from an uneasy sleep. He had a pounding headache. 'How long was I out?'

McKay looked at his watch. 'We got back here at four o'clock. It's now ten-thirty.'

'In the morning?' Patterson looked around the cavernous cellar. 'You'd think it was midnight in here.' After a moment he leaned towards McKay. 'What's that?'

McKay showed him a notepad on which he'd drawn a map. 'I've been doodling.'

'Wilhelmstrasse, right?' Patterson touched the tip of his cigarette to the pad. 'And that's the place.' McKay nodded.

'Thoughts?'

'Our problem,' McKay said carefully, 'is how to get the dynamite down to the crucial room. It's too much to carry. If we blow it in the courtyard the explosion dissipates. Even if it brings down the building the underground room is untouched. So we've buried the thing, but not destroyed it.'

Patterson looked at McKay's doodle as if it would answer the question. 'So?'

'Remember what our friend Dettke said about courtyards? Horses have no reverse gear; they need room to turn around, right? Practical, right? Well, the research centre is below ground

210

in what used to be the palace stables. Horses don't go up and down stairs, so there must be a ramp. There has to be a ramp. Neisen tells me the machinery in this laboratory is pretty hefty. My guess is the ramp is still there, though perhaps sealed, like a big root cellar.'

'In which case . . .'

McKay smiled. 'No problem. We drive the ambulance down. Shut the doors tight. Confine the blast. Take out one former stable.'

'What does Neisen say?'

'I pumped him without raising the issue with him.' McKay smiled again. 'I wanted to leave something for you to do, group captain,' he smiled.

'Kind of you, colonel.'

McKay handed Patterson the pad. 'By the way, I meant to tell you last night. I thought you did damn well.'

Patterson shrugged, although McKay's compliment pleased him. 'It was Dettke's show, start to finish. I never saw any better than him. Did you?'

McKay shook his head. 'But now he's a problem.'

Patterson dropped his cigarette into the dregs of his coffee. It sizzled. He watched it turn black. Then he said, 'I don't know, Mac. He seems . . . all right to me.'

'He's a Red.'

Patterson didn't respond.

'We can't trust him.'

'Maybe we need him.'

McKay stared at Patterson. 'Are you prepared to revise the orders?' he asked softly, no hint of challenge.

'Look, Mac, we're in Berlin now. On the spot some things which were obscure in London become obvious. Dettke is a German. I don't care if he's a Communist, and neither will the Russians. To them he's just a Kraut.'

'We don't know what he is to them.'

'We know what he is to us, though. We could not have pulled that off last night without him.'

McKay stood up. He loomed over Patterson. 'We don't need him tonight.'

Patterson stood too. 'It's not at all clear to me, colonel, that we can find that palace without him.'

'I can find it. Wilhelmstrasse is like Madison Avenue.'

Patterson snorted. 'This isn't New York, my friend. It isn't

211

even Berlin anymore. We neglected to anticipate at Jed that the shape of a city changes somewhat when it's obliterated. It's been five years since the maps we memorized were drawn. What do you use for landmarks? Can you tell me where the tank barriers are? And what do you do if your route is blocked by rubble? And if an SS patrol stops us, you can pass for German, can you?'

'Neisen can.'

'Good Christ, man, Neisen has never seen action. We can't depend on him. Be serious.'

'Do I gather that the C-in-C has made up his mind on this question?'

'Come off it, Mac. Don't "C-in-C" me.'

'No, really, group captain, I wouldn't think of pushing my point of view if I thought the matter was settled.'

Patterson recognized McKay's ploy. McKay didn't think he had the nerve to exercise his authority over him. 'The matter *is* settled,' he said. 'Dettke's coming. I'll talk to him.'

'And tell him what?'

'Leave it to me.'

McKay turned to go.

Patterson grabbed his arm. McKay always made him feel he had to prove himself. 'And, colonel, if Dettke turns out to be a problem, if, that is, you're right, I'll kill him.'

'My thought was to avoid that, group captain.'

'You Americans are so bloody humane.'

'Yes, we're famous for it.'

'Famous for what?' Dr Neisen asked from the doorway on the far side of the cellar. He crossed towards them. McKay and Patterson separated awkwardly.

'Improvising, doctor,' Patterson said jovially. 'We were discussing jazz music, and we agreed that improvisation is what makes it unique.' He lit another cigarette. 'How are you?'

Before Neisen could answer him, Patterson turned to McKay. 'Mac, would you raise Jedburgh on Dettke's wireless and find out the latest on Zhukov's breakthrough?'

McKay stared at Patterson in surprise. Communications intelligence was McKay's responsibility. He did not need to be told how to exercise it. 'Yes, your Lordship,' he said. He saluted and left.

The door closed behind him soundlessly. Patterson and Neisen took chairs at the table. Patterson adjusted the flame on the oil lamp to make it brighter. Next to the lamp was a green wine bottle with a single red rose in it. Patterson fingered the flower. 'Roses. This place has ruined them for me.'

Neisen stared at the flower but said nothing.

'My mother cultivated roses . . .'

'I still do,' Neisen said. 'I suppose my garden is a bramble by now.'

'Everyone's is. We should all have nuns for our gardens and our laundry.' Patterson smiled, but Neisen did not. 'What sort of day is it?'

'Grey. Cold. But cheerier than here. You should come upstairs.'

'I just woke up.'

'How can you sleep, Group Captain Patterson? How can you be so calm?'

'What is it, doctor?'

'Professor Isenberg just came up to me in the chapel. I was sitting by myself. It's quite a lovely room, perfectly proportioned, lined with delicately carved reliefs from the Passion of Jesus. I'm not religious, of course. Certainly not a Christian. But I found it soothing, sitting there. It reminded me of the tapestry room in the British Museum, where I often went as a young man. Not the room. The feeling.' He took his glasses off and pressed his slender fingers against his eyes.

'You say Professor Isenberg came up to you?'

Neisen looked directly at Patterson. 'He knows who I am.'

'Really? How?'

'When I was here at the institute I lectured on occasion at the university. He was on the philosophy faculty there.'

'And he attended lectures in physics?'

Neisen shook his head. 'Apparently we met at a reception. I don't recall it.'

'What year?'

'I was at the *Kaiser-Wilhelm-Institut* from 1922 to 1927.'

'That's a long time ago.'

'Not so long at our age.'

'What did you say?'

'I told him he was mistaken. He pretended to believe me, but he didn't. I'm afraid I gave myself away, stammering, blushing, and so on.' He put his spectacles back on. 'I'm not the sort for this.'

'Would he be able to deduce from your reputation at that point what you might be doing here now?'

'If he knows I worked with Otto Hahn, perhaps. Atomic science itself was primitive in those days.'

Patterson thought for a moment, then said, 'You and Isenberg seemed before to have hit it off.'

Neisen shrugged. 'I admire a Jew who has stood his ground in this inferno. But we have other things in common besides Abraham. I have a daughter, too, though no grandchild. I like the man. It bothered me to lie to him. Do you think it's a disaster that he knows?'

'You're a better judge of that than I am. What could he tell the Russians?'

Neisen shook his head. 'It will be the end of this century before the Russians have the scientific base necessary to take advantage of uranium science. They don't even know the rudiments of the language.'

'Then, forgive me, sir, but why are we here? The Prime Minister made it sound quite important to keep the Russians in the dark.'

'Of course it is. You asked me what Isenberg could tell them.' His eyes widened and he spread his hands. 'Were they to capture the research centre intact, the records and so on, and not only that but also, say, a scientist intimate with the material, then . . . well, that's what they call a shortcut, isn't it? Only if we keep them ignorant of the basic principles of uranium science can we discontinue its development in America. And, believe me, Group Captain Patterson, discontinue it we must!'

'You mean if we destroy the Nazi research . . .'

Neisen nodded gravely. 'Then we can destroy our own. Many of us would never have agreed to work on the project at all were it not for the Nazi programme. You know they could have had the weapon by now' – Neisen smiled – 'but too many of us are Jews.'

' "Jewish physics . . ." '

' "*Jüdische Physik*", Hitler called it. By the time he realized what a mistake it was to dismiss a whole wing of science because Jews dominated it, it was too late. Some of my colleagues in America believe that my work here is the most important work of all. I would never have come, not even for Churchill, but my colleagues convinced me. This is perhaps the last moment in which the process can be stopped. Naturally I cannot say more. I am honour-bound. But, believe me, uranium science has a devil in it. You know that expression? A *dybbuk*?'

'The Americans have this weapon?'

Neisen pointedly stared at Patterson, not speaking.

'Forgive me, I didn't mean to put you in that position. I am not unaware that we have so far avoided this conversation. I too consider our mission here the most important work, even if I have to take it on faith. A terrible weapon, involving the splitting of the atom, the very structure of the universe, I can imagine . . .'

'No, Group Captain Patterson, you can't.'

'But if we succeed here, the Americans have the weapon alone, to use against Japan and thereafter . . .'

'No! We have been Jews working against Hitler. The premise has always been that Hitler would have it. Not Japan.'

'I see.' Perhaps the scientists were still in control. Patterson knew that Groves's project was several years old. He found it difficult to believe that scientists would simply disavow, and had he said 'destroy'? the results of their own work. Would Groves permit that, or Marshall or Roosevelt? Christ, Roosevelt was dead; he could not get used to it! But perhaps his incredulity was a measure of his ignorance. Neisen's horror was palpable. Perhaps they all shared it – scientists, generals and politicians alike. 'You raise an interesting question, doctor,' Patterson said, tacking. 'Where is Otto Hahn, do you suppose?' Patterson knew from his own sources that Hahn had only that week been captured. He wondered if Neisen would tell him.

'If I was Hahn I would be making my way west as quickly as possible. I would think he got out of Berlin some time ago. There will be a brisk trade, don't you think? in providing certain Germans with the accoutrements of new identities.'

'I suppose. Cigarette?'

Neisen declined.

After he'd waved a match out Patterson asked, 'Have you discussed politics with Professor Isenberg?'

Neisen shook his head, but said, 'He's rather devoted to Mother Russia.'

'I gathered. I find that a bit shocking, don't you?'

Neisen shrugged. 'Why should they be more devoted to us? After Dresden? After what we've done to this city? Have the Russians lost the capacity to distinguish between civilians and combatants? It's not clear to me that they have.'

'You're saying that we have lost that capacity?'

'Yes, of course I am. Do you doubt it?'

'I can still make that distinction. And do.' Patterson pushed out of his consciousness an image of the face of the child he'd killed the night before.

'Perhaps so, but you are anachronistic. You fight the war personally. You can see the faces of your enemies. Those bomber pilots can't. And neither do the men who make the bombs. Wars should be personal, in my opinion. That's how to limit them.'

'In all trenches Tommies and Krauts knew each other by name.'

'What happened in the trenches will seem benign one day.'

Patterson and Neisen stared at each other for a moment.

Then Patterson said, 'As for tonight, we find that the simplest is often the best. You know that the ambulance outside carries nearly a ton of dynamite. Our plan is to drive down the former stable's ramp. Once you have satisfied yourself as to the Nazi research, we will simply withdraw and, at a safe distance, detonate the dynamite by means of an electric charge from –'

'I am aware of the technique.'

'Fine. Our thought is that the underground quarters will serve to restrict the force of the explosion. Sergeant-Major Cooper expects that the blast will be sufficient not only to destroy the targeted material, but, with luck, to attack structural elements of the building itself, bringing on at least a partial collapse.'

'The old stables, in the conversion, may have been massively reinforced. In which case . . .' Neisen did not finish his sentence.

'In which case what?'

'We would have to improvise, wouldn't we?' Neisen stood. 'But that's all right. The Americans are famous for it. And we're learning from them, aren't we?'

'Indeed.'

'And what am I to do about Isenberg?'

Patterson put his cigarette out. He was not unaware of the subservience implicit in Neisen's having stood and in his waiting now for direction. Neisen would not so much have glanced at a dandified ne'er-do-well like Patterson when they were both at Cambridge. Now Neisen deferred to him. Patterson said, 'You are here, remember, as the Prime Minister's personal representative to the ceremonies of surrender. You must simply conduct yourself as if that were the case. Professor Isenberg has other matters to contend with besides his vague memory of having met you several decades ago. It means nothing.'

Neisen nodded, apparently reassured.

'Now, doctor, one other thing. I must insist that you get some

216

sleep. There is no other use to be made of the daylight hours. It won't do to have you nodding off tonight on your Geiger counter.'

'I think perhaps I could sleep in that chapel. Do you think they'd mind?'

'I'm sure they wouldn't. I'll ask Dettke to mention it to the Sisters.'

'Thank you, Group Captain Patterson.' Neisen grasped Patterson's hand and shook it warmly.

Patterson thought, Now this is a man of my father's generation. They aren't all trivializers, you see.

'I'm looking for your husband,' Patterson said.

Anna-Lise backed away from the door. 'He isn't here.' Patterson saw behind her their bed and near it a carved wooden cradle. Next to that a small table was wedged into the crevice under the eave. Above the table an uncurtained peaked window offered a view of such startling unreality as to seem a vision out of Brueghel. It was the first time Patterson had seen the city in daylight, and the sight transfixed him, as if it were a painting his father had just brought home from a visit to Montmartre.

Smoke curled upwards from dozens of smouldering fires. There hadn't been an air raid since the one in which they'd arrived the evening before, but the Russian artillery was still firing relentlessly. Patterson was already accustomed to the distant booms, and only by his deliberate act of concentration did they register now. The district in which the convent was situated, Schöneberg, had yet to be targeted, so the artillery seemed more background effect than threat. Patterson stepped towards the window, unconsciously entering the woman's room without having been invited, but he was in the grip of that vista of ruins. Dramatic as the sight had been at night, with fires blazing against the darkness, Patterson was stupefied by it now. The window of that garret was on a level several storeys higher than any other building in Schöneberg, although across a cobbled square immediately below was a public building with a tall Florentine bell tower. It had not been damaged and neither had the immediate neighbourhood, but beyond lay a broad wasteland of charred, roofless half-buildings. 'Good Lord,' Patterson said softly. What had they done?

'America,' Anna-Lise said. 'A gift from America.'

Patterson looked at her. Yes, it was. Without the Americans the Germans would have done this and worse by now to London.

We've beaten the Nazis, he thought. But the Yanks have beaten all of us.

She was looking at him as if he were an American. He looked out the window again. His dramatizing mind inclined to see that chaos, that plain or rubble as more than a city. Neisen was a fool if he thought Americans were going to draw willingly back from the power to do this or worse. Once havoc has been loosed on this scale it will be loosed again. The starting point for each generation is the end point – the limit of horror – of the last. The power to do this resides not in the technical capability, as if the destruction he beheld was caused by gears, winches, gyroscopes, wings, and nitroglycerine dispersed in porous matter, but in the simple human willingness to do it. If we will do this, Patterson said to himself dully, we will do anything. And it didn't begin with Hitler. Neisen's word – *dybbuk* – came back to him: an evil spirit released from the corpse of one unjustly dead. The corpse of a city. Or a century. I have seen this before, he thought. Coventry. London. But I have never until now *felt* it. What obscene creatures we are! All of us!

He faced Anna-Lise and repeated, as if he were in a trance, 'I am looking for your husband.' He looked at her hand, expecting to see a wedding band, but her fingers were bare. She and Dettke were not married? Patterson blushed. Whose imbecile innocence if not his?

The woman was not embarrassed, however. What is a wedding in wartime? What is Patterson's opinion to her? Her direct gaze, her strong green eyes, did not waver. She was only three feet away from Patterson, and suddenly he was acutely aware of her body, the curve of her breast, the line of her cheek. He could smell her, a fresh lively natural scent, the very opposite of the odour of ash that hung over the grey city. Patterson thought ordinarily that he had in his time stepped cavalierly near the very limits of experience, but this formal young woman, barely out of childhood herself, made him suddenly feel that he had been protected and immune. A city had been levelled at the very sill of her window. He wanted to ask her, was it like beholding Vesuvius? Or the salting of Carthage? Was it like standing on the Temple Mount when the Romans came? Jerusalem! Blake's verse broke like a wave over his mind. To him Jerusalem was the subject of a schoolboy's favourite hymn. The lyric threatened to unroll across the spindle of his memory even then. But to the Jews – she didn't look Jewish with that extraordinarily blonde braid, but

Isenberg was her father. Did it make him an anti-Semite that he thought Jews had no right to such hair, such skin? Of course it did – Jerusalem was the ravaged city left without stone upon stone. And he was himself one of the destroyers. We British have perfected the Roman terror. Giles shuddered with the horror of it.

He shook himself and looked around her room as if he didn't know how he'd got there. 'Forgive me, but the sight of such destruction disorients me. I shouldn't have intruded.'

Anna-Lise softened. 'It disorients us all.'

'Has it been unbearable?' he asked inanely.

'We have borne it.'

Giles looked through the window again and realized for the first time that he wanted no part of what had done this. Americans, British, Russians – all *dybbukim* alike. 'It shames me,' he said quietly. He could feel himself draining away, his soft core.

'It frightens me,' Anna-Lise said, 'for what my child will see.'

The future, yes, the future, Giles thought suddenly. That alone deserves our loyalty now. And he saw with clarity that the purpose of their mission, in Neisen's terms, was not to uphold one nation against the others but to protect the future from this madness. All the nations have gone berserk! But the future! At that moment the word embodied for Patterson the only cause left that required his commitment and his sacrifice. The fight for England had not purged him of his ambivalence, but deepened it. The fight for the future, though, now, was absolute and for the first time in his life he felt absolutely an urge to serve. He looked at Anna-Lise. 'We have to stop this, don't we?'

'Yes. But how?'

'First, by seeing it. By knowing what we've done. What we can do.' Giles stepped solemnly to the window again. For him the moment was a turning point. He vowed to oppose what caused what he beheld. Oppose it always and with everything. Anna-Lise joined him, and they stood together, silently, searing their eyes on the sight of the ravaged city. He felt her presence like a ratifying witness to his oath.

Finally he said, 'Now I must see Herr Dettke.'

'I will take you,' she said. She brushed by him. He looked in the cradle. It was empty, bare even of linen. Of course, she wouldn't have her infant there, so far from shelter. He glanced out the window once more, saw smoke and dust kicked up a few

219

blocks away by an artillery shell, the closest yet, and he followed her.

She led him to a narrow staircase at the opposite end of the building from the large, public staircase he'd ascended, and they wound down five floors in silence, and then crossed a broad polished corridor on the main floor to a pair of huge doors that opened, Patterson guessed, on the refectory.

Even before Anna-Lise pulled the heavy metal latch to swing the door on its wrought-iron hinges the size of books, Patterson could hear the children. At Callow's End each Christmas in the late morning of the day of the Christmas ball, Patterson's father had thrown open the great festooned hall to the families of the servants and tenants. It had always been an excruciating humiliation to Patterson to have to face boys and girls his own age as the son of the man who owned them. He was somewhat slow in coming to understand that ownership was not precisely the appropriate category in which to locate the relationship between the servants and his gentle, well-loved father, but by the time he had substituted for it the constitutionally defined notion of peerage, he had a fixed repugnance for the happy sounds of children gathered in a hall.

He followed her into a room that, despite the black cloth that sealed shut the floor-to-ceiling windows, was nearly as bright as daylight. Dozens of oil lamps and candelabra jutted from the panelled walls and hung from the moulded ceiling. Their light reflected off the host of luminous creatures swirling like angels. He could not count them all. The tables and chairs were pushed against the walls. The bare floor was a gleaming parquet. Dozens, a hundred perhaps, even two hundred children, from very small ones to adolescents, all in simple muslin shifts, all girl-children, dashed cheerfully back and forth and in random circles with aimless energy like minutiae under the microscope. No, like seabirds behind the fleet. Here and there, exactly like their name-sake channel markers, stood nuns, three of them, no, five, six, in white robes and black veils which framed their faces beautifully. They were waving their arms and clapping, giving orders, but as far as Patterson could tell no one paid attention to them. The children danced around them, dodging, tagging, racing, skipping, bumping each other, falling, getting up, leap-frogging, all the while squealing deliriously. The nuns were enjoying themselves too, but their handsome posture and their creased gestures indicated what the pandemonium really was: a deliberate, ordered exercise in release. Christians believe, don't they, that when the spirit hovered over chaos, chaos ceased to threaten?

When the children saw Anna-Lise they swooped towards her. Immediately her arms were filled with round bodies, cherubs, who grinned over her shoulders at Patterson. Anna-Lise waded through the white-clad throng and Patterson followed. He was unsure how to see this woman. Was she a surrogate mother for orphans or a dogged resistance fighter? She was both, he saw then. His admiration for Dettke was established, and now he decided that Anna-Lise was worthy of him. They crossed to a mound of children who were happily writhing, rolling, playing on – it took Patterson a moment to recognize it – the form of a man.

Anna-Lise spoke loudly.

The man freed his head and looked up. Such joy was in his eyes, such peace and happiness, that Patterson had to stifle a wave of a most surprising envy.

Hitler's pilot?

An accomplished secret agent?

The grim resistance leader?

The Conductor of the Red Orchestra?

Europe's one real hero?

No, a man with his children.

'Herr Dettke,' Patterson said, smiling, 'I hardly recognize you.'

CHAPTER EIGHTEEN

'You have children?' Dettke asked the question without looking at him. He and Patterson were standing side by side. Dettke had his arms folded. He was freshly shaven and was wearing yet another clean white shirt. He had all these nuns to do his laundry, and they had all these girls to help them.

'Not married,' Patterson replied.

Dettke did not acknowledge that he was not married either.

Anna-Lise had replaced him. Neither she nor the girls were playing with the glad abandon that had been tangible when Dettke was at the base of the heap. Patterson estimated that Dettke was ten years older than he was, which would make him forty-five, though what had first struck him about the lean, blond Prussian was his youthfulness. His eyes and mouth, however, could be seen now to have been harshly touched by time. The night before, in impersonating the Nazi general, Dettke had drawn on a world-weariness that could not possibly have been manufactured. But what would fiercely age a man if not a decade underground in Hitler's Berlin? How was it then that Patterson had observed once more, watching Dettke with those children, an attractive boyishness that made him feel old by comparison?

Perhaps the answer was in the children themselves. Can one imbibe youth? Was that the point of generation? Patterson had quite frankly never understood what was in it for adults to have children. But now he sensed, in the midst of Berlin's massive obliteration, that renewal was. Dettke had asked his question to learn if he and Patterson shared that rejuvenation. He was a new parent, Patterson reminded himself, and he believed no doubt that the male of the species were divided between men who were fathers and men who weren't. He was like McKay.

'I'm sorry to take you from this, Herr Dettke. But we must talk.'

Patterson realized that Dettke was watching not the children, but Anna-Lise. Her skirt had been pulled up so that most of one of her shapely legs was visible, and from beneath the scampering girls came a white flash of the inside of her thigh. Her body was ripe, and it was easy for Patterson to imagine a man desiring her. But her youthfulness, unlike Dettke's, was no illusion. She was young enough to be his daughter. Patterson imagined how they had come together. Were they tumbling in a pile once, like that, both pretending that she was just one more of the convent's brood? When suddenly a shell fell nearby and frightened her? When suddenly his hand brushed against her breast and then did not move? Had she rescued Dettke from his hatred, his discouragement, his resistance? He had not resisted her. Patterson had sensed his attachment to her at the meeting the night before, and he sensed it now, but not as mere attachment, as worship.

When he let his eyes drift across the room Patterson saw that many of those girls were on the brink of womanhood. He saw suddenly among those hundreds of pairs of jiggling legs dozens of well-turned calves; he saw waists and bosoms and shaped buttocks. He saw even in that muslin the toned and flushed skin of bodies which, despite themselves, had grown ready for another kind of play and argument. Patterson wanted suddenly and desperately to protect these girls, to save them, to care for them.

What dangers awaited them! He'd had the feeling only once before, in relation to his nephew, but that only after his nephew's having been crippled. This was the first time Patterson had allowed himself to feel a rush of paternal anxiety towards anyone who was whole, anyone who was not his. These children were the future to which he would give himself.

Dettke abruptly turned and strode out of the room.

Patterson followed him across the broad hallway, through a low door and into a narrow ill-lit corridor, which led down a flight of stone stairs into a catacomb tunnel, which opened in turn, finally, on a small cubicle with a low-arching brick ceiling and bricked-in gothic windows. It was a space that once might have held vintage wine or the convent's treasures but that now was dominated by a white marble altar against its far wall. Dettke lit the pair of candles, as if for liturgy. The altar was draped with a purple cloth along the fringe of which were the words *Sanctus Sanctus Sanctus*. A crystal vase holding half a dozen red roses sat between the candles. A plaster crucifix, perhaps three feet tall, the top of which nearly touched the ceiling, stood on the back lip of the altar. Its painted Christus rendered that writhing suffering so starkly and so literally – his mouth gaped to drool, the irises were turned up into his head – that the effect was the opposite of what the pious artist intended. Such mawkish realism invited disbelief.

Dettke faced Patterson with his back to the altar in his characteristic posture, arms folded. He waited.

The flame of the candles cast shadows on the granite walls and masonry ceiling. In the ancient catacombs below the streets of Rome, Patterson, as a twenty-year-old tourist, had had his first bout with claustrophobia. An electrical short had extinguished the string of naked light bulbs and he had panicked in the abrupt darkness. Whole moments had passed in which he was certain he was sealed in his tomb alive. When they finally made their way out he and his companions had laughed about it. His chums had no idea how afraid he'd been, and that taught him that he could keep even the most intense of his fears in check.

To master his uneasiness now, Patterson tried quickly to estimate the dimensions of the room. From the vaulted ceiling to the floor was perhaps nine feet. A set of three velvet-padded *prie-dieux* lined the wall opposite the altar, leaving an open space of only five feet by five feet.

'This was the private chapel for the priests where they made their Masses alone. Now, during the air raids, they bring their

Sacrament down here and the Sisters kneel in vigil.'

'I'd have thought they'd have it down here now.'

'They will tonight. I encouraged them to be upstairs today. I wanted the children to play. Who knows how long the siege will last when it comes?'

Patterson leaned back, half-sitting, on the arm-rest of a kneeler. Could the rote prayers that had been offered there for the children of St Magdalene's be said finally to have gone unanswered? 'I wanted to talk to you about something.'

Dettke nodded carefully but remained silent.

'Having to do with the brigadier. We weren't, I'm afraid, quite forthright about him, Mr Dettke. Brigadier Bard is in fact a civilian scientist who has accompanied us as a resource for a secondary mission.'

Patterson was watching for an indication that Dettke already knew who Neisen was. Surely Isenberg had told him. But Dettke stared impassively at Patterson. The shadows from the candles played eerily across his face.

'Do you know of the Ministry for Armaments and Munitions?'

Dettke didn't respond.

After a moment Patterson said, 'I'd like to have a frank conversation with you. After last night it seems quite clear we can trust each other, I'd say.'

'Last night you and I read each other with great precision.'

'Well, I can't read you unless you answer me. Do you know of the ministry?'

'Of course. *Das Ministerium für Wisssenschaft, Erziehung und Volksbildung*. A multi-department bureaucracy with laboratories under the authority of the *Heereswaffenamt*, the Army Weapons Department, at Number 69 Unter den Linden.'

'I thought Wilhelmstrasse, the old palace.'

Dettke nodded. 'A large building. The entrance to the court-yard is on Wilhelmstrasse. What is your interest?'

'I'm sure you can guess. The data from all Nazi research in weaponry is on record there. A central archive, very well organized, very German. We are interested in particular in their work in rocketry and jet propulsion. It would be a great loss if the information accumulated were to be destroyed.'

'Surely it is already destroyed.'

'Perhaps. My orders, however, are to take advantage of the small chance that it has not been. And I need your help.' Patterson paused, watching him. 'I intend to go there tonight.'

'Tonight? But the last battle begins tonight. One can hear the guns moving closer. Better to wait and go to the ministry once the city is secure.'

'My orders are to prevent the Nazis from destroying the ministry archives.'

'Good luck.'

'And to hold it until Marshal Zhukov's representative can take over.'

Was Dettke that naïve? Patterson tried to read him but couldn't. He said, 'After last night I am quite certain we cannot find the ministry or negotiate the city's chaos without you. I am asking you to help us through Berlin.'

'Unter den Linden and Wilhelmstrasse – that intersection will be the Russians' objective. The artillery will be fierce, and the soldiers will have in mind the siege of Stalingrad. Heinrici will be fighting to the death.'

'You're saying there's a risk. I haven't noticed you shirking risks.'

'What I have done has been for one purpose, the defeat of Hitler. You are concerned with something else now.'

'That's true. Nevertheless I am asking you to help me.'

'Tell me about Brigadier Bard.'

'His name is Neisen. He is the director of the Clarendon Laboratory outside of London where our research into various forms of propulsion is conducted. In England we have had personal reasons to want to learn about German rockets. For example, a V-2 destroyed my sister's house and crippled her son. That was last year, when he was about your daughter's age. That boy's father, by the way, is Colonel McKay. The sight of healthy, active children such as those here is difficult for him. You may have noticed that. In any case, Neisen is a physicist who has specialized in rocketry. He is with us because he was in Berlin as a lecturer at the *Kaiser-Wilhelm-Institut* in the twenties. He knows what to look for. It also happens he is a personal friend of Churchill, and *is* prepared to offer his services to Marshal Zhukov as a representative of the Prime Minister.'

'That does not concern me. Neither does your mission.'

Patterson straightened up. 'I understand. Thanks anyway.' He turned to go.

Dettke took his arm. 'But I will come with you.'

'Why?'

'Because you waited a few seconds last night and let me live.'

Dettke let go of Patterson's arm and walked out of the chapel.

Good Lord, Patterson thought, here I've been trying to deceive the bastard when what moves him is an impulse of simple gratitude. That his offer comes as such a shock indicates what damage the war has done me.

Patterson followed Dettke, but at the door was met by Karl Schott. Schott was holding a bunch of fresh roses with which to replace the stale ones on the altar. What was he, a sacristan? He waited for Patterson to move out of the doorway, but Patterson stood there. 'I'm sorry about last night,' he said. 'I know you were counting on going.'

Schott shook his head. 'You were right. I am not a soldier. I am a gardener.'

'And a very good one, I'd say.'

'It would be better,' he said, appraising his roses, 'if I could tend them in daylight.'

'Perhaps soon you'll be able to.'

Schott entered and went to the altar. Patterson watched him, was touched by his deliberation. Clearly the flowers had taken on extraordinary significance. Schott faced him suddenly and asked, 'Will the Russians harm us?'

Patterson did not answer.

Schott said, 'I am not a Communist. Neither are the Sisters. It is natural to think if the Russians are against Hitler they are good, but now I ask myself, is that so? Should we be afraid? Most Germans, you know, are afraid.' Schott took his spectacles off and rubbed his eyes.

'How old are you, Herr Schott?'

Schott looked up in surprise. 'I am forty-five. Same as Jörg.' Schott laughed. Dettke seemed a full generation younger.

'I admire enormously your efforts here.'

'It has been the others. Those who are dead. And Jörg, of course. Him, you should admire. Me, all I do is hide.'

'You grow roses.'

'I never struck a blow. Hitler is finished, and I never struck a blow.'

'You can hold that against me, for stopping you last night.'

'I hold it against myself. I permitted Hitler.'

'The world permitted Hitler, Herr Schott.'

He hooked his glasses carefully over his ears and turned to his roses again. 'I thought for a long time – for a long time I told myself – that bringing forth even a little beauty was an act of opposition. Beauty is the opposite of evil, I said. But it is not so. No doubt there are roses in the Führer-bunker.' He looked sharply across at Patterson. The light from the candles glinted off his glasses. 'Do you know what I learned? I learned it is a mistake to wait until a morally pure act of opposition presents itself. I waited and I waited. There is no such thing.'

'You were prepared to destroy a hospital.'

'Yes. The last acts are the worst of all. I would have done that because up to then I had done nothing.' He shrugged. 'You spared me, but not before I learned. I always thought the difference between me and Hitler was my moral purity, but my moral purity allowed him to exist.'

'For a gardener you have a philosopher's bent.'

Schott smiled for the first time. 'Gardeners are philosophers.'

Patterson had taken up a position between a nun and a delicate plaster column in the oversized refectory. The children had been organized into two large circles, which revolved, one inside the other, in opposite directions. In their midst, in the dead centre, stood Anna-Lise, blindfolded. Dettke had joined one of the circles, and Patterson was not altogether pleased to see that so had Cooper and Nichols. But hell, what was the harm? It would reassure the children to have the strangers playing with them. The room was bright with high spirits. Everyone knew it was only a question of time before the last Nazis fled or surrendered, and then they could play their games in the streets.

McKay, approaching from behind, touched Patterson's sleeve. The nearby nun smiled as they moved away from her.

'Zhukov is in Prenzlauer Berg. Koniev is in Pankow. They've suffered over fifty thousand casualties already. Heinrici has his men lined around the edge of the centre city. The fighting is street-to-street and house-to-house. It could be days before they take the Chancellery. It could be tonight.'

'What about Schöneberg?'

McKay shook his head. 'The thrusts are only from the north and the east. They won't get to this district until after they've taken the centre.'

Patterson stared at the children, in their wheeling circles. They were singing now.

McKay studied notes on a pocket-sized pad.

'These little girls are oblivious,' Patterson said absently.

'They'll be waving red flags when the Russians arrive.'

Patterson looked quizzically at McKay, who explained, 'I came upon a pair of nuns who were cutting old vestments, red silk, waterstains and all, into dozens of little flags. They said that Hitler was the Antichrist, and anyone who opposed him did the work of the Lord.'

'It's a luxury, isn't it, to fight one war at a time? Here's hoping their flags do the trick.'

'The nuns are lucky it's not our boys. How could they make the Stars and Stripes or the Union Jack?'

'Listen, Mac. I had that conversation with Dettke. He's coming tonight. He thinks we're after rocket research. We can keep him at a distance.'

McKay closed his notepad emphatically. 'That will be your job.'

'As I see it we have no choice!' Patterson's anger flared. He could tolerate neither McKay's reticence nor his own need for McKay's approval.

McKay maintained his brisk demeanour, an implicit criticism of Patterson's emotion. 'You've become too dependent on him. It's the first thing we warn the Jed-boys of; you're out of your element, alien country, strange language, the enemy everywhere. It's natural to attribute superior resources to native operatives. But they know less than we do. Locals always know less than we do. It's the first rule, group captain, and you've forgotten it. I think you've made a mistake with Dettke. He's going to be very cosy with the Russians. They'll use him. He's probably already in touch with them.'

'That's ridiculous. You're overestimating the Russians. You Yanks always do. Zhukov is wielding a sledgehammer, not a rapier. His army has no intelligence capacity and barely the communications required to talk to his own commanders, much less a Kraut who claims to be a Red. Hell, they'll all claim that now. Zhukov will never have heard of Dettke. There's only one way a German like him can establish bona fides with the Russians, and that's through us.'

'Perhaps, but perhaps not.'

'He's not stupid. From what I told him, he'll think that Neisen is his ticket to a meeting with Zhukov himself. He needs us, Mac, as much as we do him. I can feel it. What the hell should I trust, after all these years, if I can't trust what I feel?'

'Trust the orders, Giles. The orders involve what you and I don't know about.'

'The orders are mine now. I don't want you kibitzing, *versteh*'?'

Jörg Dettke had pulled out from between his two partners in the circle and was now crossing to Patterson and McKay. He approached, smiling broadly. 'You gentlemen should join us.'

McKay, hands behind his back, rocked on his toes and heels. 'We'd rather stand on the side and kibitz, right, group captain?'

'I didn't mean "kibitz", Mac.' Giles lowered his eyes, conveying his apology.

Dettke sensed the tension between them and started to excuse himself, but then he said to McKay, 'I'm sorry about your son.'

McKay looked sharply at Patterson; how have you put Jake to use in this?

Dettke went on, 'Don't you find that when he grasps your finger in his fist with the clutching reflex, your questions are all answered?'

'My questions about what?'

'Why, about your existence.'

'I don't have any questions about that.'

Dettke raised his eyebrows slightly, opened his hands, turned and walked away.

'Christ, McKay,' Patterson said quietly. 'For all your righteousness, you are one cold son of a bitch.'

McKay took Patterson's upper arm in his right hand and squeezed it. 'You are not to refer to Jake with him again. Is that clear? I will not have you using Jake's leg to ingratiate yourself with him.'

'Let go of my arm, Mac.'

'What happened to Jake is my pain, Giles! Not yours!' McKay released Patterson and stepped back. He was now blushing furiously and showed signs of not knowing what had come over him. His outburst startled him even more than it did Patterson.

'No, it isn't yours, Mac. Jake's pain is Jake's. That's your problem; you don't know that yet. The Germans didn't do something to you, not even to Eleanor. They did it to Jake. If I told Dettke what happened, it's because he's a man who could understand that. Even if he is a German, you could learn something from him.'

Patterson sensed how close McKay was to striking him and, perversely perhaps, Patterson wanted him to. This was the first time in over a year that McKay was showing him his real face. Mac's rage frightened Patterson, but it reassured him, too, because it meant they could touch each other still.

Patterson turned and walked through the twin circles of children to their very centre. He touched Anna-Lise's shoulder. She stopped spinning and fell against him. The children laughed and clapped.

Patterson was conscious of the delicate feel of her body. She was dizzy, and as he helped her undo the blindfold he had to support her with an arm around her waist. He held her more tightly perhaps than he had to, and he felt a rush of desire for which, given the setting and what had just happened, he could not account.

When the blindfold was off she looked up at him and surprise showed for a moment in her eyes. Then she kissed him on the cheek and began to tie the blindfold around his eyes. When his hand went to the place on his face where she had kissed him, he was aware of it, but as a gesture a youth would make, a naïf, a boy, a person he hadn't been in years.

The children could have played on for hours, and the adults were far from inclined to discourage them. On the contrary, Giles Patterson, after his stint as the hub of the wheels, went to the upright piano in the corner of the refectory and began to play ragtime tunes to which the girls began to hop. If they'd wanted then to listen to the distant booming cannon, they couldn't have heard them for the music.

Which is why the explosion came as such a shock.

A shell landed very close by. The noise was louder than any they'd heard. Schöneberg had so far, by the grace of the Virgin, been spared except for the occasional random stray. The convent had suffered no damage at all, and neither had the Town Hall across the square. But this shell seemed to have landed on their very heads.

Everyone froze.

Patterson sat with his hands depressing the keys of the last chord he'd played.

Within seconds another shell exploded. One of the huge blacked-out windows was blown in, but the shards of glass were absorbed by the stout woollen material – the cloth from which the Sisters made their veils – which covered the windows. The children began to scream.

One of the nuns, the Mother Superior who led the prayers when the priest was absent, recited loudly, '*Introibo ad altare Dei.*'

The other nuns and the older girls answered automatically, '*Ad Deum qui laetificat juventutem meum.*'

As they continued to recite the psalm antiphonally with the Mother Superior, the girls formed their lines, with the Sisters herding like collies. By the time they were arranged two by two, the youngest first in a rank which began with small children but ended with tall young women, everyone was reciting obediently.

A third shell fell, and a fourth, but no one screamed now.

A pair of nuns led the line out of the refectory and across the hallway to the chapel.

That alarmed Patterson. They should have proceeded directly to the cellars. Psalms were one thing, but not above ground. Patterson guessed that the Russians had successfully advanced their artillery units, but the gunners had yet to readjust their range. Surely they would do so soon. They wanted to bombard government buildings and holdout barracks, not convents and orphanages. Or was it that Russians, like British and American air squadrons, were bombarding the city at random now?

The line of girls was leaving the chapel as quickly as it had entered and then crossing the hallway again to the narrow stairway to the cellar. Several dozen pairs of girls waited patiently, with great discipline, while ahead of them the line briskly but decorously wound into the chapel and out. Patterson squeezed ahead of the girls to enter the chapel himself.

Each pair was entering the chapel, genuflecting towards the sanctuary, in which a large candle burned through red glass, then dipping their right hands in the shell-shaped holy water font at the head of the aisle and carefully blessing themselves before genuflecting again. The genuflections, right knee to left heel, were precisely executed. The signs of the cross which left drops of water on each brow were heartfelt. The girls seemed uniformly free of panic, but they glanced, also uniformly, with intense pleading towards that red candle suspended above the altar at the far end of the chapel.

Patterson saw Neisen standing in the right rear corner beyond the curtained confessional booth. He was watching the procession with tears in his eyes. Patterson crossed to him.

'This is why we must succeed,' Neisen whispered.

They watched the girls enter, genuflect, bless themselves, and leave until at the end of the line a pair of nuns appeared and did likewise. Then the Mother Superior. She glanced at the sanctuary lamp too, but then she turned as another shell exploded perhaps a block away and addressed her pleading look to Patterson and Neisen.

She left. It seemed no one else would enter.

Patterson saw what Neisen had meant about the chapel. It was a jewel of Gothic proportion. It soothed.

Someone else entered, stoop-shouldered and shuffling. It took Patterson a moment to recognize Anna-Lise's father. He did not notice Neisen and Patterson in the corner. At the head of the aisle he donned a yarmulke, then approached the sanctuary. He stopped only at the gleaming brass railing, and he looked up at the sanctuary lamp. One could imagine him closing out of his mind the statues and the crosses. *Yahweh is a Pillar of Fire*. It was the fire he'd come for. Isenberg began to bob slightly in the rhythm of his prayer.

'I thought he was a Marxist,' Patterson whispered.

'First he is a Jew,' Neisen said.

In the foyer outside the chapel, Dettke was waiting for Patterson and with him were McKay, Cooper, Nichols, and, holding her infant daughter, Anna-Lise.

McKay said to Cooper, 'Sergeant-major, perhaps you'd explain to the group captain what the problem is.'

Cooper seemed short of breath. 'Sir, it's the ambulance. You know how it's loaded up. I was just agreeing with Mr Dettke here that if it was to take a hit there wouldn't be nothing left of this place to put a cross on.'

McKay said icily, 'Herr Dettke was about to move it. I forbade him to do so without clearing it with you.'

Patterson addressed Cooper. 'Even the north wing cellar is vulnerable?'

Cooper snorted. 'I tell you, Group Captain Patterson, when that many sticks go at once they'll feel it in China. Every kipper down there will be blown to smithereens. Not to mention us. This old place could stand an odd shell or two, but nowhere near that dynamite. I agree with His Nibs here, if you'll permit me to say so.'

Patterson asked Dettke, 'Where were you going to take it?'

'Anywhere. Away from here.'

'Is there another place where it would be off the street?'

'No. But it makes no difference. We have no use for it now.'

'That is not for you to say. On the street now a working vehicle would be seized immediately.'

232

'Let them have it! Let the SS be blown up, not our children. What possible use remains for it now?' Dettke's stare implied the rest of his question; your purpose tonight is to prevent the archives from being destroyed. Therefore? Dettke pointed at Cooper. 'The sergeant agrees with me!'

'Sergeant-Major Cooper has spoken out of turn. We shall all repair to the cellar now. The ambulance stays where it is.'

Dettke leapt at Patterson, grabbing his lapels. 'There are children here!'

'You should have considered that before you made this your headquarters, Herr Dettke.'

A shell exploded, no closer than before, but still in the neighbourhood.

The infant pulled away from Anna-Lise's breast and began to wail. Dettke released Patterson and crossed to Anna-Lise. He put his arm around her and offered the tip of his small finger to the baby. She took it.

Patterson faced McKay; you, at least, agree with me, Mac, don't you?

Another explosion. The walls shook this time. McKay pointedly refused to meet Patterson's eyes. He was ashamed of himself for agreeing with Patterson.

Dettke guided his daughter's mouth back to Anna-Lise's breast, kissed Anna-Lise, then turned to leave.

Patterson drew his pistol. Dettke stopped. 'You're married to me for the next few hours, Mr Dettke. Corporal Nichols, I want you to find Herr Schott. Consider him under arrest. Stay with him. Be polite.' John McKay crossed to Dettke and felt in his shirt for a pistol. He was unarmed.

'Now, please, everyone,' Patterson said. 'We should join the Sisters and the children downstairs where it is safe.'

Professor Isenberg went to his daughter and, like an usher, led her to Jörg Dettke. Isenberg and Dettke embraced Anna-Lise and the sucking baby. Isenberg's head bobbed as if he were still praying. Dettke by comparison was restrained. He was content to place his cheek against Anna-Lise's and let that simple contact speak for him. Finally, ignoring Patterson and Patterson's weapon, he turned Anna-Lise and Isenberg towards the door and eased them forward. He followed them down the stairs.

John McKay crossed to Patterson and said quietly, 'We're both cold sons of bitches, Giles.' Then he walked into the chapel, genuflected, and crossed himself as the children had.

Patterson holstered his weapon and looked at Neisen who was nodding at him and off whose eyes the light glanced.

CHAPTER NINETEEN

Not far from Baker Street were the London offices of a special unit known in the Intelligence community only by its code name, Alsos. Acquaintances of Patterson's from the SOE had been recruited for it the year he and McKay went to work on Jedburgh, and he knew that Alsos had a priority rating that equalled theirs. But throughout 1943 and '44 dozens of top-secret projects having to do with the coming invasion had sprung up in London. Patterson was familiar with the existence of most of them, but also preoccupied enough with his own work to rein whatever curiosity he might have felt about other operations.

But Alsos.

Something about Alsos pricked his curiosity after the late March meeting he and McKay had with the Prime Minister, and it took him several weeks to realize what. It had to do with Greek. Patterson could barely remember from his schooldays which of the Greek prepositions took the dative case, but for some reason, one day, the meaning of the word *alsos* popped into his head. It meant 'grove'. The olive groves of Delphi.

The Leslie Groves of Downing Street, the stout and surly general of the US Engineers.

Patterson made discreet inquiries. Several things were quickly and easily established. Alsos was a joint British-American effort designed to gather information about the Nazi effort to build a uranium machine. After D-Day Alsos teams, which consisted of scientists supported by OSS and SOE operatives, accompanied the advance units of the invading army, and once the Allies had crossed into Germany itself, Alsos commanded all the resources it required to carry out its mission. By the time Patterson and his team had left Tempsford on April 28 he knew through his own sources that their mission was one part of a massive joint effort to prevent the Russians from capturing any part of the Nazis' so-called 'U-Project'.

On March 15, for example, a single factory in a Berlin suburb, the Auergesellschaft in Oranienburg, had been the target of an

Eighth Air Force raid led by General Carl Spaatz himself and involving 612 Flying Fortresses, which dropped nearly two thousand tons of high explosives and incendiary bombs. At that factory were manufactured uranium metals needed for the construction of the super-weapon.

By March 30, the week of the meeting at Number 10 Downing Street, Alsos units with Eisenhower had already occupied physics laboratories in Heidelberg and rounded up several top Nazi scientists, including one of the two directors of Berlin's *Kaiser-Wilhelm-Institut*. Documents captured there indicated that some research activity had been recently evacuated to several locations in the Redoubt area in Bavaria, but also that while various other aspects of the project were being conducted in Frankfurt, Leipzig, and Vienna, overall control was still being exercised from Berlin.

In mid-April an American force, arriving just ahead of the Russians, captured a salt mine near Stassfurt in which the Germans had stored 1200 tons of uranium, almost the entire supply of the metal in Europe. Alsos was able, without nearby Russians knowing anything about it, to truck the uranium to Hannover, whence it was flown to the United States.

By the last week of April, in actions completed just before Patterson's force left Tempsford, Americans had seized a primitive uranium pile hidden in an old schoolhouse in Frankfurt, a large laboratory concealed in a tunnel in the Alps, and a large chemistry lab in Tailfingen presided over by Otto Hahn himself. In addition to Hahn, Alsos had by then captured von Laue, von Weizsäcker, and Weitz. On April 26, the heavy water used as a controlling element in the activity of the uranium pile in Hargerloch was found hidden in a cave beneath an old mill, and buried in a nearby field one and a half tons of small metallic uranium cubes were discovered. From captured documents, including signed receipts for all the reports that had been sent on to Berlin, it was apparent that by the time Patterson's mission embarked, all of the important scientists – they had called themselves the *Uranverein*, the Uranium Society – had been captured except one, and likewise all of the important facilities were occupied by then except one. The missing scientist was Friedrich Nagel, the second director of the *Kaiser-Wilhelm-Institut*, and his laboratory and archives beneath the Ministry for Armaments was the one facility the Allies had yet to take.

When Patterson had begun to outline these discoveries of his

235

to McKay, McKay had refused to listen. At first Patterson thought he was simply being peevishly self-righteous about the breaches of security implied in Patterson's knowledge. But then McKay explained his reticence. Clearly an Alsos unit would have more logically conducted this raid into Berlin. It was flattering to think that Churchill had selected them because of their achievements with Jedburgh, but wasn't it more likely that they had been selected precisely because they were not Alsos? All of the other Alsos efforts had been carried out in the womb of, or at worst on the lip of, the advancing army. But the Berlin operation was different. They were dropping into the midst not only of the old enemy, but also of the new one. There was every likelihood that, if they were lucky enough to survive the Nazis' last spasms, they were still going to be found and detained by the Red Army. Their very presence in Berlin would be a violation of the agreements arrived at in Yalta. How did Patterson suppose the Russians would react to the discovery that senior British and American officers, with a combat force, however meagre, had arrived in Berlin before they did? At very least, the Russians would interrogate them aggressively. The rules of war and the courtesies of allies did not extend to guerrilla fighters, and Patterson knew it. What was to prevent the Russians from taking extreme measures against them? And what precisely made Patterson immune from the tortured prisoner's ancient willingness to talk?

McKay, in short, agreed with the Prime Minister and with General Groves; in Berlin ignorance was to be prized above either courage or honour.

As for Neisen, Patterson understood by the time they took off for Berlin that the scientist's main burden was *his* knowledge. By then Patterson's inbred inquisitiveness had faded and he had no further inclination to learn from Neisen anything about uranium or its uses. He'd decided, in fact, that compartmentalizers like Groves were probably correct. These *were* secrets of a special kind. He should not have made his inquiries. He should not have broached the subject with McKay. Why was that bastard always right?

Patterson had no real idea what, besides files, they would find if they successfully made their way into the caves below the old Hohenzollern palace. His intuition had prepared him to be alert for Friedrich Nagel, but he wouldn't know the scientist from the janitor. And the laboratory? He wouldn't know fission from fishing, radiation from the radio. He wouldn't know a cyclotron if it snapped its heels and said, '*Sieg Heil!*' All Patterson knew by the time they left Tempsford was that he already knew too much.

At midnight, in the first moments of April 30, they set out from the Convent of St Magdalene. Dettke drove the automobile in which rode Neisen, Nichols, and Patterson. McKay drove the ambulance, and at his side was Cooper. They were all dressed innocuously, like labourers, except Dettke, who wore the uniform of an SS major.

Compared to the night before, the passage into the centre of Berlin was tranquil. The streets were quiet, if barely passable. Remnant SS units were nowhere to be seen. Tank barriers were unmanned. There were no other vehicles in motion whatsoever, and even the artillery had died down. Now only occasional rounds could be heard. That relative silence was the sign that the troops of the Red Army were moving in, and it was what told Patterson and McKay the time had come.

Still the unerring cockiness with which Dettke drove, his knowledge of the streets, confirmed Patterson. Even in the ghostliness of Berlin that night, or especially in it, they'd have been lost without him. It took less than half an hour to arrive at Wilhelmstrasse. The once-elegant avenue down which the elite of Germany's armed forces had goose-stepped in the moon's light had the eerie look now of the moon itself. Countless craters, concrete rubble, twisted tangles of iron, the skeletons of automobiles, the wreckage of tanks, and the charred stumps of trees testified to what had happened, but so grotesquely as to make even men who'd inflicted such damage forget for a moment why. Here and there fires still blazed. The artillery barrage had only within two hours eased off. The sterile rectangular concrete buildings inspired by Gropius and Behrens loomed over the waste endlessly, for miles it seemed, like the walls of a new canyon looming over the fissure of the earthquake which had just created them.

The two vehicles drove slowly up Wilhelmstrasse. Each man strained to take in what he was seeing. As they drove by the *Reichskanzlei* Dettke pointed to Hitler's balcony, but did not speak. It struck Patterson that the balcony was undamaged. Even the eagle with its swastika was intact. Hitler could have safely stood there throughout years of bombing raids and now a whole week of close-range artillery, watching everything as if it were an electrical storm. But Hitler was in hiding. Even as they left the

Chancellery behind, Patterson reflected that Hitler was hiding in rooms below them. When does one's shelter become one's grave?

In the block before Unter den Linden, Dettke slowed and McKay in the ambulance did likewise. The building on their right was set back from the avenue more than the others, and even in the dark its contrast with the sluggish Bauhaus gloom of the government buildings was striking. This was Albert Speer's Ministry for Armaments and Munitions, but first it had been the eighteenth-century palace of the last Hohenzollern. A huge five-storey building that occupied several acres, it nevertheless achieved an effect of relative modesty in part by the delicate rococo ornamentation of its façade, and by the fusion of different architectural elements. From Wilhelmstrasse the structure was dominated by a single-storeyed portico with an elaborate gable arching towards a much higher peaked roof of gracefully framed opaque glass. It seemed to have been added, perhaps in the nineteenth century, as a canopy over the inner courtyard. The central section of the building was flanked on both sides by imposing wings, which ended at the corners in pavilions three storeys higher than the rest of the building. Their round turretlike roofs suggested a medieval fortification. Patterson knew that the building was laid out in a square and so assumed that its character, a subdued monumentality, was the same from Unter den Linden, though from that side, he knew, the elaborate portico housed the main stairway entrance, while here it served as the gate to the courtyard.

Dettke pulled the car up to a position twenty metres away from the wrought-iron grillework. The ambulance stopped immediately behind. Neither Dettke nor McKay shut his engine off. Patterson got out of the car, approached the gate, attached a small device to the foot-square lock-box and then quickly stepped back. A small explosion jolted the gate. Then Patterson opened it. The car and the ambulance drove through. Patterson closed the gate behind them. He had to stifle a shudder that their entry was achieved so easily. They were moving at exactly the moment between the defenders' flight and the conquerors' arrival.

The vehicles pulled up side by side in the middle of the glass-covered courtyard. Patterson opened the car door for Neisen and said, 'Your show, doctor.'

'Right.' Neisen got out smartly, carrying a flashlight and, hanging from a strap around his neck, a canvas-covered case the size of an auto battery, the colour of fatigues. He looked around the courtyard, then pointed. 'North-west corner.'

McKay drove the ambulance the forty metres to that corner. A huge bulkhead with a pair of steel doors covered an area large enough to accommodate a truck even larger than the ambulance. There were handles for four men on each door. Neisen, McKay, Patterson, and Cooper each took one and, with a common heave, opened first one door, then the other, exposing a steep, cobbled ramp.

Nichols stayed in the back seat of the automobile with his pistol aimed at Dettke.

McKay and Patterson unloaded four jerricans and two dozen sticks of dynamite. Then McKay got back in the ambulance and drove it slowly down the ramp. Within moments he reappeared on foot.

'I'd say a storey and a half. There are sealed lead doors down there.'

'That's it,' Neisen said.

The four men closed the steel bulkhead again.

Cooper, staring up through the glass canopy at the corner pavilion, said, 'Couldn't be better. That tower will fall like cards.'

'Give us a cap or two for these, sergeant-major,' Patterson said, indicating the sticks they'd kept out.

Cooper went to work on the sticks, wiring them into bundles and preparing detonators.

Patterson and McKay, each carrying two jerricans, followed Neisen into the palace. In the shadows a broad marble staircase led up to the main level where the great hall with its legendary candelabra and magnificent statuary in grandiose baroque interiors displayed the vitality of another failed empire. But Neisen, holding his case to keep it from banging against his stomach, cut behind the staircase and ducked into a narrow basement corridor. If Neisen knew exactly where he was going, it was because German physicists captured only weeks before had described the network of tunnels that wound beneath the ministry.

The group had descended, in Patterson's estimate, the equivalent of two storeys when the spiralling iron staircase in its cement sleeve ended in a steel door. Neisen found the latch and tried to open it, but the door did not budge.

Patterson, standing right behind him, thought immediately of going back for Cooper. They'd have to blow it. But Neisen took a key from his pocket, applied it to the lock, and the door opened.

Neisen looked back quickly at his two companions. 'Otto Hahn, bless his soul.'

The door opened on a small chamber six feet long, at the end of which was another heavy metal door. This one, Patterson realized, was not steel but lead. Neisen had a second key out now, but he faced Patterson and McKay. 'You may not want to come in here. There's no telling what it will be.'

'You mean radiation,' Patterson said.

'Yes.'

'The risks have been explained to us,' McKay said.

'We agreed' – Patterson touched Neisen's elbow – 'if it's safe enough for you, it'll do for us as well.'

Neisen untied the canvas flap that covered the box at his chest. He withdrew a small rod, adjusted dials, and ran the rod along the threshold of the door and up both edges. A series of faint but distinct clicks came steadily from the instrument. Patterson had never seen a Geiger counter before.

Neisen faced them again. 'Even through lead, unless the seams were airlocked, which these aren't, we can get a reading. The clicks count the charged particles being released from radioactive material. If it was contaminated in there, you wouldn't hear them as clicks, but as a whine, an unbearable sound.' He turned the machine off. 'I think it's safe.' He turned the key and opened the door about two inches, then he switched on the counter again. The clicks were somewhat louder and coming more rapidly, but not so fast that Patterson didn't suspect he was imagining the difference.

Neisen turned the machine off and pushed the door open. It led on to an iron balcony. Even though Neisen presumably knew what to expect, he seemed as surprised as Patterson to find that they were standing near the gently arching ceiling of a dimly lit two-storey-high room the walls of which were covered entirely with row upon row of books. It was like the scriptorium of a monastery, with that medieval tranquillity, but there was the unmistakable odour of dung and urine. Before books, horses. From the balcony on which they stood, an iron stairway led down to a catwalk about halfway between the ceiling and the floor. The catwalk, circling the entire room, offered access to the upper bookshelves and, immediately across from their perch, to a pair of large metal doors in front of which stood a crude elevator. On the floor of the room, where one might have expected other shelves and tables if it were only a library, there was a gleaming stainless-steel machine the size of a ship's boiler and consisting in large part of a pair of tubes a yard or more in diameter. A set of pipes like ordinary heating ducts led from the machine up to the ceiling. Wires and switches and smaller metal tubes were everywhere around it.

'What the hell is that?' McKay asked, despite himself.

'A cyclotron,' Neisen answered. And then he added absently, 'An atom smasher.' He gazed around at the shelves. Not only thousands of books, but also hundreds of boxes of documents yet to be filed. 'This is the archives of the *Uranverein*. Everything is here.'

'Is that the "uranium machine"?' Patterson asked.

'The "uranium machine" is many machines.' Neisen began to lead the way down the iron stairs.

They were just below the level of the catwalk when the lights in the room went out. Each froze where he was. They could hear a soft whirring, a motor pumping air into the room.

After perhaps two minutes during which nothing moved, the faint squeak of leather could be heard below.

Neisen said, 'Friedrich, it is me, Eric.'

There was no response.

Neisen repeated himself.

And a voice said, 'Eric Neisen?'

'Yes, Friedrich.' And then he spoke in German. It was Friedrich Nagel.

Nagel said, 'Who's with you? Americans?'

'Yes,' McKay said. 'I'm Colonel John McKay, the United States Army.'

'Turn on the lights, Friedrich, so you can see.'

After a moment the lights sputtered on, still dim, but by comparison to the pitch-black, the room was brilliantly illuminated now.

Nagel stepped out from behind the machine, a short bald man meticulously dressed in a dark suit and vest. A gold watch chain curved across his belly.

Neisen whispered to Patterson, 'Dr Nagel and I were the only two in our group' – he mimed the act of drinking – 'who believed the elbow was as important as the brain.' He leaned over the railing towards Nagel. 'May I see your work, Friedrich?'

Nagel waved him down.

Patterson and McKay, still carrying the cans of gasoline, stayed where they were until Neisen had joined Nagel, then they descended the remaining stairs carefully. Nagle had just opened a heavy metal chest, and as Patterson and McKay approached, he said to Neisen, 'Four milligrams.'

Inside the chest was a small lead box. Neisen leaned over it as if a closer look would tell him something. Then he switched on the Geiger counter and brought the small rod close to the box. The clicks were about as before.

Nagel shook his head sadly. 'We are not ignorant. You think we have less regard for life than you? Turn off the *Geiger-zähler*.'

'What is it?' Patterson asked. He put his jerricans down and drew closer.

Nagel answered promptly. 'Plutonium, four milligrams.' He gestured at the cyclotron. 'Extracted from uranium by the centrifuge method.'

'Four milligrams?' Patterson said dumbly. He had never heard of plutonium.

'Yes, four, like several grains of salt, my friend. Although this is in the form of dust particles, thousands of them. It is as close as we came. It would take several pounds to produce an explosive reaction, but a millionth of a gram is sufficient to poison you. There is enough here for everyone in Berlin.'

'How long did four milligrams take?'

'One year,' Nagel said. 'Our purpose here was simply to develop the information needed to design and build a plant for large-scale conversion of uranium into plutonium. And in that we have succeeded. The Furies spring from the blood of the dying Uranus, whose name, you know, means "heaven".'

But Pluto, Patterson thought, was the god of the underworld.

Neisen said, 'Friedrich, we expected that you would have moved to production by now. Everything we find indicates you haven't.'

'We could have. Of course we could have.'

'Why didn't you?'

Nagel fixed Neisen with a stare. 'For the same reason you didn't.' He picked up the small lead box. 'What man of conscience would loose this on the world? You think I should have come to America like Firsch and Bohr, don't you? I stayed and Heisenberg stayed and Harteck stayed to control the research. The U-Project remained at the institute. The *Wehrmacht* never could take it from us. Speer would have given Hitler the weapon, but we fooled him. We made it impossible. We slowed it down

242

at every point. We did so deliberately! Such a weapon in Hitler's hands! In any man's hands! It would turn him into Hitler!'

Patterson and McKay exchanged a look. How often had they heard collaborators argue that effective resistance comes only from those who pretend to co-operate?

'And now we must destroy it, yes?'

Neisen nodded. 'But I want a summary of your findings.'

'No,' Nagel said.

'Verbally then. Have you used the centrifuge to obtain U-235?'

Instead of answering, Nagel crossed to the jerricans that Patterson had put down, hefted one, and began to splash gasoline on the nearby rows of files.

'We'd better move,' McKay said.

Neisen said forlornly, 'I wanted to see what they had done.'

'No, you didn't, doctor,' Patterson said. 'You wanted to destroy it.'

Neisen stepped towards the cyclotron. 'I wanted to see.' But then, as if shaken by the lapels, he snapped upright. He pulled the leather strap over his head to free the Geiger counter, and he put it on the metal table near the chest that held the plutonium. He lifted a can of gasoline and joined Nagel in splashing the documents. McKay and Patterson watched them. This was their work. They knew where to concentrate the flammable liquid, and they were the ones for whom the frenzied asperges was cathartic.

'We'd better get the door, group captain.' McKay led Patterson up to the catwalk. Feet clanging, they circled to the pair of huge leaden doors. They threw the bolts and swung them back easily, opening the room to the ramp on which, at that very point, the ambulance sat. When Patterson turned back to the room, he was transfixed by the sight of Neisen and Nagel systematically dousing the papers. Nagel was bawling like a child.

'Dynamite,' McKay said.

'Right.'

By the time he and McKay returned to the cavernous chamber, each with an armful of bundled sticks, Neisen and Nagel had emptied all four jerricans and were now bent together on their knees in the far corner of the room. From the stairs it looked to Patterson as if they were praying, but when he approached he saw that they had lowered into a lined compartment in the floor the sealed chest that held the plutonium. While McKay placed the dynamite sticks at various places under and around the cyclotron, Patterson watched as Nagel with liturgical solemnity closed the heavy latch and sealed it. Plutonium, Patterson repeated to himself, as if to carve the word in his memory. Named for Pluto.

Patterson touched their shoulders. 'We must go.'

Neisen looked vacantly up at him.

'We must go, doctor.'

Neisen started to help Nagel up, but Nagel shook him off and stood by himself.

At the top of the spiral staircase, Nagel turned abruptly. '*Der Geigerzähler!*' he said and pushed by the others. Rapidly he descended the stairs again. A moment later he returned, clutching the Geiger counter.

At the door, Nagel, with a courtly bow, insisted the others precede him. They did. But Nagel didn't follow. At the threshold he handed the counter to Neisen. 'You should check afterwards, to be certain.'

Neisen nodded, and then he threw something past Nagel into the room. It bounced off the iron railing with the ping of a coin.

McKay and Patterson realized at the same instant that Nagel intended to remain behind. They moved forward together, but Neisen blocked them, and the door slammed closed.

Patterson shoved Neisen aside and threw himself futilely against the door. 'Herr Nagel! You can't!'

They could hear the sound of the man's footsteps clattering down the stairs.

'Give me the key!'

Neisen shook his head, and Patterson realized that the key was what he'd thrown inside. Neisen said, 'He doesn't want to be taken. He knows they'll make him work on it.'

'Tell him the Russians won't capture us,' McKay said. 'We'll get out tonight.'

'We can't let them at either of you,' Patterson added.

Neisen seemed amused. 'He doesn't want to be taken by our side either. In his opinion, there is no difference.'

Patterson banged on the door. 'Nagel! Nagel!' He roughly grabbed Neisen's sweater. 'Call him, doctor!'

'Herr Nagel's decision merits your respect, young man! If I were he I'd be doing it myself.'

'How do you know he's not slipping out some tunnel?'

'You'll know in a moment. We would do well to remove ourselves from here. There will not be oxygen enough in there to feed the explosion and the combustion of the gasoline. The vacuum created will multiply force many times.' Neisen freed himself, then led the way up the stairs.

Halfway up they encountered Cooper on his way down. 'I was just going to check the detonator.'

'That won't be necessary,' Neisen said, and squeezed past him.

'What gives?'

'The Kraut's going to do it,' McKay said.

'Without a transmitter?'

'He'll find a way, sergeant-major. About-face now, old boy, and double time, chop-chop.'

In the courtyard everyone piled into the car except Patterson and Neisen. Out of Dettke's hearing Patterson asked, 'What about the plutonium?'

Neisen answered, 'Won't explode. The danger is release. We'll know after.'

'He meant it then, about slowing the project and deceiving Hitler?'

Neisen nodded. 'Would that we had all done as much.' Neisen turned and got into the car.

Patterson stood on the running board. Dettke dutifully started the engine and backed the car out of the palace courtyard. Patterson leaned in towards Cooper. 'Sergeant-major, how far?'

'One thousand metres, sir.'

'That's you, Herr Dettke.'

A thousand metres down Wilhelmstrasse, in the canyon of government buildings, they stopped.

'Give it sixty seconds, sergeant-major,' Patterson said. 'Then blow it.'

But only seconds later there was a clap, a sharp sound followed by an instant of silence and then the familiar low rumble of an explosion rolling across the night city. The palace itself was not visible, but suddenly the sky above it shone with stark red light in which splinters of glass and tumbling shards of stone and wood glowed spectacularly.

They watched until the light faded and the debris disappeared and the roar was swallowed by the night's peculiar calm.

'Go back,' Patterson ordered.

The pavilion at the north-west corner of the palace was gone. A plateau, not a pile, of rubble from which smoke and, here and there, flames licked at the wind had replaced it. The main body of the palace with its exposed wings yawned over the waste.

Neisen got out of the car. Patterson and McKay followed him.

They drew as close to the ruin as the flames would allow, and far enough from the car so that Dettke could not see what they were doing. Neisen adjusted the dials on the Geiger counter and held the rod up as if to read the wind.

The Geiger counter was silent. 'Nothing,' Neisen said. He looked at Patterson bitterly. 'So we succeeded.'

In Patterson's opinion, it seemed an altogether perfunctory check, but what else could they do? He said nothing.

As they approached the car again, they noticed a strange noise echoing down Wilhelmstrasse from the direction of the Potsdamer Platz.

It was the direction in which they had to go now, so Patterson ordered Dettke to approach slowly.

'Christ,' McKay said. 'It's the army.'

But it appeared to be a mob, hundreds of crazed, charging men, storming the *Reichskanzlei*.

'It's the Russians,' Dettke said. He slumped on the wheel. 'Let him be alive! Let the devil be alive!'

If there was pleasure in seeing with his own eyes the very moment of Hitler's defeat, if there was relief, Dettke could not savour them. Patterson pressed the barrel of his pistol against the SS insignia at his throat. 'You wouldn't want to greet your liberators dressed like that, *Herr Oberbannführer*. Turn around. Take us through the Tiergarten.'

CHAPTER TWENTY

It was easier, as it happened, to get into the Tiergarten than it was to get out. They'd entered at Unter den Linden through the Brandenburg Gate and were able to drive rapidly down the East-West Axis because, as Hitler's airstrip, it was still free of craters, fallen trees, and piles of rubble. At the Victory Column they stopped. They heard the rattling of tanks coming at them, but from which direction they couldn't tell. Oil fumes, faintly at first, then rankly, filled the air. Dettke cut back towards the familiar ground near the zoo.

But that brought them to the flak tower near the Zoo Station. Now they could see the tanks rumbling into position; the creaking steel of their treads jarred the earth. In the darkness the armoured machines presented otherworldly silhouettes that seemed unconnected to the grunting motors. They looked like moving coffins.

On that first night when Dettke had pointed out this flak tower as the twin of the one in which Hitler's airplane was hidden, it had seemed a monumental sepulchre, but now, to Patterson it seemed familiar, almost friendly, perhaps because its dozens of steel-plate shutters were open and light shone from the apertures cut in the thick concrete. The ghostly shades of figures could be seen waving squares of cloth, red flags perhaps or white ones. Patterson recalled that having been abandoned by the *Wehrmacht* days before, the ten-storey bunker was occupied now by several thousand civilians who'd sought refuge from the bombardment.

The Russian tanks, with a stupefied deliberation, half-encircled the tower. Foot soldiers whose steel helmets resembled the helmets of GIs, not Nazis, slipped in beside the tanks. The tanks found their positions and stopped. When the noise of the creaking, rattling motion fell away, the shouts of the people in the huge bunker could be heard.

From the top of a hill several hundred metres removed, over-looking a ravaged forest and the remains of two zoo buildings, Patterson and his party watched as the tanks – he counted seventeen of them – began blasting the tower with their cannon. A pandemonium of splitting noise broke loose, and flames snapped out of the muzzles like tongues.

Snakes' tongues. Patterson shifted in his seat to look at McKay. It was like a memory from boyhood, that one of Mac from only a night ago – 'Together now, one, two . . .'

McKay, sensing Patterson's stare, returned it.

'Jesus, Mary, and Joseph!' Nichols said.

The heavy doors of the tower swung open, even as the shells riddled the bunker, and panicked civilians began to stream out of it. They ran, ducking, while cement fragments and pieces of shrapnel flew around them. The gunners in the tanks and the foot soldiers crouching at the iron treads opened fire with their machine guns and rifles. The volleys rattled against the concrete like silverware in a drawer. Ejected cartridge cases could be seen against the light of the firing, jumping like sparks.

'Murder!' Nichols said. 'Murder!'

In a matter of moments hundreds of bodies, mostly of women and children, lay strewn on the ground around the tower, and all of them seemed to continue to writhe and bounce and jerk beneath the conflagration. Still, terrified inside that mammoth tomb against which the artillery pounded as if it were a beast that refused to fall, people pushed savagely to get out. From the upper storeys people leapt. Soon the entranceways began to be blocked by piles of corpses.

Patterson looked at McKay again. He took refuge from the horror of what they were seeing by focusing on this man who had caused him such distress. But now he could not remember what had gone wrong between them.

What they were watching seemed to push the ordinary constraints of consciousness aside. Patterson could feel the profoundest ache rising in him, and if he looked from the sight of the massacred civilians across the shadows to the face of John McKay, it was because for a long time now his dream of having such an ache soothed was a dream of that man. He wanted to ask him to define the meaning of what they were seeing. What could they do against such evil? He wanted to ask what a child would ask his father if he had the words.

Patterson's dilettante father had been a geyser of expressiveness compared to McKay. Patterson had never thought to question his father's love. Why, then, was he so desperate now for a modicum of affirmation? But he knew. His gracious, large-hearted father loved everyone, the servants and the townspeople and the cousins and the patrons of his salons and the young artists he supported. His love was spacious and uncritical and could do everything for a lad but make him feel unique.

What one needed was the love of a man who hoarded himself. Patterson believed that when McKay at last unchecked himself, his affection would sustain its object forever.

What the hell should we do, Mac? How shall we stop it? Absurdly, Patterson believed that McKay had answers to such questions. He could stop the fiery flight of the tracer shells in their tracks. He could make the Russians see what he, Patteron, was only seeing now for the first time. Even if they are Nazis there, those targets, those flaming bodies, they are just men, not devils; the sons and daughters of men, not devils; the wives and mothers of men, not devils.

The guns, in a permanent riveting staccato, continued.

Corpses in mounds below the apertures from which they fell like overripe fruit continued to writhe long after they were dead as bullets by the hundreds pumped into them.

Not devils, Patterson repeated to himself. But then his mind began an argument with itself, an argument behind which it could take shelter. This was pandemonium if ever anything was, and *pandemonium*, the argument ran, is from the Greek and means 'abode of all devils'.

Patterson poked Dettke. 'Let's move.'

Dettke only swung at Patterson, as if to underscore his unwillingness.

Patterson levelled his pistol.

The German moved slowly, then swung the car around and retraced the route towards the Victory Column, but they were cut off again. That quarter of the Tiergarten was swarming with troops who, after a week of awful fighting, had finally overrun the centre of Berlin. Now, apparently disoriented by the utter collapse of their enemy, they were converging on the flak tower. The flak tower was what remained to them of war. Surely every victory involves for a moment a loss of purpose, of clarity, of drive. Now what?

Hundreds of soldiers moved en masse or in isolated bunches towards the raging ranks. From the vantage, always at a distance, of the automobile, the victors were queerly silent, as if bewildered by the scorched landscape. Their progress behind horse-drawn gun wagons and creaking motor vehicles was not disciplined, precisely, not a march, but from a distance it had the unity of that trancelike sway one notes in a cortege winding its way through a cemetery. And, as over a throng of mourners, the question hung: What will we do when it's over?

That was not the question of the men in the automobile. Dettke drove alternately slowly with the headlights out, or rapidly with the lights on, depending on the proximity of Russians. If there was an order to his turns and U-turns, stops and starts, the others could not sense it. They were lost in a maze of roads and garden pathways, but Dettke never hesitated, succeeded repeatedly in avoiding the Russians, and no one dared ask where they were or if they could get out.

They came suddenly upon a squad of soldiers who, when they saw the large, official-looking car, raised their weapons and began to rush them. Dettke stopped the car and frantically began to unbutton his Nazi officer's tunic. But Patterson jammed him with his pistol. Dettke shifted into reverse and plunged the car back into the pitch-black centre of the Tiergarten.

*

'We have to wait it out,' Patterson said. The car was hidden in a tangle of shrubs. A Russian patrol had just missed them. It was clear now that they were surrounded by thousands of Red Army soldiers.

Dettke raised his hands off the wheel in a gesture of resignation. 'We should find an officer and identify ourselves.' He started to get out, but Nichols garrotted him from behind.

'I think Herr Dettke is right,' Neisen said.

'You're speaking out of turn, doctor,' McKay said. 'Group Captain Patterson is C-in-C here.'

Patterson said briskly, 'They'll understand soon that they've won, that it's over. In the daylight they won't think twice about us.'

Nichols released Dettke, who said, 'I propose leaving the car here. We can return to Schöneberg on foot. It is less than five kilometres.'

'Out of the question. We'll need this car to leave Berlin. It's your best chance of getting rid of us. We stay with it and for now we stay together.'

Dettke looked back at Neisen. 'So, brigadier, you were to make contact with Zhukov, representing Churchill.'

'He never believed it, doctor,' McKay said. 'Don't let him play you.'

'I won't, colonel. Never fear.' Neisen smiled weakly at Dettke. 'Deception is merely one of many sins, and far from the gravest, that we have made our peace with. Don't you agree?'

Now Dettke did take off the SS tunic. He bundled it and threw it out the window.

It no longer served Patterson's purposes to have him vulnerable to the Russians, so he said nothing.

When they set out again, well after dawn, Patterson was at the wheel because of his knowledge of Russian. They crossed the park without incident. In a steady drizzle, the victorious army had apparently taken cover.

But from the perimeter road they saw ahead a contingent of troops lounging on the quays of the Landwehr Canal. Patterson drove directly up to them, put his head out the window, ignoring the rain. As he slowed the car to a halt he asked several sharp questions. The soldiers tried nervously to come to attention. They wore the brown uniforms, stars on their breasts, of the Red Army, but they were Orientals.

In response to Patterson's questions, they only shrugged, looked at one another and giggled boyishly.

Patterson said to his companions, 'They don't speak Russian. They're Mongolians.'

Cooper exhaled audibly, but his relief was premature.

One of the Reds approached the car with an arm behind his back.

McKay and Nichols both had their weapons ready.

But then the soldier brought his arm forward with a flourish and offered them a bottle of champagne. The soldiers behind watched Patterson anxiously, and when he took it, they laughed in relief. Patterson thanked them. As he drove slowly across the canal, the Mongolians, without concealing their bottles now, waved happily.

'You expect them to be animals,' Dettke observed. 'That is Goebbels' lie about them.'

No one in the car replied, and no one seemed inclined to drink the champagne.

In order to avoid unnecessary contact with the occupiers, they set out for the Schöneberg district in the south by heading west on the Kurfürstendamm. Progress along that heavily bombed street was slow, but the only Russians they saw were looters too intent upon ransacking the remains of the once-fashionable stores to notice them. At the end of the Kurfürstendamm they drove south on the Avus, Hitler's showpiece Grand-Prix highway that bisected the Grunewald. In the morning rain, with the mists rising off the nearby Wannsee towards a pewter sky, the huge Berlin forest seemed, especially by comparison to the ravaged city around it, enchanted.

When they came to the bridge that led out of Berlin towards Potsdam – it was how they would flee the city – Patterson turned east again, but with a reluctance that surprised him. They had to return to the convent to replenish their supply of gasoline for the dash towards the American lines. Otherwise Patterson would have dumped Dettke and fled across the bridge. He had been numb for hours, but now a fresh feeling ambushed him. He wanted out of Berlin, out of this bloody war, out of the company of ruthless men, and out of the frigid presence of John McKay. Ironically Patterson had hoped this mission would rekindle their old friendship, but it had, instead, finally made Patterson feel that their relationship was too complicated ever to succeed. Out, he thought while turning in, just get me out!

In the broad cobbled marketplace between the Schöneberg Town Hall and the imposing façade of the Convent of Sancta Magdalene which neither Patterson nor McKay had seen in daylight before, were drawn up in no particular order several vehicles of the Red Army. From the tower of the Town Hall was hanging a large red flag, and from several windows of the convent opposite, small red flags could be seen.

Columns of smoke rose from between the trucks and horsecarts and half-tracks, but these were campfires protected from the rain by canopies strung between the tops of the vehicles. The odour of cooking meat could be distinguished from the more pervasive odour of sodden ash. As Patterson drove into the square itself, they saw soldiers with blankets over their heads against the rain idling by their carts and horses. From truck windows the boots of sleeping men protruded. Patterson had to bark an order at a circle of soldiers who were blocking the way. As they moved aside they stared glumly at the car and its occupants. These were Russians, not Mongolians, and they were not drunk.

Driving past the main entrance of the convent, they stared up at it. Two dozen rain-washed stairs led up from the square to a pair of oversized oaken doors in front of which three soldiers were posted with their rifles unslung. Rain dripped off their helmets. Patterson drove slowly to the corner and took it. Halfway down the block he turned into the courtyard.

'Why isn't the gate shut?' Dettke asked no one in particular, and he craned forward to look up at the windows.

A soldier, his rifle ready, stepped out of the doorway and shouted, waving them off.

Patterson called back at him, then said under his breath, 'Off limits, he says. Give me a minute.' He got out of the car and crossed to the soldier.

He returned to the car a moment later and, leaning in, said to Neisen, 'I told him you are the Archbishop of Berlin come to see the nuns. We're your priests. We are dressed like this because of the Nazis. Weapons away. Let's go.'

The guard averted his eyes as they filed past him.

The first person they came upon was Professor Isenberg. He was sprawled across several of the topmost stairs that led up to the main hallway. The stairwell was dark. Patterson and Dettke approached Isenberg together and stooped over him. He seemed to be staring up at them, but he was dead. Dettke raised him by the shoulders to hug him, while Patterson touched his hand. It was cold and hard. He'd been dead for hours. When Dettke released the corpse, blood, dark and sticky with coagulation, stained his shirt. He said, 'The SS must have come at the end.'

Each of the six stepped carefully over Isenberg and ascended the remaining stairs.

Dettke pushed against the door, but something blocked it. He pushed harder, then Patterson and McKay pushed with him. Light from the hallway poured into the stairwell as they forced the door open.

Blocking it had been not one corpse but two. A hulking, brown-tunicked Russian soldier with his trousers bunched at his thighs lay with his hands locked around the throat of a naked old woman, whose own hand, even in death, clutched at the Russian's. Her face was grotesquely frozen, gasping for air. They lay together on a bed of the nun's robes, white and black, but also red with blood which had poured from the Russian's chest, from which protruded the handles, only the handles, of a seamstress's scissors.

'*Mutter*,' Dettke said softly. '*Mutter*.' She was the Mother Superior.

Then they heard the soft whimpering, the stifled sounds of children, many children, who were trying not to weep. Dettke led the way across the hall towards the chapel. Its heavy doors had been rammed open, and now were splintered and barely ajar. When Dettke swung one of the doors towards him, a single piercing wail went up in the chapel and was followed by the loud cries of dozens of girls. They were huddled in the sanctuary at the far end, holding on to each other as if that platform were a raft. The room was in chaos. Pews were upended. The stained-glass windows that had survived two years of bombing had been shattered by benches and *prie-dieux*. The arms and legs of several small bodies could be seen protruding from beneath the upturned pews. Stations of the Cross had been ripped from the walls. Incongruously, the white porcelain tank of a toilet lay amid the shattered wood and glass.

The corpse of a man in a Russian uniform lay crumpled in one corner. Lying near him was Karl Schott, clutching a heavy candlestick. At first it seemed he was dead, too, but when Dettke lifted him, he opened his eyes, or rather an eye. Half of his battered face was horribly swollen and that eye was altogether closed. Blood streaked from it. Dettke spoke his name. Schott pulled himself up and looked around. He saw the dead Russian, then looked at the candlestick in his own hand. He dropped it. Dettke hugged him.

Patterson and McKay approached the sanctuary. McKay said to the children, '*Angst haben Sie nicht!*'

But the girls shrieked louder the closer they came.

There were more than forty of them, including the youngest girls in the orphanage, five-year-olds. Most still wore their white muslin shifts, but some were in underwear and some had wrapped themselves in towels and sheets.

'*Angst haben Sie nicht,*' McKay repeated.

An older girl, perhaps fourteen, stood apart suddenly. She was half naked. She began to wave a red square of cloth frantically and to cry in a singsong, '*Hitler ist kaputt! Willkommen Russe! Hitler ist kaputt! Willkommen Russe!*' Some of the others picked up the chant.

Dettke had helped Schott to his feet, and they now approached the sanctuary too. The sight of the panicked girls brought Schott back, and he immediately began to go from child to child, soothing them.

Dettke too walked among the girls, but more purposefully, Quickly it was obvious that the one for whom he was looking wasn't there. He began to call, softly at first, then loudly, 'Anna-Lise! Anna-Lise?' Then he bolted from the chapel.

Nichols, who'd remained by the door, went after him.

'I've got him, Mac.' Patterson went after Dettke and Nichols, while McKay, Neisen, and Cooper joined Schott in trying to comfort the children.

In the hall Nichols was just coming out of the refectory. 'I thought he went in there, but he didn't.'

'Check the cellars!' Nichols started to go off, but Patterson stopped him. 'And, corporal . . .'

'Sir?'

Patterson's mind settled finally on the grim fact. The Russians simply could not learn about Neisen's mission.

'We have to kill him.'

Nichols stared at Patterson for a moment, then said simply, 'Well, fuck.' He turned and dashed down the stairs.

Patterson drew his pistol and went up.

On the fourth floor a curtain wafted from behind an open door just off the stairwell. It was a nun's cell, and a throaty slurping sound was coming from it. He put the muzzle of his pistol in a fold of the curtain and jerked it aside.

A naked man lay on the floor, his face resting in a pool of vomit which, in respirating, he sucked in and out of his mouth and nostrils. A stench rose, apparently from the vomit. It seemed he'd been grievously wounded because blood fresher than either Isenberg's or the Mother Superior's oozed out from under him.

On the bed was a brown jacket with epaulettes and tarnished bars; the man was an officer.

Patterson lifted him with his foot.

The officer rolled over and uncovered a girl on whom he'd lain, an unclothed child without even the first hint of breasts or pubic hair, from whose vagina all that blood had flowed. It was not flowing now. She was dead.

The Russian looked up at Patterson groggily and he said in his own language that the first ones to reach the convent were dogs, filthy dogs. He looked at the dead girl, then, bewildered, back at Patterson. We posted guards, he said, so this wouldn't happen.

Patterson shot him.

As gently as he could he lifted the dead child and put her on the bed. A cross hung on the wall just there; it had no *Christus*, and in the back of his brain that triviality jarred Patterson, who thought Catholics were devoted to the ravaged body of Jesus. He took the cross down and placed it on the child's breast, and folded her hands on it. As he covered her a mournful tune crossed his consciousness like the shadow of a cloud. The words came. 'Comfort ye, comfort ye my people, saith your God; speak ye comfortably to Jerusalem; and cry unto her that her warfare is accomplished.'

As Patterson approached Anna-Lise's garret room he could hear the voices of two men arguing fiercely. They were arguing in Russian. Patterson stopped at the door and listened.

One was viciously denouncing the other as a disgrace to Russia and the martyrs of the Revolution. In reply the other whimpered that he had saved the youngest, that he had driven the pigs off and posted guards. It wasn't his fault. The men were intoxicated with victory.

And what are you intoxicated with? You have proven the worst lie of Goebbels about us to be the truth!

The lies of Goebbels! With a shock Patterson realized that the first voice was familiar. He pushed the door just enough to see into the room. The second man was naked and on his knees in front of Jörg Dettke. And Patterson understood.

Jörg Dettke was Russian! A Russian agent all these years in Berlin!

He was standing over the officer with the officer's own pistol. Beyond them Anna-Lise was sprawled across her bed, naked, her face and body horribly bruised. She was curled, spine-out, around her chest, but was twisted enough to reach a hand into the nearby cradle. She lacked the strength to rise to see her baby.

Dettke, speaking softly, still in Russian, told the officer that the woman he raped was the mother of his child.

The officer clutched at Dettke's legs. But I saved her! I saved her from the pigs! I came up here with her to protect her!

Dettke shot him.

The gunshot startled the infant and she began to cry. Anna-Lise struggled to reach her. Patterson saw that her sheets were blood-stained.

Dettke stepped over the Russian's body, went to the cradle, and picked up his daughter. He offered her his finger, which she took hungrily. Then he sat with her on the edge of Anna-Lise's bed. Anna-Lise had collapsed and lay inertly by Dettke and the child, unable to acknowledge them.

The child shook her head away from Dettke's finger, his useless finger, and began to wail again.

Anna-Lise raised a hand towards her. With a tenderness that moved Patterson to the edge of tears, Dettke brought his daughter down to Anna-Lise.

Anna-Lise rolled towards them, exposing her wound to Dettke apparently, and apparently for the first time, because Dettke cried out and pressed the sheet against her body to stop a flow of blood.

The child wailed. Anna-Lise insisted on taking her.

Dettke turned, a frantic expression on his face, and he saw Patterson. 'Bandages! Get bandages!' he cried.

Patterson ran headlong down the stairs and back to the chapel. Karl Schott had already obtained gauze, ointment, and bandages, and with the others was binding the wounds of children who'd been hurt.

Schott returned with Patterson to the garret room. He moved with surprising swiftness, considering his own wound, that eye.

The confidence with which Schott attended to Anna-Lise, and the fact that Dettke deferred to him, made Patterson think that Schott was perhaps a doctor.

Schott gently handed the infant to Dettke. The baby protested, but Dettke rocked her while Schott deftly wrapped Anna-Lise.

Patterson watched Dettke comforting his child. He decided it didn't matter a tinker's damn who Dettke was or what he knew.

I won't kill this man, he said to himself. Not now or ever.

CHAPTER TWENTY-ONE

Patterson waited quietly in the corridor until Karl Schott came out. They nodded at each other, and Schott started to pass. Patterson touched him. 'You should see to your eye.'

'Yes.' Schott went down the stairs.

Patterson waited a moment more, then discreetly knocked on the half-open door. 'It's Patterson. May I talk to you?'

Dettke pulled the door towards him. He was barechested, having just buckled the Russian's trousers. He was donning the dead man's uniform. Contradicting the imposing effect of his lean, muscular chest and arms, an expression of rank helplessness flickered across his face. 'You must do something for me,' he said in English.

Patterson replied in Russian that he would, happily.

At his own language, Dettke flinched. He turned slowly away. He put the brown tunic on and began to button it. He asked carefully, also in Russian, if Patterson had heard them.

'Yes. You've been here since before the war, I assume. Does she know?' Patterson nodded at Anna-Lise.

Dettke shook his head. 'No one knows.'

'Well done, major.' Patterson indicated the rank insignia of the uniform Dettke had just put on. He wore it naturally, as if it were his. But he had done as much with the Nazi general's. Patterson guessed that he held the rank of colonel or above. An NKVD agent operating for a decade in Berlin, surveilling Nazis and simultaneously playing as if they were timpani – Red Orchestra indeed! – the OSS and the SOE . . . It would rank as one of the espionage coups of the war.

Dettke ignored Patterson's compliment and crossed to sit by Anna-Lise. He touched the back of his hand to her brow. He looked at Patterson, needfully again. 'You must help us. She needs treatment, needs it gravely.'

As if to underscore his statement, Anna-Lise stirred and groaned. She had either lost consciousness or, like the baby, fallen asleep.

'She'll never get it here. There will only be more . . .' Dettke's eyes fell contemptuously on his dead comrade. 'They prefer it with the dead.' Looking desperately at Patterson, he said, 'Take her with you? Take the child?'

'You come too,' Patterson replied. Strangely he was not surprised by the attachment he felt towards this man.

Dettke stood. He fastened the collar hook at his throat. 'I must stay. First, to keep the animals away. For the children and the Sisters.' He stepped over the dead Russian. 'We are not all like him, but apparently enough are.' At the pointed garret window he paused to look out at the grey city. The rain had stopped falling. As far as one could see were rubble and the roofless shells of buildings.

'And second?'

Dettke faced Patterson. 'My duty to report.'

'Report what?'

Dettke thought before he answered. 'The events of nine years. But certain things do not concern my superiors.'

'Like what?'

'My love for Anna-Lise and . . .' Emotion pulled on his face. He looked towards her and the child. When he faced Patterson again, he said, 'Nor does my debt to you concern them. I will not mention Neisen or that you destroyed the rocketry research. It will not matter.'

Rocketry! Patterson was surprised that he had believed that, but also relieved. 'Would you like me to forget that you are Russian?'

'That does not matter either,' he said wearily. 'Hitler is defeated.'

'We defeated him together.' Patterson paused, then said, 'It's a shame, isn't it, that our partnership is over.'

Dettke stared at him in reply, then said finally, 'If it were possible to continue, I would welcome it.' He put on the officer's peaked hat. Its red star was what impressed. 'Will you take Anna-Lise and the child?'

'Of course.'

Dettke picked up the baby and handed her to Patterson. 'You will have to find milk along the way.'

Patterson looked over at Anna-Lise. 'Her milk will come back. They always have enough.' He smiled at Dettke while enclosing the child in both his arms. 'It's a miracle of nature.'

Dettke said harshly, 'But my compatriots bit off her breast.'

Patterson gasped and crushed the child against himself. 'Christ, what will become of children who have seen such things?'

'We have seen them. What will become of us?' Dettke returned to Anna-Lise, dressed her as well as he could, wrapped her in a blanket and picked her up. She awakened.

When she saw who was carrying her she said, '*Ich liebe Dich.*'

Patterson followed Dettke down the stairs, each one with his bundle. But the weight of the child was no weight. Patterson thought of his nephew, of that tiny misshapen leg, and he wondered if the impulse to take care of needs this limitless could substitute for love.

Dettke led them down to the catacomb-chapel in the sub-basement of the convent. As they approached, light from its candles flickered out into the corridor.

In the chapel Karl Schott was waiting by the altar, in front of the roses and the crucifix. It had never occurred to Patterson that Schott was a priest, but when he saw him now in a flowing white gown, a red stole around his neck, he was not surprised. Karl Schott was the convent chaplain. His vestments contrasted cruelly with the bruises on his face.

Jörg Dettke and Anna-Lise Isenberg exchanged their vows in German. Having blessed the couple, Father Schott turned to Patterson. 'You are the witness.'

'Proudly,' Giles Patterson answered.

'May I have a word with you, group captain?' McKay had just closed the right rear door of the automobile after helping to settle Anna-Lise in the back seat. Cooper and Nichols were still funnelling gasoline from jerricans into the auto tank. Neisen was already sitting in the front seat.

Patterson followed McKay to a corner of the courtyard. Behind them, Father Schott, still vested, was holding the infant, while Dettke, in his major's uniform, leaned into the car to comfort his wife.

'I'm sorry, Giles,' McKay whispered, 'but we simply cannot do this.'

'Do what, Mac? For Christ's sake!' Patterson responded brusquely, but an old feeling welled in him, the dread of his own softness, his soft middle. He had always known that at some point a pressure would be brought to bear on him and he would break under it. Not break, but leak, ooze like the liquid centre of a golf ball. John McKay could bring such pressure to bear on him. Patterson held himself rigid.

'Leave him. We cannot leave him.'

'Dettke?'

'His name is no more Dettke than mine is. He's a Russian. Did you hear him with those guards? Those *Russian* guards. He has them petrified. He's the real thing.'

'Of course he is, Mac. I'm surprised it took us this long to see it. How, precisely, does that affect the situation?'

McKay stared at Patterson in disbelief. 'He's not a Kraut whose tales to the debriefers will be dismissed as self-serving bullshit. The NKVD will know in detail what we did and whom we did it with. It was an explicit order of Churchill's. You involved Dettke, or whatever his name is. I warned you.'

'He bought the line about rocket research. He can't hurt us. It's not reason enough to kill him.'

'We could bring him with us.'

'What, in the boot, tied like a cowpoke?' These fucking Americans! Patterson's rage flew. 'Suppose we did! What happens to Sancta Magdalene then? Would you like to go back inside and explain to those girls that the show has only just begun? Yes, I saw Dettke speak to those guards! Now perhaps they'll protect these children instead of taking turns with them!'

'The priest can protect them.'

'You Catholics overestimate the power of your clergy. Father Schott is a badly wounded man. He doesn't speak Russian, and he's terrified.'

Patterson started to turn away, but McKay grabbed him. 'Giles, listen! I didn't want the hospital blown, remember? I don't want these children harmed more than they already have been. But Dettke has it in his power to ruin us! We have to cross that bridge at Potsdam. You know it. I know it. And he knows it. Our first concern has to be Neisen. Somehow the lives of children, of many more children than this, depend on his getting out of here. The Russians will stop at nothing to get him if they find out. What's to prevent Dettke from making a call?'

'The same thing that prevents him from calling those troops out in the square right now. He doesn't have to wait for us to get to the bridge. He won't do it then for the same two reasons he hasn't already done it. Anna-Lise. The child.'

'You believe him?'

'That he loves them? That they are more important to him than

260

Mother Russia or the Revolution? Why else would he have delivered them, the perfect hostages, into our care? Yes, damn right I believe him. Maybe a man can have a loyalty beyond his nation, to human beings instead of to governments.'

'You're more naïve than I thought, if you believe him.'

'I'm famous for it, Mac. I used to believe in you.'

McKay flinched. 'What the hell does that have to do with anything?'

Patterson ignored his question to continue his own thought. 'But here's the difference. If I'm wrong about Dettke, we can do something about it.'

'What?'

'We can kill the woman. We can kill the baby. What the hell, Mac, we're bloody well made of steel, aren't we? We're making the world safe for the next war. What could be more important than that? What's a little more carnage compared to what we've seen, what we've done? And Dettke knows it. We have his woman and his child, not only until we reach our own lines, but for as long as we want them. It's the perfect set of screws to turn on him.'

'Perfect if he loves them.'

'And as a Russian, of course, he couldn't. You know what, my friend, I've thought for a long time that your problem was with me, that it was *me* you couldn't respond to, couldn't, yes, love! But that isn't it at all. You don't respond to Eleanor or to Jake or to anyone. You've a stone for a heart. You wouldn't know an act of love if it fell on you.'

'Don't you dare refer that way to Eleanor and Jake, you bastard, after what you pulled! On them too you pulled it!'

'You mean in Piccadilly?'

'You know damn well I do!'

'Well, finally it comes out! At last the issue! I made a thought-less pass at the wrong chap and for the rest of my life I'm to be punished, and everything I do or say or decide, even including whether Dettke lives or dies, is to be seen in the light of that one moment. Christ, Mac! It was a mistake! I admit it! Let it go!'

McKay lowered his voice suddenly and forced himself to speak calmly. 'You've no idea, Giles, even now, what a blow it was. It was more than an idle pass, more than a thoughtless act, more than a mistake. You made me feel that I'd been foolish to trust you. Yours was my first real friendship, and you sullied it. You

261

ruined it.' McKay's voice, to his evident horror, began to waver. He stopped, collected himself, and said, 'Look, I'm sorry. I really am. I *should* let it go. I will.'

Patterson was affected by McKay's emotion, and for the first time it occurred to him that he had not understood this man. 'But you're saying nonetheless that it's ruined . . .'

McKay nodded, almost apologetically. But he had withdrawn again. He said, 'I wish you well, Giles. Truly.'

An image of McKay walking out into the rainswept London street flashed before Patterson's mind. Patterson felt air escaping a cavity in his chest. Not deflation; it was release, at last. He knew that he would never be disappointed like this again. Now the change in him that he would spend a lifetime understanding was complete. 'We blew it, Mac, didn't we?'

McKay did not respond. He was stolid again, the bastard.

Patterson turned and walked back towards the car. As he did so every impression registered, and he saw clearly the man he would be now; his callow days were over. The horrors he had seen would fuel his determination to prevent their recurrence. His determination would make Mac's resoluteness pale. He would return home not a servant of the Empire, but a servant of all humanity. If Neisen and Nagel could unblushingly embrace such an ideal, so could he. He was a changed man and he knew it, but he was not unfamiliar to himself. He was like Dettke now. Like Dettke he would risk everything for what he believed, trusting the risk itself to sustain him.

Cooper and Nichols had finished gassing the car, and had taken their places in the back seat beside Anna-Lise. Dettke was leaning across Cooper to be sure her blanket covered her. Father Schott was standing by the car, holding the child. Patterson joined him and lifted a corner of the linen wrap to look at her. She smiled at him, generously, he thought.

'She likes you,' the priest said.

'No, she's just farting.' He regretted the cynical crack as soon as he'd made it. He looked at the priest apologetically, but the priest had fixed his one eye upon the child. This Englishman's despair was no concern of his.

McKay joined them, then Dettke turned with palpable reluctance from Anna-Lise. Dettke took his daughter from the priest and offered her to Patterson, but Patterson declined. He had to drive.

Dettke looked hesitatingly at McKay.

McKay put his arms out and said, 'My son is just a little older. I need the practice.'

Dettke handed her over. 'I wish your son well, colonel.'

McKay nodded and got into the car.

Patterson crossed to get in behind the wheel.

Dettke leaned in to kiss his child, and then reached back to touch his wife one last time. She was asleep. He straightened and stepped back beside the priest. They watched impassively as Patterson drove out of the courtyard.

John McKay was the only one to speak. He was staring at the baby and he said, having just noticed, 'She's beautiful.'

BOSTON/BERLIN

1980

CHAPTER TWENTY-TWO

'So what we have seen accomplished in the period of our readings from Hawthorne through James is the utter abasement of ethical emphasis. What in Hawthorne was the temptation to defy the cosmos itself – has shrunk in James to the temptation not to behave like a decent chap.'

McKay stopped, leaned forward on his cane, and let his gaze drift across the hall full of students. This was the last lecture of the term, the one in which he made explicit the themes they'd spent the summer stalking. It pleased him not only that even the dull students had paid attention throughout his remarks but, more, that the sharp ones had stopped their furious note-taking just to listen. It surprised him regularly that these polished banalities of his could seem fresh, even important, to wide-eyed classes semester in and semester out. They had seemed important once to him. Now what mattered was getting through each class and then each term without giving himself away.

'And in our era even decency, that impoverished standard, is under assault from all quarters. But its defence today is another story, isn't it? Not the subject of this course or even of our literature so much as the first purpose of our lives.'

He stopped again. That was it. He knew it and they knew it, but together they let the silence hang for several moments.

The silence at the end of his lectures was what Jake McKay still did this for.

He stared at the students, three hundred and forty-two of them, some dabbling adults, but mostly undergraduates of Tufts University in Medford outside Boston. Jake McKay perennially drew more students to his lecture courses in American literature than anyone in the department. He felt a twinge of regret that the term was over. He preferred the informality of summer school, and the chance it gave him to concentrate on teaching, as opposed to the chores of administration. He admitted again that, despite his notion of himself as a worldly intellectual, he loved these kids for their eagerness and would have even if they did not hang on every word he said.

'Good luck in your exams. See you in the fall.'

He turned to pick up his blazer from the back of the chair. Ordinarily, unlike his laid-back colleagues, he never lectured in shirt-sleeves, but it was August and the hall wasn't air-conditioned. Even so, he wore a tie, firmly knotted.

The room exploded with the noise of the students rising, talking, and exiting as one creature.

While McKay donned his blazer his eyes were drawn through the open window to the figure of a woman cutting across the quadrangle towards East Hall, where his office was. She was blonde, tall, slim, and, compared to the girls swarming behind him, elegant-looking. Her hair was pulled into a knob at the crown of her head and she wore a tan summer dress and heeled sandals. Why was she familiar?

And then he forgot her as she disappeared from view and students crowded him to ask about the exam. Their preoccupation with grades always exasperated him, but he answered each question courteously. Generally he tried to reassure students. It was well known that he rarely gave failing grades but also that he almost never gave excellent ones.

Outdoors, the warm August air was less oppressive, and it refreshed him. Abundant shade trees sheltered the pathways from the afternoon sun. The lawn, surrounded by stately old brick buildings, offered a classic college scene, even including English ivy. But the charm of the Tufts campus, like that of beauty queens, had no edge because it was the stereotype. Small-town colleges and better prep schools all aspired to look like this. McKay often wished the place were a little seedier, and the bright scrubbed students too for that matter. Still it was impossible not to feel benign towards the scene that day.

As he crossed towards East Hall his graduate assistants trailed him. Other students waved at him from clusters on the grass. It was easy to win the affection of kids. Jake McKay was still thin, still good-looking, still, in his subdued way, a dandy who carried his slim mahogany stick with flair. That he was also smart, literary, and witty made up for the fact that he held himself slightly aloof. People had their theories about what that aloofness protected. For a man as accomplished as he was – he'd been appointed Chair of the English Department four years earlier at age thirty-three – it was widely assumed at Tufts that he couldn't be all that outstanding or he'd have been snatched away by Harvard.

His was the corner office on the third floor. Access was through his secretary's office adjoining. He paused at the door when he saw farther down the corridor the woman in the tan summer dress. She was reading notices on the bulletin board. He stared at her, somewhat rudely, but she didn't turn. He could not place her.

'Cheers, Malcolm,' he said to his secretary, a bearded young man who had dropped out of a doctoral programme years before.

'You have a visitor, prof,' Malcolm said and he winked. 'Isn't she out there? She was waiting in the hall.'

'Somebody's mother?' Jake asked. He picked up the pile of mail on the desk.

Malcolm smirked. 'She said it's personal.'

Jake stood there for a moment, undecided. Then he stepped back to the doorway and looked out into the corridor again. The woman was still at the bulletin board. He looked back at Malcolm. 'Did she say her name?'

Malcolm looked at his notepad and read, 'Dettke.'

Jake started. 'What?'

'Magda Dettke, she said.'

Unconsciously his hand went to the watch pocket of his trousers. The rush of his surprise could have cost him his composure, but he controlled himself. He fingered the lump of his father's watch. It had become his when his father died in 1962. He carried it to remember him.

He approached her slowly. Her figure seemed more youthful to him than it should have. The smooth curves of her legs and ankles; her ass. How she had aroused him! The memory of his rampant sexuality amused him. She was still angled away from him, but he knew exactly what she would look like when she faced him. That Degas dancer. That tilt of the nose. He had not thought of her in years. But neither had he forgotten her.

An observer, knowing only that this woman as a girl had smitten him one afternoon in a museum, would have misunderstood. His acute emotion at seeing her had nothing to do with a nostalgic longing for a lost infatuation. Magda Dettke? The Degas dancer, yes. But not a figment from his dreams. Rather a player in mysteries he had never plumbed and from the spell of which, therefore, he had never freed himself. His father died. His uncle disappeared. His mother lost her grip on the rail. His sisters, Dori on the verge of spinsterhood nursing their mother in Virginia, and Cicely, married and divorced three times before thirty, both lived in the cold shadow of that mystery more nakedly than he did. Jake

McKay had once regarded it as the central task of his life to understand what had destroyed his family. Yet he had not directly addressed that question in twenty years.

Approaching Magda he understood for the first time that he had always expected her to do this. And now that she had, he was in danger all at once of having to look directly at what had happened not just to his family, but to him.

'Hello, Magda,' he said.

He saw in the way she turned to face him that she had already been aware of his presence.

Green flecks in blue irises, her eyes locked on his. He remembered their last moment together, in the doorway of that clapboard house in Georgetown. She had closed his hand on a piece of paper and looked pleadingly at him. There was nothing pleading in her now. She was looking at him with curiosity and a hint of bashfulness, but without insecurity.

'Hello,' she said. Even in that one word he heard her accent. Because of the association with Degas, perhaps, he'd thought of her as French, but she was German. Her omission of his name seemed both pointed and natural, as it was with adult students who rankled at calling a peer Professor. She offered her hand.

He took it. 'It's been a long time, hasn't it?'

She nodded and smiled. 'You look good.'

'You look great!' His effusiveness surprised him, and he was aware suddenly of students in the corridor. 'Come into my office.' He stepped aside for her, but for a moment she hesitated, apparently just to look at him. He studied her. Her earnestness had a purity about it which moved him, but he was also aware of her extraordinary sensuality. Yes, of course, he thought, Degas's girl would have grown into a woman like this. Her hair, the pale brown tone of her skin, the sharp features of her face, her long slender throat, the curves implied at her breast, her waist, her hips all combined in a physicality that was more than mere bodiliness, in the way that certain rare fragrances combine in an effect that is more than perfume. It was easy for him to remember that his first sense of her was as an artifact.

As he walked behind her towards his office he was conscious of his limp, a rare thing for him, perhaps because her stride was so perfect. She walked erectly, like an African maiden. Had she been a model? Christ, he thought, I know from nothing! He felt suddenly inadequate, as if the white-washed bricks and the worn linoleum of the corridor, and, in his office, the old chairs and the lumpish desk piled high with books and papers under glaring fluorescent ceiling lights would seem tacky to her. When he was eighteen years old, hadn't his promise pointed to grander surroundings than this?

Malcolm stood up when Magda entered, and McKay said, 'You've met my hippie secretary?' Magda smiled. McKay reached past her to open the door to his own office. 'Malcolm is my revenge on the women's movement for calling me a chair.' As he closed the door behind him he said to Malcolm, 'Don't interrupt, champ, okay?'

'What a charming office,' Magda said, taking it in. It was air-conditioned and bright. There were two walls of books, two walls of windows, a view in the distance of the skyline of Boston, and a tree nearby.

Jake offered her the soft chair, but on the corner of his desk was a copy of the late edition of the *Boston Globe* and a headline held her attention.

Jake craned to read it. 'Gdansk Strike Spreads.' When she looked up at him he said, 'Amazing, eh?'

Magda shrugged. She sat on the edge of the chair, awkwardly.

He took the padded Windsor, the college chair, and adjusted it to face hers.

She said, 'The Poles attacked the Nazi tanks on horseback.' But it was clear when her eyes darted back to the newspaper that she was far from indifferent to the events in Poland. While she read the news story, she raised her hand absently to gather a pair of loose strands of yellow hair and tuck them behind her ear. Only then did McKay notice that her hair was subtly rippled with grey.

'Forgive me,' she said when she sat back.

'I think they might pull it off. The Russians have their hands full in Afghanistan.'

Magda's silence was like a dismissal; his opinion was banal.

She let her gaze fall on the photos displayed on the shelf behind his desk, one of his two children, the other of his wife leaning on a picket fence, the fence that surrounded their house in Maine.

'They're lovely,' Magda said.

It was true. His son and daughter were startlingly handsome, and his wife had a rare dark beauty that photographed uniquely.

'She is a dancer,' Magda said.

'My wife? Yes, she is.' Jake was startled by her deduction and showed it. He studied the photograph. 'You're just surmising that?'

'I knew it. She teaches dance, I believe.'

Jake nodded slowly. 'Yes. At a local college, Simmons College. How do you happen to know that?' He paused. 'Forgive me, but it's just now dawning on me that you're here. How in the world did you find me?'

Magda smiled. 'Because this is so far from Washington?'

Jake stared at her quite openly.

Magda's gaze was fixed upon the photograph of his children now. 'I don't know about your children. Could you tell me about them?'

'As if we'd just met each other, on an airplane?'

'Yes.'

After a moment he said, 'All right. Robert begins the second grade next month. He's already trying to teach himself his signature, and he collects maps. He wants to be a geographer.' Jake smiled. 'Whatever that is.'

'A geographer,' Magda said affectionately, 'shows the rest of us where we are.'

'I suppose.' Jake looked at their photo. His daughter was in his son's lap. 'Maureen worships him. Last night she had a bad dream and she wanted to sleep with her brother. I asked her why and she said because behind her eyes he got lost. She's the one who's afraid of getting lost, of course. She starts nursery school next month.'

'You must be very happy.'

Jake held her eyes. 'About my children? I am. Very.'

She said in her careful English, 'I find it difficult to remember that we were not good friends, that we knew each other for only two days.'

'Where did you go?'

'England, at first. Then I lived in Paris for many years. Now I live in England again.' She shifted in her chair and crossed her legs.

When she placed one leg over the other, the effect in his mind was cinematic. For an instant he saw her unclothed. He focused on her heeled sandals. The perfect brown tone of her ankle was from the sun. She was not wearing stockings. He had not been so conscious of a woman's body, apart from Linda's, in a long time.

'England? Is that so? I'm half English.'

'I know that.'

'You know more about me than I do you.'

'How is your mother?'

He opened his hands. 'Her life is difficult. *She* should have returned to England. She never would.' Jake stopped, heard his mother screaming, How can I go home after what my brother did? He said, 'She still lives in the house I grew up in, with my sister.' Jake's concern for his recluse mother had at some point taken second place to his concern for Dori, but he had for a long time now felt unable to help either of them. 'And your mother?' he asked, to deflect his sadness.

'She died some years ago.'

'I'm sorry.' Jake fingered the polished black arm of his chair. Ordinarily he was adept at steering conversations, but now he kept running aground.

Magda shifted in her seat again, and her eyes wandered back to the pair of photographs. He had been right to remember those eyes as extraordinary, and now they conveyed a depth of feeling that drew him and unsettled him.

'And your father died,' she said.

'Of a stroke, a pair of strokes, actually.'

'I suppose that affected you . . .'

'Of course. It took me a long time to come out from under the cloud.'

'You came out because of your wife.'

'That's true. I can't imagine how you know it, but I'm glad you do.'

'Marriage should do as much for everyone.'

'Do you think everyone needs . . .' What he intended to ask was, Did you?

Magda studied the seam of her skirt. She traced it with her long elegant forefinger. She wore no rings. 'The loss of a father is the loss of a father, no matter how it happens. It leaves us all chilled.'

He remembered that her father had died in the war. Not a loss, therefore, but a permanent absence. Which, he wondered, was worse?

After a moment he said, 'You won't tell me how you know. Perhaps you'll tell me what else you know?'

'I know that after your father died you left Washington and you go back only to see your mother.' She let her gaze drift around his office. 'I know that you are an eminent professor.'

Jake laughed. 'Come! Come!' His face reddened, not at the compliment but at the contradiction it was to how he felt. The modesty of his office and of his accomplishment was embarrassing

273

to him. More than that, since being named chairman he hadn't focused his energies to do half the things in the department, much less on his own work, that he'd intended to do. Half the time, in others words, he felt unworthy even of this distinction.

But Magda insisted on the point. 'You are the head of your department.'

'Yes, at Tufts. Had you ever heard of Tufts College?'

She didn't answer.

He smiled. He knew that his dissatisfaction with himself would be unattractive. Usually he pretended to a certain smugness. 'Don't misunderstand. I am content here. But, well, it hardly represents the fulfilment of one's ambition.' He tried to deflect this train of thought, but couldn't. Why was he talking in this way to her? 'I was going to write significant books and publish in great journals. I was going to gather about me the luminaries of literature. I settle for amusing undergraduates.' Usually Jake had a drink in his hand when he made such statements. He turned in his chair to look out a window. 'It's a tidy little corner of the world. Mostly, I like it.'

'I can see why.'

'I don't believe you,' he said quickly. 'But never mind. What else do you know?' It excited him disproportionately to think that she had been aware of him all those years.

She replied solemnly, 'I know that you suspected at first that your father was murdered.'

Jake showed no sign that what she said registered, but inwardly it was as if a wrecker's ball had been swung against the structure of his defences. Girders shook.

'I know that you are still obsessed by what your uncle did.' She paused to let the radical novelty of her statement sink in. 'You never refer to it or to him. You have never been associated with his notoriety, but you are acutely conscious of his status, with Philby, as one of the great traitors of the century.'

'That's true,' Jake said quietly. He could feel himself retreating.

'You blame him for what happened to your father and your mother and your sisters. You have never forgiven him.'

'How do you know that?'

'Your uncle told me.'

Jake stared at her impassively.

'He assumes it to be the case. Is he correct?'

Jake stood, placed his stick carefully, and walked the half-dozen paces to the near window. He leaned his forehead against the glass and let his eyes drift across the city in the distance. The Hancock building. The Pru. Now, instead of trying to keep his emotions at arm's length, it was a numbness he was trying to resist. He sensed it rolling in on him like fog. And he knew why. It was in that numbness that he had sheathed the blades – Giles, his father, what had happened to his family, to him – that Magda now flourished at him. He shouldn't have been surprised. She was no harmless fantasy. She was what she had been in the beginning, his link to the mystery. What surprised him was that the mystery still existed! But of course it would have! Because Giles was still alive. He said without facing her, 'I have no particular feelings about Giles Patterson. I rarely think about him.' He shifted the focus of his gaze to the nearby clustered roofs of Medford and Somerville. Roofs. What was it about roofs?

'I find that surprising.'

'Good. Your omniscience was beginning to bother me.' He faced her and raised a finger. 'I am going to insist that you tell me every bit as much about yourself.'

She was not charmed. 'Your uncle betrayed you. And your father was destroyed. And so was your family. And you never think about it?'

He replied flippantly, 'Does an oyster think about the grain of sand it can't digest? No, it spins a little pearl around it. That's what I've done.' He gestured grandly around his room and out the window that faced the centre of the campus. 'I never digested what he did. But I have not let it obsess me.'

A word as if shouted from a hill across a valley echoed faintly through his mind. Liar! Liar! *This* was what went wrong not in his mother's life or his sisters', but in his! The familiar if vague dissatisfaction. The restlessness that made him prefer teaching in the summer to idling on the rocky coast. But also the sense of drift that prevented the accomplishment of significant work. The dull pain his drinking was intended to assuage. The offensive habit of deflecting awkward feelings with literary cracks. Grains of sand? No. Shards of glass, slicing away in there.

Magda was staring at him without any display of sympathy. She reminded him of the therapist he'd had as a young man. If you are not angry, why are your lips white?

Pretend that she is a coed who wants her grade changed. 'You want me to tell you that I hate my uncle? I could tell you that. But what purpose would it serve? He thinks I won't forgive him? He's probably right. But perhaps it would wound him more if you told him I haven't bothered to take a hard and fast position on the question.'

'But you would like to wound him.'

Jake stared at her in silence for a moment, then slowly shook his head. 'Magda Dettke. I always imagined that if I ever met you again you would not only have lost that strange sparkle of yours and, perhaps, have gained weight or grown warts, but also, like the rest of us, have settled into the mundane routines of ordinary life. I gather not. Why don't you tell me now who you are?'

She stood up. As she approached the edge of the desk – he had to approach from his side; it was between them now – she withdrew from her purse a folded leather case the size of a bill-fold. She held it out to him, held it steady until he took it.

Only with some effort could he focus on the credential. The image of a lion, rampant, standing on its left hind leg with both forelegs elevated, its plumed head in profile, was elaborately engraved in pale green ink, like money. Imposed over the lion in bold black letters were the words, *Her Majesty's Secret Intelligence Service*, and in smaller plainer letters, the name *Magdalene des Andelys*. In the left-hand corner were a seal and a signature and in the right-hand corner was a photograph of Magda Dettke.

'What am I to make of this, Magdalene des Andelys?'

'I kept my former husband's name.'

Jake had an impulse to flip her credentials across the desk at her, but he checked it. Still, when he handed them back to her he dropped them. They fell on the *Boston Globe*, on the front-page picture of the moustachioed Polish strike leader.

'Sorry,' he said. He picked up the folder and handed it to her. She put it back in her purse. He sat in his swivel chair, hooking his stick on the desk drawer. When she sat she seemed more suppliant, but Jake knew it was the large desk that did that. 'Nothing is what it seems, eh? That was one of the rules of my father's world, as I recall. It used to make me very angry that I never knew what was what, and, forgive me, but you've made me feel that way again. Do I call you Fräulein or Madame? Des Andelys or Dettke? Are you German or French? Do you mean to be taken as an emissary from my uncle? If you have a message for me, why don't you just deliver it?'

'Because it is not that simple.'

Jake laughed. How often had his father said exactly that! 'I'll wager that you were an agent then, at sixteen, when we first met. Do you call yourself an agent now? Is that the word you use?'

She did not answer him.

He leaned back in his chair, made a steeple of his hands and positioned it at his lips. 'Magda Dettke,' he repeated. 'Or do you call yourself a spy? My father loathed the word. I suppose you all do. "Hello, my name is Magdalene Dettke des Andelys. *Ich bin eine* spook."'

'You asked me. I told you.'

'You're going to tell me everything, aren't you?'

'Yes.'

'What if I don't want to know? I say, let the dead bury the dead. Things are fine for me the way they are. What if I ask you to leave, now?'

She snapped her purse shut. 'Then I leave.'

Neither moved for a moment. Jake could feel the pulse in his temples.

He swivelled to look out his window, at the buildings in the distance. Jake recalled staring down from the Monument at the parchment-coloured buildings on the edge of Foggy Bottom. '*Sub Rosa*,' his uncle had said. He had smelled faintly of alcohol. That detail, that fragrance of his uncle's breath combined with his cologne, startled Jake now, so acutely could he remember it. His uncle had leaned in on him while saying, 'Because Cupid gave a rose to the god of silence to keep him from revealing the indiscretions of Venus.'

Jake turned towards Magda and said abruptly, 'How do I know it's you, since you didn't bring a rose?'

'You knew about that?'

'I saw my father give you a rose in the museum. He gave one to your mother. He told me once that she worked for him.'

'She worked for SIS. The same as your uncle at the time. The same as me now.'

'What do you want?'

'I want you to help me bring Giles Patterson back from Moscow.'

Jake and his uncle had huddled close together, this time just out of the rain, staring in at the revolving bronze globe that loomed in the cavernous hall of the Foreign Service School. Enchanted balloon, Giles had called it. Jake could recall the exact tone of voice, its mordant dullness, with which his uncle had said, 'Do you notice that every nation disappears from view but one? Bloody waste of the earth's surface!'

'What are you going to do, kidnap him?'

Magda shook her head. 'He wants to come home. He's an old man.'

'Has anyone told him there is no home to come back to? His family estate has tract houses on it now.'

'It's all relative, don't you think? Moscow isn't the Riviera. He hasn't been on holiday, you know.'

'I don't know that.'

'Well, I'm telling you.'

'I gather you've seen him.'

'Yes.'

Jake stared at her over his hands. He didn't move, but it felt to him like the building under him was shaking. That wrecker's ball kept slamming into it.

'Don't you want to know how he is?'

'Frankly, I'm not sure I do. You said he assumes I haven't forgiven him. Since you've asked for an honest statement, that puts what I feel mildly.'

'Still, he is your uncle.'

'And what is he to you?'

Magda lifted her shoulders. 'My mother and I had a debt to him, from the war.'

Jake tried to make it true, what he'd said before, that he didn't care. He leaned towards her. 'This is not my business. You have your reasons for involving yourself in this. I have mine for refusing to do so.'

She let her eyes trail around his office. 'You have moved so far away, haven't you?' She looked back at him sharply. 'Yet you hang on every word I say. You tell me you don't care, but you press your fingers together until their tips are white. You have your reasons for refusing to involve yourself? What? Classes to attend? Courses to assign? Papers to grade? Children to take to the beach? A wife who is waiting with your supper?' She stopped. Her stare bored into him. When he didn't react she went on. 'Once, I stood behind you while you watched through a crack in a door your father and my mother on their knees, feeding documents into a fire. What were those papers? You saw agents of your own government inject a drug into your father and drag him away. Why? I saw you transformed by that mystery. Now you claim you have made a snug, quotidian life for yourself. You don't care? I don't believe you. You hate your uncle? Perhaps. But more than that, you want to know precisely what he did and what your father did, and what they did to him. I was there too. I saw

278

what you saw. I am exactly like you, except it was my mother. I was drawn to that mystery like a moth to a flame. It was my reason for coming to this, and it will be yours for joining me.'

Jake said very quietly, 'I thought you'd never come.'

'I knew I would eventually. And I knew' – she dropped her eyes – 'you would resist.'

'My father made me promise to keep those papers secret. What were they?'

'It is not for me to answer you.'

'But was my father . . .' How could he ask if his father had lied to him at the end of his life? Jake felt the seals on his every pore open as he asked, 'Was he with Giles?'

'Come with me. Ask him.'

Jake had stopped breathing. His voice was barely audible when he asked, 'But why?'

Magda stared back at him.

'Why do you need me?'

'I don't.' She looked up at him. 'It's your uncle. He is terrified of being found out by the KGB. He believes they have infiltrated us and the CIA. Many believe that. It doesn't make him paranoid. He has made it a condition for his return that you be his contact and his escort. He believes that if you are involved in the arrangement, then he can trust it. He trusts you.'

'But you said he knows how I feel.'

'Yes. He is hoping, I think, that in addition to the other things, you remember that once you loved him.'

CHAPTER TWENTY-THREE

Linda was waiting for them when they arrived. Jake greeted her more affectionately than he usually did because Magda's presence put him in touch with the implicit guilt he felt. They had been married ten years. It had never occurred to him to want someone else. They would both have insisted that their life together, with the children, was satisfactory. But he knew that Linda, more than he, was disappointed. Of course, they loved each other. But their love was stunted by the same vague unease – his unease – that had stunted everything.

Linda was not glamorous in the mode of movies or magazines,

but she had the vibrant body of a dancer and to him, since he'd first laid eyes on her in college, she was beautiful. Yet in the instant it took Linda and Magda, shaking hands, to acknowledge each other, Jake found himself comparing them. His wife was taller but her features were less delicate. Her dark hair lacked the lustre of Magda's, but her face sparkled with curiosity and friendliness. Magda's manners were perfect and her smile was easy, but she was contained, aloof, and Jake remembered what always drew him to Linda. She had no capacity for reserve. He always knew what she was thinking. That meant that he always knew when he had hurt her, but also how much she loved him.

While he was getting ice from the refrigerator, Linda, on her way to serve a plate of crackers, poked him and whispered, 'An old friend, you said. You didn't say she looked like Catherine Deneuve.'

'You expected Max von Sydow?'

Linda poked him again and slid off.

They sat down with their drinks on the deck off the living-room. On the far side of the adjacent fence, children coud be heard at play in the driveway that ran behind the house. The McKays lived in an elegant old colonial house on secluded property on Belmont Hill. Jake's family money supported them in a style well beyond what they could have afforded on his salary.

A boy called out.

'That's Bobby,' Jake said.

They listened.

Bobby was encouraging his sister to go faster on her Big Wheel.

'They sound happy,' Magda said.

Linda reached for Jake's hand. 'We think they are.'

Jake pressed her hand in return, but remained silent. He was embarrassed by the smugness of Linda's remark. It was excruciating to him that Magda should be seeing the smallness of his world. Undergraduates, children, an ivy campus, and a wooded suburb.

'You are a dancer,' Magda said.

Linda nodded.

'I wanted to be a dancer once myself. I suppose we all did. You're lucky.'

'I am. I love the teaching too.'

This banal exchange shocked Jake because it made him realize that though in his dream of her he had always seen Magda as that dancer of Degas's, he had never associated the statue with his wife. Was that fantasy the basis of his attraction to her? No wonder they were disappointed.

Linda looked sharply at Jake. 'Oh, darling, I nearly forgot. Your mother called. I said you'd call her when you got home.'

Jake dropped her hand and reached for his drink. 'Christ,' he said softly, as he brought the liquor to his mouth. Straight scotch, no gin-and-tonic for him. He took a large swallow. 'I'll call her later.'

'I did promise, Jake.'

'Then you call her.'

Linda did not reply. Magda stared at her hands, and Jake imagined what she was thinking about him. Wife-beaten, mother's boy. He was weak, peevish, and rude. He stood up. 'You're right. I'm sorry.' He smiled thinly at Magda. 'My mother thinks she's dying. She's thought so now for seven years. She likes to say good-bye before she goes to sleep. Just in case.' Jake usually indulged his mother without resentment. Now he felt angry. That he should appear callous towards her, even while appearing dominated, mortified him.

He excused himself and went to his study. Here the book-shelves were full of first editions and leather-bound volumes. On the walls were framed autographs, with photos. Melville. Whitman. Dickens. Joyce.

The phone was answered on the first ring. That meant she was in bed. It wasn't dark yet.

'Hello, Mother.' He tried to line his voice with affection. None of this was her fault. ''Tis your loyal subject.'

'Why didn't you call before?'

'How are you, Mother?'

'You don't care.'

'Tell me what your day was like.'

'Dori brought me tangerines. And apricots.'

'Wonderful. You loved that, I'll bet.'

'They have seeds, terrible seeds and pits.'

'Oh.' His wit failed him. Usually he could banter with her, control their exchange, make it warm, reassuring. But now he held the phone futilely. His mind was blank. An entire city's worth of structures, walls, sealed rooms was crumbling inside him. He swallowed more scotch.

'Jake?'

'Yes, darling?'

'I thought you'd gone away.'

'No, I'm here.'

'When are you coming?'

'Soon, Mother.'

'You always say that.'

'And I always come, don't I?'

'Not since June.'

'I'll be there. You know I will.'

'Don't bring her.'

Who, Magda? He panicked for a moment, that she knew. It had always unhinged him, when she knew what he was up to. But, of course, not Magda. She couldn't tolerate Linda, though Linda was unfailingly kind to her. His mother was a bitch. No. This wasn't her fault. 'Sometimes I bring her, Mother. You know that.'

'But not this time, Jakey. We have to say farewell. It should be just the family.'

Linda's the family, God damn it! 'What farewell, Mother? Come, come.'

She was weeping now. 'You know.'

'Mother . . .'

'What time are you arriving?'

'Mother, I don't know.'

'But tomorrow, right. You're coming tomorrow.'

'No, I'm not, Mother. I can't.'

'She promised you would.'

'Who? Linda? No, she promised that I would call.'

'Oh.' Silence. 'I suppose you want to speak to Dori.'

'No. I want to speak to you. I'm calling to say I love you. And to wish you a good night. If I was there I'd tuck you in, like you used to me.'

'But you're not, are you?'

'No.'

'Well then.'

'So sleep well. Okay?'

'Goodnight.'

'Goodnight, Mother.'

Now she would wait for him to hang up. It used to infuriate him that she would never hang up first. She had to feel abandoned. He listened for a moment. If he'd heard a click, it would have seemed a miracle, as if she'd been healed. Nothing but her breathing.

He hung up. And he felt it again. The stab of truth. He *had*

282

abandoned her. Her masterful re-enactment of that act was how she punished him.

When Jake returned to his chair on the deck the two women fell silent.

He sipped his drink calmly, but his feelings were stampeding, and he had no idea how to rein them. When Linda looked at him he knew she saw how helpless he felt.

'How is she?' Linda asked. Her sympathy was for him. She was on his side no matter what.

Jake smiled at her weakly. 'Depressed.'

Linda said to Magda, 'She's clinically depressed. That's her problem.'

'No,' Jake said, snapping out of his mood. 'It's her solution!' He stood up. 'Let me freshen those drinks.'

'No, thank you,' Magda said.

Linda shook her head. Neither woman had dented her gin-and-tonic.

Jake went in and poured himself another stiff scotch. By the time he returned he was resolved to take control and had decided the way to do that was to drive immediately to the issue at hand. 'Before the kids come in,' he said, 'we have to talk.'

'About what?' Linda seemed vulnerable suddenly.

'About who Magda is, for one thing. I said on the phone she is an old friend. That overstates it.' He turned to Magda. 'Don't you agree?'

'Yes.'

Jake took Linda's hand. He wanted to lay aside everything but his concern for her. She had a right to a cogent explanation.

'We were acquainted for a total of two days. Magda's mother worked with my father and my uncle. Do you remember what I told you once, about seeing my father dragged out of a house by his own people?'

'Of course I remember.'

'Magda was there. It was her house.'

Linda looked at Magda. 'Well, that qualifies you, I'd say, as an old friend.'

'Magda walked into my office today, and it all came back. I asked her to come home with me to explain to you what brings her here.'

'Frankly,' Magda said, 'I did not want to. I have no authority to speak of these things to anyone but your husband. He insisted.

283

It is a condition on which he insisted.'

'A condition for what?'

Magda lit a cigarette. Ordinarily, Linda would have dashed for an ashtray. She didn't move. Magda held her match and ashes in the palm of her hand. She spoke slowly and carefully. 'As your husband said, my mother was a colleague of his father and his uncle. The three of them, together with my father, were involved in underground activity against Hitler. My father was killed. After the war, Mr McKay and Mr Patterson helped my mother and me. We lived in Cologne, but her family lived near Meissen in the Eastern Zone, and it was possible for her to help establish an intelligence network. She did not hesitate to work against the Russians, but also she was devoted to Mr Patterson. We went with him to Washington. But then . . .' Magda stopped. An undefined emotion threatened to overtake her, but she fended it off. '. . . When he defected to Russia, my mother was afraid.' Magda looked at Jake. 'Your father could not protect her. Once Mr Patterson was gone, the KGB would surely have killed her. She went into hiding in England. I lived in Paris with my grandmother. I finished my schooling there. I married a French film-maker. You may have heard of him, Andelys?'

Linda shook her head, barely.

'When, eight years ago, my marriage failed, I went to England to be with my mother. We became very close. She told me the whole story, and for the first time I understood the strange events in the shadow of which I had lived my first years. When my mother was killed in an accident, it seemed very natural for me to take her place in the service, first as a translator, as she was by then. Only later as an officer. My mother believed in her work, and I believe in mine.' Magda stopped. 'All this sounds very strange to you, doesn't it?'

Linda replied, 'I have never succeeded in imagining what Jake's father could have been like. And as for his uncle, I'm not sure I ever really believed it . . . I'm quite dumbfounded, Magda, by what you're telling me.' Linda laughed. 'My father was a bank teller.'

Magda said, 'So was your husband's grandfather, in Newport, Rhode Island.'

Linda was shocked. She looked at Jake. 'You never told me that.'

'If I knew it, I forgot it years ago.' Jake continued to hold his wife's hand, but the warmth had drained out of it.

'My point is,' Magda said steadily, 'that events like defection do occur, and persons engaged in the secret work of governments do exist. And we have bank tellers and porcelain-makers in our families.'

'So what is your secret work?'

'Beginning several years ago, I have travelled regularly to Moscow. My purpose has been to contact and establish a relationship with Giles Patterson. For a long time he refused to meet me. Because of the memory of my mother, he finally agreed to. It was neither a surprise nor unwelcome when he admitted at last that he wants to return to England. He regrets his defection. He would like to undo it. I encouraged him that he can. Ironically, he would be an invaluable source of information on the inner workings of the KGB where he is employed as an analyst.'

'So he is coming back?'

'Yes, if we meet his one condition.' Magda paused. 'Your husband must participate in his return actively.'

Linda dropped Jake's hand and fell back against her chair. 'What?'

'Giles Patterson wants your husband as his escort.'

'I never heard anything so ridiculous.' Linda waved her hands in front of her body, like a stubborn child, then became aware that she was doing so and stopped. Then she looked at Jake. 'Good Lord, can you imagine!'

He smiled faintly. 'Barely.'

No one spoke.

Then Linda leaned towards him. 'Wait a minute. You're not considering it?'

'Of course I'm considering it.' He gestured at Magda. 'Do you think I brought her home to entertain you?'

'Have you already said yes to her?'

'I wanted to talk to you about it. I wanted your advice.'

'That's easy; hell no!' She faced Magda. 'He's not going to Moscow with you or anyone!'

'It isn't Moscow,' Magda said. 'It's Berlin. Giles Patterson arrived in Berlin this afternoon.'

'I don't care where he is. It's the Iron Curtain. It's going to blow up over there. They're on strike in Poland. Everyone says the Russians will invade. Those people are at war practically.'

'I'm not talking about Poland,' Magda said calmly. 'And not about Russia. I'm talking about Berlin, where to go from East to West is a simple matter of a subway ride.'

285

'They let him go to Berlin?' Linda's incredulity flew about, Jake thought, like a loose halyard. 'They let him out of Moscow?' He had raised the same question himself.

'Patterson is a specialist on the political affairs of the EEC, and he is presenting a paper at a Party congress. In fact, he is regarded as a less likely candidate for crossing to the West than other officials who do not, after all, have severe prison terms waiting for them on this side.'

'But I thought those people spied on each other . . .'

'One assumes he will be well watched.'

Magda's cigarette was down to a stub, and she looked about for a place to put it.

Linda now stood and crossed into the house to get an ashtray. In her absence Magda and Jake exchanged a look. When, exactly, had they become conspirators?

He said quietly, 'You make it sound exciting.' He'd been aware as she spoke of his growing infatuation with the idea of going. It would be better than correcting papers. Better than calling his mother.

Magda did not comment.

Jake felt foolish. Had he said 'exciting'? Would she think him puerile if he displayed eagerness?

Linda returned. When she was seated again, Magda said to her, 'In point of fact I am violating the law and my oath by telling you these things. I am doing so because your husband has given me no choice.'

Linda looked coldly at Jake. 'Should I be grateful?'

'I knew if it was me telling you, you'd think I'd lost my mind.'

'I think you have anyway.' She reached across to touch him. 'It's just taking me by surprise. I'm sorry. I've lost my stride. It sounds like a bad movie.'

Jake stroked her hand, but he resented her.

'You would go . . . soon?'

'Yes. Tonight. Right away.'

'Would it be dangerous?'

Jake looked across at Magda; yes, would it? Was fear more fitting than eagerness?

'Not at all. The hardest part, as you guessed, was getting Patterson cleared to travel to Berlin. Now it is simply a matter of following a routine. We have prepared for him documents that identify him as an ailing East German pensioner, who has been granted – and this is no longer unusual – an exit visa to live with his daughter and son-in-law in Switzerland. The key is the computer at the border, and we have agents who have made the proper adjustments in the data bank. When the officials check Patterson's papers against the control, everything will be confirmed and he will certainly pass through without incident. The pensioner's daughter and son-in-law will have travelled to East Berlin from their home in Zurich, as is customary, to accompany him across the border. His daughter, myself, and his son-in-law, your husband.'

Magda lit a second cigarette.

Linda looked at Jake. 'She explained this to you?'

'Yes.'

'And your thought is . . . ?'

'It seems preferable to a dash across the Wall.'

'It is impossible,' Magda put in. 'The Wall is impossible.'

'I was joking.'

'Very funny,' Linda said. 'You think you can pass for German, do you?'

'I would be a Swiss citizen, but a British expatriate. A tax exile.' He withdrew from his inside coat pocket a worn passport and he handed it to his wife.

When Linda opened it, she said 'Good God!' Jake's photograph was embossed with the seal of Switzerland. 'You people are serious.'

The gate in the fence behind them crashed open. Bobby burst in on them. 'Maureen's cut!' he cried with alarm.

Linda was off the deck before Jake and met her daughter at the gate. The child had scraped her knee, not badly. 'You didn't cry!' Linda said proudly and hugged her. Maureen pulled away to go to Jake, who scooped her up, though his sympathy was for his wife. He wanted to exchange a look with her, but she averted her eyes.

Jake examined his daughter's knee. 'Gosh, we better fix that, huh?'

Linda went ahead of them to the bathroom for the Band-Aids. Before following her, Jake looked at Magda, who smiled sympathetically at Maureen. 'You are very brave,' she said.

Jake could feel his daughter brighten at the compliment. Even she seemed aware of Magda's special authority. Jake appreciated the affirmation of Maureen, but for himself he felt more intensely than before Magda's judging aloofness. How banal this must all seem to her.

He let Maureen down, but held her hand. He would have loved to carry her in to the bathroom, but it had been a long time since he could do that. He couldn't walk while carrying his child, even if she were hurt. No wonder he felt, under this strange woman's gaze, as if he had large things to prove. What surprised him was how she made him want to.

While Jake showered, Linda stuffed the side pockets of his suitcase with shirts, underwear, and socks. From this closet she called into the bathroom, 'Your gaberdine and your blazer?'

The rushing sound of the water stopped. A moment later Jake appeared, naked, at the door, towelling his hair. 'Did you say something?'

'I said, your gaberdine? And your blazer? I don't know what people wear in that business.'

'Try to restrain your sarcasm, will you?'

'I'm trying to help!'

'It doesn't help for you to be angry.'

'Well, I don't like it.'

'Sweetheart, this isn't my doing.' He started towards her, conscious of his limp, as he was only when naked. 'I didn't pick the family I was born into.'

She stopped him with a cold look. 'You picked this one. What am I going to tell the children?'

'You needn't tell them anything. I wouldn't think of going without explaining it myself.'

'Explain it to me.'

'My uncle is a member of my family, like you are. Like Bobby and Maureen are. Doesn't that explain it?'

'And this woman, what is she to you?'

'Oh, Christ, Linda.' He threw his towel down and turned to the bureau, to dress.

'No, really, Jake. You're like a twelve-year-old who's been invited on a camping trip. You brought her home, expecting me to listen sedately, then give you my permission.'

Jake whipped around. 'Permission? I'm not asking your permission!'

'Then what the hell did you have her tell me all that for?'

'Because you have a right to know what I'm doing.'

'I don't want to know.'

'You don't mean that.'

'You pretend to consult me, to seek my advice. I dare to be less than enthusiastic and you reveal that you've already decided anyway. You'd decided to go with her before you came home.'

'Yes! I decided twenty years ago. What are you afraid of? I'm going to hop in bed with her first chance I get, like a sailor who's hit port?'

'No, I'm not afraid of that.'

'What, that I'll discover that I like the world of international intrigue, and I'll join up?'

'No, I'm not afraid of that.'

'Well, what?'

Linda's lips quivered. She covered them with clenched fists. 'I don't know. I'm just afraid.'

Neither moved.

In the reading-room of the B.U. library that day thirteen years before, she had crossed to his table and said in a whisper, 'How can I study with you staring at me?'

To which he had said – a calculated impudence; they had never laid eyes on each other before – 'I'm in love with you.'

That night in her small graduate-student apartment in Brighton they undressed each other. When she saw his leg she touched it. No one had done that but his mother and doctors. She said, 'I want to know about it.' She lowered her face to his knee and kissed it. 'But not now.'

For years she had driven like that without a hint of coyness to the very heart of things, and her innate, brave directness had asked as much from him. But he had dodged her until finally she too accepted deflection, not directness, as the mode of their relationship. 'I'm in love with you,' he'd said, trying to be a card, trying to avoid feeling embarrassed. But he had uncovered despite himself his rawest feeling, though it took him a while to know that was what he'd done. He had a smaller gift than she had for the truth.

She was afraid. So was he.

Why couldn't they cross the room and embrace?

Their anger, when they let it flare, always immobilized them. It always took them hours to recover the ground they lost to harsh exchanges. But now, unfortunately, they didn't have hours.

Jake went to his closet and pulled on his shorts and trousers. Then he swung out his tie rack and began fingering through his ties without thinking, or rather, thinking about her.

Unconsciously, his fingers fell upon a narrow blue tie, his only old one. Jake McKay replaced all of his ties every few years, but he had never discarded this one. He pulled it out. 'Georgetown University, 1964.'

And he realized he had never told Linda about hazing, about his first victory, his speech. 'We claim our place in the world,' he'd cried. But he never claimed his.

As a kid, the purpose of his existence had seemed clear; now it was unfocused. He had a career, wife, children, two houses, and the feeling it all belonged to someone else. He was barely part of his own life. And he had never said any of this to Linda, his only friend.

Was she afraid that what for her was total was for him only partial? Had she always sensed the gap? The something missing? He could never finger it, except in an abstract way. In starting out, Jake had missed a beat and he'd never been quite in step again. Linda knew it. That was the source of her disappointment. She was attuned to what was lacking not in her or in their life together but in Jake himself. In their worst arguments she would accuse him of being unhappy, as if that were the worst treason. 'It has nothing to do with happiness!' he would yell. It has to do, he thought now, with this. Why can't she understand that of course I have to go?

'Are you taking that one?' She was beside him now, indicating the tie.

'No. Just reminiscing.' He folded the tie back into the thick of ties.

'Magda brings back memories, does she?' Linda was trying to be light.

'I should have told you more about my uncle and my father.'

'I should have asked. I should have asked your mother.'

'She could never have talked about it.'

'I know what I'm afraid of, Jake. I'm afraid of ending up like her.'

He faced her and took her gently by the shoulders. 'With Maureen taking care of you?'

'And Bobby being only dutiful.'

'Is that what I am?'

She placed her palms against his chest. She smiled. 'It was dutiful of you to bring Magda home. At least now I know what I'm up against.' She said that in a way that made it clear she wasn't serious. Magda Dettke was not the issue and they both knew it.

'You know, my mother used to be like you are. Everyone who ever knew her loved her.'

'But I don't care about everyone. I only want you to love me.'
She slid her arms around him.

He kissed her. Still he felt guilty. Christ, he was sick of feeling
guilty.

As they crossed to their bed he leaned on her, and, once there,
he sat while she helped him remove his trousers.

She remained standing before him while he undressed her. Not
dutifully, he told himself, not dutifully.

Linda had always been self-conscious about her small breasts,
and so he habitually began with them. Often, as now, when she
lowered herself on him, he touched her nipples with his lips and
tongue.

They proceeded deliberately, with a matching lack of passion,
a mutual act of will.

In their lovemaking they were always agile with each other,
even athletic. She had a dancer's knack for articulating each
movement of muscle and limb, and he knew just how to touch
her. Sex was the last thing left in which they were direct with each
other. At one point, as she often did, she tumbled over him and
brought her face down to his withered leg. In kissing it was she
saying, Remember I am the one who loves what is ugly about
you?

He put that question away.

He always put it away. It was too easy to use his leg against her.

He drew her up. 'Linda, I do love you.'

'Of course you do. I am just terrified of losing you. A whirlwind
has come and scooped you up! I don't believe her, that it isn't
dangerous. Russia is dangerous. Everyone knows that.'

'But Berlin, darling, I'm going to Berlin.'

'Oh, Jake! Jake!' She kissed him. Her passion quickened his
and they clung to each other fiercely.

Afterwards they both lay looking up at the ceiling. Linda asked
innocently, 'What are you thinking?'

Jake wished he could lie to her: About you, my love. Or about
Bobby, I hope I'm not a mystery to him.

But instead he told her the truth. 'My ebony stick, I was
thinking about it.'

'I've never seen you use that one.'

'I haven't used it in twenty years. My uncle gave it to me.'

Linda snuggled against him. 'Just like a twelve-year-old,
thinking about what to wear.'

CHAPTER TWENTY-FOUR

Magda dozed fitfully on the flight from Boston to Zurich. Jake
was aware of it each time she stirred. He had no inclination to
sleep, but with a pillow crushed beside his ear he leaned against
the window staring into his own image in the black glass.

How had this happened? Only hours ago the great question in
his mind had been about final exams. *Comment on Eliot's statement that people cannot bear very much reality.* Now his mind was
a wilderness of memories and impressions, and he was
periodically frightened by an acute shortness of breath.

He resisted the impulse to look at Magda again, but his
awareness of her nearness calmed him. It had surprised him, how
familiar she seemed, how well he remembered the slight nuances
of her beauty, the stretch of skin across her cheekbones, the
barest upturn of the outside corners of her eyes, a faint hint of
the Oriental. It was as if they had been lovers once, so efficiently
had he recovered each impression she had left him with. He
remembered vividly what it felt like that time she had kissed his
cheek. He recalled the thrill of his own reaction fondly, with the
self-accepting bemusement of a grown man who has long since
resolved the agonies of youth.

But of course they weren't resolved and that was why he was
here. He had misled Linda. He had agreed to do this not because
of responsibilities he owed his family, his uncle, father, mother,
and not even because he needed answers to old questions that
only Magda could provide. He had agreed to do this because he
had to learn what he was made of. This was the great passage rite
he should have accomplished years ago. Was he his father's son
or not? Would the long-postponed test, whatever it involved,
shrivel him or free him? He had to know. He had to be here.

And yet, he wondered, did he really? Was he a fool to drop
everything and fly away simply because an old heartthrob asked
him to? In fact wasn't this mere escapism, a flight into melodrama, into fantasy, as if a trip to Berlin would relieve his
claustrophobia? Even if his uncle had asked for him, what did he
owe Giles? Nothing. Not a bloody thing. Fuck Giles.

The more Jake recalled the consequences of his uncle's act the more angry he got. But it wasn't his anger that unsettled him. It was his fear. One thing about dull old Tufts and Belmont, fear wasn't a feature of the landscape in either place. But here! Underneath all of his reflections, memories, and emotions was a layer of fright unlike any he'd known before. Linda had felt it before he had. She was right. She was a good woman. He was wrong to be unhappy with her. Already he understood that the farther away he got from his family the more he was going to love them.

He kept sliding back towards his fear but then scurrying away from it. He had nothing to be afraid of, he insisted. But he knew better. He was right to be afraid of what he would learn about himself.

But hell, he was no adolescent, and it was *not* just for himself that he was here. He *was* doing this for his family. For his uncle. He was doing it for his father.

John McKay had endured his illness, in Jake's opinion, nobly. The first stroke had ravaged him. His entire left side, from the muscles of his face to his arm and leg, had been paralysed, and it had seemed likely when he was first home from the hospital that he would spend the rest of his days bedridden. And he might have, had not Jake withdrawn from Georgetown to be with his father, shepherding him through the daily routines of physical therapy, and to help his mother and sisters cope with the stresses of what had happened. For one full year Jake and his mother had put his father through the rigorous round of prescribed exercises. For months there had been barely a sign of progress, but then slowly function had begun to return to his father's muscles. As his body improved, so did his mind and will. Before long he was surpassing the doctors' expectations, though not Jake's.

The greatest satisfaction of Jake's life had been in standing at his father's side, holding his arm, while he tried to learn to walk again. Each morning Jake would offer him with a flourish the choice of his own collection of walking sticks, and whenever his father referred in his slurred speech to the sticks as canes, Jake jokingly rebuked him. By that spring progress came quickly, and they promised each other that before summer's end they would be playing golf together again.

As if Jake needed to be confirmed in the essential cruelty of life, just when his father could be said to have recovered – he limped, but could walk; he could speak with relative clarity; he napped often, but passed his waking time lucidly and in good humour –

he suffered the second stroke and it killed him. Jake's mother had renewed her happiness in caring for her husband, and with his each step towards recovery she had brightened. When he died it was as if an armoured visor fell across her face. No one would see, except in rare flashes, the witty, strong-hearted and tender Eleanor Patterson McKay again.

Throughout the time of her husband's illness neither she nor he nor Jake nor Jake's sisters had ever once mentioned Giles. But when Jake went through his father's papers he found a sealed note-sized envelope on which was typewritten, 'Dear Jake, I'd be grateful, if the occasion ever presents itself, if you would hand this personally to your uncle. As ever, Dad.' Jake had that envelope, still sealed, in his suit-coat pocket now.

The airplane banked slightly and under the wing the first sharp light of dawn appeared. Shortly after that the cabin lights were brought up full, and the Swissair stewardesses began to pass out hot towels.

Magda stretched and craned across Jake to look out the window. '*Bonjour, mon cher,*' she said, and she pecked his cheek. Her hair, down now in a luxurious cascade, brushed him. It smelled faintly of perfume, but also of tobacco.

He smiled at her, but the kiss, even that one, made him uneasy. He implicitly flagged the awkwardness he felt with an ironic tone when he said, 'You did that to me before.' He touched his cheek. 'I never washed.'

Magda took a towel from the stewardess's tray and reached up to wipe Jake's cheek. '*Voilà!* Now you are chaste once more.'

Jake smirked. He applied a towel of his own to his face. The heat revived him. When he lowered it, Magda was gone.

When she returned from the lavatory her hair was pulled tightly into a prim fold behind her ears again and he was, to his surprise, disappointed.

When the attendants served coffee, juice, and croissants, he said, 'It's absurd, isn't it? We had dinner only three hours ago.'

'Still, it helps with jet lag if you pretend it's breakfast.'

'You travel regularly?'

'Rarely to America, although I like your country.' She took a bite of the croissant, then put it down. She wasn't going to eat more, either.

'Have you known many Americans?'

'No.'

'You've never been married to one before?'

'Before you? But you are British, darling.'

'In fact I spent summers in England. Quite happy ones, at my uncle's estate. He was always after me to go to Cambridge. Perhaps I should have.'

'Why did you choose to be an American?'

'In 1964, it wasn't much of a choice. Imagine, we could refer in public discourse to "the Great Society" without blushing. Besides . . . as a family we did not feel precisely celebrated in England at the time. I gather Giles's defection put the whole network on its collective ear.'

Instead of commenting Magda moved her eyes to the seats in front of them. Both were empty. It was for this relative privacy, he saw suddenly, that she'd arranged to travel first-class.

'You are a British subject?' he asked.

'Technically.' Magda put her head back. 'But many of us are citizens of nations that no longer exist. That is a European phenomenon. You Americans would not understand it.'

'Some of us feel that way about our own country.'

'Do you?'

'When I started in graduate school my purpose was not to titillate undergraduates.'

'What was it?'

Jake did not answer. He remembered that speech he gave. *We are responsible for the world.* He had wanted to ask the great questions and answer them.

Magda poked him. 'It is what people our age do, have always done, to think nostalgically of our lost ideals.'

Why, Jake wondered suddenly, won't she use my name? Then he wondered why it mattered that she didn't. Neither spoke for some moments. Then he said, 'You've told me nothing about Giles.'

Magda turned in her seat. An old lady was sitting alone behind them. She was asleep. Still, Magda lowered her voice.

'He has done well in Moscow. He was given a meaningless position in the bureaucracy in the beginning, but he became an expert on the structures of the Common Market as it developed Obviously, as an Englishman he grasped the nuances.'

'And that's what qualifies him for this congress in Berlin?'

'Yes. It is a meeting of economic ministers of the bloc countries. Giles is addressing them on the EEC. His subject, I suppose, is more crucial than ever, because Poland's economy depends so much on Europe.'

'I hope the Poles keep calm for a few more days, don't you?'

Magda raised an eyebrow. 'The Poles?'

'Well, all of them.'

'You asked about Giles. Do you know he is a homosexual?'

'Yes, I know that. It's not important.'

'On the contrary, it has been very important. He had for a long time a relationship with a senior official in Moscow. That accounts for his relative privilege.'

'You say "had".'

'The man is dead.'

Jake felt a wave of sadness for his uncle. Why hadn't it occurred to him that Giles's life in Moscow would have its loves, triumphs, satisfactions, losses, worries, and griefs? He knew why. He'd long regarded Giles as dead. He said, 'I think of him the way he was when he left. He would be an old man now, I suppose.'

'In his seventies. He is still a lovely man . . . to look at.'

'You don't like him?'

'I don't have that sort of opinion about him. It is not my business to like or dislike.'

Her cold statement disappointed him. 'I don't have the knack for such detachment. I always like or dislike the person whom I'm with.' He smiled, as if to reassure her. 'I had the impression from what you told me before that you felt a certain compassion for him, and that your interest in him was somewhat personal.'

'I was assigned to his case, if that's what you mean.'

'And mine, therefore?'

'Yes.'

'Whose idea was it, that we should be married?'

'The idea suggested itself.'

'To you?'

'It doesn't matter.'

Jake was suddenly awash in feelings he hadn't expected and didn't understand. 'I am travelling with you as your husband. I've had to explain to myself half a dozen times in as many hours why that is.' What had gotten to him? Her stated indifference to Giles? Or her implied indifference to him? 'Perhaps the present circumstance is not extraordinary to you, but it is to me.' His fear surged in him. A canoe guide had told him once it wasn't the rapids themselves that freaked people, but the sound of the rapids approaching.

Magda looked wearily away. 'The present circumstance is always extraordinary, in my opinion.'

At first Jake dismissed her statement as a cheap banality and nearly called it that, but then he thought, Christ, maybe her life is different than mine. Maybe physical danger, adventures behind the Iron Curtain, were commonplace to her. Adventures behind enemy lines – it was what his father did in the war. He said, 'I get introspective on airplanes in the middle of the night. I apologize.'

'You are worried about your wife.'

'No, not at all.'

'That I understand about her, I mean. About your attachment to her.'

He shrugged. 'That goes without saying.'

'You want me to understand that you intend with me only what the liberation of your uncle requires.'

'Why do you think such a statement is necessary?'

She returned his stare. 'Because your wife is the only woman you have been with.'

In Magda's eyes, it seemed to Jake, were displayed, as if photos on flash cards, the faces of all the men she'd been with.

He felt suddenly ashamed of his fidelity. He said as lightly as he could, 'And here we are having breakfast with each other.'

'But you are not eating.'

He shrugged. 'Airplane food.'

The stewardess took Magda's tray away. Magda replaced her tray table and lit a cigarette. It was a French brand, without filters. Short and stubby with black tobacco, the cigarettes must have wreaked havoc on her lungs. That Jake hadn't smoked since the Surgeon General's warning went on the packs seemed to summarize the difference between them. What he wanted was a drink.

Magda said, 'Once you asked me to go with you. Do you remember?'

'No. I asked you to go with me?'

'To find your dog, Cooney.' Magda's face broke into a friendly smile.

He laughed. 'I do remember, yes.'

They basked for a moment in the warmth of that memory, the autumn field, the swings on which her white skirt billowed, the overgrown shrubbery through which they'd 'searched'.

Magda touched his sleeve with the fingers that held her cigarette. 'But this is different. I have not deceived you.'

'I never regretted deceiving you that time.' Since, he went on to himself, it was how we met. He was aware of the intensity of her gaze. Why are you looking at me like that, he wanted to ask, if it is not your business to like or dislike? He dropped his eyes. 'That man in your mother's house? Who confronted my father? His name was Yeats. Did you know that he was killed?'

Magda nodded. 'A hunting accident, wasn't it?'

'In New Hampshire. Did you believe that?'

'Even spies and counterspies die in accidents.' She turned away. 'My mother was killed by an automobile.'

Jake could feel himself flowing towards her. The smart canoeist pulls to the bank when the river quickens, then walks ahead to look. 'And you didn't wonder about her death?'

'Would it have been better, in your opinion, or worse, if her death was someone's deliberate act?'

'You're right. Better or worse doesn't apply. But one obsesses anyway.'

'I don't.'

'Well, perhaps we're different.' Now he wanted her to feel rebuked. He wanted her to sense his contempt for her detachment, as if detachment was not a mode of his. 'It still matters very much to me whether my father was murdered or not.' Murdered? Had he said *murdered*?

'I assumed you'd let go of that.'

'It hasn't let go of me.' He had not admitted this before. He could hardly breathe.

Magda shrugged, and she seemed more aloof than ever.

Jake took refuge in his bitterness, his old bitterness. It had always confused him; should he resent his ignorance or the men who condemned him to it? He watched her while she smoked her cigarette. She had used that hand to touch him. He was aware of her mouth, her lips, the smoke curling past her teeth, down her throat. Smoking had never seemed so physical to him, so sensuous. Finally he admitted that he wanted to part those lips with his tongue. He leaned back against his seat. 'Perhaps you're right. Perhaps it doesn't matter.'

'I did not say that. I said knowing does not make it better or worse.'

With his eyes closed he said quietly, 'I'd like to ask a more personal question.'

Magda waited.

'Were your mother and my father lovers?'

298

'Never.'

'It was a pose of theirs?'

'My mother was always faithful to my father.'

Hadn't Magda just mocked him for his fidelity to Linda? He opened his eyes. 'But your father was dead, killed in the war.'

'She was faithful to his memory, I mean. She was devoted to his memory.'

Jake tried to square that with the image he had of that woman, easy in his father's arms. 'Do you think she and my father had conversations like this?'

'I hope not.'

They smiled at each other.

Jake went on, philosophically, posing somewhat. 'The Great Society was a long time ago. The hideous secrets of our parents' business, of their world, had not been laid bare. We could pretend before Vietnam and Nixon that the creatures in the shadows were not people we loved.'

Creatures in the shadows. It was a melodramatic phrase and Jake had used it deliberately, a goad against Magda, for what was she if not one of them? It was not her business to like or dislike. Was that what her mother said? Was it his father's business to like, at least, his son?

Magda's aloofness was what made him angry. It made him angry because suddenly he realized that his own aloofness was not unlike hers. She was hoarding her information and disguising her attitudes, the way he did with students. That gave her the advantage, but for some reason, perhaps the one she'd offered – that Giles made it a condition – she needed his co-operation. He would give it to her, but a step at a time. In order to protect what little power he had he would not trust her. For all his apparent callowness he would refuse in principle to believe fully anything she told him.

Callowness. Where had that word come from? But he knew. *Callow's End.* It shocked him to realize that circumstances had invited him to assume the stance – see how inexperienced I am; my wife my only woman! – his uncle had perfected. But his uncle was a master. One could do worse than imitate him. One could, for example, imitate his father. The unflappable iron man had been soundly defeated in this shadow combat.

'Don't you think,' Magda said slowly, 'that much bewailed pre-Vietnam innocence of yours – America's, I mean – was somewhat false?'

'Of course it was, but that didn't make it less compelling. It's our illusions we live by.'

Magda's silence both indicated her disagreement and forced Jake to admit that if he wanted to live by his illusions he would not have come with her. He was being professorial, and he stopped before she could express her disdain.

Magda surprised him by touching his sleeve again and saying with an apparent fondness, 'You're right. Twenty years ago we needed the illusion that there was a Cooney.'

'Oh, there was a Cooney, but he wasn't a dog. He was a class-mate of mine. He was with me when I first saw you at the Phillips Gallery. He thought you were beautiful.' Jake grinned at her.

'How nice of him.' Colour came to her cheeks, but she did not release his sleeve.

'You were wearing a white pleated skirt and carrying books and that red rose. Your hair was in a pony-tail.' Jake stopped. That she was blushing and had averted her eyes moved him. Despite an implicit resolve he said, 'I thought you were beautiful too.'

Magda nodded and whispered, 'I was then.'

Magda had a car in a parking lot at the Zurich airport, an innocuous small sedan. Dawn was just breaking as they pulled away.

'I don't understand why we don't go on to Berlin right away.' It irked Jake that she kept their agenda to herself.

'We won't be here long,' was all she said. She drove in silence, away from Zurich. Soon they left the four-lane highway for a country road, and within half an hour the suburbs had given way to dense fir forests and deserted hilly terrain that struck Jake as unfriendly. The roads wound so and their route involved so many turns that he wondered if she were deliberately complicating it so that he would be unable to retrace it later. Finally they arrived at a modest cottage set well back from the road, made of precut cedar logs and surrounded by a blanket of pine needles that had dropped from the overarching trees. The place had its charm, but it seemed gloomy to him in the early morning mist and he had to stifle an ominous shudder.

The ground underfoot was damp.

Magda unlocked the cabin door and went in ahead of him. She snapped on several lights. That there was electricity surprised him.

The main room was furnished cosily with a pair of couches

arranged in front of a wood-burning stove. At the opposite end was a counter that separated the room from a small kitchen. A pair of stools stood at the counter, but Jake had the feeling that when she used this place she was alone.

A short corridor led away from the main room. Jake followed Magda past two closed doors to a third, which she opened. 'You will use this room.'

It was cheerful enough. He saw a bed, a bureau, an open closet, which held several men's suits and jackets.

Magda opened the top drawer of the bureau. 'You will find shirts here, and personal articles in the other drawers.' She indicated the clothes in the closet. 'And these are for you also. You should select what you need.'

'I don't need any of it, thank you.'

Magda spoke brusquely. 'When we leave here you are not to bring anything of your own. Not even toiletry.'

'Don't be ridiculous,' he said, but something in him welcomed her authority. Tell me what to do, and I'll do it.

She stared at him. 'It is a question of labels. All of your labels are wrong. Beginning today you are Harold Davidson. These are *his* clothes. They are all in your size and they reflect, I believe, your taste. Because now they are yours. And here' – she crossed to the bed and picked up a stapled sheaf of papers – 'are facts about him and his wife with which you must now become familiar. It is your first task.' She handed him the papers, then looked at her watch. 'Later we will review the Davidson family history together. I assume you will be ready to do so. Between now and then you should learn what's written there. And you should sleep.'

'In that order?' Sleep seemed inconceivable to him.

She shrugged. 'The WC is there, and my room is next to it. I sleep lightly. I will hear you if you leave.'

'Leave? Where in hell would I go?'

She looked at him impassively. He imagined her saying, You might run away, you coward!

He started past her, towards the main room, but she stopped him. 'I need my bag, darling,' he explained.

She shook her head. 'Use what's in the room.'

'I have a bottle in my bag. I want a drink.'

'Harold Davidson never touches alcohol. Can you accept that? If not, this is as far as we go.'

He forced a smile. 'You want me stone sober, eh?'

301

She didn't answer, but of course that was it.

He shrugged. Suddenly he felt his weariness. 'Yes, I can accept it.' But, he wondered, could he? What the hell had he let himself in for? The thought of spending time in that room alone terrified him. And he knew why. Time with those papers and that clothing would change him into a man who would encounter what Jake McKay had painstakingly constructed a life to avoid.

The sound of water running through pipes elsewhere in the cabin woke him up. He raised the shade at the window. The sun was high in the sky. It had been years since he'd slept in the middle of the day, and it heightened his sense of unreality that he'd been able to now. He listened to the water sounds. A shower. Magda was in the shower.

An image of her naked filled his mind, water coursing down her body, making it shine.

When she turned the shower off he got up, found a blue silk bathrobe in the closet. It did fit him. There were slippers, and so did they. He opened his door just as she came out of the bathroom. Her hair was wrapped in a towel. When she saw him she closed her terry robe at her throat.

'Hello, Sigrid,' he said.

There was such convincing domesticity in the scene that all at once they both laughed.

'Did you sleep?' she asked, managing to convey a certain concern.

'Soundly,' he said. 'I feel much better.' She was barefoot but the turban on her head made her seem much taller. 'And I must say, my dear,' he spoke with the unpronounced British accent it was his intention to use from now on, 'the robe fits perfectly, and I approve the wardrobe utterly. My compliments to whoever made the selection.'

'I did.'

'Really? I'd have assumed an underling . . .' She stared at him. He asked abruptly, 'Are you working on this alone?'

'Yes.' She smiled. 'You expected henchmen?'

'Of course. And helicopters. And weapons.' He paused. 'Are there weapons?'

'No. We will depend utterly on our ability – and your uncle's – to appear to be what our papers claim. And so we have a little work to do, yes?'

He nodded. 'I'll be right along.'

'Dress to travel,' she said.

While he showered he realized that he did feel better. Her competence reassured him. If she thought he was up to what was coming, maybe he was.

Jake dressed in a top-quality lightweight tan suit that bore a Monte Carlo label. Though the cut was a hint more European than his own clothing, it was apparel he might have chosen himself. In the mirror it was the difference he noticed and liked. With the bright blue tie, it felt like costume, and for an instant it occurred to him that this might be fun.

'So.' He sat at the counter opposite her. Tea was set, and sandwiches. 'You made tea for me years ago.' He touched the cup to his lips. 'I remember your family dishes. Meissen, wasn't it?'

She nodded.

'Do you still have them?'

'There hasn't been room in my life for heirlooms.'

'That's too bad.'

'Yes, but not relevant. Can you tell me where we met?'

Books and papers away, class. Take out your blue books. 'How could I forget? You were a Lufthansa stewardess on a flight from Frankfurt to London. I was a first-class passenger.'

'When was that?'

'Seven years ago. You loved your job but after you married me I made you quit, and now you are part owner of a boutique in St Moritz.'

'And your profession?'

'Trust officer, is how I always answer the question. In fact I manage the family money. My father was an oil speculator in what is now Qatar, and he left me and my two sisters small fortunes. Some of it in unexpired oil leases. Just before he died in 1969 the three of us became Swiss citizens to avoid losing more than three-quarters of it in taxes. I manage my sisters' portions of the estate as well.'

'What is the capital of Qatar?'

'Doha.'

'What is our address?'

'Waisenhausstrasse 23, 8820 Waedenswil. Our phone is 01-780-2531. We have a schnauzer named Igor and a maid named Helga. Your name was Sigrid Schmidt and you first contacted your father in 1972 and have visited him nearly every year since. I have never accompanied you until now.'

'Why is that?'

303

'I don't know.' Jake panicked suddenly. The answer wasn't in the papers she'd given him. What, he should make an excuse? That wasn't supposed to be in the exam. He was a humiliated undergraduate. Perspiration coated his palms.

'Don't ever say "I don't know"!' she commanded. 'Think about it! Why haven't you accompanied me?'

'Because my doctors advise against it. I have a genetic heart defect and must avoid unnecessary stress.'

'Then why are you coming with me now?'

Jake answered automatically, surprising himself. 'Because this is different. Not "unnecessary" at all. I know what your father's coming over means to you and how worried you are. You are terrified for him. It is unthinkable to me that you should have to deal with it alone. I love you.'

Magda startled both of them by smiling suddenly. 'That was very good. *Very* good. You convinced even me. You see, you *can* do it!'

Jake was not relieved by her compliment. He was trembling inside. He thought of a crack to make – Besides, my doctor doubled my Valium dose – but he said nothing. He could imagine that his 'wife' would be terrified because he was.

At the Zurich airport late that afternoon, they responded to each other not with indifference, but with an easy, almost callous familiarity. This couple, their manner said, had been together for years. Magda carried the heavy canvas tote and, in her oversized purse, both their passports. Jake followed with a nylon suit-bag hooked over his shoulder, a newspaper and magazines in French and German under that arm, and in his other hand, his silver-handled ebony stick. Magda, wife that she was, felt no compulsion to wait for her limping husband. She was a German émigrée preoccupied, presumably, with the imminent reunion with her aged father. To observers, Jake sensed, she was a nervous traveller, while he was himself a calm, perhaps resigned, man who had long since grown accustomed to his own limitations, physical and otherwise, as well as to the envious glances strangers cast continually at his high-strung gorgeous wife.

As they checked in at the airline counter, Jake felt an exquisite tension. Once it was clear that his new identity had been unhesitatingly accepted by the airline clerk, his spirits soared. Beneath his cool demeanour an excitement surged such as he had never experienced before. All at once Jake McKay, the well-liked but vaguely disappointed professor, no longer existed. Not that his place had been taken by Harold Davidson, but that Jake felt somehow that he had finally joined the select company he had grown up worshipping. Now it did not matter that he limped. If anything, since everyone knows that spooks aren't gimps, it helped the subterfuge. And now it did not matter that he had long since repudiated the assumptions of the world of secrets – secret identities, secret missions, secret agents. Now that he had entered it, he felt more alive than he ever did at Tufts or at home. He was learning something new about his father.

But then, at the security check as he stepped through the wired door frame, the alarm went off, a loud buzzer and a flashing light. He jumped, and his hand shot involuntarily to his heart, as if he *did* have heart disease. He stood guiltily in front of the policeman. Magda had preceded him through and was waiting with studied patience. Her steely expression said, You're on your own, chum.

The guard addressed Jake in French, but much too quickly for him. But the guard was indicating Jake's stick. Of course! The silver handle! That would do it, wouldn't it? He smiled wanly. 'I almost never carry this one. All my other canes are wood.' He handed the ebony through to Magda and crossed back to the other side of the threshold. Unsteadily now he went through again. And the alarm rang, this time, it seemed, more excitedly. Jake froze. There was an explanation, but he couldn't think of it. I'm not armed! he wanted to cry. If anyone's armed, she is!

Magda took his elbow as if he were an invalid. 'It's your leg, darling. The pins in your leg.' She led him aside and spoke to the guard in French. The guard frisked him perfunctorily, but discreetly felt his leg through his trousers to satisfy himself that the deformity was real.

Jake, when he recovered, was mortified. As they walked towards the gate he said, 'That's never happened to me before. I've gone through dozens of those things.'

'Yes. But this is Europe. The detectors are much more sensitive because the threat of terrorists is much more real. In America you worry about ageing Black Panthers. Here we have the PLO, the Red Brigades, and Punk Rock stars.'

On the airplane this time, Magda sat at the window because that's what wives do.

The ease with which she took his hand during take-off, as if they always did that, as if she were frightened of flying, instructed him.

More than halfway between Zurich and Berlin lies the border

between the German states. At about the point where he guessed it might pass below them, Jake leaned across Magda to look out of the window. What did he expect, minefields? Guard towers? Rows of tanks? A barren swath of ploughed land, barbed wire? Giant firebreaks in the forest? In fact the border between the Germanies consists of all these things, and it remains the one frontier in the world which from the air might verify the naïf's impression from pastel maps that the borders between nations are dramatic.

Jake was disappointed. Visible below them was a carpet of clouds. He smiled at Magda. 'I wanted to see that Iron Curtain.'

'You will see it, I promise you. Our first stop will be the Wall. I want you to see what we are dealing with.'

Soon the plane began its descent, and when it finally broke through the clouds Jake McKay, almost despite himself, leaned across Magda again. On the pastel map, what colour would that land have been? Owing to the overcast and the fading sunlight, not politics, it was grey, and that seemed perfect. The plane was banking over a quilted countryside on which suburban tracts of houses and apartment buildings were interspersed among patches of farmland.

'It looks like the exurbs anywhere,' he said.

'Except for history, I suppose, it is.' She pointed. 'That is Oranienburg.'

Jake stared down at the town famous as the site of the first death camp. What the Nazis began there they perfected later at Buchenwald. As the plane angled lower he said, 'I guess they don't get an inch away from history here, do they?'

'They shouldn't.' Magda did not speak again until the airplane was making a broad turn above the centre of Berlin. 'Tempelhof,' she said, pointing to the downtown airport.

'I've heard of it.'

'Of course you have, the Airlift. Planes approaching Tempelhof dropped raisins and candy for the children. "Raisin bombers", they were called.'

'Don't we land at Tempelhof?' The plane, in its steep approach, was leaving the famous airport behind.

'No. Tegel.'

'Never heard of it.' He pointed past her. 'What's that?'

'That's the park in the centre city.'

'The Grunewald?'

'No, no. The Grunewald is a large forest straddling Wannsee

to the southwest. What you see there is the Tiergarten. The famous zoo is in the Tiergarten. Forgive me, I think everyone knows Berlin like I do. Look there, you can see the Victory Column.'

'Which victory would that be, darling?' Jake's sarcasm registered in her face as a blow. Whatever her attitudes about the recent history of her country, she was still a German. He reined his manic agitation. He might have apologized for the crack, but the chime sounded and the no-smoking light went on. They brought their seats forward and waited for the landing. *Flughafen Tegel* abutted the residential section known as Wedding. The plane seemed to brush its rooftops.

Rooftops, what was it about rooftops?

He remembered looking down on Washington, on the terracotta roofs of the official buildings, and the dull grey roofs of the old tempos and the yellow-tiled roofs of the CIA Compound on its knoll above Foggy Bottom. And he remembered Giles Patterson quoting Churchill, 'To the roofs, London!'

Suddenly that bold wartime esprit seemed to fill the cavity in his chest, like air to a man who hadn't breathed, and Jake experienced in a wholly new way his own resolution, his own will, his own – yes – courage. He too had survived the Blitz.

Magda took his hand just before the wheels touched, skipped, caught. Her palm was wet with perspiration. Was that an act as well? If she was afraid, what right had he not to be?

CHAPTER TWENTY-FIVE

The Wall is not just a wall. It is a stretch of no-man's-land thirty, forty, and in many places more than a hundred yards wide. To come from East Berlin one must first climb an eight-foot chain-link fence topped with barbed wire, then cross a broad strip of sand, which collects footprints to alert the jeep patrol. If one gets by the watchdogs on the running leash, it is only to dash across an open space, tripping an electronic sensor, which signals the guards in towers spaced at intervals of two hundred yards. The guard who brings the fugitive down will receive a bonus, so none hesitates to activate the automatic machine guns emplaced in pill-boxes at a distance calculated to provide fire cover all along the border. The machine guns send out sprays of bullets at the height of an average man's chest. If somehow one survives that, one comes at last to the poured-concrete wall itself, which by now, if it is night, is brightly illuminated. Scaling it to its height of twelve feet, one encounters the last obstacle, an ordinary cement pipe that tops the wall off, but is too large and smooth to offer a handhold.

Jake and Magda were standing, faces into the wind, on a high wooden platform overlooking that gash. It was nearly dark now. The platform, sturdy and unornamented, was almost two storeys high and built like a gallows at the spot just beyond the Tiergarten where Bellevuestrasse achieved its dead end in the Wall. From where they stood, they could see the centre of East Berlin. Lights were on in all the buildings, but it was the brilliantly illuminated armed wasteland immediately in front that held their attention.

'I'd have been disappointed,' Jake said after a long silence, 'if it wasn't hideous.'

Magda was looking at a feature of the landscape of her home-town, as if it were a given of nature, a river at floodstage, a stirring volcano, a dark canyon. She said, 'People come to this spot – not Berliners – and are amazed. What do they think the argument is over?' She faced him. 'You must keep in mind whom we are dealing with. Things must go according to plan. We must make no mistakes.'

Her words registered, but remotely. The death strip itself monopolized his attention. It was the one sight in the West, Jake realized, that explained her choices. He could imagine her thinking, like every general, that every recruit and every critic should be brought here and made to look and to contemplate. No differences worth protecting? What end justifies our means if not the one of resisting this?

Jake raised his eyes. East Berlin was spread before them with its share of new, tall buildings, including a soaring television tower, which, with its bulbous observation deck, restaurant included, looked like an inverted scallion. Red warning lights flashed on top of it. His surprise at East Berlin's apparent prosperity – it looked like any modern city at night – did not distract him for long. He looked at the Wall again, then let his eye flicker from pillbox to guard tower to tank barrier. 'I understand,' he said.

'Good. From now on you must obey me in everything, however minor. I will not feel obliged to explain myself.'

'All right.'

His willingness seemed to surprise her. A hint of gratitude flickered across her face. Her voice softened when she said, 'It doesn't need to be dangerous.' She looked out across the Wall again. The wind whipped at her hair and countless little strands of it had worked loose and fluttered around her face. 'Only fools attempt to cross here. It is not a problem to bribe officials for the proper papers with which to pass through the checkpoint. Greed is the opiate of the revolution.'

Jake appeared to mock himself, saying, 'I don't ordinarily condone bribery, mind you, but what's good enough for Boston politicians is good enough for the Politburo.'

'Politburo?' Magda asked carefully. 'Why do you say Politburo?'

Jake sensed that Magda was suppressing a surge of feeling, and that made him curious. He shrugged, but he was watching her. 'I used the word innocently. Aren't the officials one must bribe in the Politburo?'

'The Politburo are the Party rulers, and you know it.'

'Unless we use the language precisely, my dear. In 1952 I know that the Politburo as the Central Committee was replaced by the Presidium.'

Magda turned away. 'You are ingenuous.'

He put his arm on her shoulder. 'No, I'm not. I'm nervous.'

'You think to disarm me by a pretence of naïveté and ignorance.'

'Yes, I do. Why should you be armed with me? I thought we were in this together. I look out over this minefield and I think if I am going to mess with these people I'd better have a partner I can trust. I don't think you've told me everything.'

When she didn't reply he took his arm from her shoulder and leaned on his stick half a step behind her. He too fixed his eyes on the death strip.

And he found himself asking his oldest question. How could his spirited, eccentric, gregarious uncle have willingly imprisoned himself on the far side of that barrier? Once, in an effort to identify the appeal, Jake had even dedicated a sabbatical to the study of Marxism. But at the end of the year his head was stuffed with platitudes that, given the realities of Soviet application – their praxis – left Jake more convinced than ever that Giles could not have been motivated by an intellectual ideal. And now Giles wanted out. Well, that made sense at least. It was the one item on his list Jake didn't wonder about.

Magda said something.

'What?'

'Potsdamer Platz,' she repeated. 'It was the most fashionable square in Berlin.'

Jake saw the old trolley tracks bisecting the no-man's-land, pictured the ladies dismounting their limousines in their evening gowns on their way to the opera. 'Before the Wall?'

She smiled and shook her head. Berlin had layers of history. 'Before the war.' She pointed across the strip. 'Do you see that mound?'

Jake looked to his left, to a low dark hill, an unclothed pile of dirt rising beyond a set of white criss-crossed girders. The mound was in the very centre of the illuminated forbidden zone.

Magda continued, 'That is what remains of his bunker.'

Jake's eyes fell involuntarily to the relic trolley tracks. Paving-stones showed beneath cracked patches in the asphalt. Jake imagined he could hear the clacking of hooves.

Magda went on dully, as if she were an ill-paid guide, 'All the great buildings were here. The *Reichskanzlei*, the Gestapo Office, Goebbels' Ministry of Propaganda . . . Standing here we would have been in easy sight of Hitler's balcony.'

Jake's eyes fixed finally on that mound. He couldn't picture the grand buildings or the hellish crypt in which Hitler died, but all at once he could hear resounding in that very air the cry of thousands, '*Sieg Heil!*'

Jake clutched his stick; these were the people who had crippled him. But that resentment was a mere complaint compared to the evil they had accomplished. 'Christ, it's possible to believe he really existed when you see the very spot.'

'Yes. That too is why I brought you here.' She touched his arm. 'So now perhaps you are ready.'

'Are we going across now?'

She shook her head. 'Think about it. What would Harold and Sigrid be doing?'

He surprised himself by answering without hesitation. 'They would be crossing in the morning. Tonight they would stay in a hotel here in the West. A first-class hotel, with a good restaurant.'

When she nodded he smiled, pleased with himself. As he followed her down the wooden stairs he felt his wariness lift somewhat. He was relieved to leave the Wall behind, if only for the night.

'Where are we staying?' he asked as she pulled the car into traffic.

'The Kempinski, on the Ku-damm.'

'Sounds Polish. In honour of Walesa?'

'You joke, but Walesa may be our only problem. The GDR is more threatened by the Polish workers than the Russians are. If the strikes spread . . .' Magda downshifted and took a corner just as the light changed.

'If the strikes spread, what?'

While Jake waited for his answer he noticed that her eyes kept returning to the rear-view mirror, dartingly, compulsively. When she took the next corner at top speed and then accelerated, he turned in his seat to look out the back window. 'Is someone following us?'

The realization slammed him. A grey Mercedes took the corner behind them, and it was travelling at high speed too. The menace of Berlin overtook him. Spies everywhere. And danger.

But as they went up the ramp on to a congested super-highway, Magda said, 'No one is following us, Jake. They won't follow us until we are in the East.'

Jake lost the Mercedes. He had the intuition that she was not levelling with him, but he was also aware that she had just called him by name for the first time. That defused his suspicion, though he guessed it was supposed to. She's good, he thought. He said, 'You drive superbly.'

She was in the passing lane, blinking her lights for gangway. Their car was flat out. 'Near here is the Avus, Hitler's first great highway and racecourse. I saw the Grand Prix there once. It inspires me.'

When a car ahead refused to pull over, despite her flashing lights, Magda leaned on the horn and drove so close to it, even at a hundred-forty kilometres an hour, that their bumpers almost touched. The car swerved into the next lane and Magda, stone-faced, shot by it.

'Maybe you ought to take it easy,' Jake said.

'Driving fast!' she exclaimed. She threw a look at him. 'It makes me feel wonderful.'

Her rush communicated. Colour had filled her face, and the tension in her arms and hands, rigid on the steering wheel, seemed electric. A new energy overtook Jake's fear. He pressed

311

his right foot hard against the floor as if there were an accelerator under it. Things were about to happen, dangerous things, once-in-a-lifetime things. Jake felt it too. He grasped the handle in front of him and pressed his own emotion into it.

When she looked at him, he nodded. She laughed delightedly. Her hair had come half undone. She pushed it back from her face and tucked it behind her ear, but she wanted her hands for driving. When her hair fell again, Jake reached across and tucked it back for her.

When they arrived at the hotel and went to the desk to check in, there was no clerk. It took a moment for them to realize that he was standing, together with a dozen guests and other employees, in the cramped office behind the wall of mail slots. The sound of a television could be heard.

Jake hit the bell.

The clerk came out, wearing a perplexed and concerned expression.

'*Was ist los?*' Magda asked.

'*Polen,*' he answered, and added a sentence Jake didn't get. He and Magda then checked in. But the clerk's preoccupation didn't lessen, and when he rang for the bellhop, he too came out from the room with the television.

At the elevator Magda said, 'A general strike is declared for tomorrow in Poland.' She spoke quietly so that the bellhop, standing aside, wouldn't hear.

'The whole country?'

'Yes.'

'What will that mean for us?'

'Less grievous trouble than that has closed the border.'

'If the Russians invade . . .'

She cut him off and said with a hint of condescension, 'The Russians are already there. They don't need to invade. Our problem is the GDR. Honecker must control *his* people. East Germans must not be tempted to imitate their neighbours. At a certain point the first thing he will do is close the border to demonstrate, no, to flaunt his control.'

'When does that point come?'

The elevator doors opened. They stepped inside with the bellhop and fell silent. All three watched the number lights indicate the floors.

When the bellhop, having led the way into their room, went to the window to open the curtains, Jake said in his British accent, 'You can leave those drawn, my man.' He held out a ten-mark bill. 'Thank you.'

The bellhop took his tip and left.

Jake had assumed there would come a moment when they would be alone together in a room with a bed. He had expected it would be excrutiatingly awkward, but it was not. For one thing there were two beds, and for another Magda went immediately into the bathroom. Jake unpacked his second suit and hung it in the closet. They would be going down to dinner now, wouldn't they? He had to check a wave of resentment at her for keeping him so utterly in the dark.

He moved casually towards the window. He had no idea what view the curtains obscured. The Kaiser Wilhelm Church, perhaps?

He put a finger in the curtain and drew it back slightly. The colours of the Kurfürstendamm, the automobiles, the kiosks, the bright shop windows, the brightly lit neon signs, the peddlers' pushcarts, first struck him as a wild abstract splattering. Restaurants and cafés bristled with dinner trade, well-heeled pedestrians crossed the broad avenue in the centre of which elm trees dominated a bench-lined strip. The colour, the crisply modern buidings, even the towering trees, he reminded himself, were all new since the war. West Berlin's happy thronging prosperity was the touted evidence of our system's superiority to theirs. But that scene suddenly struck Jake as frantic, and he could feel welling in himself a desperation which, though he had never consciously felt it before, he recognized. A like desperation, he was certain, sloshed like bilge in the hidden spaces of every person he could see from that window. Superiority for what, exactly? For racing? For manic speed? For endless efforts to rebuild the world? But the world, West Berlin and Boston, the Ku-damm and Beacon Street and the Kremlin and the Berlin Wall, for that matter, all inexorably unbuild themselves. The world has contempt for the efforts of men. Why, then, are men contemptuous of each other? And why, when they are all so lonely and afraid, are they at war?

Subversive thoughts; he banished them.

Half a block up the Ku-damm towards the not quite visible Kaiser Wilhelm Church was a gaudy theatre marquee and above it a two-storey-high billboard which featured in floodlit Day-Glo a nude woman brazenly displaying her pubis. With her right hand she was touching herself, and with her left she was aiming a Luger across the avenue at McKay. Her tongue showed between her teeth.

He wondered again if Magda was armed. Because of airport security her weapon, if she had one, would have to be in her luggage. Could he bring himself to search it?

He was about to let the curtain fall shut when something caught his eye across the Kurfürstendamm. He looked again.

A grey Mercedes. It was parked, but the driver was at the wheel. Magda was good, but so were they.

Something about the driver, a well-groomed man of middle age, was familiar. Was he looking up at the Kempinski? Jake tried to make out the man's features in detail, but couldn't.

He swallowed and noticed that his throat was dry. He needed water, he could use a drink. Would she let him have a drink with dinner? His shirt was soaked with perspiration.

He chastised himself. She was right about the booze. He *didn't* need it. He had to control himself. Fear and paranoia would not do. This was Germany. Grey Mercedeses were ubiquitous. The Communists had no reason to follow them until they were in the East.

He closed the curtain and stepped back.

When he turned, his eyes fell involuntarily on Magda's suitcase. It was still closed where the bellhop had put it. He looked in the direction of the bathroom. No sign of her. Search her suitcase? Wasn't it the point of his life that he did not do such things? But that was before. Before, for one thing, she'd lied to him.

'No one is following us, Jake,' she'd said with a hint of affection in her voice, using his name.

He crossed quickly to her bag and unzipped it.

Seconds later he closed it and straightened up. In the mirror he saw her watching him, and he jumped.

'What did you find?' she asked.

'Nothing,' he said.

She nodded. 'I told you. Our only weapon is our skill.'

At dinner they hardly spoke. The dining-room was crowded, and the adjacent tables were very close by. A harpist played in a nearby corner and it was natural that they should seem to listen to the music. Sigrid and Harold Davidson, too, would have had their reasons to be preoccupied. Jake realized after a time that, however awkward he felt, no one could have guessed from watching them that they were frauds.

After they'd finished eating and Magda had lit a cigarette, Jake said, 'I'm sorry I did that upstairs. I feel rotten about it.'

'I expected it. You should have asked me.'

'But you wouldn't have told me. You've told me almost nothing.'

'It's best that way.' She looked off across the room, cutting even that talk short.

A man who might have been an Arab was sitting alone at the next table. He stared intermittently at Magda. She was wearing a pale blue linen dress, without jewellery, and with only the barest hint of make-up. Her hair was pulled even more severely back, but the effect of her appearance was stunning. Jake let his eyes fall for an instant to her bosom. Even tastefully clothed as she was, Magda's sensuality asserted itself, as if despite her.

'You have an admirer,' Jake said, indicating the Arab. It was easy to picture her at the dark man's side, at a blackjack table. And then suddenly, just as easily, Jake pictured the Arab slipping a loop of piano wire around Magda's throat and choking her.

He reined his craziness.

Magda had ignored his comment. She smoked distractedly. He recognized, besides his paranoia, his resentment that she had been with other men and would be again.

'Darling, I must say,' he offered blithely, 'you don't look like anyone's idea of an East German worker's daughter.'

'We daughters of East German workers make a point not to.'

He reached across the table for her cigarettes. 'May I?'

'I thought you were above smoking.'

'I was.' He leaned towards her to light his cigarette from her lighter. 'I was above a lot of things. Perhaps if I smoke it will make me better at this stuff.'

'No. It will just make you dead sooner.' Before the shock he felt at her cruel statement registered fully she reached across the table for his hand. 'I'm sorry,' she said. 'I didn't mean that. I don't know why I said it. I'm not myself.' She pressed his hand. 'You've been so good. I'm sorry.'

Jake stared at her. This was the first hint of feeling she'd displayed. A small corner of her surface calm had been ripped back by her inadvertent flippancy about his death. Was his death in fact an issue? And was this emotion Magda's? Or Sigrid's? Was she apologizing to a husband with a heart condition? Or to an out-

315

classed amateur whose teacher must not frighten him? Either way, it was an apology and he accepted it. 'Only your presence,' he said, 'makes what I'm feeling bearable.'

Magda blushed, but she did not release his hand. After a moment she said quietly, 'Yours helps me too.'

'It does?' Jake grinned. He felt a sharp stab of happiness in his chest.

She grinned too and nodded girlishly. 'It shouldn't, you know. I'm not supposed to need help. Usually I don't.'

'But you do now?' He could not conceal his pleasure. He'd not dared hope to be anything but her pupil, her burden.

She nodded again, but solemnly. 'Don't ask me more.' Her voice now was the barest whisper, and it was sad. 'Just hold my hand a moment longer.'

But it was Magda who was holding. Jake returned her pressure, but he kept his hand inside hers.

Soon they left the dining-room. They rode the elevator in silence, and walked the length of the corridor to the door of their room without touching each other. As Jake turned the key, Magda stood on her toes to put her mouth at his ear. She whispered, 'In the room now we cannot presume to be in private.'

Jake displayed his surprise, then drew her away from the door. He whispered, 'What do you mean?'

'There has been time now to plant a device.'

'But you said before they wouldn't bother with us until we're in the East. They were following us, weren't they!'

'Don't tell me what I said before! And don't question me!' The brisk authority which once he'd welcomed now deflated him. Clearly he'd misunderstood the moment of tenderness, of friendship, they'd just shared in the dining-room. She was still in charge. They returned to the door. Jake unlocked it and pushed it open. Both beds had been plumped and turned back, but otherwise the room appeared undisturbed.

Jake went automatically to the window and looked out. There was no sign of a parked grey Mercedes on the Ku-damm below. He drew the curtains closed.

When he turned Magda was lifting her dress over her head. She did it exactly the way Linda would have, without coyness, as if the act of disrobing in front of him promised nothing out of the ordinary. Then why was he riveted by the sight of Magda naked from the waist up? Her breasts were perfectly shaped. Suddenly his anxiety about the menace of Berlin gave way to his complex feelings about her. He watched her blatantly.

She turned her back to him and sat on the edge of her bed to remove her half-slip and stockings. Then she unfastened her hair and shook it free. She was naked now except for her underpants, but it was the sight of her hair, unrestrained, loose on her shoulders, that seemed most sexual to him. Her hair underscored her great beauty, but the way she had been wearing it, tightly gathered above her nape, had underscored her control. Now it was not gathered but her control was intact. In a quick movement which displayed her breasts and torso and the beige splash of her underpants against the tan flesh of her trim abdomen and thighs, she leaned across the bed towards him to snap out the lamp.

In the darkness he heard her settle beneath her blanket and he sensed that she did so on her side, facing away from him.

This is the moment, the only moment of which Linda will require description in detail from me. In fact, he would admit, I was sexually interested for a moment. He would not tell Linda that Magda had aroused in him a desire the acuteness of which he had not felt in years. He had felt it before, but not for Linda. Then for whom? Why, for this woman, of course, when she was a girl.

It pained him that he was with his *danseuse* whose intensely sensual image he had carried faithfully in his subconscious all these years. Her presence now seemed a rebuke that his life had not turned out differently. He was with his *danseuse* and yet enacting perfectly the stale, mute ritual of marital ennui. With what sublime indifference had she undressed herself and turned away from him! Linda would be amused, would think it hilarious if she knew how perfectly Magda Dettke, *femme fatale*, had played the role of blasé wife.

Jake took off his jacket. Before draping it over the edge of a chair he withdrew the envelope from the inside pocket. He balanced the letter in his hand as if the weight of it would tell him something. For the first time in eighteen years he felt an urge to open it.

By now his eyes were adjusted to the dark and he could make out the shapes of the room's furniture. He tossed the envelope on the dressing-table and efficiently, quietly took off his own clothes. He sat on his bed to take off his socks, and with a gentleness he rarely exercised towards himself he caressed his

317

own left leg and for once allowed his fingers to trace the ridges of the scars of countless scalpels. In the dark, depending on his sense of touch, his leg seemed uglier than ever. It felt like the skin of a reptile. He grasped his leg at the shinbone, now without gentleness, and could practically encircle it with his fingers. He felt an urge to raise that leg in his hand, as if it were a club. Primitive men wielded bones for clubs, didn't they? The bones of their victims, yes, but not their own bones. He wanted to smash it down on his enemy, but what enemy if not his leg itself? For once he had not cut short his emotion. His leg had ruined him, had made him weak, a man without substance, sturdiness, or courage, a man who had fled the one test life required of him, taking refuge instead with stifling sincerity in a pale trade and a calculated domesticity.

He released his leg abruptly. It wasn't his leg's fault. His leg was his great excuse. It excused him not from winning races, but from running in them. It excused him now from standing and crossing the room and saying to Magda Dettke, 'All my adult life I have wanted to be with you.'

When Linda asks me, he said to himself as he lay back on his bed, I shall tell her, 'No, I was not faithful to you. But out of gratitude for all your pity, my leg was.'

He lay there in silence, not moving, not covering himself, not even listening particularly to the sound of Magda's breathing. He lay there for a long time, and perhaps he slept.

What he dreamt of was Degas's *danseuse*, the delicate mesh of her skirt, her ribbon, her bronze skin. He dreamt of a boy drawing near and touching with his forefinger her stiff leg from her ankle wrapped in the ribbons of her toe slippers up along the back of her calf-muscle and into the faint hollow behind her knee.

He opened his eyes and sat up, then carefully lowered his legs over the edge of his bed and crossed to hers. He lay down behind her, spooning her, though she was under the sheet and he was on top of it. He put his mouth by her ear to whisper, 'Magda, we must talk.' He said that as if he had lain down beside her because he was afraid of being overheard.

She rolled on to her back, brushing his cheek with her hair, then gathering it. She lay staring at the dark of the ceiling. The silhouette of her profile conveyed a depth of unhappiness that moved him. He touched her cheek.

She did not react.

'Why are you unhappy?'

318

'Because I hate what I am, and I don't want to do it anymore.'

'Tell me,' he said softly.

'I wanted this to be my last time, but now I feel . . .' Her sentence trailed off.

'Trapped?' he offered.

She nodded.

'I feel that way too. Isn't that funny? My life is so different from yours, but I feel trapped by what I have become. Not by my family or my wife or my job. By me.'

She nodded more vigorously. 'It's the same. I am alone, but it's the same.'

'Why do you want out of it?'

She looked at him. 'You see what it makes me. Merciless. Hard. I want to love someone. I want to learn how to do that.'

She raised her eyes to the ceiling again. She was afraid, he guessed, that he was one of those men who would want to talk about his wife. He wasn't. His wife, he saw finally, had nothing to do with this. If there were ghosts inhibiting him and Magda, they were ghosts of his father and her mother.

'Why weren't they lovers?' he asked quietly.

'I told you. My mother loved my father.'

'But he was dead.'

'No, he wasn't,' she whispered. 'He was in Russia. My father was Russian.'

'I think I had guessed as much. And he brought Giles across when Giles defected.'

Magda nodded. 'My father and your father and Giles were together here in Berlin at the end of the war. They destroyed Hitler's airplane, preventing his escape.' Magda let her face fall towards Jake again. Their faces were almost touching. 'Your father and Giles brought us out, my mother and me. They saved us. Your father was very good to me, always. I was very sad when he died.'

'You knew when he died?'

'My mother told me. From an early age she told me everything.'

'Unlike my experience. My father's silence was absolute.'

'My mother only told me because she had no one else. Secrets must be shared with someone.'

'My father never told my mother secrets.'

'He had Giles.'

'Was my father working for the Russians too?'

Magda didn't answer him.

'I think I could have forgiven that if he had explained himself to me.'

'Jake, you were a child. How could he explain . . . ?'

'Yes, *his* child! He owed me explanations.'

'He owed you nothing. It wasn't family secrets he was keeping from you. It wasn't trade secrets, or a recipe for sauce. People would have died if your father's silence had not been absolute.'

'Who?'

Magda didn't answer him and Jake knew that he was lying side by side now with the very secret he had been raised to hate. 'I recognize the tone of your silence,' he said. '"Secrets must be shared with someone," eh? Who do you share yours with? I've had enough of being the odd man out with all of you.' He sat up abruptly, swung off her bed and crossed back to his own. He lay on his back and closed his eyes.

A moment later the television was snapped on and turned up loud. Inane music, an advertising jingle, filled the room. He sensed it when she pulled the set into the space between their beds, and even through his eyelids he registered the peculiar light of broadcast colour bouncing off the ceiling. He felt her weight on his bed and he was conscious suddenly of his own nakedness and he was embarrassed.

Her mouth was at his ear. 'I told you my secret.' He could barely hear her, though her breath moved the hairs around his ear. 'You did not listen to me. I have decided to quit the service. This is my last mission, and that frightens me.'

Jake laughed. 'It frightens me because it's my first.'

'But you know what the world holds for you. I have no future. I feel suspended, lost already. And if they learn, they will try to stop me.'

'Who are "they"?'

She did not answer.

'You have yet to trust me with anything. I don't even know who you are.'

'But don't you see?' she said urgently. 'If I stop doing this neither will I. I want out of it. I want to start over.' She seemed about to sob. 'I want a different life.'

Jake was moved by her emotion and he believed it, but questions popped open in his mind and he had to ask them.

'My uncle is afraid of the KGB. Hence my presence. But your

father was his KGB connection. Hence yours? Tell me the truth, Magda. Am I the bait in your trap?'

'No.'

'Are you KGB?'

'No,' she answered wearily.

'Why should I believe you?'

'There is no reason why you should. You'd have to trust me.'

'You people make a point to trust no one. My father trusted Giles and it destroyed him. Giles doesn't trust you. Why should I?'

'Because you are outside of it.' Magda leaned over him. When her hair brushed his face he turned his head slightly. He did not flinch to find her right above him. 'You,' she went on, 'have not been corrupted by this business. That is why your uncle wanted you.'

'And you?' He curled his finger in her hair. 'Tell me more, Magda.'

'All right. Giles is leaving Russia now because my father has recently died. My father was a senior official of the KGB, a member of the Politburo. That is why I was startled when you referred to it. He always protected Giles. Before he died he arranged for Giles's assignment to the Party congress here, and he provided him with the necessary false documents to come across.'

Behind them the television, more advertising, boomed. No wonder she was afraid of being overheard. 'The documents aren't from you?'

'No.'

'Then why does he need us?'

'He does not need me. He needs you.'

'And he expects me to protect him?'

'Yes.'

'From you?'

Magda didn't respond.

'Are you supposed to arrest him?'

'Of course I should. If I followed procedure I would call in my colleagues when he is across the border.'

'And will you?'

Magda fell back on the bed, but Jake turned towards her so that they lay on their sides, facing each other. She said wearily, 'My father did not want him arrested, and neither do I. He would spend the rest of his life in prison. I told you, I want to stop it. I will not help them take him.'

Jake felt an abrupt surge of concern for his uncle. 'You mean I can just take him home?'

'You'd have to protect him. Would you do that? Could you?'

'Yes.' It was a surprise to him. He would do anything for his uncle. But of course he knew his sentiment was ludicrous. And so did she.

'It would change your life,' she said, as if he *could* protect him.

'My life could use changing.'

Magda touched his cheek. 'You *are* like me,' she said.

That she abruptly displayed her affection for him unsettled Jake, and instinctively he deflected it. 'Besides, how can I do less for my uncle than your father has? Tell me about him.'

'What can I tell you?' She withdrew her hand.

'Why you work for the British if he was KGB.'

'Because of my mother. She hated the Russians. There was a virtue about her hatred of them. The Poles could learn about the Russians as invaders from stories my mother told. She lived for the day that my father would come over.' Magda shrugged. 'I never thought he would. I am loyal to my mother, but I get the quality of my loyalty from him.'

Jake timidly wound his fingers through her hair. 'Magda, you and I were born on opposite sides of the same street. What a terrible burden you've been carrying all these years.'

'You too.' Magda's eyes filled. 'I knew you would understand me. I always knew you would.'

He moved closer to her, and they kissed. Jake closed his hand on her breast.

But Magda pulled back and whispered with a sudden desperation, 'It isn't that I don't trust you. My habit is to guard secrets because secrets protect us. Now they protect your uncle and the memory of my father. He wanted, even in death, only the good opinion of his countrymen. If it were known that in the end he helped Giles . . .'

'I understand that. Now that I know what we're doing, it's all right.'

'I could learn to trust you, I think.'

'Use my name.'

'I could learn to trust you, Jake.'

While kissing him then, Magda let Jake guide her body on to his.

The novelty struck him. Magda's lean, toned body was similar to Linda's, but it was as if no woman had lain on him before. He explored her skin, her breasts, waist, hips, the rise of her buttocks. The bristly thatch of her pubic hair scratched his thigh, then his erection as he pressed his pelvis up at her. Her hand cupped his face. She played her kiss out, rolling her head slightly and slightly groaning. He could not help but think of Linda, who never curled her tongue around his, who never made a sound.

Jake turned her on to her side and with one hand found her vagina and with the other began to trace down along her thigh a line, barely touching her, until he found the hollow behind her knee. As if that were the secret spot for her as well as his, she bent her leg back sharply and caught his hand.

When she began to move her face down across his body, trailing her tongue through his chest hairs, leading with a hand that closed around his penis, he guessed that she would end at his leg, that she would caress it, that she would curl her body around to kiss his scars. Wouldn't it be every woman's need to demonstrate to him first that she was not offended by his limb, that such were her womanly resources that she could even love it? Magda brought her mouth as far as his penis, kissed him, moistened him, but then, pressing lightly to turn him on to his back again, she brought her face back to his and found his mouth again. She sealed the length of his body with her own. Her right leg lay across his left, but made nothing of it. She didn't even rub it with her foot. He stopped thinking of Linda when he realized that Magda had made nothing of his leg and would continue to. It had never occurred to him that was possible. That it was, released him.

My dream! he said. My dream! His mind burst with the realization that at last she was his. The woman he'd always longed for, and this was how! Her face, her breasts, her hair, her glistening skin, her legs, those thighs, her cunt, her juices, his prick inside her! The taste of her saliva, the stench of sex. He gorged himself while she devoured him. My dream! he said, fucking her.

Afterwards Jake realized that the television was still blaring. He got up, but went first to the window, and drew the curtain back enough to look down on the gaudy Kurfürstendamm. The grey Mercedes was there, with its driver, and the sight of it plunged him back into his panic, but more terribly than before because now he sensed that in some way things had begun to depend on him. The television announcer behind him made it worse. Certain words flew like warning flags above the unintelligible surface of the brutal German: *Polen. Russland. Überfallen. Angst.*

323

CHAPTER TWENTY-SIX

It is not difficult to cross from West Berlin into East. Non-Germans can do so either at Checkpoint Charlie in tour buses, private cars, or as pedestrians, or at the Friedrichstrasse railway station, a stop on the S-Bahn line.

When Magda and Jake went over the next morning, their journey began at the West Berlin S-Bahn station at the Zoo, only a few blocks from the Kempinski.

'Much is made here,' Magda said once they had their tickets and were waiting on the crowded elevated platform, 'of the fact that the East Berlin government runs the S-Bahn even in the West, and that is why the stations are so dingy.' Magda laughed. 'They should see New York.'

The drab station had hardly registered on Jake. He was more curious about the rush-hour passengers who were about to cross willingly behind the hideous barrier he had seen the evening before. Some, with their knapsacks and cameras, were easily identified as tourists, but others, stout women with string bags stuffed with vegetables or colourless men in shapeless suits, carrying old leather satchels, were clearly Germans. 'Who are these people?' he asked.

Magda looked indifferently around the platform. 'West Berliners. Perhaps they have relatives on the other side. They are bringing food.' She fixed her eyes on a particularly old man who was stooped, weary-looking. 'Perhaps he is visiting his children for the day. He might be an East Berliner who was allowed to leave when he became a burden to the state.'

'Like your "father".'

'Precisely.'

'But he would go back?'

Magda looked at Jake. 'It is all in having the proper papers. The border guards are German; they have a German regard for *Ausweise*.' Magda smiled and looked at the old man again. 'We may not all believe in God, but we all believe in our documents.' Then she added, with an instructor's note in her voice, '. . . which are, of course, cross-referenced by computer. The border guard can press buttons and know instantly everything about this man, where he was born, what his work was, how he was rated, when his *Ausweis* was issued.' Magda laughed. 'At Friedrichstrasse they have the best equipment made. American, naturally.'

'What will the computer say about you?'

'It will have the record of each of my visits, naturally. Ironically enough, for background the computer has the truth, that my mother and I were in the Western Zone when the war ended.'

'And about me?'

'Also the truth, that you have never crossed over before. When you enter now, the computer will be informed. When you leave later they will check. If there was no record of your entry, you would not be allowed out.'

'German faith in documents? That sounds like the faith we all have now in our machines.'

'Either way,' Magda said, 'we are depending on it.'

The red train rattled into the station, and as Jake followed Magda into the car he, like the other passengers, fell silent. It was not, for all appearances, just another stretch of ageing urban rapid transit. He sat next to Magda on a wooden bench and the train pulled out of the station. He stared out the opposite window. In the distance he saw the jagged tower of the Kaiser Wilhelm Church and behind it the giant Mercedes star revolving on top of a modern building. The neon lights of West Berlin were all extinguished now. In the morning sunlight the city seemed less callous. Slowly the train left West Berlin behind. It stopped once at the Tiergarten, but no one got on or off. The passengers in the railway car, even the young tourists, seemed sullen and unfriendly. Jake had to remind himself that these were not East Berliners. They were not the Communists.

Soon the train was crossing the Spree River, and Jake realized that they were about to enter East Berlin. At that moment they passed another train coming out and Jake immediately imagined a fugitive having dropped on to the train from an overhanging apartment house and now clinging to a stanchion on its curved roof, riding the S-Bahn to freedom. But at the far bank of the Spree, the first thing Jake saw was a screen of barbed wire suspended between the nearest building and the elevated track. At the point where the railroad bridge ended stood a guard tower, and even though the tower passed in a flash, Jake saw its soldier and his weapon, and he was sure the soldier saw him.

For the few moments that the train careened above the streets of East Berlin Jake stared down at them trying to see the difference. But all he saw were snatches of cityscape like what he could have seen from a train anywhere. The prefabricated apartment houses were drab-modern with balconies and abstract splashes of colour, which were intended to relieve monotony, but only drew attention to it. Still, he'd expected tenements.

The train slowed and then pulled into the great cavern of the Friedrichstrasse station with a screech, and Jake realized that though they had entered East Berlin they had not actually crossed through that curtain yet at all.

When they stepped on to the platform Jake's eye went automatically up to the soaring roof, which, as in railway terminals everywhere in Europe, was made of countless panes of grimy glass. The soft light of early morning was filtered to seem dull and ominous. He saw a soldier on an iron bridge halfway between the track platform and the arching ceiling. His uniform was the colour of the dirty light.

Jake and Magda fell into line with the other passengers and filed down a flight of stairs into a windowless hall. Signs directed foreigners into one room and Germans into another. Magda touched Jake's arm. 'I go over there. When they ask your purpose, say tourism, and that we return this afternoon.'

'Tourism!' he blurted. 'What do you mean, tourism?'

'Keep it simple,' she said. 'It is not going in that there are problems.'

'But you should have told me we go in separately. What if . . . ?'

'Harold! It's routine!' She gunned him with her stare.

He nodded, and said as casually as he could, 'Yes, love. Sorry. See you on the other side.'

He took his place in line, but his heart sank when Magda disappeared through a cloudy glass door. He concentrated on the people immediately in front of him, a pair of young women, one of whom was wearing a brown wooden cross at her throat. When she approached the stern-looking pair of guards Jake paid close attention. The guard took her passport, then, addressing her in French, asked what her business was. She replied that she intended to hear Mass at St Hedwig's. The guard did not react. He filled out the form in front of him. When he finally looked at her, it was only to compare her face with her photograph. He gave the passport back, then held out his hand for McKay's.

He read it, then asked in English without raising his eyes, 'You are Swiss?'

'I am a citizen of Switzerland, yes.'

The guard filled out the form without any further comment.

Magda and Jake were reunited in the next hall. They stood in line together at the currency exchange, where they were required to obtain East German marks. 'It was six marks fifty before, less than five dollars. Now it is twenty,' Magda said.

'Before what?'

'Afghanistan.'

'Oh, God,' Jake said under his breath. 'I don't believe I'm doing this.' He wiped his brow furtively.

Magda seemed alarmed by his nervousness, but she heightened it when she leaned in to him to say, 'And the frontier with Poland, don't forget, is less than an hour from Berlin.'

'By air?'

Magda gave him a quick look of disdain. 'By auto,' she said, and she moved ahead in line, leaving Jake to realize that his American ignorance appalled her. And he was sure that she was wondering if he was up to what was coming.

They exchanged their currency without incident and were quickly on the bustling sidewalk outside the train station. Despite his anxiety, it had been simpler than Jake expected and he was relieved. He looked around, trying to take in every detail of what was before him, but the first person on whom his eyes fell was the young woman who had preceded him in line. She was walking briskly away from them.

'Do you see her?' He pointed. His impulse came, as far as he knew, only from the desire to tell his omniscient guide something she did not know. 'She's French. She's going to hear Mass at St Hedwig's.' Then he stopped, realizing the anomaly. 'Mass? In East Berlin?'

'Yes. St Hedwig's is the cathedral for the whole city. The Archbishop has refused from the beginning to recognize the division of Berlin. As the shepherd, he says, he must tend the entire flock. He has always travelled freely between the halves of the city, the only East Berliner who does.'

'The Russians let him?'

'He is not an ordinary priest. He is the *Rosenpater*.'

'The what?'

'The Rose-father, that was his code name when he was a member of the anti-Hitler underground. He is still called that.'

'But roses . . . !' Jake was stunned. The memory of how all of this began, his father holding roses, came back to him. He was in no way prepared to discover that someone else survived what his father had been part of, and his uncle. 'Roses!' he repeated. 'Was he involved somehow with *Sub Rosa*?'

Magda nodded. 'Your father, your uncle, my father and mother, and the *Rosenpater* were all together at the end of the war.'

'Can we see him? I want to see him.'

Magda looked at her watch. 'I allowed extra time in case we were held up coming over.' She looked at Jake, and nodded. Her eyes glinted. 'I'd like to see him too.'

They took a taxi to the cathedral, a homely green-domed edifice that was set well back from Unter den Linden, East Berlin's main boulevard. As he pulled over, the taxi driver spoke to them in German. Jake didn't understand him, but he seemed friendly, and he used the word *Rosenpater* twice.

On the sidewalk Jake asked, 'What did he say?'

'That this was the first Catholic church built in Prussia after Luther. That it was rebuilt with donations from the West.' She smiled. 'He said that he was a socialist himself, but as a German he revered the *Rosenpater* as a hero.'

'I'm amazed.'

'We Germans don't have many heroes of the struggle against Hitler.'

'Do you know him?'

Magda smiled. 'No. Although he married my parents. My father was a Communist. My mother was a Jew. But they were both very proud of that. Come. I'll show you why.'

Magda led him into the vestibule of the church, to a wall display that featured old photographs and documents.

In one grainy photograph Jake saw a large building with a stone cross mounted on top of it. Magda pointed to it. 'That's where I was born. The Convent of Saint Mary Magdalene. My namesake,' she added solemnly.

Other photographs showed individual nuns, their faces framed in white, and groups of little girls in first-communion dresses. There was a photograph of a priest, a gaunt strange-looking man whose clerical collar was too loose. Next to it was a faded handbill in heavy Gothic script.

Magda began to translate the handbill. 'Roman Catholics!' she read. 'Hitler is reaching for a crown! He wants to be omnipotent. His striving is arrogance. It conflicts with human and divine law. Christ is king! Therefore bear witness for him! Remember those who have borne witness with their lives! Bear witness against

Hitler! In the name of God, resist him! Your brother in His Holy Name, *Rosenpater*.'

Jake looked at Magda and then at the cleric's photograph again. 'Why didn't the Nazis kill him?'

'The nuns hid him. And my father protected him.'

There was another photograph, a more recent one, of a cleric in red robes, with a gold cross. He was not gaunt now, but ascetic. The piercing hollow stare of the young priest was gone, replaced by an unfocused, vacuous expression. 'This is him today?'

Magda nodded. 'He is old now. He refuses to retire. They say even the Pope can't make him resign. I think Catholics are embarrassed because he denounces détente. He remains strongly anti-Communist.'

'But the Russians let him travel back and forth?'

'Not Russians. The GDR. They are Germans. You heard the taxi driver. And of course the Archbishop criticizes the West as well as East.'

'A curse on both our systems. I know the type.'

'No, you don't.' Magda smiled. 'He is not a type. He is the *Rosenpater*.'

'Frankly, in this photograph, he looked a little unsettled.'

'His left eye is glass, and that side of his face is frozen. It gives him a peculiar look. He was badly beaten.'

'By the Gestapo?'

'By the Russians. To them he was just a German. But he showed them what he is. You could say he shows Germans what we might have been.'

Jake had to suppress an urge to touch her. He'd heard a note of penitence in her voice. She was a German. Germans had crippled him. He would have forgiven them all by touching her.

The door from the street opened behind them and the wedge of light startled Jake. He whipped around to see who had come in, prepared for . . . what? Gestapo? Russians? He was more on edge than ever.

It was the Frenchwoman with the cross at her throat. She must have walked from the station. She was startled too. Jake and Magda must have seemed menacing figures in the shadows. She quickly crossed through the vestibule and into the church.

Jake wanted to follow her. He wanted to slide into a pew, anonymous and passive, and let the old words and silence hover there on the edge of his worry as they always had when he was a boy.

He wanted to think. What was happening to him? Was he uncovering truths about himself, or lies? What did it mean that his feeling for Magda Dettke, in the charged field of his conflicting emotions, was now the only one he trusted?

What he wanted, he admitted, was to pray. He was not man enough for any of this. He would never have defied Hitler or Communism. He could barely bring himself to defy the habit of his own disappointment. He felt inadequate and paralysed. He was in over his head. He had to pray for a way out! No! No! He had to pray for help. For the wisdom, he suddenly recited to himself, to know what was right, and the strength to accomplish it.

Magda touched his arm.

He said, 'Can we go in for a minute?'

She hesitated, looked at her watch.

'Please,' he insisted. Even he was shocked by the urgency in his voice. He was pathetic.

She stared at him. He knew she was thinking she had made a mistake in bringing him. Still, she nodded. She wanted to see him too. 'We only have a moment.'

The Mass was being celebrated not in the main body of the cathedral but in a sunken modern chapel situated in an open well like a spacious orchestra pit in front of the main sanctuary. A pair of circular stairways descended to the chapel, but even from the main church one could look down on it. Magda and Jake stood at the railing. Two dozen worshippers, including the Frenchwoman, were gathered in a semi-circle around the altar.

The celebrant was a bent old man on whom the green vestment hung, cockeyed somewhat, like a folded tent. Vestments are supposed to disguise the uniqueness of the person wearing them, but these highlighted this man's by the very contrast. His head and thin neck poked out of the chasuble like a knob. His translucent pallor, a void of colour, seemed even more wan by comparison to the deep green. He was standing before a lectern on which an oversized Bible was open. He was fiercely gripping the edge of the stand, whether for balance or out of the vehemence of his preaching, Jake could not tell. He was not speaking loudly, but his voice, charged with feeling, carried easily up to the main floor. Jake found it difficult to focus on his face, which was turned to a peculiar angle. Priests were supposed to look like figures from El Greco, lean, feminine in the perfection of their proportions. But this one's face was askew. From that distance Jake could not tell which of hs eyes was glass.

He could read the Archbishop's fervour if he couldn't understand what he was saying. The setting, for all its transcendent associations, had long since bent before this proclaimer. *Bear witness against Hitler!* Yes, this man, Jake saw in a glimpse, could have said that. He could be saying it still.

A robed usher approached Jake and whispered sternly. Jake gathered that he wanted them to go down the stairs with the other worshippers. Magda whispered an impatient question and the man replied with a curt phrase. She thanked him, then turned and walked out of the church.

Jake would have genuflected if he could have. He wished Magda hadn't left. He wanted to descend those stairs and take a place among the faithful and let the *Rosenpater*'s barrage fall against the wall of his own implacable insecurity.

Outside Magda said, 'They don't allow spectators. One must worship or leave.'

'Jesus Christ, spectators! Do you feel like a spectator?'

'Calm yourself,' she ordered.

He inhaled deeply, to deflect his resentment. It was enough to feel this tension without being rebuked for it. But she was right. He inhaled again. To show her that he had hold of himself, he asked, 'What was the *Rosenpater* saying?'

'That freedom is the gift of the Holy Ghost. That authentic human impulses are sacred.'

'Did he mention Poland?'

'He didn't have to.'

Because she was eyeing him carefully, evaluating him, he said, 'Magda, I'm all right.'

'Don't call me that! You are not to call me that!' Her reaction was extreme. For an instant she shook with anger. She too was on edge.

'Right,' he said simply. 'I won't.'

'Are you ready? It is time now.'

'Good. Let's get it over with. Can you tell me where we are going?'

'To where "my father" can see you. He wants to see you before he tells us where to meet him.' She turned slightly and let her eyes rise to the thousand-foot television tower half a mile away. With its bulbous capsule it seemed less an inverted scallion now than a sphere, the world itself, that bronze globe from Georgetown

331

years before, stabbed by a giant's pike and now displayed like a severed head. 'There,' she said. 'Up there.'

The television tower drew crowds of tourists all day long, not only from West Berlin, but the Bulgarians and Rumanians and Poles and others from East Bloc nations, many of whom had come to Berlin for the economic congress that was to open that day. Though it was early still, tourist buses were already disgorging sightseers. Magda and Jake had to wait in line, and by the time they crowded into the elevator Jake was already feeling queasy. He fixed his eyes upon the indicator above the door. International symbols indicated a restaurant floor and an observation deck. When the elevator doors closed he felt claustrophobic, and the first lurch of the ascent unsettled him further. Somehow, in the throng, he found Magda's hand. He didn't care if she knew how his palm was sweating.

When the elevator bounced to a stop and the doors opened at last, he and Magda were among the few to get off at the restaurant. It was late for breakfast, but too early for lunch, and the room was half-empty. Yet even the vacant tables seemed ominous to him, as if people knew to stay away. While they waited for the maître d', he fixed his gaze on the view and concentrated on how ordinary it seemed, how unthreatening. It was what one saw from the sky restaurant over any large city. Buildings far below stretched out endlessly to the horizon, which on that morning, because of haze, was not a line, but a blur of mauve.

When the maître d' had shown them to a table by the window and they'd taken their seats, Jake immediately leaned towards the glass so that his forehead touched it. After a moment he looked up at her. 'I'm not afraid of heights at least.'

Magda lit a cigarette. He reached for one. As she leaned to light it for him she said, 'You should remember that with our papers what we're doing is entirely legal.'

'Sigrid, darling, do I seem nervous?' He smiled, but his hand shook slightly as he put the cigarette to his mouth. He immediately began to scan the faces of the other diners, to find his uncle. What would he look like now? Would he recognize me? Jake wondered. *British Diplomat Defects!* The shock of that headline came back to him. 'Do you see him?'

'No,' Magda said. Instead of looking for Giles Patterson she'd been reading the menu.

The waiter came. Magda ordered a pastry, juice, and tea. Jake ordered coffee, but he couldn't imagine drinking it.

'There's the Wall,' Magda said, pointing through the glass.

Was she trying to distract him? To remind him not to make mistakes? The Wall was like a faint scar which wound across the city, disappearing at intervals behind buildings, but never for long.

'Bloody damn thing, isn't it,' Jake said. He could try to be relaxed as she was.

But she was posing. The Wall held no more interest for her than for him. She leaned forward and said quickly, 'Whatever happens today, you mustn't think that last night is not sacred to me.'

'Of course I won't.' He reached across the table and covered her hand.

She stared at him, dry-eyed, but reminding him how vulnerable she had made herself to him, how strong she'd made him feel. She was warning him of something. The unimaginable was going to happen. His heart rose in his chest like that elevator. He could not ask.

Nor could he breathe suddenly. He withdrew his hand from her. Across from him a Berliner sat at a table alone, reading a newspaper. The bold headline read, '*Moskau: Die Katastrophe Kommt!*' Jake had to look away. *British Diplomat Defects!* He looked out the window, tried to focus on the Wall, but couldn't find it. His eye fell to the ruins of a medieval cloister immediately below the television tower, and in front of it a grey automobile. A grey Mercedes?

He pushed away from the table and stood. 'Magda, I'm sorry.' He knocked his cane to the floor. He was going to be sick. He had to get air. He had to get away from that table and that window and that room and her. He had to get out!

'You can't leave just now, darling.' She smiled at him calmly, then indicated her plate. 'I'm not finished.'

Her poise salvaged his. 'Just for a moment,' he said. How would Harold Davidson put it? 'I have to use the facilities.' He forced a grin, then bent for his stick, but Magda picked it up. She did not give it to him.

She refused to let him rush her. She looked closely at the engraved silver handle.

Jake could feel himself calming somewhat, but still he had to get out of there. He needed the movement, the distraction. He'd be all right in a moment. 'I'll be right back,' he said, and he nodded at her.

She held on to his stick. He had to convince her he was all right. He had to make her give it back.

'Did I tell you my uncle gave that stick to me, Sigrid, dearest? He used to wear it to the Alhambra to see the Ballet Russe.'

'It's lovely, isn't it? I've always admired it.' She handed it to him. 'And you carry it so gracefully.'

'It carries me.' He bowed, and made his way among the tables. Other diners had been watching them, and he sensed that all the men had noticed Magda, and they envied him.

He went to the men's room and splashed water on his face. He dried himself, then studied his eyes in the mirror. So this is what a coward looks like, he thought.

As he passed the elevator on his way back, the chime sounded and the doors opened. On an impulse he got in. The elevator took him and its crowd efficiently up to the observation deck. What was he doing? When he saw the telescope by the window he knew.

It took fifty-pfennig coins, which he obtained from the souvenir stand. He inserted one, heard the lens click open, and then applied his eye to the scope even while trying to find the ruined cloister below.

The grey automobile was gone.

That was that, he thought.

Surely he would have relaxed some then if he hadn't smelled that cologne and heard that familiar voice behind him saying, 'How beautiful are the feet . . .'

Jake froze, but he responded automatically, 'Of them that preach the gospel of peace.'

'Alleluia,' Giles said. 'We are risen indeed. But don't turn around, old boy. Don't move for a moment.'

Jake didn't. He felt a hand at his jacket pocket, and then in the window's reflection he saw the vague figure of his uncle slipping away. Even that quick exchange had been indiscreet, but it sufficed to call powerfully to mind that other time, above that other city. His uncle had whispered, 'I would love you no matter what you did. Could you say as much for me?'

How had he answered that question? Jake could not recall.

His uncle had disappeared. Jake wanted to run after him, to throw himself upon him. But he knew better. He stood there, frozen, trying to think, trying to keep himself from turning numb, turning into a statue. How had he answered his uncle's question? How could he possibly be of any use to him now?

He wanted to put his hand in his pocket, to see what Giles had given him. But what if he were being watched? Instead he put his hand into his inside coat pocket to touch that other envelope as if, since it was his father's, it would give him the wisdom and the strength he had prayed for, but did not have.

CHAPTER TWENTY-SEVEN

They took a taxi to a block of old housing off Karl-Marx-Allee, one of the first apartment complexes built after the war. In those days Party functionaries had lived there, but now that the structures were faded and decrepit, manual labourers had been moved in.

Magda compared the street sign with the address on the paper Giles had slipped into Jake's pocket. She told the taxi driver to wait. They would get in and out. It would be simple, quick. Still, Jake felt a visceral pumping.

As they crossed the dreary paved apron that surrounded the building, cement instead of grass, he realized the glum scene satisfied a need he had to perceive life behind the Iron Curtain as unbearably ugly. The building they approached would have compared favourably to any of dozens of housing projects in Boston, but he barely noted the fact.

He followed Magda into the building. The assurance with which she opened the door and strode up the narrow stairs was in pointed contrast to his own nervousness.

On the third floor she knocked twice on a door and it opened immediately.

A cadaverous old man nearly as tall as Jake stood there as if he'd been waiting. His skin was the colour of French mustard, and it hung from his cheeks and slack jaw as if those bones had only borrowed it for the occasion. A baggy suit draped his body, and the collar of his white shirt, though buttoned, sagged. He wore no tie. The pupils of his eyes were tiny black dots peering out from the twin hollows under his brow. But those eyes nevertheless flared with intelligence and acute emotion. The man said something.

Jake panicked. They had the wrong apartment. The stench of the man's illness reached him, and Jake wanted to turn away.

But Magda, at that moment, threw herself against that man,

who, instead of falling back, embraced her. He pressed his eyes shut and leaned on Magda. He was completely bald. Even the hair of his eyebrows was gone. Veins, like cracks, zig-zagged across the loose yellow flesh of his skull.

Magda was whispering repeatedly, 'Papa! Papa!'

Jake wondered why, since he had never anticipated this, he wasn't surprised.

He looked past Magda and her father into the apartment. It consisted of a single room with a bathroom off one side and a kitchen off the other. A huge walnut wardrobe dominated one wall. Otherwise the only furniture was a narrow iron bedstead, its mattress covered with a brown blanket, and a deal table with two straight-backed chairs.

Jake entered and closed the door. As if that were his signal, Giles stepped out of the kitchen, holding a cup and saucer. He wore the familiar rakish moustache, but it was grey. Though much older, he looked healthy, chipper even, like the senior master of a good boys' school. He was dressed impeccably, of course. The knot of his tie rode perfectly between the wings of his collar.

Giles ignored Magda and her father, who stood in each other's embrace just inside the door. He touched the cup to his lips, then said to Jake, 'A bit of tea, old man?' Both his position in the doorway and his statement, their studied casualness, seemed rehearsed.

'Hello, Giles.' When had he decided not to call him uncle?

Despite his offer of hospitality, Giles did not move. He and Jake waited silently in deference to the monopolizing event of Magda's reunion with her father. Jake watched them, to his own amazement, without feeling.

Finally Magda hooked her arm through the old man's and turned to Jake. 'This is my father,' she said quietly.

Jake looked at him again. His eyes were glazed. He barely seemed aware of Jake's presence.

Magda went on. 'It is what I could not tell you. We are going now.' She dropped her eyes. 'Without you.'

'What?'

She leaned towards him, still holding her father, and kissed him on the mouth.

He stopped her from pulling away by taking her free arm. 'Magda . . .'

But she pulled free of him.

'Magda . . .'

'Just listen now! We must cross separately. The visas require it. Me with my father. You with your "father".'

'Wait, explain to me . . .'

Magda's father commanded, 'Don't question her!' And his feebleness disappeared.

Jake fell silent. In truth, he had no questions.

Her father went on in heavily accented English, but with authority. 'Explain to you? What? That her father whom all Moscow mourns is not only alive but has in his last days betrayed the motherland by fleeing it? No! She should not explain to you!' He looked at his abject daughter. 'Can he be trusted?'

Magda nodded, met Jake's eyes, and said in a firm voice, 'Yes, absolutely.'

It stunned Jake that she meant it.

Magda said, 'I will see you at the hotel.'

But if she trusted him absolutely, why had she lied to him? Jake felt more bewildered than ever. He wanted to take her by the shoulders and shake her and say, Magda, you mustn't be like this with me! Because I love you!

Magda turned.

Her father crossed to Giles, who still held the cup and saucer. The Russian drew close to him as if he were going to kiss him, but instead he rested his head for a moment on Patterson's shoulder, and Patterson inclined his own head so that his cheek touched the other's scalp.

Then the Russian, stooping now as if mourning himself, rejoined Magda, and without a further glance at Jake, they left the apartment.

Giles sipped at his teacup, then made a face. 'Wretched stuff.'

'Jesus Christ, Giles.' Jake stared at the closed door. 'Her father! Did he come with you? He's a Russian!' Jake faced his uncle. 'If I start asking my questions I'll never stop, and we'd never get out of here.'

'There's time,' Giles said.

His casualness jarred Jake. 'Do we have a plan?'

Giles shook his head.

Jake had to deflect the feeling that she'd left him in waters he couldn't handle alone. 'We can cross at Friedrichstrasse,' he said. 'By the time we get there they should already be through.'

Giles was still shaking his head, now sadly. He said, 'You shouldn't have believed her. I'm not going back with you.'

'What do you mean?'

Giles crossed in front of him and took one of the chairs. Indicating the other one, he said, 'Sit down.'

Jake stared down at him, not moving.

'Forgive me, nephew. I did this to you. Magda didn't.'

'You mean that' – Jake could barely bring himself to put into words what he saw now – 'she isn't going to be waiting for me?'

'No, she isn't.'

'Oh, my God.' He collapsed into his chair. His stick clattered to the floor. He struck his clenched fists together.

Giles watched him, silently.

When after a moment Jake looked up he forced a laugh. 'Sap. I think the word is *sap*. You're looking at one.'

'It's my fault. I forced her to lie to you.'

'It got a bit more complicated than you think, Giles. You weren't the only subject of her deception.' Jake's face displayed a new question suddenly. 'Was it the plan that I would fall for her?'

'No. No, it wasn't. If that happened . . .'

'Never mind. Forget it.' Jake shook himself. 'That isn't an issue between you and me. But your crossing over is. What the hell do you mean you're not coming? That's what I came for.'

'No, you came so that we might sit together for a moment and talk. I had an intuition that you needed it as much as I do.'

'Oh Christ, Giles.' Jake slammed his hand on the table. 'Jesus Christ! You're like her! You people keep hitting me from behind!' When Giles didn't respond, Jake slumped. Talk? How? How even to begin? He looked at his uncle helplessly. He felt bereft and humiliated.

Giles said at last, 'I need you.'

'Bullshit,' Jake said bitterly.

But Giles pressed. 'I brought you here because I'd like to make you understand. It's how I could make peace with myself.'

It took a moment for Jake's own longing to penetrate his defences, but when it did, it shot through him entirely. 'Oh, Giles, I'd love to understand.' What went wrong with me? he added silently.

Giles said, 'I'm not a traitor, Jake. I've never betrayed England or the family or you.'

'You haven't?' Jake felt a hope stir that he'd thought dead. He stared at his uncle mutely.

'It begins with Sergei . . .'

338

'Magda's father?' Should I believe him? Jake thought. But then he dismissed that question. He had to try to listen, to understand. Belief or not would be for later.

'Yes. His name is Sergei Sebalov. He was a Russian agent here in Berlin. At the end of the war your father and I came here to destroy the Nazi research into atomic weapons, to prevent the Russians from getting it. Without appreciating fully what he was doing, Sergei helped us, and that compromised him. Combined with the shock he received when he saw his fellow Russians rape this city brutally – they raped his wife – that made him seem a candidate for a possible conversion. So your father and I resolved to stay in touch with him.'

'You stayed in Germany. You went to Bonn.'

'Yes. And Magda and her mother were with me, or nearby.'

'In Cologne.'

'That's right. When we finally made our approaches to Sergei, Anna-Lise and Magda were the important considerations to him.'

'Because he loved them?'

'Yes. And because we told him that we would kill them if he did not co-operate.'

Jake sensed that his uncle was waiting for him to react. He was beyond shock now. He asked numbly, 'Would you have?'

Giles nodded. 'We couldn't rely on his nascent disillusionment. It was a ruthless trade, my boy.'

'So he went to work for you?'

'Yes. After the war he remained in Berlin to run an NKVD operation. His job was to train and dispatch agents into the Federal Republic. Our arrangement with him involved his claim to his own superiors that he had recruited me' – Giles bowed gracefully – 'a well-placed English diplomat. Since I was a lapsed Marxist from my time at Cambridge, it seemed credible that I would sign on as a Soviet agent.'

'But eventually you did sign on! Otherwise why . . . ?'

'Please, don't jump ahead.' Giles smiled, but he was doing this carefully. Jake sensed the man's intelligence, his control. 'My "recruitment" was a coup for him, of course, and it led to his appointment as the head of the NKVD in Berlin. We realized we had struck a rich and potentially long-playing vein, and at that point it was decided that the most extreme security would be imposed on the operation. Only the head of my service was aware of it in Britain, and that remained the case. In the States, since the CIA was only just being organized, General Donovan, Allen

Dulles, and your father were able to limit the secret to themselves. Of course, General Donovan died, and Dulles was director all those years. The year your father died, Dulles was forced out by the Bay of Pigs. The Bay of Pigs, of course, was what first opened the Agency to the scrutiny of the Congress and the press. Dulles anticipated that scrutiny, and he wisely decided on his own authority to leave the operation entirely to us British. Therefore no one has known now for years except the head of SIS.'

'Known that you've been . . . ?' Jake could hardly breathe. This revelation would change the meaning of everything he'd experienced for twenty years. It might even change the meaning of what Magda had done to him.

Giles nodded. '. . . a triple agent.'

How was this possible? Jake's mind refused to focus. He posed the first question that occurred to him. 'But doesn't the Prime Minister know? Or the President?'

'They each know just enough to appreciate the reliability of the arrangement, and also to keep at arm's length from it. It would never have survived otherwise. Politicians, the good ones, understand that better than anyone.'

'I'm still not clear what the arrangement is.'

'I'm ahead of myself, but only to impress upon you the extreme secrecy of what I'm saying.'

'I understand that.' But in fact he wasn't sure he did. He wasn't sure he understood anything. He felt like the class dunce getting tutored after school. Only the prospect that his humiliation could be redeemed by what Giles was saying enabled him to listen at all. He had to force himself not to think of Magda, what she'd done to him.

'Good,' Giles continued. 'Back to the early fifties, then. By feeding Sergei strategic information, we could see to it that he continued to impress his superiors. We wanted him in Moscow, of course, and so we took a chance. I was promoted and sent to Washington as head of MI-6 liaison.'

'I remember when you came.'

'Indeed so. My being there with you and your family was more important to me than you know.' Giles paused, in the grip of feeling that prompted him to ask, 'How is your mother?'

'Not well, Giles. She hadn't been well for some time.' Her humiliation had been total and permanent. Jake's sadness snagged him.

'I'm sorry.' Giles fingered the table's grain.

'Sometimes it's easy to blame you.'

Giles looked up sharply. His expression said, Blame? What has blame to do with it? Neither spoke for a moment, then Giles resumed. 'My transfer worked. Sergei was returned to Moscow as deputy chief of the KGB Illegals Directorate. His main responsibility was to nurture his contact with me.'

'Were you still threatening to kill Anna-Lise and Magda? Is that why you brought them to Washington?'

Giles smiled. 'Sergei is a fox. To guarantee that we would treat Anna-Lise well, he required that she alone know the key to the code he used in his messages. Anna-Lise was in Washington because we needed her.'

'And later Magda took her place?'

'That's right. She has had the key since Anna-Lise died. Her father gave it to her himself when she first travelled to Moscow posing as a tourist.'

'He was a KGB official, but he could meet with a tourist?'

Giles smiled. 'It can be simpler to avoid the police in Moscow than the press in Washington. Magda and her father knew how to manoeuvre.'

'And now that he's out of the business, she wants out too.'

'Does she?' Giles watched Jake carefully for a moment.

Jake realized that he'd been a fool to believe even that. Everything she'd told him had been a lie. The bitch, the fucking bitch!

Giles said, 'To resume.'

Jake had to jolt himself back to the train of thought. He said carefully, 'So it was deciphered messages from Sergei that Anna-Lise was passing to my father in the museum that day.' Giles nodded. 'I saw them burning papers at her house before they took my father away.'

'Your father kept the file of Sergei's transmissions. He couldn't be seen destroying them at the Agency, given what else was happening.'

Your defection, Jake thought, was happening. He knew his uncle's explanation was pointing to that, and he waited.

Giles, however, was distracted. 'You were very concerned that your father might have betrayed your mother.'

'I suppose I was.' Now that Magda was gone, Jake knew he would be helpless before his guilt. 'Marital fidelity used to be a value of mine.'

'Is your mother well physically at least?'

'Yes, she is. Forgive me if I seem surprised at your concern.'

We are all betrayers, Jake thought. It was how his mother saw it, and she was right.

Giles refused to register Jake's cut. He said, 'And you have a family of your own now. Magda tells me you've given me a great-nephew and a great-niece.'

Jake stiffened. His children had nothing to do with this. It seemed dangerous even to mention them.

'Do you have a photo? May I see it?'

Jake was torn. Giles seemed old suddenly and Jake sensed his loneliness. He wanted evidence of his progeny, even if it was indirect. Jake reached for his wallet and only then remembered that *his* wallet was in Zurich. He panicked, as if in having left the photo of his family behind he'd abandoned them. He had never been without his pictures before. Don't hurt them! he wanted to say. He checked himself. Linda, Bobby, and Maureen were safe at home. 'I'm sorry,' he said. 'I don't have my pictures with me.'

Giles said broodingly, 'It breaks my heart not to have met them. And I've never sent them presents. They must think I'm horrid.'

'The children have never heard of you.'

'Oh,' Giles said, but he couldn't conceal how it devastated him. He looked at Jake helplessly. 'That's the worst part.'

'No, it isn't. It's been worse for Cicely, who's been through three marriages and twice that many psychiatrists. Dori still lives with Mother. You're not the only exile. One can be in exile without leaving her bedroom.' Or his campus, Jake added to himself. 'Everyone's life turned sour,' he said.

Giles nodded slowly. 'I see.' But he was pulling back from his emotions. He collected himself and sat up straight. 'Sergei's career progressed steadily, with our help, but he'd have distinguished himself in any case.' Giles resumed his narrative, but his voice was not calm as it had been before. 'In 1957 he was made head of the Directorate, and we realized then that he had the potential of moving to the very top of the Russian intelligence apparatus.'

'But then in 1960, something happened.'

'I should say so.' Giles nodded vigorously.

'That's when I came in.' Jake remembered how ambushed he'd felt. 'I've been off the track ever since.'

'I can't believe that. Off the track?'

Jake looked at his uncle impassively.

'I knew there were consequences for you.' Giles hesitated. He lowered his eyes. 'I always regretted them.'

'What happened?'

'Sergei had his rivals. One of them, a man named Andrei Antipolya, head of Counter-intelligence, suspected the truth, that Sergei was my agent, not vice versa. Sergei moved against him. Antipolya became desperate to prove his theory, and so he informed my own shop that I was a Soviet spy. Naturally, since only my chief knew the truth, the others were bound to believe it. Then Antipolya arranged to have me warned that he had blown me. It was the perfect way to smoke a grouse.'

'A mole.'

'If you like,' he said, but conveyed his disdain for the cliché. 'An ingenious move in any case. If I was what Sergei claimed I was, I would have had no choice but to defect to the USSR, and when I did exactly that, Antipolya was destroyed.'

'Jesus Christ! So all this time you've been . . .' Jake stopped. He was unable to utter the words that came to mind: hero, patriot, martyr. The enormity of his uncle's act overwhelmed him. He listened, dumbfounded.

'Sergei, his bona fides established beyond doubt by my defection, was shortly thereafter made head of the First Chief Directorate with control over counter-intelligence, with control, that is, over anyone who might find us out. From then on he was secure.'

'What about Philby and the others?'

Giles smiled and raised his eyebrows. This was a point of pride. 'Kim never suspected. None of them did. Their credibility only added to mine. And I was, forgive me if I seem smug, the ace of trumps.'

'And Sebalov . . . ?'

'In 1967 he was made chairman of the KGB, *chairman*, mind you, and a member of the Politburo, thus justifying not only the hopes your father and I had, but also the, well, sacrifices that had been made.'

'My father was dead by then, of course.' The memory tripped him. His anger reasserted itself. He and his father were victims of this shit!

'Yes.'

'And my mother was completely wrecked by what had happened.'

343

'I'm well aware.'

'And my sisters . . .'

'I told you, Jake, how much I . . .'

'You think the ruined lives of four people, four at least, were worth this victory of yours, this – what do you call it – grand slam? You're the ace of trumps? You've been rehashing the finesses, crossruffs, and sloughs of a bridge game to me.'

'No, I haven't, Jake.'

'You've been totting up the score . . .'

Giles banged the table. 'No, I haven't! I have been accounting for myself to you! You will be the only one who knows it all!'

'Then I should be the one to decide what can be justified, not you!'

'Perhaps you didn't hear me. I said he was head of the KGB! And he was working for us. I am not indifferent to what happened to my sister and to you and to Sissy and Dori. But neither should you be indifferent to what I'm telling you! Because of Sergei our side has known at critical moments what the intentions of the Russians have been. The intentions! The most important and the most elusive intelligence of all. No one knows with reliability the intentions of his enemy. But we have! Therefore? Who can say? But possibly it is true that, for example, because of Sergei, Israel continues to exist! What is that worth? Because of Sergei, London and Washington knew what Moscow intended throughout the crisis in Iran. In arms negotiations, Sergei has made it possible for the West to tilt things towards the moderates in the Kremlin. What is that worth? You wouldn't ask if you knew the generals! Look at Poland! As that crisis worsens, what would it be worth for Washington to know what, at each stage, Moscow intends?'

'I don't believe even Moscow knows what it's going to do in Poland. Intentions elude everyone.'

'You're wrong,' Giles said brusquely. 'Please do not presume to tell me about Moscow. The point is that at a moment like this the world has only one hope, that the two sides not misunderstand each other. That the two sides not surrender to their extremists! That the two sides act from, yes, intelligence, and not from fear! The two sides! You see, that's the problem! When I met Sergei in Berlin years ago, something happened between us in which it stopped mattering that he was Russian and I was British. We both discovered together something bigger than our "two sides". I am convicted, in London, of being an agent of the East, though my secret in Moscow is that I'm agent of the West. But, don't you see I'm neither! Sergei and I could have reversed roles and have been doing exactly the same thing. We are neither traitors *nor* patriots. We are not on one side or the other. We have been working for the world, Jake! The world!' Giles stopped and forced himself to say coolly, rationally, 'It is not inconceivable that on three, perhaps four, occasions over thirteen years, a nuclear exchange has been avoided because of the channel provided by Sergei. What is that worth? My life? Yes, without a doubt.'

Jake was affected by what his uncle was saying and by the passion with which he said it. But his oldest question launched itself, despite him. 'And my father's life?' he asked.

'What do you mean, your father's life?'

'Who killed him?'

'Killed him?' The question stunned Giles. 'He died of a stroke. You know that. Multiple strokes.'

'Don't use that word with me as if it means something. Strokes can be induced. Who gained most from what happened to him? Obviously Sebalov. My father's disgrace was essential to bolster the credibility of your defection. And his death made it even better. You and Sergei, your noble endeavour!'

'We would not have harmed your father.'

'Why not? You'd have murdered Anna-Lise and Magda. A ruthless trade, you said. I know it was ruthless! I was there, remember?'

'We wouldn't have harmed him because he was one of us. He was part of it.'

'He considered you a traitor.'

'He did not.'

'What, he was lying to me? It was the basis of our affection then, our first real closeness. You're telling me my father was lying to me at the end of his life?'

'Of course I am,' Giles said coldly. 'How childishly naïve you are! You have not been listening to me. Will you *listen* to me! Your father was the key to all of this. He enabled it. He *wanted* it! It all went the way we prayed it would. Your father was not wronged and neither have you been!'

The bald statement stunned Jake. This was the secret he'd always wanted to know. But now he saw: he hadn't wanted in on it at all. He had preferred being a victim and a victim's son. Yet his father was not a victim, but a man whose first loyalty was neither to himself nor to his son, but to, as Giles put it, the world.

'He couldn't explain that to you any more than I could.' Giles softened. 'That doesn't mean your closeness with him was false. And that his choice involved tragic consequences for his family doesn't mean he didn't love you all. He could only trust you to make the best of it. As he did me.'

Jake shook his head slowly. His grief rose in him as he said, 'We made the worst of it. We could not forgive him for putting us second to something, not even something noble. Oh Christ, Giles.' Jake slumped over his arms on the table. Off the track? Yes. Where he deserved to be. He had lived by his illusions. But now he was stripped of them. He stared at the shell of his own life, brutally.

Giles touched him. 'You feel this way because you love your family so much.'

Was it true? Had he ever loved anyone or anything, save his wound? He looked up at Giles. 'Will you come home with me?'

'For your mother's sake?'

'Yes. You could redeem what time remains to her.'

'I can't. If I returned with you, the Russians would realize that I never truly defected. They would conclude quickly, even after all these years, that Antipolya was right. They must never know that Sergei betrayed them.'

'You're protecting Sebalov, but he's gone. By now he's at the checkpoint. Why does he have the right to put a personal motive first? If you can't come out, why could he?'

Giles raised and lowered his shoulders, which were bony, angular. His body was still like Fred Astaire's.

'Because he can leave without jeopardizing his secret. He has leukaemia.'

'It's obvious.'

'It has been well known for some time that he is dying. No one was surprised in Moscow when his death was announced three days ago. His ashes were entombed with honours in the Kremlin wall day before yesterday. Even in the West it is not doubted. Everyone thinks he's dead.'

'How is that possible?'

'I told you. In Moscow, for one who knows how to use the inefficiencies of the state against itself, anything is possible. Doctors and clerks were bribed to alter procedures and records, but not one of them knew the final outcome of what they'd done together. The man who helped Sergei was a fellow patient who'd become his friend. It was he who died and he who was buried in Sergei's tomb. No one knows but Magda and me. And now you.

346

But his secret is safe only as long as no one takes a second look. If I left, they would. Unluckily for me, I do not have leukaemia.' He paused, studied his hands, then went on, 'Circumstances have made it possible for Sergei to go now to be with his daughter. One must not begrudge him that.'

Jake was silent for a moment, then asked, 'What will it be for you?'

Giles shrugged. 'I live alone, in my own flat, which is of course a privilege. And I am allowed to shop in the hotels. I never miss the ballet.'

'But Sebalov was your friend?'

'I will miss him.'

The simple statement moved Jake.

'You were close friends with my father.'

Giles nodded stoically, now fingering the teacup.

'Never close enough, frankly. We came to a point of personal stand-off. By the end what we had in common was . . . what you called our "noble endeavour".'

Jake reached into his coat pocket, withdrew the sealed envelope, and put it on the table in front of Giles. 'He gave me this for you before he died.'

The old man did not move a muscle towards it.

'Uncle Giles?'

'Open it for me, would you? Read it to me?'

Jake hesitated, then picked up the envelope and opened it. He unfolded the single piece of paper across which was scrawled – Jake had forgotten how unsteady his father's hand had become – a single sentence. Jake read it aloud, quietly. 'Dear Giles, what my Jansenist forebears would never let me say, I love you, J. B. McK.'

'Oh, John,' Giles whispered. His eyes were fixed on the table. 'Oh, John.'

Jake had seen such sadness only in his mother. He could imagine her saying, 'Oh, John,' in just that tone. John McKay's Jansenist forebears had been her great enemies too.

After a long time Giles looked at Jake. 'Thank you very much.'

Jake had to look away from his uncle because he remembered the moment in the Washington Monument when Giles asked, 'Will you love me no matter what?' Jake had never answered him. Why? Because he was his father's son. Jake saw that he had suffered nothing compared to what his uncle had suffered for years. And his mother and sisters. They had been burdened but not sacrificed. They could have recovered. Wives live on after such losses. Daughters and sons realize their promise. If they didn't, who was there to blame? No one.

Giles reached across the table for the letter. He folded it without reading it again, put it in its envelope, and put the envelope in his coat pocket. Then he smiled pleasantly and nodded at Jake's silver-headed cane. 'I admire your stick.'

'Do you remember it?'

'Of course.' Giles took it, deftly twirled it, then examined the engraved silver. 'Did I tell you about it?'

'You said you used to wear it to see Diaghilev.'

'Good Lord, Diaghilev! To think I loved the Russians as a young man.' Giles grinned at Jake, savouring that irony. He fondled the cane.

'But did I tell you its secret? No, of course I didn't. Your mother would have killed me.'

'Its secret?' Jake didn't move.

Giles twisted the silver handle, saying, 'I used to call it Messiah's Handle.' He twisted with great effort until the handle loosened, and then he turned it twice quickly on its threads and pulled it out of the ebony shaft. Attached to the engraved handle was a gleaming slender blade, perhaps a foot long. Giles flourished it like a bandit. '*Voilà!*' he said. 'Stiletto! From the Latin *stilus*, the same root that gives us "style"!'

Jake stared at his exuberant uncle, dumbfounded. His stick! A stick he'd rarely used, but still his oldest one. He'd thought he knew it.

Giles continued to display the blade, admiringly, as if he were that young dandy who'd purchased it. But then Jake's stunned expression registered on him, and Giles lowered the thing.

Jake whispered, 'How could you not have told me?'

'Nephew, you were a child when I gave you this stick. It would have been dangerous.'

'Dangerous? Dangerous?' Jake's voice rose sharply. 'My stick is a weapon? Even my stick is a lie!' Jake gripped the table, stood and leaned over his uncle, screaming, 'Everything you've ever given me is a lie! You! My father!' Jake threw his arm at the door. 'Her!'

Giles raised his hand sharply. 'Remember where you are!'

'Where am I?' Jake cried loudly. 'Tell me where I am!'

'You are in East Berlin! East Berlin, son!'

'Son? Don't you dare call me son!'

'Nephew,' Giles muttered. 'I meant "nephew".' He replaced the blade in its shaft, tightened the handle, and placed the stick on the table between himself and Jake.

Jake slowly sat. If that cane had become a serpent and wriggled away he would not have been surprised. He picked it up, balanced it on the palm of his hand. He touched the silver handle timidly, then turned it. The thing unscrewed easily. He looked up at his uncle. 'How could you not have told me?' he asked again, but quietly now.

He drew the blade out. It had the edge of a razor.

And he slammed it back in its slot. 'Jesus Christ,' he said. 'Jesus Christ.' When he looked up at Giles now he burst into laughter. Soon he was laughing hysterically. 'All these years,' he managed to say, 'I've been the Count of Monte Cristo! And didn't even know it!' And he laughed and laughed.

Giles sat impassively at the table.

While Jake finally wiped the tears from his eyes with his handkerchief, Giles looked at his watch. 'I am due at a meeting.'

'You're serious, then, about not going with me?'

'Why is it so hard for you to listen?' Giles asked wearily. 'Have you understood nothing?'

Jake lowered his eyes. He could speak only with difficulty. 'Unfortunately, I understand it all.' His tears welled again, but not from laughing. He forced a jovial note into his voice. 'All but the cane.' He fondled the ebony shaft.

Giles stood. 'Don't call it a cane, Jake. It's a stick.'

Jake's tears overflowed now. He stood too. 'I hate you, Giles,' he said, but as he did he fell on his uncle, fell into his arms. 'I hate you,' he repeated and then while his uncle held him, he sobbed.

'I hate you too.' Giles stroked his nephew. 'I assault your innocence. You assault my complacency. Of course we hate each other.'

'Giles, come home with me,' Jake said with a desperate rush of feeling. 'Not for Mother's sake, for mine!'

'I can't, Jake.'

'I could do it, Giles. I could get you out.'

Giles pulled away from him. 'I must go. Everything fails if I don't go.'

Jake held him. 'I need you! I need you, Giles!'

Giles grabbed Jake's shoulders and shook him roughly. 'No, you don't. You are strong, Jake. You don't need me! You didn't need your father! It's been too long, Jake! Let go of it! Be like him!'

'I can't be!'

'You can be!' Giles shook him. 'You are!' And then he took him into his embrace again. After a moment he said quietly, 'Now I have to go and finish what I've begun. That's all any of us can do.' Giles released Jake and moved towards the door.

It was a shock to Jake to realize that he was standing alone and steadily, without arms to support him, or a cane. 'Giles,' he called, 'I loved him and I love you! I've always loved you, and always will.'

'Thank you, Jake,' Giles whispered. 'It's what I'd hoped to hear from you. I'll cherish that you said it.' And then he opened the door and was gone.

It wasn't clear to Jake how long he'd been sitting at the table. When he heard the footsteps in the stairwell he stood up. It was Giles coming back, and Jake thought, Perhaps now I can help him. He crossed to the door and opened it.

Magda was there with her father. He was leaning on her. 'He has to rest,' she said.

Magda and Jake lifted Sebalov on to the bed. Immediately he went to sleep.

Magda looked helplessly at Jake. 'They're harassing at the border. All GDR Special *Ausweise* must be reapplied for and reissued,' she said. 'Because of Poland.'

CHAPTER TWENTY-EIGHT

'What does that mean?' Jake asked. They had moved into the small kitchen to talk without awakening her father.

Magda's eyes filled and she looked at him helplessly. 'That there are no other moves to be made. I can't do it.' Tears overflowed her eyes. 'I can't get him out.'

'You can't get a new visa?'

'It takes weeks, months.' She fell against him, sobbing.

Jake absorbed her weight, held her, moved his hands lightly on her shoulders. 'Maybe he knows someone, or has a contact who could . . .'

'I can't do it!' she cried. 'I can't do it!'

He remembered how she'd looked at him when she'd said she wanted out, a new life. This was to be it, a beginning. He'd believed her, and he'd wanted to help her. To his own surprise, he still did. 'You can, Magda,' he said.

She pulled away from him. 'No!' she said bitterly. 'You don't understand. There are no moves, no choices. I promised my father they would never take him. If anything went wrong I had to . . . Don't you see? I have to kill him.'

'No.' Jake grabbed her arms.

'I promised him! He made me promise! I never thought I'd have to!' Now she collapsed in his arms, sobbing.

He felt her despair. She shook with it.

And he felt his own. Of course the old man would prefer death to capture now. It had been absurd to think Magda could free herself from the awful bondage of her life. The terms were clear. Either rescue her father or kill him. Either salvage her life or ruin it forever.

Shudders rocked her, and no wonder. He tried to stop them by holding her more tightly. Instead of stopping hers, however, he began to shudder himself. He felt *his* rage, *his* shame, and *his* bondage. And he felt his wariness of her. Magda, like his father, had put him second and made him face the fact – the source of all his fear – that he was alone.

But now he refused to let any of those feelings swamp him. He shook himself and he shook her. 'No, Magda,' he said firmly. 'No.'

He held her at arm's length, pressing her fiercely. 'You will not kill him! I won't let you!'

She stared at him, mystified.

'We'll get him out!' Jake said. 'We'll take him across.'

'How?' Magda asked weakly.

Jake had to answer something. There had to be a way. He had spent too long coming to this moment for there not to be. But he couldn't think of it, so he said, 'How would your father do it if he were young? He never just quit, did he?'

Magda shook her head.

'How would my father do it?'

They stared at each other. Magda wasn't going to answer. It was clear to both of them that now she was waiting on his initiative. Magda Dettke was out now. Jake McKay would have to go in. He said slowly, 'I know.' And as he realized that indeed he did, he said it again. 'I know.'

351

Her expression changed slightly, just enough to let him see that, though she had no will to resist him, she did not believe him.

He didn't care. 'Listen, you wait here with your father. If he wakes up, give him tea. All right?'

Magda nodded.

'I'll be back as soon as I can. We're going to get him out, Magda.'

'Or we die trying to?' she asked with bitter irony.

He shook his head. 'No. We're not dying. Not today. None of us. Do you know why?'

She shook her head.

'Because we've just begun to live. I love you, Magda.' He kissed her. She hesitated at first, but then, in returning his kiss, overcame herself and gave him everything.

Jake dipped his hand into the holy water font as he entered the cathedral, but he did not cross himself. He approached the edge of the sunken chapel and looked down into it. The noon Mass was nearly over. The celebrant was not the Archbishop, but another priest, a stout middle-aged man. He was rubbing the chalice with a white cloth. When he addressed the congregation of perhaps forty-five people, a gold tooth flashed in his mouth. While he said the closing prayer, Jake carefully descended the stairs and slipped into a rear pew.

The priest left the altar.

A woman of about fifty got up, genuflected, walked soundlessly to the corner in the rear of the chapel in which were three purple-curtained confessional booths. She lifted a curtain and entered one of them. Above it was a sign plate on which were engraved the word '*Erzbischof*' and a coat of arms that included a bear and a rose.

A young man, a student perhaps or a seminarian, entered the confessional after the woman left. He was followed over the next few minutes by half a dozen other penitents.

When it seemed no one else would be going to confession, Jake stood and approached carefully himself. He hadn't been inside such a booth in years, but that was irrelevant now, as were all other reasons for being intimidated.

The only light in the confessional came through the grille from the priest's side. Jake knelt awkwardly. The cramped space barely accommodated his stiff leg. To his surprise he blessed himself, a reflex. He remembered wanting to be an altar boy at St

Thomas's Church, the priest explaining to him that he couldn't since he couldn't genuflect. He overheard that priest tell his mother that liturgy required gracefulness, and it wouldn't be fair to the boy or fitting to God; what if he fell?

This priest said softly, '*Gott sei mit Dir.*'

'May I speak in English?'

'Yes, of course.'

'Is this the Archbishop?'

'Yes.'

'The *Rosenpater*?'

'Yes. God bless you, my son.'

'Father, I am not here to confess. I must speak urgently.'

'This is a good place to speak urgently.'

'I am an American. You knew my father. My name is McKay. My father was John McKay. He was here at the end of the war.'

After a moment the Archbishop said quietly, 'Yes. I knew him.'

'You may also remember from the same time Giles Patterson, a British officer, and a man named Dettke.'

The Archbishop did not reply.

'You joined in marriage Herr Dettke and a woman named Anna-Lise. They had a daughter, Magda. Do you remember?'

'I remember everyone I have married. Even those who have died.'

'How freely can I speak?'

'You need have no concern about our privacy. I make certain of that.'

'Dettke is here.'

'In Berlin?'

'In East Berlin. He was turned back at Friedrichstrasse this morning. Magda is with him. He has leukaemia. He wants to spend what time remains to him with her.'

There was no response from the other side of the grille.

'Father?' Jake had to press against the shelf of the confessional. He had never been more frightened in his life. But neither more in control. The combination of fear and self-possession that defied it was exhilarating.

'He sent you to me?'

'No. I came on my own initiative. I thought there might be some bond between you. He wants to cross.'

'I do not involve myself in such activity.'

'I am sure you don't, but . . .'

The Archbishop was gone.

Jake left the confessional and saw a short, angular man in a black cassock and crimson skullcap striding across the chapel. Jake followed.

In the sacristy, a vacant room just large enough to accommodate a vesting case and a small sink, the Archbishop stopped.

As Jake approached, the Archbishop turned towards him. The cleric's face, seen from so close, shocked him. The vacancy of his one eye was made horrible by the passion in the other. Half his face seemed made of plastic, like a mask, but a mask of someone dead. His intense emotion flared, but only on one side of his face. 'Get out of here! You have no business in here!'

Jake closed the door behind him. 'I insist that you listen to me!'

'I do not engage in illegal activity!' the Archbishop sputtered, and then he began to berate Jake in German.

Jake shook his head. 'I do not speak German. I am telling you the truth. I am not from the police. I am not trying to trap you.'

The Archbishop stared at him. 'Let me see your passport.'

Jake took out his passport, but it was the false one. He handed it to the Archbishop. 'My real passport is in Zurich.'

'Where are you staying?'

'A hotel in West Berlin.'

'What hotel?'

'The Kempinski.'

The Archbishop studied the Swiss passport. Then he looked pointedly at Jake's leg, at the silver-handled cane. 'What happened to you?'

'My leg was crushed when a beam fell on it during the Blitz in London. My father was stationed in London.'

'I knew that. I knew about your leg.' He handed the passport back and with his peculiar gaze studied Jake carefully. 'If you were from Security you would have papers that lent more substance to your story.'

Jake tried to look into the priest's good eye, but his own gaze kept drifting to the dead side of his face.

The Archbishop put his finger to his lips and whispered, 'Offences against the state require a little more privacy than mere sins against God.' He indicated that Jake should follow him. They went through a door that opened on to a brightly lit narrow corridor. It led to the rectory. While Jake mounted a flight of stairs he realized he was crowding the Archbishop. The old man, well into his eighties, took the stairs more slowly even than Jake did.

Once they were in his small book-strewn apartment, the Archbishop led the way into the bathroom, a cubicle barely large enough for the two of them. He closed the door, turned on the shower and aimed the nozzle so that the water struck the cloudy plastic curtain, noisily.

'To discuss what you propose there is no safe place.'

'Can you help?'

'I have never involved myself in escape.'

'I understand that . . .'

'I doubt it. Escape is impossible! What do you think? A ladder? Some rope?'

'But you cross freely. I've been told they let you cross freely, back and forth, by auto.'

Archbishop Schott laughed. 'You think they don't search me? My car?'

'I thought perhaps they did so perfunctorily.'

He laughed again, a short dismissive laugh. He took a handkerchief out and pressed it against his pale, lifeless cheek, then against his false eye.

Jake looked away from him and said softly, 'If he can't cross, then Herr Dettke's daughter intends to kill him.'

'How?'

'I haven't asked. Some kind of pill perhaps.' Jake's mind dodged away from that. The cascading water of the shower reminded him of the time he'd stood in the shower fully clothed at Georgetown, leaning against the tile, clenching his fists. *The next son of a bitch who touches me gets this stick across his face!*

He looked at the Archbishop, found his good eye, and what he saw surprised him. The *Rosenpater* was helplessly in the grip of an emotion of his own.

'So it is impossible, then?'

The Archbishop said solemnly, 'There is one chance. If they thought I was leaving permanently.' He hesitated, then went on more quickly, 'If I told the Chief of Security that the time had come for me to retire, but I wanted to leave discreetly, secretly almost . . . you see, I have always sworn I would never leave the East. I could imply that His Holiness has insisted and I have yielded. His Holiness has ordered me to leave, and I am embarrassed . . .'

'So you would like to bring a few possessions with you, but not

355

have them found. A border search would draw attention . . .'

'Yes. I have always made a point to return here at night. I never brought even one valise with me.'

'Would they believe you?'

He shrugged. 'They know that Rome wants me replaced. I am past the age. And I' – he shrugged again – 'am out of step a bit. You say out of step?'

'But would the turmoil in Poland make it impossible?'

He thought a moment. 'No. Poland works for us. Everyone is afraid I will speak my mind. If there was an invasion, or if there were workers' strikes here in Germany . . . His Holiness sent me word himself. "*Prudentia*," he said. "*Prudentia* . . . Pray for our Polish brethren but do not speak of them." Honecker would give anything to have me in the West if the worst should happen. I say so in all modesty. Newspapers make more of me than I deserve. Yes. Yes!' His one eye flashed with the realization. 'Poland makes it possible! The government will want me out! I could ask the general to escort me himself. He might agree! He might!'

Jake stared at the Archbishop. Even with the water drumming off the shower curtain he lowered his voice. 'You know who Dettke really is?'

'Of course.' The Archbishop pressed his handkerchief to his cheek again, as if he were mopping perspiration or tears, but his plasticine flesh was dry. 'He is my oldest friend. That he should need me today is the answer to my oldest prayer. He is the only person for whom I would abandon my pulpit.'

'But do you know . . . ?'

'I know everything!' He touched Jake's shoulder. 'And nothing.'

'But do you understand the risks?'

'What, imprisonment? Execution? There is no imprisoning the Word of God, and, as for the other, I should have been executed forty years ago. I wasn't, because Herr Dettke risked his life to save me. He did so many times. The risk? The risk was that I might have said no to you.'

The Word of God? Jake thought. Who's talking about the Word of God? The old man's vehemence unsettled him.

'But there would be a risk for my driver, and I cannot involve my priests in this. So you will have to drive us.'

Jake's heart sank. Drive? 'What kind of car is it?' It was like admitting he could not genuflect when he added, 'I cannot drive a manual shift.'

'Manual shift?' The old priest smiled. 'Would the Archbishop of all Berlin have a manual shift?' He clapped a hand around Jake's neck. It was like receiving a sacrament from him. The man's power communicated. Jake thought that at his urging even he might have borne witness against Hitler. If even I would have, he wondered, why didn't everyone?

'Go to them,' the *Rosenpater* said. 'Bring Herr Dettke here. The girl can cross on her own?'

'Yes. She has papers.'

'Tell her I remember her well. She was a beautiful child.'

Magda leaned into the taxi to kiss her father. She whispered something in his ear.

Then she straightened, closed the door, and faced Jake. 'I will wait for you at the Victory Column.'

Jake smiled. 'And then I'll know what victory it celebrates.'

Magda lowered her eyes. 'You make me think all things are possible.'

One thing at a time, Jake thought.

Magda's glance went to her father, who was leaning back against the seat with his eyes closed. When she looked at Jake again her eyes widened, and she kissed his cheek, lightly. '*Bonne chance*,' she whispered.

He crossed behind the taxi and got in on the other side.

The Archbishop was waiting at the rectory door. He was dressed formidably in a red cassock now and a red skullcap. A heavy gold chain arched across his chest and a jewelled cross protruded from his cincture. '*Wie geht's, Jörg?*' he said simply, and he embraced Sebalov, but perhaps because the Russian looked so sickly he did so lightly, as if he were passing along the Pax at liturgy. But Sebalov gripped the Archbishop's arms fiercely. The two men were visibly suspended for a moment in the rigid emotion of their reunion.

The Archbishop led them through the rectory, across the kitchen, and down a flight of stairs to a garage in which four cars were parked. Three were small and nondescript. One was a highly polished black Mercedes of medium size. The Archbishop walked behind it and opened the trunk. He brought out a black cassock and collar and handed them to Jake. 'Father,' he said amiably and bowed.

'What if they ask me for papers?'

The Archbishop shook his head. 'They won't. The general will

357

be with us. Besides, all of my priests are known to be citizens of West Berlin. I alone am a citizen of the East. They are accustomed to me. You are a priest now.' He indicated the collar. 'That is your *Ausweis*.' The Archbishop helped him to put it on.

Jake gestured with his cane. 'Do the clergy use walking sticks?'

'I suppose so, if they have an accident. But not such a fancy one, perhaps.'

If you only knew, Jake thought. The blade in his stick made it feel like someone else's.

They helped Sebalov climb into the trunk, which the Archbishop had lined with pillows and cushions.

The Russian held on to the Archbishop's sleeve. 'Karl,' he ⁿegan, and then went on in German. The Archbishop pressed his hand reassuringly. Sebalov looked at Jake. 'If there is trouble – and it is possible – you should leave me.'

'There won't be trouble,' Jake said. 'The *Rosenpater* has seen to everything.' He fastened the last of his cassock buttons.

'Nevertheless,' Sebalov said. His eyes brightened momentarily with what Jake sensed was gratitude. Then he curled around his own knees. He looked more frail than ever.

The Archbishop laid his hand on Sebalov's head. '*Gott sei mit Dir, mein Freund.*'

Jake felt an urge to kneel before the old prelate and ask his blessing too. No, his forgiveness. Bless me, Father, I have sinned. I have blamed the world, my father, mother, uncle, and wife for all my weaknesses. I have wallowed in self-pity. Jake saw his sense of being a victim for what it was, and he set it behind himself forever. For the first time in years he was crossing into the free world too.

The Archbishop slammed the lid down on the trunk.

He and Jake exchanged a look and then, each to his place, one at the wheel, one in back, they got into the car.

Jake drove on to Unter den Linden, saw the linden trees and thought, Linden trees, Linden Street; if only all things were so simple. They left behind the television tower and, at its base, the looming bronze façade of the Palace of the Republic, where, presumably, Giles was even then in his meeting. Jake tried to picture him lecturing a hall full of delegates on . . . what? The decadence of Western family life? As he drove down the stately boulevard, he kept brushing the rear-view mirror with his eyes, catching glimpses of the palace, but wanting one of his uncle.

'Do you see the Gate?' the Archbishop asked.

'Yes, of course.' Driving towards the Brandenburg Gate suspended theatrically across the avenue some blocks ahead was like the driving one does in dreams.

'Beyond, in the West, this boulevard was Hitler's airstrip. Herr Dettke and your father and Patterson prevented him from using it.'

My father, Jake thought.

The Archbishop was oblivious to Jake's emotion. He said, 'On this side of the Gate the Russians crushed a demonstration once. Our dear Herr Dettke was still in Berlin and was the only Comrade to denounce that brutality. It was the work of Beria. Herr Dettke denounced him publicly.'

'And he survived?'

'Beria himself was liquidated. He had overreached himself. The NKVD was dismantled. A more humane approach developed. Herr Dettke was part of that. In Berlin we remember.'

The KGB more humane? Jake looked in the mirror again, expecting to see someone following them. The palms of his hands were wet. He would have welcomed a silence as he inched through the mundane midday traffic, but the Archbishop continued to speak.

'First Berlin, then Budapest, then Prague, now Kabul. And any time now, Warsaw.'

'You think the Russians will invade?'

'Not only the Russians, but also the East Germans. Once again, Germany and Russia against Poland. Of course they will invade! That is why General Schwerin was delighted that I am leaving. It will be sting enough for them, what the Pole, Wojtyla, says in Rome.'

'It's surprising to me that the Church emerged with so much power.'

'It is the power of the Cross.'

'I suppose.' The Archbishop's certitude, his moral absolutism, was what put Jake off, but that was what made him the *Rosenpater*.

He rattled on. 'We must be in constructive opposition not only to the stern atheism of the East, but also to the unchecked materialism of the West. We must withhold our loyalty from all earthly kingdoms. Just because we are leaving now does not mean our mission is finished.'

'I'm sure it doesn't.'

'I must denounce the works of Satan wherever they are found.'

The Kurfürstendamm, Jake thought. Let's start with the fifty-foot nude, pubis and pistol.

'Do I turn on Friedrichstrasse, Archbishop?'

'Yes. That leads to the checkpoint. General Schwerin will be waiting.'

'What is he like?'

'He is a German, do you understand? A German! We are a people who have made a profound evil of accommodation. We accommodated Hitler, that Austrian. Then half of us like Schwerin accommodated Stalin, while half accommodated Churchill and Truman.'

'What was wrong with Churchill and Truman?'

'Ask Dresden!' the old man answered fiercely. 'Ask Hiroshima and Nagasaki!'

Ordinarily Jake would not have engaged such vehemence as the priest exhibited. He could feel, it seemed, his heat on the back of his neck. Jake took for granted the ambiguous character of all human situations, and he wanted to face the Archbishop with the ambiguity of the one they shared at that moment. 'But sometimes one must accommodate. You are, for example, accommodating Herr Dettke.'

The Archbishop replied even more fiercely, 'He gave me the last forty years of my life! Can't I give him the last few months of his?'

'Yes, of course. I agree. That's why I'm here. I . . .'

'I owe everything to Jörg!'

'I understand,' Jake said. It had been a mistake to raise the point.

Jake turned left on Friedrichstrasse. With a quick glance to the right he could see a block away the shoddy railroad station where he and Magda had arrived early that morning and where Magda and her father had been turned back. Ironic that he should be leaving East Berlin just when he was learning his way around.

For two blocks the traffic was slow and heavy, but after three it stopped dead. The checkpoint was still several blocks away, but they were in line for it already. Dozens of automobiles were ahead of them.

'It looks,' Jake said, 'like everybody's leaving.'

'Berliners have a special sense.' The Archbishop leaned forward to look. 'Everybody who can leave probably is. If the border closed . . . When the Wall went up many from the West were caught.'

'These are all West Germans?'

'Look at the licence plates. Ours is the only auto in the line from the GDR. These people have been taking their holidays with relatives and now they fear being held here if something happens.'

The image that came to mind was of a huge vault door slowly swinging shut, and Jake had to squeeze his eyes against it. He felt that claustrophobia again, that lack of air. His cassock was soaked through now with perspiration.

'Pull over there.' The Archbishop pointed across an open lane to a turnout, and Jake drove to it. 'Now shut the engine off. We wait. No more English, Father.' The Archbishop opened his breviary. Jake watched him in the mirror. The old man's lips moved while he read. Jake would have given anything for pages to turn, beads to finger.

The autos in line did not advance. Jake realized it would take them the entire rest of the day if they had to wait. From his vantage the checkpoint consisted of a pair of low makeshift buildings straddling the roadway. Beyond those, a hundred yards ahead, across the border, were the American equivalents. The buildings called to mind the old tempos that had lined the Mall in Washington. The Agency had had many of its offices in buildings like that, though not his father's. For the relief it gave him Jake pictured that yellow stucco compound on the hill where he had gone after school, where he had met Allen Dulles, where he had learned to think of his father as an agent of God's. Jake remembered with what pride he had always presented himself at the compound gatehouse, with what cocky verve he had always greeted the guards. The thought of guards now filled him with panic.

A dark brown automobile pulled up next to them and the rear door opened even before the car quite stopped. A tall man in a green uniform, wearing sunglasses and smoking a cigarette, got out and crossed to the Mercedes. He smiled ingratiatingly at Jake and said, '*Guten Tag, Pater*.'

Jake nodded. Please, God, don't let him ask me anything in German!

The general leaned on the sill of the rear window and addressed the Archbishop. '*Excellenz*,' he began. The rest of his remarks were lost on Jake, but the man's tone was amiable. When the

Archbishop replied in an equally friendly voice, the general opened the door and got in next to him. The Archbishop caught Jake's eyes in the mirror and said, '*Bitte, Pater, fahren Sie.*'

Jake started the car. Please, God, let it mean 'go ahead'! He put the car in gear and drove slowly down the vacant lane, by-passing the other waiting autos.

The general and the Archbishop conversed casually. The general's car fell in behind them.

Jake was conscious of the stares of the people they were passing. He imagined how they felt. They would wonder – rightly, in Jake's opinion – why the clergy should take precedence even here. For his part, Jake resolved never to criticize clerical privilege again. He had to keep wiping the sweat from his hands on his cassock. He hoped the general didn't notice.

'*So, Pater . . .*' The general touched Jake's shoulder, pointed to the right, and gave him an order.

Jake guessed that he was telling him to pull behind a yellow corrugated plastic screen and he did so, holding his breath. Please God! The screen cut off from broader view a good-sized lot in which a pair of tour buses were parked alongside three automobiles. The passengers on the tour buses were peering nervously out their windows. The three autos all had both their trunks and hoods open. Luggage was stacked on the asphalt. The occupants of the cars waited anxiously while policemen dressed in grey trousers with green stripes and matching green wind-breakers with epaulettes and grey peaked hats searched through their possessions. Their jackets half covered pistols in holsters on their belts. One policeman was guiding a six-foot pole-on-wheels along the ground, and it took Jake a moment to realize that a mirror was attached to it. He was running the mirror under the vehicles to see if anyone was . . . what? Clinging to the muffler? Oh fuck, he thought, we'll never get away with this!

The general got out of the Mercedes and went into the adjacent building.

Jake noticed that red flowering plants grew in window boxes on each side of the door. Not roses, impatiens. He was still surprised by any sign of humanity in such a place. He focused on the flowers. Flowers don't shoot.

The general came out again, and behind him an officer, who leaned slightly to salute the Archbishop. But his eyes went immediately to Jake's ebony cane on the front seat. He looked at the general, who shrugged. He addressed a brisk statement to the Archbishop. It was impossible not to guess his meaning. *I never heard of a priest with a cane*.

The Archbishop patted his own leg, groaned for effect, and, whining slightly, complained. Arthritis? *It's my stick, don't you know?* The Archbishop nodded sadly. *I'm getting old*.

The officer bowed politely and stepped back.

The Archbishop waved casually. The officer gestured at Jake, indicating he should drive on.

The general saluted in farewell.

Jake put the car in gear and drove slowly along the corrugated fence that isolated the lot in which the police did their work. But the fence had another function, which was to block any view of the Wall. At the end of the fence a guard raised a barrier. Jake picked up speed as he drove through and swerved out into the street again. Only the greatest act of will kept him from flooring it. Were they going to make it? Were they actually going to make it?

Now theirs was the only car. There were no buildings on either side of the street, and Jake realized that they had crossed into the stretch of no-man's-land. He saw the Wall, but peripherally because he focused entirely on the modest guardhouse directly ahead. Above it an American flag was flying. A large, tan-uniformed MP, a black man, was watching them approach.

When Jake finally pulled the car to a stop in front of the GI, he was not prepared for it when the military policeman, smiling broadly, leaned towards him and said, 'Hello, Father.' With a snappy salute he addressed the Archbishop. 'Good day, Your Excellency. Nice to see you again. Welcome back to the free world.'

Yes, Jake thought. He slumped over the wheel, quivering. Relief, gratitude, happiness. Thank you, God. The free world at last! Oh, Jesus Christ, it's sweet!

Jake turned in his seat. The Archbishop's appearance shocked him. The colour had drained completely from his face and all of its muscles had sagged. His jaw was slack. He seemed much older than he had even moments before, and he was limp in the corner as if he'd fainted. His eyelids were half shut, but he acknowledged the soldier by raising his hand. His hand, Jake saw, which shook.

A tear had overflowed his glass eye and now coursed singly down his artificial cheek. Because he had no feeling in that side of his face, the Archbishop was oblivious to it. Jake realized that the tear-function of the old man's false eye had no relation to his emotional state. In his own rampant emotion Jake wanted to reach back and wipe the water away, but he couldn't. One doesn't touch a man like this, he thought. Not that he was an archbishop. But that he was the *Rosenpater*.

CHAPTER TWENTY-NINE

'It looks somehow grander from over here,' Jake said about the Brandenburg Gate as he pulled the Archbishop's car on to the East-West Axis.

The Archbishop said from his corner, without looking, 'Vanity from either side is still vanity.'

Jake drove west through the tailored woods of the Tiergarten towards the monument over which it seemed to him, despite the Archbishop's iconoclasm, the golden woman, *Viktoria*, soared, truly soared. As he accelerated he realized that this was Hitler's airstrip. Yes, he could imagine a light plane taking off here. He felt a kind of flight already.

He sensed a nearly mystical connection suddenly with his father, a profound satisfaction that at last he knew who his father was. He knew it not from information gleaned, but from the experience at last of taking a terrible chance and winning.

Jake had successfully crossed the most rigid border there is, an iron curtain exactly. And he had enabled the escape of one of the most important spies the West had ever had. Yet even in his musing that word – spy – seemed alien, melodramatic, silly. He could barely apply it to the sickly man crouched in the trunk of that very car. Spy? He knew the meaning of what had just happened. Sebalov, finally, was an old man who wanted out, out from all of it. He wanted to be with Magda.

And so did Jake. She would understand this feeling he had, this happiness. He gunned the Mercedes at the monument. Wasn't she that golden woman? That *Viktoria*? He remembered running after her in that park in Georgetown twenty years before. How he had feared losing her! When he fell she came to him; that was how he had always won his victories. But he did not need to fall anymore; that was what he felt! It was a feeling he had never had before.

*

'Why don't you bang on the shelf behind you, Archbishop? To see how your old friend is doing?'

The Archbishop twisted back to strike the shelf three times briskly. Almost immediately Sebalov responded with three blows of his own.

'*Gott sei Dank*.' The Archbishop brightened as if he'd just remembered what their purpose was. He jovially addressed a sentence to the shelf. When he faced forward he found Jake's eyes in the mirror. 'I told him soon he would have fresh air to breathe.'

'As soon as we pick up Magda we'll go somewhere discreet and we'll all get out. We'll all breathe easier.'

Jake slowed the automobile as they approached the traffic circle that wound counter-clockwise around the monument. He craned to look up at the column as he drove. 'From up close it's rather small, isn't it? I always measure these things against the Washington Monument. I grew up in Washington.' He felt expansive and talkative. 'The television tower in East Berlin, for example. That's two Washington Monuments, same as the Hancock building in Boston.'

The Archbishop grinned at him. 'I measure things against Saint Peter's.'

'The only thing I ever really wanted to do but couldn't was walk up the Monument stairs.' It was unlike Jake to refer to his disability. His leg injury, as a relic of the war, seemed all at once puny to him, nothing compared to what this man and countless others still suffered. The Archbishop's half-frozen face moved him finally more than it unsettled him.

He added in the same light tone, but now it was forced, 'I also wanted to drive a clutch car.'

'You drive very well.'

Jake cut smoothly into the circle traffic and began to ease towards the kerb. The Victory Column was surrounded by a broad well-kept grassy apron. Here and there tourists sat on the grass in small groups. A row of tour buses was parked on the far side of the circle. Once they were near the kerb, Jake cruised slowly along it with his eyes peeled for Magda.

He had made one full circuit and was just about to cross a second time through the mid-afternoon shadow that the column cast. But he saw her, looking stylish in her tan suit, walking in that shadow away from the column towards the kerb. Why in the shadow? he thought at once. But he slowed the car to a stop exactly in it. He put the gear in park, but didn't shut the engine

365

off. Without thinking to bring his cane he opened the door and was out, limping towards her, but not conscious of his limp, not conscious of the priest's cassock he wore still.

The sight of him so unselfconsciously anxious to be with her demolished the reserve in which Magda had resolved to hold herself. She ran to him and they caught each other in the middle of the grass, just out of the monument's shadow. They swirled each other. Jake kept his balance and they kissed.

We will always be together. This moment will last forever. The dream we had is true now. Everything is possible. Oh, Magda! Oh, Jake!

Magda came up for air before he did. She laughed and fluttered her eyes at his collar. '*Guten Tag, Pater!*'

Tourists were gawking at them. Not only at Magda's beauty but also at Jake's garb. He didn't care. He resolutely did not care. He kissed her again.

But out of the corner of his eye he saw, slowing to a stop on the circle fifty yards across the lawn, the grey Mercedes.

Jake continued to kiss Magda, but now he focused everything on that automobile and the man who was getting out of it.

He was dressed in a dark suit. He walked casually across the grass towards them. A light wind feathered his hair.

I know him, Jake thought. I know him!

'Who is that?' he whispered to Magda, turning her enough to see.

'Oh,' she said softly, a profound exhalation. For a moment she slumped against Jake. 'The Americans,' she said.

'Americans? The Agency?' Jake remembered then from his time at Georgetown. What was that fellow's name? Yeats. The son of his father's enemy. Fred Yeats. After all these years.

Magda said, 'I never thought the Americans would track us. How could they know? They will take my father.'

Jake turned her and leaned on her and they walked as quickly as they could back towards the car.

The man began to run after them. When he'd nearly closed the distance he called, 'We should leave the Archbishop out of this!'

Magda freed herself from Jake. She had to reclaim her old identity. It was the loss of it that had led to this mistake. 'Go quickly!' she said.

Jake did not hesitate. He hurled himself in his ungainly off-balance stride towards the car while Magda crossed to intercept the man.

366

Two other men were racing towards them on foot from across the circle, but traffic slowed them.

Jake's momentum brought him hard against the Archbishop's car. He opened the door, got in, dropped the gear lever into drive, and floored it. He nearly ran the two men down. After he passed they cut back across the circle towards their car, a staid blue Ford.

Jake looked over his shoulder and saw the first man dragging Magda towards the grey Mercedes. He was about forty years old. That would have been right. Was it Fred Yeats? Jake was certain that he knew him.

The Archbishop leaned forward, gripping the seat by Jake's shoulder. 'The Grunewald! Go to the Grunewald!'

'You direct, Father. I follow.'

'Just straight! Just go straight!'

The boulevard took them quickly out of the Tiergarten and into the thick of downtown Berlin, but traffic in the lull before rush hour was light, and they were able to make speed. Eventually the boulevard spilled on to a super-highway and Jake assumed that was where they were headed. But the Archbishop directed him away from the access ramp marked 'Avus'. Jake realized that the Avus was the famous stretch of highway, pure straightaway, designed for Grand Prix races, but they bypassed it for a narrow road that plunged them into Berlin's huge forest.

It was immediately evident what the Archbishop had in mind because the Grunewald, unlike the manicured open acreage of the Tiergarten, was a tangle of trees and undergrowth. A maze of roads and trails wound through thousands of wooded acres. Such wild ruggedness was the antidote to the claustrophobia of life in Berlin.

Jake cut quickly off the road and into a grove of willow trees. The curtain of limp downhanging branches and leaves slapped at the car as he pulled through it. He stopped and turned the engine off. He and the Archbishop both faced the rear window to watch. In moments the blue Ford shot by on the far side of the willow screen. Before long the pair of men in that car would be hopelessly lost. Or would they double back? Were there others he hadn't seen?

'Bang on the shelf, Archbishop!' How was Sebalov holding up?

The Archbishop did so, but there was no response.

Oh God, Jake thought. He considered letting Sebalov out right there, dressing him in the priest's garb and leaving the Arch-

367

bishop too. But how would they fend for themselves in those woods? How soothing to have stayed hidden in that snug grove. But it was urgent, he saw, to find a better place. He had to get the old man out of that trunk. 'We have to get Herr Dettke somewhere safe,' he said.

But where was the grey Mercedes? Had it simply given up? Or had the man – who was he? – taken Magda off to work on her? Would the Americans do that? Would the British intervene for her? Or would they disavow her? But Magda could not be Jake's concern. And, he reminded himself, she was better at this stuff than he was.

'I know a place,' the Archbishop said. 'We can be there in a few minutes.'

Jake started the car and put it in reverse. When he looked back his eyes and the old prelate's met. The more animated one side of his face became, the more inert the other seemed. 'Does it matter to you,' Jake asked, 'who they are who want him now?'

'They are all the same,' the Archbishop said fiercely. 'Herr Dettke has the right to die in peace!'

As Jake backed the Archbishop's car out into the road the grey Mercedes approached from behind a curve. 'Fred Yeats, you bastard,' he said to himself, and a vision of Yeats's father hauling his own father out of the house in Georgetown filled his mind.

He jammed the accelerator down. The car roared powerfully and leapt forward like a jungle animal. Jake worried that Sebalov was being jolted violently, but it couldn't be helped. They careened around a downhill curve and, as quickly as it had appeared, the grey Mercedes was gone.

Fred Yeats had said to him in that bar called Tehan's, 'I always thought you were on the team.' And Jake had replied, 'How can I be on the team, Fred, when no one tells me what we're playing?' He remembered standing fully clothed, drenched, in a shower stall, shaking his ebony stick at Yeats. 'Next son of a bitch who touches me is going to get this stick across his face!' Yeats had flinched and backed off.

He dropped his eyes momentarily to his stick on the seat beside him. Its hidden blade made him shiver.

And as for team! He was gripping the wheel so tightly his hands were turning white. Magda Dettke told me what we're playing, so I'm on her team.

After a series of reverse curves the road straightened, and the grey Mercedes came back into view less than two hundred yards behind them.

'How many are in it, Father?'

The Archbishop squinted back. 'Two. Only two. The woman and the man.'

Jake turned sharply on to an unpaved road, which led soon, unfortunately, into a broad meadow in the centre of which was a small lake. Out of the forest he felt exposed. Long shadows fell from isolated trees across the grass, but it was sunny, and the sunlight seemed wrong for what was happening. He gunned across the meadow at a hundred kilometres an hour. The car bounced across the terrain. Poor Sebalov, he thought. Oh fuck, don't let me be hurting him! The dust behind billowed enough that his view of their pursuer was obscured. The woman and the man, he thought. Magda and Yeats. But Yeats had flinched. Why not stop and take him on?

Because this is not hazing.

This is not a game.

But the unpaved road began to play out. A strip of grass bisected the two tyre tracks, and the grass grew higher as they went. Soon it was slapping at the car and he had to slow down. Up ahead the road, a mere trail now, hooked over a ridge.

When they went over it Jake saw a stand of poplar trees beside a lake. The air shimmered above the reflecting water and the trees swayed slightly in the breeze.

The road ended just beyond the trees at a cluster of picnic tables on the shore of the lake. There was a stone fireplace. Beyond, a thick wood blocked the way. There was no choice but to stop.

All right, he thought, take him on. Your whole life has been pointing you to this. John Kennedy says we are responsible for the world . . . we claim our places here . . . we are the new generation!

He stopped the car and shut the engine off. He removed the Roman collar and unbuttoned the cassock while he waited for the grey Mercedes to pull up. It was like taking off the freshman tie.

He gazed around the spot where they had stopped. Birds that had scattered a moment before were coming back. A breeze wafted the grass, which was tall everywhere except immediately at the picnic tables. The same breeze dusted the surface of the lake. The afternoon light was stark.

'So, Fred,' he would say, 'we get to finish what we started.'

But his mind gave him no image of how Fred Yeats, grown, might respond. He faced the Archbishop, who sat impassively, waiting, holding his handkerchief at his cheek. He wanted to apologize for involving him in this further escapade. Hadn't crossing through the Wall been enough? 'The man after us is an American. I think I can talk to him. I think it will be all right.'

And then, grabbing his stick, he got out of the car, shrugged the cassock off, bundled it, dropped it on the car seat, and closed the door. He looked at the trunk. Just a few minutes more, Sergei. He felt a terrible pang for what the old man must have been suffering, but he had to lay it aside. He rolled his shirt-sleeves, assumed a casual pose, leaning on the car, and watched the grey Mercedes approach. The birds scattered again. Tall wild-flowers bent as the breeze picked up. The poplars whistled. After the grim scene in East Berlin and the frantic chase through West Berlin the pastoral setting for this encounter seemed like a reward.

'So, Jake,' Yeats would say, 'you're still bucking it.' They would grin at each other and shake.

This was not Russians coming at him. It was someone he knew, someone from his own world, the world he'd grown up in, the world he'd once loved.

Jake stared at the driver as he slowly pulled alongside.

The man, even as he stopped the car, had a gleaming black pistol pointed at Jake. The sight of that weapon dispelled Jake's calm, blew it away like fog ahead of bad weather. It wasn't Fred Yeats.

'Hello, Jake.'

It was Dwight Houseman, his father's trusted aide, Jake saw it again with fresh pain, his father's favourite son.

'Hello, Dwight.' Jake let his eyes fall to the gun. 'You don't need that thing.' He held himself ruthlessly in check. Dwight Houseman! Jesus Christ! How could I have made that mistake?

Houseman got out of the car carefully, still aiming the gun. Magda got out on the far side of the automobile and remained there. Jake sensed that she was trying to catch his eye, but he could only stare at Houseman.

He was thinner. What at a distance had seemed trim elegance could now be seen as a form of gauntness. The veins stood out in his neck. His mouth was set, but his body was loose. He held the pistol as if he always led with it. He peered into the Archbishop's car. 'I'm sorry, Your Excellency. I won't delay you long.' Then he faced Jake. 'So you finally joined the family trade, eh?' His words conveyed measures both of fondness and regret.

Jake smiled. He was still leaning casually back against the car, idling his stick in his right hand. 'I'm a small-time teacher, Dwight, but even I know you have no authority here.'

Dwight Houseman began to laugh, then he stopped abruptly, an ominous shift. 'I don't know why you're here, McKay, but you've made a bad mistake.'

'I'm here because of my father. Perhaps you remember him.'

Houseman stared at Jake.

Jake realized that his reference to his father threw Houseman off balance. He had to keep him that way. 'I remember how surprised and disappointed he was to realize that you had betrayed him. How is Mr Yeats, by the way?'

Houseman did not answer. He would not be so easily deflected. He looked briefly at Magda.

Jake pushed away from the car. What could Houseman know? Certainly not the truth about his father or his uncle, and that made him seem inferior.

But Houseman surprised him then when he said, 'I want Patterson, Jake. You and the lady can leave with the Archbishop. But Patterson comes with me.'

What was this? Jake had to take it an inch at a time. 'Why is it up to you to take Patterson?'

'The breaks, I guess.' Houseman gestured at Magda. 'Over here, please, miss.' She crossed in front of the grey Mercedes to stand by Jake. 'Breaks we owe to you, actually, Jake. We thought your uncle might try to get out when he came to Berlin. When you showed up, we knew he would.'

Jake and Magda exchanged a look. The grey Mercedes had been tailing *him*. Magda hadn't blown it.

Jake knew he had to slow things down. 'My uncle?' he asked. 'How could he get out?' Jake took a step towards Houseman, but Houseman jerked his pistol at him.

'With the *Hochwürdenträger Rosenpater*, anything is possible.' Houseman backed away from them with his pistol level, and he glanced through the rear window at the Archbishop. 'He never put his privilege at our service before. He could have helped us out a lot.'

'He could only have done it once, and he knew it,' Jake said.

371

'Well, he picked a good one, in my opinion.' Houseman was at the trunk now. 'We've been waiting twenty years to get your uncle, Jake.'

'Isn't it a British matter? He's a British citizen. He was convicted under their laws, not ours.' Jake nodded at Magda. 'Shouldn't you respect your colleagues' prerogatives?'

Dwight stared at her. Colleague? 'Patterson burned more of our people than theirs. Right, miss? Ask her. She'll tell you why. Because SIS is KGB-West. Every tenth agent in the SIS has been turned, Patterson has a host of friends in England. We couldn't have him just return to his manor house, now, could we?'

''d have thought if there were KGB in England they'd kill him.'

'Also a possibility.' Houseman glanced at Magda again. 'You're a fool, Jake, if you've trusted her.'

'I have, Dwight.'

'No matter now. The point is, Patterson comes with me. No manor house, but no murder either. We won't mistreat him. You know that.'

Jake let his eyes fall to Houseman's gun. Houseman still handled it confidently. He had not even been tempted to lower it. An enormous sadness, a fundamental regret, filled Jake, and he recognized it immediately as the feeling he had structured his entire life to avoid. He regretted what had happened, and what had to happen now.

Houseman bent to press the button of the trunk lid.

Jake moved towards him along the side of the car. As he did so he fingered the silver handle of his stick.

The passenger door brushed him when the Archbishop opened it, and Jake wished that the old man would stay in the car where it was safe, wished he would get down on the floor. But he ignored the Archbishop to keep moving slowly, working his stick handle, towards Houseman.

When the trunk lid popped open, Houseman aimed the gun towards the man in it, and at that moment Jake lunged at him, pulling the handle out of the ebony shaft. The Messiah's Handle! And brutally, without thinking – the only way to do such a thing – he thrust the blade into Houseman's forearm.

He plunged it into the flesh as if it were a hypodermic needle, at that same shallow angle. A needle full of air! An embolus is any foreign particle circulating in the blood, as a bubble of air

. . . not cane, my lad, but stick! A bloody stick!

Houseman fell back, cried out, dropped the pistol.

Jake locked his free arm around Houseman's throat, and pressed the point of the dagger into the skin under his jawbone. 'Don't move! Move and you're dead!'

Magda crossed quickly to pick up Houseman's gun, but the Archbishop had moved first and he reached it before she did, scooping it as if he were removing an obscene thing from view.

Magda leaned into the trunk of the car to help her father get out. He was even paler than before, soaked with perspiration and breathing rapidly. When he was on his feet he tottered, then collapsed against his daughter.

'Jesus Christ,' Houseman blurted. Jake tried to turn him away, but he twisted to look again. 'Sebalov!'

Magda was stroking her father, trying to calm him. If his pulse was like his breathing . . .

'Jesus Christ!' Houseman said again. 'Sergei Sebalov!' He tried to look back at Jake, but Jake choked him sharply.

It shocked him that Houseman recognized the Russian so easily. Had he been on this case all these years?

Magda, still rubbing a hand lightly up and down her father's back, raised her face to Jake. She said softly, 'Kill him.'

Such words coming from a woman who was otherwise so tenderly engaged seemed perverse, but Jake realized that he had expected her to say them. He did not respond. He did not move.

'Kill him,' she repeated. Her golden hair had come undone and had fallen across her brow. Such words from such a beauty – that was what seemed perverse.

Jake pulled Houseman a few steps away. He said, 'Magda, see to your father. Just see to your father.'

Houseman grabbed at Jake with his good arm, pleading. 'Do you know who that son of a bitch is?'

'I know exactly who he is.'

'Then help me! A former chief of the KGB? Christ, it's the most important defection of all!'

Jake jerked him again. 'More important than Giles Patterson? Are you in favour of defection or not?'

'You must kill him, Jake.' Magda's voice was eerily detached. He had heard hints of it when she'd instructed him. This was her professional voice. And her professional judgement told her that Houseman had to die.

'Magda, don't say that to me.' Is this what it means finally? Being like my father? Being ruthless? Killing Dwight?

She pressed with that same disembodied, passionless tone. 'My father will not survive the week if this man reports. You must not let him report.'

For once Jake was not standing on some platform above everything, a ridge over Washington, the Monument observation deck, the navy hospital, an office overlooking Boston, the television tower, the Victory Column, looking down on the sons and daughters of important men and how they ruin each other.

Houseman said with a calm that matched Magda's, 'Whose side are you on, Jake?'

'I'm on my family's side,' he said. His voice cracked. There was nothing calm in him. He was confused. He couldn't think.

'Then help me,' Houseman said. 'Your father would have helped me.'

Magda then said, 'Your uncle won't survive the week, either. If Washington learns about my father, the KGB will know too. Your uncle will be dead the day they learn. You must kill him.'

Kill whom? Giles? Once Jake had sworn not to forgive him. Now he wanted only to protect him. But everything in him revolted at the thought of plunging that dagger into Houseman's throat. He held him. They were locked together and would be until Jake declared himself.

Everyone waited.

When Jake spoke finally his voice, alone of those voices, shook. 'Magda,' he said, though he continued to stare at the blade at Houseman's throat, 'wasn't it that you wanted out of this shit? You wanted to stop it? Wasn't that it?' He waited. 'Wasn't it?'

'Yes,' she said finally, weakly.

'Magda, sweet Magda, you must simply stop it. You just say, "No!" That's all. Don't tell me to kill this man.'

'What else,' she whispered, 'is there to do?' Even to ask the question was for her an act of hope.

'We'll disappear,' Jake answered. 'They'll never find us.'

'And Giles?'

'Who says anyone will believe Houseman when he reports? Everyone in Moscow thinks your father is dead.'

Magda shook her head. Jake's reassurances had fallen short, infinitely short. Her voice was weighted with despair when she said, 'The Russians . . . the Americans . . . if they remotely suspect . . . disappear? Can you make your family disappear? Your

374

children? You think Berlin is so far from Boston?'

Jake shifted his eyes to stare at her. 'What are you saying? My wife and children have nothing to do with this.'

'Ask him,' she said.

Houseman's face was close enough to kiss. Houseman said, 'We leave children out of it, you know that.'

But suddenly Jake knew no such thing. 'You bastards,' he said. Jake knew that they could not leave his children out of it. Not if threatening them or even harming them meant getting what they wanted, getting Sebalov. Jake began to shake Houseman. 'All you bastards!'

Houseman stumbled, fell to one knee, clutching his wound. Jake went down with him, but he held the blade away. He checked himself. He *too* was dangerous now. He saw that. And he saw, also, something else; it would be stupid to kill Houseman. Houseman was not alone.

He released him, tossed the blade aside, and crossed quickly to the Archbishop for the gun.

But the Archbishop levelled the gun at Houseman. 'If you don't kill him,' the *Rosenpater* said, 'I will.'

'Don't be a fool.' Jake easily took the pistol from the old man.

The Archbishop didn't resist, but he looked forlornly at McKay. 'I owe it to my friend. I never helped him in the war. I never struck a blow.'

'This isn't the war now, Archbishop. And there's something else you can do, something better.'

Jake faced Magda. She was the one he had to convince. With an eye on Houseman, he said to her, 'Killing him solves nothing. His friends will hound us. They would know soon enough that Giles had not defected. They would suspect the truth, enough to stop at nothing to find us. My family would be helpless. I have to go to them.'

'Then you could join us,' Magda said.

'No, I can't. You have to go away without me. And I can't know where you are. Only if they are convinced of my ignorance will my children be safe. So you must go away now.'

'I can't.'

'Magda, you must. All your skill and all your experience – use it. It's how you get away. It's how you stay hidden. It's how you save your father. Without me you can be free. With me, they've got you.' Nothing had ever been clearer to Jake.

Jake looked at Houseman. 'I'm right, aren't I?'

375

Houseman nodded.

Magda protested, 'Don't believe him!'

'But I do,' Jake said.

She looked away.

He said to her, 'Don't go to the cabin in Zurich, or any place that might be traced from there. Once you're gone I will tell them everything I know.'

'But, Jake . . .' Magda's voice cracked. 'I need help.'

'You have it.' Jake faced the Archbishop. 'This is your blow to strike, Father. Will you help them?'

The *Rosenpater* nodded. 'The Americans, like the Russians, have nothing to use against me.'

'Do you have a parish near here where you can get a different car for her?'

'Yes.'

'Don't involve anyone else.' Jake faced Magda. 'The most dangerous part will be while you're in the car they've seen. After that, you can handle it.'

Magda nodded.

Jake sensed that he was doing for her what Giles had done for him.

The Archbishop crossed to his old friend and took his weight. Magda released her father. The Archbishop led him to the car and helped him into the back seat.

Magda and Jake approached each other. He limped unself-consciously. She started to say something in a whisper.

'Speak loudly,' he said. 'Houseman has to hear us.'

They stopped, a few feet separating them.

Magda began to cry. He stepped to her and touched the tears on her cheek. She said, 'I never used to weep.'

He saw the green flecks in her blue irises.

They kissed.

And she went to the car quickly, got in, started it, and drove away without looking back.

'Now, Dwight,' Jake said, while helping Houseman tie a tourniquet on his arm. They had improvised bandages with strips of cloth from the priest's cassock. They each worked with one hand, Jake because he continued to hold the pistol ready with his other. 'You understand how it is now. We have to kill a little time.'

'And if I force you to, you kill me.'

'That's right.'

'Once, frankly, I wouldn't have thought you could.'

Jake felt no need to put into words the certitude he felt. He stepped back and leaned against a picnic table. 'Tell me something: is it true that when you report about Sebalov, the Russians will learn it too?'

'We'd love them not to.' Houseman shrugged. 'But they probably will. It's too big.' Houseman watched Jake carefully. 'You're thinking about your uncle.'

'Yes.' Jake felt a fresh stab of fear, but now for Giles. He assured himself that Giles had already accepted the contingencies of his situation, but he hated to think that he was playing a part in the sealing of his uncle's fate. But, as Giles himself had said, he would make the best of it, whatever happened. Jake had to trust his uncle to do so as once his uncle and his father had trusted him. Still, the pain; it was the pain of his love.

Houseman examined his bandages. The flow of blood seemed to have stopped. 'What's with that goddamn cane, anyway?'

'Stick, Dwight. I call it a stick.' Jake grinned at the sound in his own voice of his uncle's inflection. 'Some fucking secret, eh?'

Duncan Kyle

'One of the modern masters of the high adventure story.'
Daily Telegraph

GREEN RIVER HIGH   £1.50
BLACK CAMELOT   £1.25
A CAGE OF ICE   £1.50
FLIGHT INTO FEAR   £1.50
TERROR'S CRADLE   £1.25
A RAFT OF SWORDS   £1.25
WHITEOUT!   £1.50
STALKING POINT   £1.75

FONTANA PAPERBACKS

Eric Ambler

A world of espionage and counter-espionage, of sudden violence and treacherous calm; of blackmailers, murderers, gun-runners—and none too virtuous heroes. This is the world of Eric Ambler.

'Unquestionably our best thriller writer.' *Graham Greene*

'He is incapable of writing a dull paragraph.' *Sunday Times*

'Eric Ambler is a master of his craft.' *Sunday Telegraph*

JOURNEY INTO FEAR   £1.25
DIRTY STORY   £1.35
THE LEVANTER   £1.25
PASSAGE OF ARMS   £1.25
THE CARE OF TIME   £1.50
DR FRIGO   £1.50
THE SCHIRMER INHERITANCE   £1.50

FONTANA PAPERBACKS

Desmond Bagley

'Mr Bagley is nowadays incomparable.' *Sunday Times*

THE ENEMY   £1.35
FLYAWAY   £1.65
THE FREEDOM TRAP   £1.50
THE GOLDEN KEEL   £1.35
HIGH CITADEL   £1.25
LANDSLIDE   £1.50
RUNNING BLIND   £1.50
THE SNOW TIGER   £1.50
THE SPOILERS   £1.50
THE TIGHTROPE MEN   £1.50
THE VIVERO LETTER   £1.50
WYATT'S HURRICANE   £1.50
BAHAMA CRISIS   £1.50

FONTANA PAPERBACKS

Helen MacInnes

Born in Scotland, Helen MacInnes has lived in the United States since 1937. Her first book, *Above Suspicion*, was an immediate success and launched her on a spectacular writing career that has made her an international favourite.

'She is the queen of spy-writers.' *Sunday Express*

'She can hang up her cloak and dagger right there with Eric Ambler and Graham Greene.' *Newsweek*

FRIENDS AND LOVERS   £1.75
AGENT IN PLACE   £1.50
THE SNARE OF THE HUNTER   £1.50
HORIZON   £1.25
ABOVE SUSPICION   £1.35
MESSAGE FROM MALAGA   £1.50
REST AND BE THANKFUL   £1.75
PRELUDE TO TERROR   £1.50
NORTH FROM ROME   £1.50
THE HIDDEN TARGET   £1.75
I AND MY TRUE LOVE   £1.50
THE VENETIAN AFFAIR   £1.75
ASSIGNMENT IN BRITTANY   £1.75
DECISION AT DELPHI   £1.95
NEITHER FIVE NOR THREE   £1.95

FONTANA PAPERBACKS

Alistair MacLean

His first book, HMS *Ulysses*, published in 1955, was outstandingly successful. It led the way to a string of best-selling novels which have established Alistair MacLean as the most popular adventure writer of our time.

*

FONTANA PAPERBACKS

Fontana Paperbacks

Fontana is a leading paperback publisher of fiction and non-fiction, with authors ranging from Alistair MacLean, Agatha Christie and Desmond Bagley to Solzhenitsyn and Pasternak, from Gerald Durrell and Joy Adamson to the famous Modern Masters series.

In addition to a wide-ranging collection of internationally popular writers of fiction, Fontana also has an outstanding reputation for history, natural history, military history, psychology, psychiatry, politics, economics, religion and the social sciences.

All Fontana books are available at your bookshop or newsagent; or can be ordered direct. Just fill in the form and list the titles you want.

FONTANA BOOKS, Cash Sales Department, G.P.O. Box 29, Douglas, Isle of Man, British Isles. Please send purchase price, plus 8p per book. Customers outside the U.K. send purchase price, plus 10p per book. Cheque, postal or money order. No currency.

NAME (Block letters) _____

ADDRESS _____

_____

_____

While every effort is made to keep prices low, it is sometimes necessary to increase prices on short notice. Fontana Books reserve the right to show new retail prices on covers which may differ from those previously advertised in the text or elsewhere.